BOLERO

JOANIE MCDONELL

BOLERO

A NICK SAYLER NOVEL

THOMAS & MERCER

Text copyright © 2012 Joanie McDonell
Printed in the United States of America.

Published by Thomas & Mercer
P.O. Box 400818
Las Vegas, NV 89140

ISBN-13: 9781612184401
ISBN-10: 1612184405

All that's bright must fade
The brightest still the fleetest
All that's sweet was made
But to be lost when sweetest

— Thomas Moore

Show me a gambler and I'll show you a loser,
Show me a hero and I'll show you a corpse.
— Mario Puzo

Beauty is my weakness, so breaking a few rules to spring a beautiful woman from being unjustly committed to a notorious psychiatric facility felt like a good deed. But it was not a good idea.

I never meant to get involved with the girl, but she was fragile and lost and she needed me.

As it turned out, I needed her more.

My name is Nick Sayler.

I'm thirty-seven years old. Blue eyes, brown hair. Six feet tall, 170 pounds give or take. No family history. No religion. Allergic to nothing. Three surgeries, right leg.

Occupation: small-business owner. Sayler Security.

Marital status: none.

And it's going to stay that way. The woman I loved died because of me. Saying love equals death is too simple; but for me, love is in a locked box. It went to the grave with her.

Sure, I'll always like women. I like looking at them, I like touching them, and I like talking to them, but eventually they want some kind of promise, and they're not getting it from me.

A couple of years ago I met Rue, who—starting with her name—is different and that's why we're friends or whatever we are.

I live at my place, and some of the time she lives at hers. That suits me best.

Edward Sloane, MD, PhD, tells me I'd be happier if I explored my abandonment issues. He knows those issues are not inappropriate for a person who was left in a cardboard box on the steps of a convent with a note to the nuns saying: 'Please take care of this baby. He is not wanted.'

I'm not interested in syndromes, complexes, or real frogs in imaginary gardens, so I never listen to Sloane, but he's a good friend. When the shit hit the fan in my life, Sloane and the Sisters of Perpetual Grace were the only people who didn't desert me. And I never forget.

PART ONE

Luck never gives, it only lends.
— Chinese Proverb

1

I live and work out of a converted barge on the Jersey side of the Hudson with a great view of Manhattan, where I spend a lot of time. I don't have a problem with the city, but I'd rather go to sleep at night with a river between it and me.

Albert Meriwether, whom I don't think of as an employee, although he gets a salary, lives on the barge too. Our relationship is pretty simple: we both know I'd pay him if he didn't work and he'd work if I didn't pay him, but so far only his goodwill has been put to the test.

Meriwether is a savant. He can remember the license plate of every car he's ever seen, he can tell you what day of the week Lee surrendered at Appomattox Court House, or how many stones are in the Kukulcán pyramid in Chichén Itzá. He can do arcane algorithms and remember weather conditions starting the first day they were reported probably by Noah from the ark. But he has few social skills, and people sometimes find him threatening since he's built like a heavyweight and doesn't like talking to strangers.

There are no phones in my bedroom because phones are for work. When I take on a client, I intend to keep him or her until the end of the job, however long it takes. And I'm almost always available to these people, but I don't encourage them to call at night. Especially late at night.

That particular Thursday night I went to bed early, just before a major storm broke. The lightning and thunder kept me from getting any sleep, so I was already in a bad mood when Meriwether knocked on my door at around twelve thirty. Since he doesn't do that very often, I was expecting a problem. But nothing like the one I got.

"OK," I said. "I hope it's important."

He handed me the phone and shrugged his shoulders when I wanted to know who it was. I've asked Meriwether to use his judgment about late-night phone calls, and he has good judgment.

"Said it was urgent," Meriwether told me. "Matter of life and death."

"It's never a matter of life and death," I said.

When it is, nobody has time to make calls.

"Hello," I said into the phone.

Meriwether walked out the door and closed it behind him.

"Hi—" A man's voice. *Hi?*

"What can I do for you?" I asked.

"My name's Justin Greenburg." He cleared his throat.

"Yes," I said.

"I'm a doctor—an intern—at Bellevue Hospital." He hesitated.

"What's the problem?" I asked.

"It's about a patient here."

"And you're calling me because?"

"Listen," Dr. Justin Greenburg said, "I could get in a lot of trouble for calling you—maybe it's because I'm tired, we never get any sleep—"

"Just go ahead," I said.

"A woman came in tonight—some cabdriver brought her to the ER and left. Nobody knows if he was really even a cabdriver because by the time security went to find him he was gone. The woman looks like she was mugged or attacked, but it could have been a domestic problem—a pretty bad one."

"Why didn't she tell you which it was?"

My first mistake. A question. I shouldn't have gone down that road or any road with this guy.

"She was in shock," he said. "She's got a concussion, and now she can't remember anything—"

"Justin," I said—he sounded like a young kid—"I don't know anything. It's late, I'm tired—maybe not as tired as you, but could you get to the point? Why are you calling me?"

"My shift ended," he said, "but I didn't leave. I keep thinking that I shouldn't be doing this."

"OK," I said. "Then don't. I'm going to say good-bye now."

"Wait a minute," he said. "The thing is the woman—the woman, is really nice—"

Jesus Christ, I thought, the health care system really is in the toilet. They're recruiting morons.

"—And she wants to get out of here."

"If she's over eighteen," I said, "she can do what she wants."

"She won't be able to get out," he said, and then all in one breath he continued, "she's been checked in and with no memory no ID and no money she's officially a Jane Doe vagrant and they're going to put her in the psych ward."

Hang up, Sayler.

"Why?" I asked.

"Because the system is fucked up," he said, hesitating for a second. "I mean it's, well, fucked up."

"OK," I said. "It's fucked up."

"I called you," he said, "because the only thing she had on her was your card. Nobody saw it but me."

"So what do you want me to do?"

"Maybe you know her," he said.

"I'm sure I don't," I said. "I have hundreds of cards."

"I did a round in the psych ward—the place really sucks—and this woman seems so…fragile."

"You're a strange doctor," I said.

"I just can't let her go up there. Can you help? Please."

"I'm sorry," I told him, and by then I actually was feeling a little sorry. "There's really nothing I can do—but good luck."

Then I hung up.

2

Why did I get involved with her? I said it was because she was beautiful—but I suppose the real question is why did I get dressed, go out into a heavy rain, cross the squally river, and then subject myself to walking in the door of Bellevue?

There are two answers. The minor one is I like to solve problems, not discuss them. But the thing that mobilized me that night was understanding how it feels to be locked up in a foul place with no way out.

Only five minutes had passed before I checked caller ID, made the call, and was once again talking with Dr. Justin Greenburg.

Nobody would complain about the huge summer storm because record-breaking heat had been laying people low up and down the East Coast for a week and a half. The temperature had never registered under ninety-five, and the days were so humid you started longing for the lesser misery of black ice and blinding snow.

The heavy rain, which broke up the heat, was welcome if you were watching it from a room with a roof and windows. Not so welcome if you were at the wheel of a boat crossing the river from New Jersey to New York.

On the way to Bellevue, I remembered going there once with a kid who got hit by a car. The hospital used to be notorious for its psychiatric facility. Now it's better known as a level-one trauma center, which makes the ER a hot spot for victims of knife and bullet wounds.

I told the cabdriver to stop at the ER entrance, where Greenburg said he'd meet me. But there were so many cars, police vans, and ambulances lined up beside the sidewalk leading to the doors, we couldn't get near the portico. The rain was beating down, and I don't believe in umbrellas. Then I regret it and resolve to buy one, but I never do.

Greenburg, true to his word, was standing on the curb in front of the ER. He was a little, oval-shaped guy whose unfortunately small head and bug eyes made him look like a turtle. His small feet were in white Nikes, and he was wringing his small hands. His white lab coat was accessorized with a stethoscope draped around his short neck. He also had a chain with a big laminated hospital ID hanging on it and a plastic name tag pinned over his heart to further identify him as an MD.

"OK," I said, shaking hands with him briefly. "I'm Nick Sayler. Where's your patient?"

"She's still in neuro. It's the eighth floor."

"Lead the way," I said.

We walked through the Emergency Room, which was, as usual, filled with too many people in too much distress, receiving too little attention from a worn-out staff.

I don't know why the elevator was full so late at night—but it was, and everybody seemed to have just come in out of the rain too. The elevator was so slow that by the time we reached eight, the floor was slick with water and I was already tempted to leave.

When the doors finally opened, Justin Greenburg, like a tour director, announced, "Eighth floor. Here we are."

As we walked down the dim and messy hall—at least it was quiet—we passed a few aides wearing an assortment of awful flowered smocks. They all said hello to Greenburg. As did the nurses at their station. Maybe he wasn't a lunatic. Just an over-wrought kid. Probably so overwrought he'd get kicked out before he made resident.

"Thanks for coming," Greenburg said.

I said nothing because I knew I wouldn't recognize whoever this woman was and I would turn around and leave Greenburg on his own again to sort out the problem. Which was not my problem, I reminded myself as I felt a chill from the rain sinking into my right leg. That leg had been repaired in four places with permanent titanium pins. My personal weather vane.

"Here we are," Greenburg announced again when we reached the end of the hall. "There's one more thing."

"Go ahead," I said.

"The attacker—whoever—cut up her back."

"What does 'cut up' mean?"

"I don't know," said Greenburg. "She's got a bandage over the wounds, and the guy who stitched her in the ER went off duty. He just left instructions about changing the dressing and antibiotics—the usual. And she's not supposed to sleep—"

He started to open the door of room 848.

"Wait a minute," I said. "You didn't say if she had been raped."

"No," he said. "She wasn't. *Thank God.*"

"Aren't you meant to be dispassionate?"

"Yeah," he said. "But wait till you see her—she's so, uh—"

"What?" I said.

"I don't know."

Room 848, a double, was lit only by the glow of a muted television suspended from the ceiling like a clumsy claw.

We walked past the other patient, an old lady who was asleep and snoring.

The girl's bed was next to the window. She was sitting up very straight, and in the dimness of the room I could only see her outline in quarter profile and her dark hair. It was long and had mostly come loose from a braid that had once started at the crown of her head. I didn't see her face until I was at the foot of the bed and she looked up at me.

Her eyes were deep violet like Elizabeth Taylor's in some of the old movies the Sisters used to watch on Saturday nights. I'd never seen eyes like that in real life until I met Julia. And I hadn't seen them again in the ten years since Julia died. Not until now.

The dark bruise on the girl's cheek made me angry. Right then was the moment I should have left.

"You came back," she said to Greenburg in a soft voice.

"I promised I would," said Greenburg, hunching into his turtle shell.

Then I got it. Not that he wasn't cut out for medicine. Not that he had been awake for thirty-six hours. Maybe he wasn't even overwrought. He was besotted.

"I'm Nick Sayler," I said.

"Do you know me?"

"I'm sorry," I said. "We've never met."

"I don't know my name," she said.

"She told the attending that her name was Jane Waters," said Greenburg. "But she saw an aide pouring water into a cup and the aide's name was Jane. It was written on her ID tag."

"And I made up an address that didn't exist. They got me on that one too," she said contritely.

"Humor, that's a good sign," said Greenburg, immediately taking a step backward as though she had shot him a disapproving look, which she hadn't.

"How did you know an address?" I asked her.

"I guess I knew there's Broadway," she said.

"But not 8700 North Broadway," said Greenburg.

"Not in New York," I said. "Maybe somewhere else."

"I didn't think of that," said Greenburg.

"Well, it's not somewhere else," she said. "I made it up."

"How do you know you made it up?" I asked. "I thought you couldn't remember anything."

"That was two hours ago," she said. "I just can't remember anything that happened before the Emergency Room. It's a horrible feeling, not being able to remember. I'm trying so hard, but nothing happens."

"It'll come back," I said.

This comment was based entirely on seeing an Australian guy get knocked out in a rugby match on Governors Island. When he came to he didn't know his name and didn't recognize his wife. I heard he got his memory back in a week, but his buddies claimed he faked the whole episode to get a break from his wife, who they all said was a bitch.

"Nobody would tell me when I'll get it back though," she said, in a quiet almost breathy voice. "And I may not actually remember anything now, but there's something I know. Something I just feel—which is I have to get out of here."

"Are you afraid of the guy who attacked you?" I asked.

"I don't know," she said. "I can't remember who attacked me. But I hate hospitals, I'm totally sure about that. I have to get out."

Greenburg leaned over to me and whispered that she didn't know they were taking her to the psych ward.

"Oh great," I said.

"What are you talking about?" she asked.

"Nothing," said Greenburg.

"Well, obviously that's not true Justin," she said, still quietly. "But it doesn't make any difference. I'm leaving."

"You have a concussion," Greenburg said lamely, "but if you could go somewhere and rest…"

The girl in the bed looked at me.

"Are you sure you don't know me?"

"I wouldn't forget you," I said.

She smiled. Maybe that's what got me. She was scared, hurt, broke, didn't know her own name, but there it was. The eyes and then the smile.

She opened the drawer in the table next to the bed, pulled out the one item in it, and held it out for me to examine.

"This is your card," she said. "Nick Sayler. Sayler Security."

"I believe you," I said. "I don't have to see the card. I've had a lot of those printed, and I can't say where they wind up. And since you can't remember how you got it, I don't have anything to go on. I'm sorry I can't be more helpful."

Greenburg was looking on sadly, shaking his head, defeated.

"Justin," she said.

"I can't do anything else either," he said. "I wish I could."

His inner battle was almost palpable. I saw him trying to square giving up all those years of school with taking her out of there, unauthorized. Taking her home with him.

"You tried," she said. "I appreciate it. I'll think of something."

She lowered the protective railing on the side of the bed and swung her legs over. I wasn't surprised that they were perfect. But her feet. Misshapen would be a compliment. It took a couple of seconds to recognize what was wrong with them.

They were ballerina's feet. I was sure because of Allegra Trent, a ballerina I knew once. For a short time, I knew her well. She had the same feet. Deformed by the many years of being blistered and bloodied and crammed into those satin slippers with steel toes.

"You're a dancer."

"A dancer?" she said.

"In the ballet."

"How do you know?" she asked.

"Look at your feet."

"God, they're ugly," she said, slipping into a pair of shoes that were by the side of the bed. They were made of some soft olive-green fabric, and I imagined that twenty million Chinese women wore them as they toiled away making sturdy sneakers for big American companies.

"Where are my clothes?" asked the dancer.

I saw her wince in pain and saw the outline of a bandage on her back as she pulled the threadbare hospital gown tightly around her. She walked slowly to the closet. There was only a pair of torn blue jeans inside, and she looked like she'd never seen them before but pulled them on anyway because obviously there was no other choice.

"Where are my things?" she asked Greenburg, who had gone over to the doorway, which he had done periodically as we were talking.

"I don't know," he said, returning to us. "Your shirt was pretty messed up, and you didn't have a coat."

"Or underwear?"

"I think there was blood from your back," said Greenburg. "The aides took everything out of the room."

They took the clothes to give to the cops, who obviously had not yet been alerted to the attack—or hadn't yet showed up. If it were a gunshot wound, they would have been there fast. Or maybe a stabbing would get their attention. But a beating with no rape and a cut-up back in the middle of a storm, late at night, no hurry. In fact, they might not even show up at all. If more people knew how arbitrary the police can be, more people would roll the dice and hope their crime was ignored.

I took off my jacket and gave it to the dancer, furious again about her attacker. The brave guy who beat and cut the hundred-pound girl.

She wasn't very sure on her ballerina's feet, and after she put the jacket on, she leaned back against the closet door. Winced again in pain. She didn't make another sound, but I saw the tears gathering first at the inner corners of her eyes like bubbles, then breaking and running down her cheeks.

"Mr. Sayler," said Greenburg. He was back in the doorway, motioning me toward him. When I got there his voice dropped to a whisper.

"They're coming for her."

3

"You're going to walk away, aren't you?" said Greenburg.

I looked out the door and saw everything was still dark and quiet. At the very far end of the long hall, I could make out a nurse and an orderly slowly heading our way in silent, rubber-soled shoes. They looked like linebackers.

"Why isn't that guy pushing a wheelchair?" I asked quietly. "What's he doing with a gurney?"

"That's how it starts," Greenburg whispered ominously. "They sedate anyone who's going up to the psych ward. They strap them on a gurney and shoot them full of Thorazine."

A shot of that drug could knock out a horse.

"I didn't think anybody used Thorazine anymore."

"Well they do."

The nurse and orderly were drawing nearer, about halfway between us and the far end of the corridor.

I went over to the dancer, still standing by the closet.

"Listen," I said to her. "Let me talk to the doctors. Justin can tell me who's in charge, and I'll go see him. Justin—" I looked at the doorway.

He was gone, the little shit. Took off in his little white Nikes. And just then the lady in the other bed woke up, thrashing around and calling for a bartender.

"Jack Daniel's and soda," she demanded. "Over here. And make it snappy."

"Goddammit," I said. I couldn't leave the dancer. "Come on, let's go."

The dancer looked young—but it was hard to tell. She could have been twenty-two or thirty-two. Enveloped by my damp jacket, she looked like a child. I knew I had to get her out of the room instantly or we were fucked.

"Hey waiter," the old lady called in a shrill voice. "Call the bartender—are you deaf?"

She threw a box of Kleenex and hit the dancer, who froze for barely two seconds. But those were the two seconds we needed to get across the hall. We had run out of time.

The fire exit was just a dozen feet across the shadowy corridor, but now there was no way we could reach it without the linebackers getting a good look at us. One call from that nurse and all the street exits would be sealed.

"We can't go now," I said, immediately trying to figure a plan B.

"Well I'm going," she said. And dashed out the door.

I ran to grab her, expecting to be tackled by the orderly. Or the nurse. But they were still down the hall and not looking our way because they were deep in conversation. Distracted by a little guy in a white coat who looked like a turtle.

In spite of the way I was brought up by the good Sisters of Perpetual Grace, I'm not one of God's children. For me, He only exists when I'm on a plane in a blizzard. What I believe in is luck. Good, bad and none; but this trip to the hospital had more to do with something like the random matrix theory. If Greenburg hadn't cared, if Meriwether had been asleep and let the call go to voice mail, if the river were at low tide and I couldn't take the boat across, if the dancer's room hadn't been at the dark end of the hall…

Whether or not all the events starting with Justin Greenburg's call can be explained by luck or abstract mathematics, the truth is if Meriwether hadn't answered the phone in the first place, the dancer would be dead and I'd be reading about it in the paper like everybody else.

It was still pouring when I got her out of the hospital through a side exit. If timing is all, it was on my side just then because a cab came around the corner and saved us from getting drenched—and being seen.

We headed to the Seventy-Ninth Street Boat Basin, where I keep my old Boston Whaler, the *Button Gwinnett*, and where I'd left it not much more than an hour earlier. The adrenaline the dancer had been running on was finally depleted. She closed her eyes as soon as she got in the taxi and was groggy when I carried her onto the boat and put her in the cuddy cabin, which isn't actually a cabin. It's more like the space beneath a canvas awning. The only thing in there to keep her warm was a tarp, which she crawled under before closing her eyes again.

I shook her since Greenburg had reminded me of what I already knew about it being dangerous for a person with a concussion to sleep too soon after a head trauma. Because I wasn't sure how soon was too soon, I didn't want to let her get comfortable.

"I'm just resting," she said vaguely. "Just resting."

I turned away from her, pulled out my cell phone, and called Meriwether. I told him briefly what happened and asked him to make up the guest room.

I couldn't watch the dancer and drive the boat at the same time, so I took her with me when I went to the wheel. I put her on the bench close to me, but immediately she began to lean to one side. There was no other way to keep her steady but to get her up and put my arm around her.

I did not need this. I didn't want to feel the heat coming from her, through my jacket and even through the tarp she had dragged along, but I did.

As we pulled away from the dock, I reviewed my position in regard to the general rules and regulations of civilized life, which is usually something like benign neglect. I had no regrets about Bellevue. Patients had skipped out before; the hospital could deal with it.

And I had no regrets about taking the dancer home with me. Just the opposite. But as infuriating as it is, sometimes I hear the voice of Sister Mary Alphonsus, my main guardian, echoing in my head. She opined by way of endless aphorisms, and tonight it was: This will end in tears.

We were a few minutes into the trip when the rain and wind finally startled the dancer. Suddenly she was wide-awake. Alert. Scared.

"Where are we?" she asked. I could feel her back straighten as she pulled away to get a better look at me.

"We're going to where I live," I said. "I'm Nick Sayler. You were in the hospital. You wanted to leave. Do you remember?"

"Yes." She paused. "Oh yes, I remember. We ran across the hall...yes, I'm sorry. I'm tired. You're Nick Sayler. I have your card."

She produced it from the pocket of the torn jeans, looked at it like a talisman, and immediately put it back.

She leaned against me and closed her eyes, but I couldn't let her sleep.

"I want to ask you something," I said loudly over the noise of the engine. "After what you've been through, why would you go off with a stranger? You could have stayed in the hospital where you'd be safe."

She paused again before she said, raising her voice several decibels, "Hospitals aren't safe. Hospitals are definitely not safe."

"But somebody hurt you," I said as loudly as I could because I did not want to lean close even though it would be easier for her to hear. "And you don't know who it was."

"At least I know it wasn't you," she shouted.

"How do you know I'm such a solid citizen?" I shouted back.

"Justin looked you up."

Endless wonders of cyberspace.

If Greenburg read the sordid details in the old stories about me, he'd see that in the end I got off. But when a case is closed the best they give you is charges dismissed. No one is ever declared innocent.

The rain and wind were too cold and the engine was too noisy for more conversation. I just held on to her and shook her a few times to be sure she didn't sleep as we headed home to the *Dumb Luck*.

I called my barge the *Dumb Luck* because I won it and most of its contents playing cards. Poker's not my game, and even if it had been, the odds were still about half a million to one against drawing to an ace-high straight flush.

But that was my hand when I got lucky around dawn at the Cobra Club, an after-hours place where I'd never been before and would never go again since it was closed down the following week by the NYPD Special Investigator's Vice Squad.

There was a rich kid in the game just shy of his twenty-first birthday, when he would be free to piss away any or all of his $40 million inheritance. Until then he was on an allowance—a big one by the standards of sane people. But even advances on the allowance had run out a couple of months before the poker game where he lost his last pocketful of money. At the end in lieu of cash, he bet the barge.

A trust officer from J. P. Morgan and a couple of lawyers from Skadden Arps tried, lamely, to squelch the deal. They knew a court battle based on a night of illegal gambling, especially with me, would dredge up all the old headlines and make it a sure thing the kid would land in the tabloids and on tabloid TV. I was bluffing when I made it clear I didn't give a shit about being back in the news, and it was no secret that the kid loved notoriety even if it was for nothing more than being an idiot.

But his parents didn't want any more public evidence about how they fucked up their son. So the bank and the lawyers backed off. And I became the legal owner of a five-ton vessel with a deck longer than a football field.

The living quarters were tricked out as a twelve-room, five-bathroom hip-hop paradise. With weird retro appurtenances. I threw out the velvet curtains, the white shag rugs, and all the posters featuring naked people of various genders.

Looking at empty rooms and bare walls it dawned on me that I'd never have enough money to transform this pleasure palace into a decent place to live, so I checked into the market for used barges. And discovered there wasn't one.

That was just before I accidentally hit a hidden panel in one of the closets and discovered a door opening onto a long, dark, sloping corridor. At the end of the corridor another door opened to reveal the panic room.

This retreat from violent trespassers was something I didn't need any more than I needed the kid's tanning room, since I wasn't worried about home invasions.

The eastern shore of Weehawken, New Jersey, isn't a destination spot. Not even a favorite with seagulls. The panic room was probably installed because it had become a status symbol, like those cement bunkers back in the 1950s built to protect against an atomic bomb attack that never happened.

This steel-walled installation was fully stocked with booze and beer and boxes of junk food. It was like what the anti-penthouse at a Ritz-Carlton hotel would look like if they ever built one. With the attention span of a dust mote, the kid had never put in any furniture, but there were other attributes. Or one other attribute.

The day after I discovered the panic room, I brought my old Ducati down there to store. The bike was a GT 1000 I'd accepted in lieu of my fee from a client with a liquidity problem. I don't use it much because, for one thing, a stakeout on a motorcycle is an oxymoron.

Rolling the Ducati into a corner, I almost stepped on a painting that had been left facedown on the cement floor. When I turned it over I saw that it seemed none the worse for wear, and I guess it was pretty if you liked naked cupids floating in golden clouds.

Looking a little closer, I could see the artist's signature in the upper left-hand corner and I recognized the name.

Less than a month later, Christie's auctioned it off, and I got $390,000 for the Fragonard.

I gave two hundred grand to the Sisters and then decided that since Madame Good Luck had laid her hand on my shoulder twice it would be bad juju to put the rest of the money anywhere but back into the barge.

I hired FAL, a construction outfit put together by a bunch of ex-cons with good skills from the outside plus a few skills they'd learned on the inside. The unions didn't want them, and builders wouldn't hire ex-convicts when they could have illegals.

Nevertheless, FAL Construction made a go of it, operating pretty much aboveboard. Now and then they got a little help from their friends in Jersey City who were in the cement or waste disposal business. Just to show a little muscle, nothing more. They wanted to stay Free At Last.

Because I offered to pay cash, half up front, half when the project was finished, I got 10 percent knocked off the original estimate. And since the original estimate was high, the discount was more like a price adjustment. Fine. Charge what the market will bear. That's what I do.

They built me an office with huge windows almost twice the size of the ones in the blueprint. The foreman took the blame, claiming to have misread the measurements. I didn't argue. I knew they had all served time in places with no light. No sky, no sun. No treetops. No weather. They liked windows.

After I got used to them, I liked the windows in my office. They made me feel like a passenger on an ocean liner. The Hudson River is not the sea, but it's good enough. Especially for me because it starts at a lake in the Adirondacks called Tear of the Cloud. Then up by West Point, long before it gets anywhere near the *Dumb Luck*, it has already passed the place along its east bank known as World's End.

When the renovation was finished, I had left only one of the original rooms intact. Clearly pristine, it was a wood-paneled library featuring custom bookshelves with sliding glass doors and a granite fireplace. There was a buttery leather sofa, a couple of comfortable armchairs, a big butler's table, and foxhunting prints on the wall. To complete the comic WASPiness of the room, the kid had left behind a brass and burl backgammon set, always closed, always calling my name.

.

4

Strong winds added an extra twenty minutes to the trip across the river, and when we finally arrived at the barge, Meriwether came out of the cabin to help. While he tied up the *Gwinnett*, I brought the dancer inside.

It was the first time I'd seen her in anything but the dim fluorescence of the hospital or the flash of streetlights as the cab flew past them.

She was a breathtaking girl. Slender and graceful. Refined even in my soggy jacket. Somebody would be looking for her soon. An explanation of how she got to the shores of Weehawken, New Jersey, could get a little dicey if Bellevue brought the cops into the picture. But I'd worry about that later.

Since Rue is a frequent visitor, she leaves things in my closet. Meriwether knows Rue is easygoing and generous (I wondered how generous she'd be in this case since she reads me pretty well), so he appropriated a pair of black jeans, a black cashmere sweater, pale-blue lace underwear, and a black silk nightgown with matching robe and high-heeled satin slippers.

Rue likes nice clothes and looks beautiful wearing them. She looks even better when she takes them off. Her things would be

·too big for the dancer, but it was all the *Dumb Luck* had to offer in the way of ladies' apparel.

The dancer looked at the Agent Provocateur lingerie. I knew the label because I gave the stuff to Rue for her birthday.

"Whose is this?" she asked, picking up the nightgown.

"Do you care?" I said. "It's clean."

"I'm sure it's clean," she said, glancing around. "And no I don't care. Does it belong to your wife?"

I shook my head.

"Your girlfriend?"

"I thought you didn't care," I said.

"I don't," she said. With that smile. "Where's the loo?"

Loo. That was a glimpse into her background. She didn't have an English accent, but maybe she trained in London with the Royal Ballet. Maybe she hung with Eurotrash. Maybe she had been pretentious in her former life. The one that had been upended just hours earlier. Whatever she was, she came from privilege.

Meriwether showed her the guest room and the guest bath where she could shower and change. He had also put out the toiletries she'd need.

He stuck his head back into the library and asked if I had a plan or wanted him to start tracking down her identity.

"Not yet," I said.

"OK," he said and slipped away like a huge cat.

I poured myself a shot of Jameson and began wondering how long she would stay in the shower. Maybe she was waiting to take a hit of cold water to get rid of the grogginess. More likely she'd think if she stood under the hot water long enough it would wash away some of the ugliness that had touched her. I knew from personal experience that one shower or two or twenty weren't enough. For a long time you think there will never be enough water to make you clean.

Justin Greenburg said they started her on antibiotics because of the deep cuts on her back, and everybody knows it's a bad idea to quit antibiotics too soon. Which antibiotics? How many, how strong, how often? And the bandage would have to be changed.

I needed help with this, so, although I didn't want to disturb him, I called Edward Sloane.

He doesn't practice medicine anymore, but he's board certified in three specialties, conversant with half a dozen more, and keeps up through endless journals and lectures.

His reading has only increased in the last few years because he's gotten too old for his real passion. He'd climbed to the peaks of Mount McKinley and Mount Kilimanjaro and to the base camps of the highest mountains on each of the other five continents. You'd never guess it from his formal manner and the bespoke suits he always wore, but the old man had once lived for the rush.

Sloane moved to the barge a few years ago, on a temporary basis after his perfectly maintained Federal-style townhouse on Sullivan Street in SoHo was destroyed by a mysterious fire. The NYPD Arson/Explosion Squad investigated because the house went up so fast and burned so thoroughly they suspected Sloane had been a victim of a crime. But there was never any proof.

After a few weeks, since there's enough room on the barge for a family of forty, I asked him to stay on. Although he would never say so, I think he was relieved. His partner was gone, his only relatives were dead, and he was feeling his age.

When I brought the dancer to the *Dumb Luck*, Sloane was in the city. He had gone to the theater with his friend Constance Cohen, and, because of the storm, he had decided to spend the night at the Harvard Club.

I knew he wouldn't be happy when my call interrupted his sleep and he wasn't, but after he heard why I needed him, he agreed to come back. He's not quite as game as he used to be, but we've been friends for a long time.

Twenty-some years ago—it was raining that night too—I turned a corner in Hell's Kitchen, where I lived with half a dozen excommunicated Benedictine nuns, and saw four men kicking the shit out of an older guy in a suit. The term *gay bashing* didn't exist back then, but that's what it was.

I knew I was fast, but being a fast fifteen-year-old street thug wasn't going to do me any good against four guys, so it was lucky I had a gun on me. An old snub-nose .38 I'd bought off a bum in Alphabet City. I couldn't take a chance and wait to see if these guys also had guns, so I shot one of them in the arm and another one in the shoulder, and they ran.

Sloane repaid the favor by taking an interest in the heretical Sisters of Perpetual Grace and has been underwriting a lot of their expenses since that night on the street. Even when I was a disappointment to all of them.

As I waited in the library while the dancer was getting dressed, thoughts I'd buried, except in dreams, were coming back.

I met both Sloane and Meriwether when they were hurt, bleeding. For them, I was in the right place at the right time. But when Julia was hurt and bleeding, I couldn't do anything. I couldn't do one single fucking thing to save her.

Ten years ago, my regret led straight to cocaine, and when that wasn't enough I went to street heroin delivered by whatever means by whatever dealer and then through any available needle.

Never again. No drugs. And except for the permanent guilt over losing Julia, there will be no guilt about anything. Being a cold son of a bitch suits my work. I don't have to be sympathetic; I don't have to feel their pain. I only have to get the job done.

I mean you're afraid your business partner who also is your best friend has been embezzling from you for years and wrecking the business. That'll be five thousand up front. And later, yes he has, the money's gone, and that'll be ten thousand plus expenses.

You want to know who your new wife's been screwing in the Southampton house. That'll be three thousand up front. Shortly thereafter, sorry to report: it's your son. That'll be four thousand plus expenses.

Too antsy to sit still in the library, I was heading toward my office to sift through a pile of old mail when Sloane called.

"I'm in the car," he said, "and there's not much traffic, obviously, since it's the middle of the night."

"I already apologized for waking you up."

"And I already said to forget it," he replied. "I'll be there in half an hour, and I'm phoning just because it's slow going on account of the rain. I didn't want you to worry."

"I don't worry."

"So you say, dear boy, so you say."

"Just get here."

"Just get Meriwether to make me a hot toddy," he said and clicked off.

I found Meriwether in the kitchen reading the fifth volume of Churchill's magnum opus about the Second World War.

"Would you go check on the dancer?" I said.

"Why don't you go?" he asked.

"I don't want to."

No wasted words. Meriwether likes it when you speak his language. If more elaborate communication is called for, we can do it. Most of the time, we operate pretty much on a need-to-know basis.

He closed the book and headed for the guest room. When he returned a few minutes later, he reported that the dancer said she was tired and wanted to take a nap.

"I told her to talk to you," he said.

"OK, I'll be right back," I said. "Then would you sit with her? You don't have to chitchat, but she can't sleep until Sloane sees her...I can't do it."

"OK," he said. "I understand."

Maybe he did.

When I went to the guest room, I found the door open. It was a simple room with gray—Rue says they're taupe—walls. So the rain pounding down outside the window was taupe too, because in the light from the deck it looked the same color as the walls.

The dancer was sitting at the edge of the bed, looking at an old issue of *Sports Illustrated* someone had left on a side table. Her long hair was wet and fell in dark ringlets past her shoulders. She was wearing the ripped blue jeans again and a sweatshirt she must have found in a dresser drawer.

"I know I'm not meant to sleep," she said when she saw me.

"Is there something else?" I asked.

"I wanted to tell you that at least I can read," she said. "But who's Tom Brady?"

She showed me the cover of the magazine, which carried a shot of Brady under the headline UNDEFEATED. SO FAR.

"He's the quarterback for the Patriots."

"The New England Patriots," she said with a faraway look. "They're bums."

I had to laugh at the incongruity. It wasn't as startling as hearing Sister Mary Alphonsus say *shit* once when she hit her thumb with a hammer trying to hang a picture of the Blessed Mother. But close.

"What's so funny?" the dancer asked from wherever she had gone in her head.

"Nothing," I said. "I'm happy because you remember the Patriots."

"Yes," she said. "And I remember they went one and sixteen this season."

"Not this season," I said. "Things turned around for them—they won the Super Bowl three years in a row."

"No—you're joking." She was genuinely surprised. "Well, maybe I got it wrong. It's so vague."

"Meriwether will know what year," I said. "I think the last time the Patriots had a season like that was about twenty years ago. You were a little kid, but at least something came back."

"We can guess how old I was then and know how old I am now. God I hope I don't have to go through fifteen or twenty years one by one. Can you imagine how it feels not to know how old you are?"

"Not exactly," I said. "But I don't know what my actual date of birth is."

"You don't know your birthday," she said. "I'm so sorry."

She had left her childhood recollection of the Patriots and returned to the present, speaking as the grown woman who seemed to understand what I meant.

"So," I said because I wanted to change the subject back to her, "you're a ballerina who follows football—I wonder how you got into that."

"My father," she said, drifting again. "He played football…he was a single wingback."

"Do you remember where?" I asked. Nobody plays single-wing defense. Nobody had for many years.

"At school," she said and paused, putting her head in her hands. Then she looked up at me and said, "I can't remember my father's name."

The dancer said she wanted to rest until Sloane arrived, but she agreed to let Meriwether stay outside her open door. Just to look in every now and then to make sure she didn't doze off.

Once he was stationed at the guest room, I went to the library and poured a shot of Jameson to help me face the weather again. A second shot was all I needed to get me to the mudroom where we stow spare parts, fishing poles, bait boxes, boots, and rain gear. Situated between the kitchen and the deck, it's much like a mudroom anywhere except for the firearms and illegal spring knives in a big lockbox against one wall. I found a long slicker, pulled it on, and went outside to watch for Sloane.

He was driving home in his chocolate-brown Mercedes 300 SE Cabriolet. Vintage 1965. Ordinarily, he'd do anything to avoid a situation where he'd get mud on the car. And since mud was inevitable in this deluge, it was another sacrifice I appreciated.

However long the trip from the city would take, I could add another ten minutes, because he'd rather get drenched himself than leave the car with no protection from the elements. So he'd have to walk in the rain after he parked the Mercedes in the garage of our closest neighbor, Pauline Prochevsky.

Pauline is a widow whose age is on the far side of indeterminate. She lives in a big Edwardian house—which she refuses to call a bed-and-breakfast, because she also serves dinner to her boarders. The house has survived the last hundred years almost entirely intact. Great for historians. Not so great if you don't like sharing a bathroom.

The Prochevsky driveway is off a narrow road that winds into a cul-de-sac. I had cut a path from the other side of the cul-de-sac down a fairly steep scrubby embankment to the hard-packed sand that, for want of a better word, we call a beach. About fifty yards across the beach there's a ramp leading up to the barge.

I spotted Sloane in the distance as he made his way down the path. He was using two canes for balance and looked like an elderly cross-country skier except without the skis.

My leg, which started hurting at Bellevue, was throbbing. But at least it didn't keep me off the slopes. Unless you've made a lot of money, people where I come from never learn how to ski. Or ride horses.

I knew better than to try and lend Sloane a hand, so I waited until he reached the bottom of the ramp, where I'd gone when I saw him.

"All right, all right," he said, "let's get inside before this hurricane kills us."

"It's a nor'easter," I said, and he glared at me.

We entered the cabin on the starboard side. That's into the house from the right. I stick with the nautical because even if the barge is in permanent dry dock, to me it's still a boat.

5

In the mudroom, Sloane leaned his canes against the wall, took off his old-fashioned fedora, shook it, and then hung it along with his lightweight coat on one of the oversized hooks.

Always a fashionable guy, even in the middle of the night, in the rain, in Weehawken. Almost regal in fact, since his hair had turned entirely white in the last few years. He had been a rower at Harvard, hadn't put on a single pound since then, and his pale-blue eyes were clear—as if by sheer force of will he refused to be visited by the rheumy look that crept up on so many old people.

"All right," he said. "What's going on here?"

"Nothing's changed from what I told you on the phone," I said. "The girl still can't remember her name."

"Evening," said Meriwether, who heard us come in.

"Hello Albert," said Sloane. "It's lucky you don't need as much sleep as the rest of us."

Sloane is the only person allowed to use Meriwether's given name.

"She's changing her clothes," Meriwether said to me. And to the grumpy doctor, he continued, "I'll make you a hot toddy. Bourbon or brandy?"

"Brandy please," said Sloane.

Things were looking up.

"Simple syrup or honey?" Meriwether asked.

"What kind of honey do you have?" Sloane responded.

What I had was a girl in the other room who'd been viciously attacked. Maybe she knew the guy who did it or got a good look at him. Maybe he wanted to take another shot at her. Maybe it was her husband. Maybe I'd get arrested. But I knew better than to interrupt this conversation.

"We have *corbezzolo*," said Meriwether.

"Good man," said Sloane. "Very good." He reached up and patted Meriwether on the shoulder. An unremarkable act, but Meriwether doesn't like to be touched. Another exception for Sloane.

"OK," I said. "What is corbezzolo?"

"It's from Sardinia," they said in unison. Frick and Frack. Jack and the Giant at the top of the beanstalk.

While Meriwether went to work breaking out the corbezzolo, Sloane and I went to the library, where Meriwether had laid a fire, and picked up our conversation where we left off.

"I don't know who was more irresponsible," Sloane said as he sat down. "You or that fellow at the hospital. If this woman has a concussion, she should have stayed put."

"Even in the psych ward?" I said, sitting across from him.

"Yes," he said. "They're overworked and understaffed as is the case everywhere, but they're not barbarians."

I didn't want to get into it with him about the Thorazine. I was sure he'd agree it was overkill, but we'd get off point, so I said nothing.

"It's unlikely," Sloane went on, "but a person can die if the concussion is severe and the condition is ignored."

"She's not going to die," I said.

"If you're so sure of that, why did you drag me out of a warm bed?"

"Well, maybe I'm not so sure."

"Honestly Nick," said Sloane, "I don't understand this."

The dancer had good timing, because when she appeared at the door just then, she saved me from having to hear about my underdeveloped risk-assessment skills.

Her hair, still damp from the shower, was pulled back into a loose ponytail, and she was dressed in Rue's black sweater, which was baggy on her, and black pants rolled up.

Sloane, who had trained and practiced primarily as a psychiatrist, was good at keeping an impassive face, but when he saw her, his eyes widened and I heard an almost imperceptible gasp.

"Now I understand," he said quietly, getting to his feet.

"That's not the reason," I muttered as I also stood.

"'O reason not the need,'" Sloane whispered, looking at the dancer backlit, framed in the doorway. "*King Lear*. Act two. Scene four. Look it up."

Then he went to her.

"Come in, come in my dear," he said. "I'm Edward Sloane. We were just discussing Shakespeare."

"Shakespeare," said the dancer, pausing for a few beats. "All I can think of is Rosalind."

"Well," said Sloane. "I understand that you are a ballerina. You may have been Rosalind in *As You Like It*. The ballet, not the play."

"Could that be your name?" I asked.

"I don't know," she said, shaking her head.

"Don't worry," said Sloane. "You know Nicky's name. And mine. Soon you'll remember yours."

"Nicky," she said with the beginning of a smile.

"That's me," I said.

"Does your head hurt my dear?" asked Sloane.

"I'll be fine," she said.

"And your back?" he asked.

"It stings," she said. "I don't know how many stitches I have, but I'll be all right."

I remembered my friend Allegra Trent from the American Ballet Theatre going on about how dancers lived with pain. Every dancer, every day. She probably would have recognized this ballerina, but I heard Allegra gave in to the pain and retired to some remote ashram in Thailand. I heard she was looking for peace. More likely opium. But I'm the last person to pass judgment on that.

"Nick," Sloane said. "Aren't there any lamps in this room? I'm getting too old to see by firelight…though it is lovely."

"It is," said the girl, looking up with her dark-violet eyes. "It really is."

I nodded. I would help this girl get back to her real life and out of mine as fast as I could. I wanted to stay in the library, but after I walked around turning on lights, I excused myself and went to join Meriwether in the kitchen.

When I met Meriwether ten years ago I was a drug addict, a gambler, and a petty thief. And I had run out of time. I was on my way to end my troubles before someone else did it for me. Inflicting extreme pain in the process.

I owed a lot of money to some guys who didn't take *not yet* for an answer, and I was entirely tapped out. I didn't even have subway fare, and I didn't want stiffing a cabdriver to be my last act on earth. So I was on foot. The clock was ticking on my last day, but it didn't matter. The bridge wasn't going anywhere.

Meriwether was lying on the sidewalk in front of Saint Vincent's, a big Gothic church on Lexington Avenue, bleeding badly from a head wound. People stepped over him and kept going without so much as a quick look back. You can find mean streets anywhere, including the Upper East Side of Manhattan.

I don't know why I stopped. There is no honor among bums, so I suppose it was fate, because we saved each other that day and now I'm probably stuck with him for life. Which isn't such a bad thing, because he turned out to be not only a genius but also a very fine cook, and in spite of what I said earlier, if he were a hundred pounds lighter and a woman, I'd marry him.

After I checked in with Meriwether, I went to my office, sat in my swivel chair, and called my friend Thomas Fallon to set the wheels in motion for a process that would send the dancer back to where she came from.

Fallon's a cop, but not like any other cop I know. He's got more lives than a feral cat and a gift for solving unsolvable crimes. People say he's lucky, but it's more like fearless. I think he was born missing a gene—the self-preservation gene.

It would have been more polite to call him after the sun came up, but the sooner I got him into it, the sooner I could start clearing my conscience, which had gotten pretty cloudy pretty fast.

I called his cell phone and it went to voice mail. I called it again, and again it went to voice mail. Three was a charm though, and he answered.

"Yeah," he said.

"Tommy," I said.

"Fuckin' A," he said. "I'm asleep." He hung up.

I called again.

"OK Nick," he said when he answered. "What happened?"

I told him the shortest version: The call from Greenburg. The psych ward. Taking the girl to the barge.

"Where's Rue?" he asked, never one to ignore a detail, which was one of the reasons he's a good detective.

"In Louisiana."

"You can be a very bad guy," he said.

"I'm not a bad guy," I said.

"Right," he said. "It don't sound like the woman you got has been missing very long—but I'll check it out when I get to work."

Then he clicked off.

I swiveled around again, found my flask in the top drawer of my desk, and discovered it empty. Got a bottle of Jameson from the bottom drawer, took a small swig, and filled the flask.

Another swivel and I took a quick inventory of my handguns. In the office, two Beretta 92SBs with left-hand safeties. In my bedroom, an old Taurus .38 and a Smith & Wesson M&P340.

I never carry a revolver at home, but *never* had pulled anchor and sailed when the dancer boarded the barge.

Meriwether and I got back to the library at the same time.

I was carrying a concealed weapon and so was Meriwether. In all the years since we met, I've never known him to be without a knife. He was also carrying a tray with drinks, a pot of tea, and a plate of freshly baked ginger cookies.

Sometimes people mistake Meriwether for a houseman, cook, or driver. It's a big mistake, because Meriwether does what he chooses as much as I do or Sloane. His choices, though, are more of a reach because he's the only one who, if he wanted, could easily pull down seven figures a year. Instead he refuses even a small fee for sharing his research on visual object recognition with the McGovern Institute for Brain Research at MIT and the Rowland Institute at Harvard. And he won't sell the motherboard he invented, which is two generations ahead of the geeks at Caltech or Microsoft. Except for me, and I don't understand IT talk, the motherboard remains a secret, and he said he'd only sell his program to keep us from a return to sleeping in the park.

We walked into the library and found that Sloane had turned on the sound system to play Chopin's Nocturne in G Major, one of his favorite pieces.

The girl was sitting next to him on the couch, and he was looking in her eyes with the help of the beam from a pencil flashlight.

Under the lamp Sloane had pulled close, her eyes, framed with black velvet lashes, looked lavender. Her cheeks were flushed, and she'd pinned up her hair.

Sloane switched off the flashlight.

"What do you think?" I asked.

"I'm not a neurologist—"

"But you wrote a paper on memory," I said.

"You have a good memory," he said.

"Thanks."

"When you feel like it."

I said nothing. I had to choose my moments with Sloane, and this was not even up for consideration.

"The paper was about repressed memory," he went on, "which is a different thing than what we have here."

"I know," I said. "But the guy at the hospital told me they gave her a CAT scan and nothing showed up, so why did she lose her memory?"

"Please don't talk about me as though I weren't here," the dancer said.

"Sorry," I said.

Sloane tapped his fingers on the coffee table.

"For one thing," he said, "amnesia is not at all uncommon after a bad concussion. There's no way to predict how long it will last, but it rarely becomes a permanent condition."

"What percentage?" asked the dancer.

"Approximately one in ten thousand," said Meriwether.

"I agree," said Sloane.

"Trust them," I said, and I felt inappropriately happy that she seemed to trust me.

"Amnesia," Sloane told the dancer, "is almost always short term, but, as I said, I can't give you an accurate time frame. There is every reason to believe you will recover, but at the moment you are suffering from declarative memory loss."

"Which is?" she asked.

"There are two types of memory," Sloane replied. "Declarative memory is for facts and events. Those memories which are accessible to conscious recollection. If you lose declarative memory, you can't call up even the simplest facts, like your name and address or birthday."

"And the other kind?"

"Procedural," he said. "Skills and operations that have nothing to do with consciousness."

"Like brushing my teeth," she said.

"Or speaking the language," he said. "Typing, playing tennis."

"Or dancing," I said.

"Exactly," said Sloane.

"Would you do an experiment?" I asked the dancer.

"What is it?" she asked reluctantly.

"Stand up," I said.

She got up, barefoot but elegant in black. I stood in front of her with my hands raised over my head, arms curved or at least bent. I stuck out my right leg with my foot pointed to the right. I had seen this done.

Meriwether laughed out loud, which is a little unusual for him.

"Can you do this?" I asked her.

All it took was her lifting her chin, raising her arms, and extending her leg. I turned in a circle. And so did she, but she did it effortlessly and on the tips of her toes. She turned again faster and then a third time even faster.

"All right, enough. Stop," said Sloane. But he was too late. She lost her balance and fell into my waiting arms.

"Nick," Sloane said, "I think you've made your point."

"I am a dancer," she said as if it were a revelation. Which, in its way, it was.

"Meriwether..." I said.

"American Ballet Theatre," he responded. "New York City Ballet, Washington Ballet, Boston, Royal Ballet, Kirov—"

He probably could have listed every ballet company in the world, including defunct or fictional ones, but I interrupted.

"There will be photographs and bios," I said.

"I'll start looking."

And he'd find whatever was there to find. He always did.

After Meriwether left I said, "Edward, I thought you followed the ballet. She—" I turned to the dancer. "I meant you—you must be well known."

"That's a very nice compliment," she said. "But I don't know. We don't know."

"I know," I said.

"Nick," said Sloane, "it's been years since I've attended the ballet. After Nureyev...well—" Then, changing gears in midsentence, he turned to the dancer and continued, "When I just agreed with Nick that you are a dancer, I was imprecise. You already know what I am about to tell you and will eventually remember, so please try not to take it as bad news—but I should have said you *were* a dancer."

"What do you mean?" she asked.

"Your musculature doesn't suggest the daily rigors of practice, rehearsals, and performances. I don't think you've danced for some time—and since you are still young, there must be a reason, but I can't imagine that it would involve...what happened tonight."

Nobody had suggested that the attack might not have been random. But she didn't pick up on his point, which was maybe someone had been looking to attack her specifically.

"So my career's over," she said. "How long do you think it's been?"

"I'd guess—and it's only a guess—several years," Sloane replied.

Except for my brief interlude with Allegra, I knew nothing about the ballet, and Sloane didn't know as much as I'd thought.

I imagine he wasn't the only one who lost interest after Rudolf Nureyev died. Allegra told me both sexes loved him. I don't know if that would be a blessing or a curse. I'd say curse.

Even though he'd given up going to the ballet, I was sure Sloane would agree that this astonishing beauty had to have been a successful ballerina. A supremely graceful prima ballerina. Somewhere.

People must be looking for her. A mother or a brother. Friends or colleagues. Or a lover. And within an hour—or less—Meriwether would find her picture, her name…and then she'd be gone.

But I was wrong about that, at least for the moment, because just as I was pouring a glass of soda water for Sloane, lightning flashed, thunder cracked, and everything, except the flames in the fireplace, went dark.

The storm had knocked out our electricity, and I wish I could say I was sorry. But the power failure took any immediate decisions out of my hands and gave me a temporary reprieve. Just a little while longer before we all returned to the real life of criminal assaults, missing persons, police reports, and ultimately the return of the dancer's memory.

6

It had been ten years since Julia's death, and, as Sloane was quick to point out when I introduced him to Rue, I'd come up with her diametric opposite.

My friend Mike Teak used the exact words.

Although I met Teak when I was selling weed in Harlem, he comes from a rich family on the Upper East Side, so he and Sloane speak the same language. The language doesn't matter though, because they are both right.

Tall and temperamental with brown skin and black eyes, Rue is nothing like Julia. She's a Creole girl from Martinique who worked her way out of the poorest neighborhood in Fort-de-France. I admire her and I care about her.

But the girl with the violet eyes…the girl with no memory… she brought everything back. I have to hand it to Sloane for not suggesting that I thought I had a chance to start all over again. Thought I'd found what he would have called a tabula rasa. A blank slate.

Meriwether came back with flashlights and said he'd checked the circuit breakers but they hadn't been thrown; the electricity from Jersey Central Power & Light was off at the source.

Ordinarily this wouldn't be an issue because we counted on our own generators—neither of which was up and running that night.

The main one had just been removed to make way for a bigger and better model, and the backup, which was about to become obsolete anyway, was recently put out of business by some visiting mice. We could do without the generators because power from outside would probably come back soon and the whole thing would resolve itself.

"Our cell phones are working," I said. "And we've got flashlights. I called Fallon, but I don't expect to hear from him for hours, so why don't we all get some rest."

"Indeed," said Sloane.

"Cell phones?" said the dancer.

"I'll explain later," I said.

"Do you think it's all right for me to sleep?" she asked Sloane.

After consulting his watch, Sloane shook his head and said she should stay awake through the night. She took the order in stride, then turned to me.

"Who's Fallon?" she asked.

"Thomas Fallon. A friend in the police department. He's going to check missing persons."

"What about the hospital?" asked the dancer.

"Don't worry," I said. "If there's a problem, I'll pay the bill."

"And I'll pay you back," she said.

"And I will pay both of you," said Sloane, "to stop talking and leave the room. By the time Tom Fallon calls, the power will have returned and Meriwether will know something."

"Probably not," said Meriwether over his shoulder as he headed back to his room.

His strange powers still did not include reading the future, but I was half hoping he was right. I wondered about the dancer's life. If it were a good life, wouldn't she have some small inkling of it?

"I am going to bed," said Sloane. "Now."

"Sleep well," said the dancer.

"I intend to," said Sloane. "And I mean it Nick. Do not wake me unless the barge is sinking."

"It can't sink," I said.

"I meant metaphorically," he said. "And in point of fact, I'd rather go down with the ship than wake up before ten a.m."

"I'm sorry," said the dancer. "It's my fault."

"Forgive me darling," said Sloane. "There's no fault. I'm just getting old and crabby. I'm glad I had the chance to meet you. Any friend of Nick's is a friend of mine."

"Good night Edward," I said. "And thank you."

"My pleasure, dear boy, my pleasure."

With that, he walked out of the room, slowly but with his usual perfect posture.

I picked up two flashlights and took the dancer down the hall to the guest room. When we reached the door she stopped.

"You do know I've been trying to remember," she said. "But the strongest memory isn't even a memory—it's just a feeling."

"The hospital," I said.

"Yes," she said. "Obviously something happened."

"Try to relax about that," I said. "You can't control the past—and tonight you don't even have a past."

"There must be a lot of people who'd be glad to wipe out the past," she said. "Make a fresh start."

"Do you want a fresh start?" I asked.

"What do you think?" she responded in a level voice.

"I think not."

"I think not also," she said. "Because people don't get fresh starts."

"You sound like me," I said.

"Maybe I am like you."

"In that case," I said, "you'll know you have nothing to be afraid of. You're safe here—but Meriwether can stay at your door and make sure you don't sleep."

"I'll be fine," she said and smiled.

I noticed her lips and her even white teeth. Her slanted cheekbones. And a small scar on her chin. Everybody who was ever a kid with five minutes of unsupervised playtime has a scar on the chin to show for it.

"Try to rest," I said. "I'll come back in a few hours. By then I'll have talked to Fallon. He'll know something. I'm sure a lot of people are looking for you."

"Thank you Nick," she said and touched my arm. "Sleep well."

I gave her one of the flashlights, and she went into the guest room and closed the door. Half a beat later I heard the lock turn and click into place.

Ordinarily I would have left Larry outside the dancer's door. But the mutt who'd turned up one morning two years earlier, starving and sick, was with Rue. She had become his first priority after she nursed him back to health. I thought Cheater was a good name for him. It seemed nobody who hadn't escaped at least one near-death episode was allowed to join the *Dumb Luck* club. But Rue insisted his name was Larry. Why? Because he looked like a Larry.

Satisfied that the dancer didn't need a bodyguard—canine or otherwise—I decided to open the bottle of Jameson Vintage Reserve I'd been saving for a special occasion. So far the night had been special enough.

After what he'd said, I was surprised to find Sloane back in the library, lying awake on the couch with his head propped up on a needlepoint pillow depicting Saint Patrick vanquishing the snakes, courtesy of the Sisters.

When he saw me, he pushed himself into a sitting position.

"There's something I think you don't know," said Sloane. "Or you would have mentioned it."

"What is it?"

"I gave the young lady antibiotics—"

"I know that," I said.

Sloane shook his head like a teacher who's just given up on teaching restraint to a loudmouth student.

"I also changed her bandage," he said. "She told me she'd been careful, but still it got wet in the shower. The one I put on is sealed with a new waterproof material. It'll be good for a couple of days. We're fortunate Meriwether has a siege mentality. He's got enough first-aid supplies to treat a small Balkan army."

"Are the wounds bad?" I asked.

"Yes," he said. "Very bad. I don't mean in the sense that they won't heal or will leave terrible scars."

"What other sense is there?"

"Her attacker very precisely carved the number 44 into her back. Why didn't that intern tell you?"

"He didn't dress the wound," I said. "Has she seen it?"

"No," said Sloane. "And I didn't mention it—because if she knew what it meant she wouldn't be able to remember it any more than she can remember who did it."

"Well thanks Edward," I said. "We'll figure it out. Or Fallon will. Now go get some sleep."

But he didn't make a move to rise. In fact, he sat back and crossed his legs. He had put on a pair of his Belgian Shoes and was wearing argyle socks.

Various shades of blue woven into complicated patterns on the Persian carpet seemed to undulate. The candles on the coffee table were burning down. And Sloane could wait me out forever.

"What?" I said.

"Do you want to talk?" he asked.

"No."

"Good," he said, slapping his hands on his thighs, preparing to get up. "If I were practicing medicine, my advice would be too expensive for you anyway."

"I'm glad that's settled," I said.

"But Nick—" he said, pushing himself up off the couch.

"Edward, I don't want to talk about Julia."

"You've never wanted to talk about her," he said, not unkindly.

"That's right," I said. And I meant it.

When Sloane finally went to bed, the sky was still dark and the rain, exacerbated by some alliance with a new storm rolling in from the northeast, had gotten worse.

I lay on my bed, tired and wired, found a pack of stale Camels in a drawer in the night table, and tapped one out.

I finished the first cigarette, lit another, and watched the smoke rise toward the ceiling.

Man is born into trouble as the sparks fly upward.

Man is born into trouble...

I hadn't stayed away from trouble. But now it was only other people's trouble. Now it was my business, not my life.

I dropped the cigarette in a glass of stale beer. No sparks there. I turned over, went to sleep, and for the first time in a long time, dreamed about Julia.

I woke up as I always do at the end of those dreams. Rather, just before the end. I'm seconds away from saving her life and something always gets in my way. Different things—bullets, wild animals, river rapids, big rigs, earthquakes.

I was only out half an hour, but I knew there would be no more sleep for me, so I went to my office, where I poured a shot of Jameson into an empty cup. Then I put my feet up on the desk and called Jersey Central Power & Light, where I learned, from a live person, there had been no power outages in our area.

Maybe I'd become a good enough detective to operate on instinct, because I don't know what else could have made me check the landlines, which did not need electricity and that is why I kept them for backup.

Line 1: dead.
Line 2: dead.

Wearing a slicker I'd grabbed on the way out, I went looking for the place where the wind might have snapped our electric line. What I found was evidence that the line had been cleanly sliced off; a simple tool could have done the job. So much for the storm.

I was pretty sure none of the wiseass locals was going to slosh down the hill through the mud and rappel up the side of the barge for some minor vandalism. Especially anybody who'd ever seen Meriwether around town.

Maybe somebody took on a stupid bet. Losing landlines and power was a pain in the ass, but I didn't think anything serious was going on. Until I glanced out through slanting sheets of rain and saw that my boat, the *Button Gwinnett*, had been cut loose and was drifting, downriver toward Port New York.

7

In spite of what I eat, drink, and smoke, and the tricky situation with my leg, I try to run a few miles every couple of days, so when I sprinted into the cabin and straight to the guest room, my heart wasn't pounding because I was out of shape.

Meriwether heard me and came running.

"Somebody cut the *Gwinnett* loose," I said.

He headed for the deck, and I stopped in the hall outside the guest room, drew a breath, and knocked softly. No immediate response. I knocked again. And again harder. I tried the doorknob and the lock was still set. Then I pounded on the door.

Like all the other doors in the place, it was solid, but I thought I could kick it down if I had to.

"*OK*, I'm coming," said the dancer. "Who is it?"

"It's Nick."

She unlocked the door and opened it. Rue's thin silk night-gown was too long and trailed behind her on the floor like the train of a ball gown. She looked at me blankly—but she hadn't lost recent memory, she had just lost sleep and it was showing.

Almost immediately her eyes focused in the half-light from a kerosene lantern Meriwether had set up in the hall.

"What's wrong?" she asked. "Did something happen?"

"No, nothing happened."

"Then why were you banging at the door?"

"I wanted to make sure you were all right."

"Why wouldn't I be?"

"Sloane was worried…"

"You know what, Nick?" she said. "I only just met you, but I already can see that you're a bad liar."

Lying was a way of life for me once, but I pretty much gave it up when I gave up drugs. It takes practice to be good at anything, and I was rusty.

"You're smart," I said.

"Please don't patronize me," she said.

"I didn't mean to."

"Will you tell me what's going on?"

"Nothing much," I said. "The *Gwinnett*—my boat—came loose and Meriwether went out to get it. Listen, we're both awake now—let's get something to eat."

"Or drink," she said.

"That too," I said.

I lit some candles Meriwether had left in the kitchen, and in the candlelight the dancer, who was wearing Rue's robe, looked like a pale waif wrapped in her big sister's silk.

She perched on a stool by Meriwether's butcher block counter, and I opened the refrigerator, which was still cold, and found the pitcher of orange juice he usually kept on hand.

"Do you have any coffee?" she asked, looking around.

"Not right now," I said. "We've got a gas stove with an electric switch—so we're limited."

"I don't care—whatever you have is fine," she said, looking out at the river. "Lightning must have knocked out your electricity. Or do you think maybe it was the wind?"

"I'm not sure what happened," I said. "But because the power's out, Meriwether couldn't look for you on the Internet." Except his stuff was juiced no matter what.

Amazing how fast an old skill can return.

"What's the Internet?" she asked. "Justin looked you up in it—and Meriwether's looking me up—is it some kind of directory?"

"No," I said, wondering how long Meriwether and I would postpone the no doubt very easy task of finding out who she was. "It's more than that—I'll explain it to you—"

"Now?"

"Later."

"It looks so nasty out there," the dancer said. "Is Meriwether going to be OK?"

"Meriwether's good," I said. "The visibility's lousy, and after he gets to the *Gwinnett* he'll have to attach a line so he can tow her back. It'll take a while, but he's OK."

"What does Gwinnett mean?" she asked.

"It's a man's name," I said. "Button Gwinnett was a politician—one of the signers of the Declaration of Independence. He got killed in a duel. We're up on those facts because there used to be dueling grounds in Weehawken where people came to fight it out."

"Like Hamilton and Burr?" she asked.

"Yes," I said. "In fact, this is where they had the duel. Do you remember their story?"

"Aaron Burr killed Alexander Hamilton," she said. "That's all."

"Well," I said, "that's progress. You've gone way back before Brady—"

"The quarterback," she said.

"Most people without amnesia couldn't say who they were and who killed who—"

"In the nineteenth century—"

"Or in which century," I said. "Can you remember more history?"

"I remember Adam and Eve," she said.

I let that go, got a couple of glasses, and poured the orange juice. Then I went back to the freezer, took out a half-full bottle of Ketel One, and added a splash to my glass. The dancer picked up the bottle and began to pour some vodka into her glass, but I stopped her hand.

"Vodka is not good for people with concussions."

"How do you know?" she said.

"I know."

"And I should follow your orders because, what—you're the boss around here?"

I didn't say anything as she daintily removed her wrist from my grasp and put a generous shot of vodka into her glass.

"I probably always have vodka with my midnight snack," she continued. Then she smiled. A mischievous smile, so familiar it hurt.

Since the kitchen was definitely not my domain, I wasn't having much luck looking around our larder for fast food.

I did spot a bottle of aspirin and washed three of them down when the dancer wasn't looking.

Finally I found some cheese and a box of Carr's crackers; but instead of eating them, the dancer broke the crackers in half and half again and sipped her orange juice and vodka.

"What are you thinking?" she asked.

I've never known a woman who doesn't ask that question. Never. Right then I was thinking about what she would look like naked.

I shrugged my shoulders.

"Tell me about your life," she said.

"What do you want to know?" I asked.

"You decide."

"This is it," I said.

She raised her eyebrows.

"Isn't there anything else?" she said.

"Sure," I said. "Like everybody's life."

"Not like everybody."

"Where do you want me to start?" I asked.

"Start where you don't know your birthday," she said.

"That's easy."

What I told her was true; omitting the sad parts, the bad parts, and the sordid parts, it was a pretty tame story. And short. I think she realized what I was doing, but she didn't say anything. I liked her more because she understood there's always a line with people, a line you don't cross unless you're invited.

Sister Mary Alphonsus would never say no good deed goes unpunished, but I would say it and have said it. She'd just ask when I was going to get tired of learning the hard way.

Not yet.

As the dancer and I talked, I stopped trying to separate the graceful woman on the barge from the graceful woman who died ten years earlier. I felt like a hidden burden of guilt and anger was lifting, and it felt good. But the relief would be short, and for me feeling good was always a foreign country.

For the moment though, I was sitting around like a guy who could afford to be on permanent vacation, where time was the only currency that mattered.

I'd found a girl with violet eyes. Not my girl. But a lovely girl. And I wanted just a few more hours before she went away.

8

"Nick, guess what I just remembered?" the dancer asked like a kid in school with the right answer.

"Tell me."

"Ship to shore radio," she said.

Antiquated equipment. But not if you're thinking twenty years ago.

"Good," I said, and nothing more.

It wasn't worth explaining that nobody used ship to shore radios anymore. She'd be back in present time soon enough.

"You must have a ship to shore radio," she said. "We can call Meriwether and see how he's doing. I can't believe he didn't mind going out in this weather—it looks so dangerous."

He's strong and silent, but he suffers like everybody else. However, since he's Albert Meriwether, not Meriwether Lewis, he is not suicidal.

"Yeah," I said. "He minded. But one of us had to go, and I wanted to stay with you."

That came out wrong.

"So let's call him and see if he's OK," she said.

"Sure," I said and pulled my cell out of my pocket. "This phone works better than ship to shore."

"That is a very small phone," said the dancer, who had been groggy when I used it earlier at the Boat Basin.

"You don't remember these phones?" I said. "It's a cell phone—a cellular phone."

"No…" she said. "I mean I can see it's a portable phone. I just can't remember anything so small."

"Here, I'll show you how it works."

I tried to ignore the force field coming off her body as she watched over my shoulder. When the phone lit up, she said, "That's amazing. I've never seen anything like that…" Then she laughed.

Good, I thought. As Greenburg said, humor's a good sign.

"So now do you tap the numbers?" she said as I paused. "Is something wrong?"

Something was wrong. The battery was fine, but there was no service. This wasn't about the storm. We were in a good spot. The wireless connection had never failed before.

"I can't get a connection," I said. "I'll use Sloane's cell phone. Come with me."

"I'm OK here," she said.

No point in letting her sense any more trouble than she already had. I'd already overreacted once when I tried to pound down the guest room door.

Sloane's quarters, built after he moved in for good, were just beyond the far end of the cabin, starboard side. They connected to the original structure by a usually well-lit hallway where Sloane had hung original posters from the 1920s Russian labor movement. I guess he deliberately chose pictures that were about as far removed as it gets from the irreplaceable Hudson River Luminist paintings he lost in the fire.

When he said it was unhealthy to try and replicate the past, he should have known he was preaching to the choir.

I walked into Sloane's sitting room without knocking and directly into another shorter hall, which ended at his bedroom door. I opened it quietly and took a few seconds to let my eyes get accustomed to the dark. Which was hard because Sloane had blackout curtains.

I could make him out, asleep in his large four-poster. I also could see his dresser across the room. I made my way over to it slowly and found the cell phone next to his wallet and his gold pocket watch. He hadn't gotten into the habit of using the phone instead of a watch to check the time, and I hadn't either, but we're a dying breed.

When I hit the Home button, the phone lit up immediately, but there was no service. Since Sloane used a different provider than I did, I began to feel the kind of uneasiness that starts somewhere in your chest and then ripples out, getting stronger not weaker.

The electricity, the landlines, even the boat could be just criminal mischief. However, jamming cell phones is more complicated than cutting towlines. And it's a federal offense.

As I turned to go, I heard Sloane's voice.

"Nick," he said, "may I ask what you're doing?"

"Sorry," I said. "I tried to be quiet."

"Not quiet enough."

"I was checking your cell phone," I said.

"For what?"

"My phone hasn't got any signal. Yours doesn't either."

"That's strange," he said, sitting up, rubbing his eyes. He was wearing his usual white silk pajamas and had barely a hair out of place.

"What's going on?" he continued.

"I'm trying to figure that out," I said. "Go back to sleep—we'll know more in the morning."

"In case you hadn't noticed, dear boy," Sloane said, looking at the clock on his bedside table, "this is morning."

"It's not light yet…"

"Because it's still raining," he said.

"Please go back to sleep."

"I will try," he said. "But tell me, how's the young lady?"

"The same," I said on my way out of the room.

"And how are you?" he asked.

"Good night," I said and pulled the door shut behind me.

I was glad Sloane hadn't started one of his lectures. Magical thinking and self-esteem are all-time favorites. If something good happens I attribute it to luck, and if something bad happens I take the blame.

The truth is simple. Skill didn't give me the winning hand that night at the Cobra Club. And I am in fact responsible for some very bad things.

As for self-esteem in general, I have more than enough. Which is usually pointed out by somebody yelling, "Who the fuck do you think you are?"

Heading back to the dancer, I went over the people who considered me an enemy. I narrowed it down to the short list of guys who might actually try to fuck with me. Then I eliminated them one by one.

It wasn't Yuri Chenvenko, the Russian mob guy from Brighton Beach who held me responsible for his first lieutenant's death. And it wasn't Roger Blatt, the private equity fund CEO who went apeshit blaming the messenger when I told him what his wife was doing with her afternoons.

And it wasn't Rue's old boyfriend, Olivier the psycho, who came at me once with a broken bottle.

Olivier wouldn't resurface because I gave him some good reasons—and one of them required fifty stitches—not to. If Blatt wanted to hurt me, he'd have the IRS on my ass. And if Chenvenko wanted revenge, I'd be dead.

Still, sometimes I couldn't sleep because of them—and sometimes I couldn't sleep or eat. And once shortly after I met Rue, I sent her out of town because sometimes private investigators, like spies, do dirty jobs.

9

In the kitchen, Meriwether was not looking like a man who'd just hauled a runaway boat through a storm. In fact, he'd already put on fresh clothes, found some kind of battery-operated hot plate, and was boiling a kettle of water.

"Boat's tied up," he said.

"Thanks. Any problems?"

Meriwether doesn't hesitate, and he doesn't lie.

But he hesitated before he shook his head, so I was fairly sure something was wrong with the boat. Whatever it was, though, I didn't want to hear it. And I didn't want to talk about the phones. Not for a while. That wasn't asking much.

Although I wanted to be alone with the dancer, I for once took the high road, which wasn't hard since I had no choice. Because for once Meriwether didn't vanish. The three of us finished the last of the orange juice, his straight, ours spiked. Besides that, all we needed was the Sunday *Times*, a bag of bagels, and a Giants game on TV.

The dancer asked Meriwether about the Internet. As he delivered his encapsulated explanation of the virtual world, he arranged a small fruit plate, obviously for her. If I wanted anything, I'd be on my own.

Clearly he was going out of his way. Which may sound easy, but Meriwether does not practice selective savantness; his pathology is equal opportunity. Except for our strange little family, he pretty much avoids everybody. If there are people aboard the barge, he's absent. His ability to disappear into the woodwork like a shadow in the dark makes him a hopeless dinner partner but a perfect wingman.

After the dancer ate a slice of apple, she took a few sips of the tea Meriwether had made for her and said, "I know this tea, it's Indian Darjeeling," again treating memory as revelation.

In a singsong way she continued, "India tea with milk—China tea with honey." She stopped. "I don't know where that came from, but at least I know what it means."

"We don't have milk," said Meriwether, who'd refilled the teapot and returned it to the hot plate.

"But we have fifty-two varieties of honey," I said.

"I'm sure I've broken worse rules than putting honey in Indian tea," she said, looking at me. "I think I'll take a chance."

Meriwether opened a cabinet and, this time skipping the corbezzolo, he chose three other bottles of honey. Nodding thistle from New Zealand, French lavender, and the only one I can ever remember, tupelo. He set them down in front of the dancer and offered her a spoon.

Sloane, I decided, had gone back to sleeping the sleep of the just. Rain drummed rhythmically above our heads, the sweet smell of lavender honey was in the air, and just for good measure, I was carrying a loaded revolver.

Again, my better—or at least tougher—self took over, and I returned to our problems.

"Meriwether," I said conversationally, "did you try to call me when you caught up with the *Gwinnett*?"

"No," he said.

"Have you got your phone on you?" I asked.

He took it out, looked at it, and returned it to his pocket. He registered that there was trouble because he knew we always had service.

"I like the tupelo honey," said the dancer.

"I'm going to take a look at the boat," I said.

"I'll come with you," said Meriwether.

The dancer was spooning honey into her tea.

"I'll come too," she said.

"You'll be able to see us through this window," I said, pointing.

"I'd like to come," she said.

"Well I wouldn't like it," I said. "Just stay where you are. Please. We'll be right back."

Meriwether and I left the kitchen, grabbed some rain gear in the mudroom, and went out to the deck.

"You were…" said Meriwether.

"What—harsh?" I asked and answered without waiting. "Yeah, well you know it doesn't matter what kind of honey she likes—and it doesn't matter if she wants to stroll around the deck or drink tea in the kitchen. She's leaving. She has to go back to wherever she came from."

"I know," he said.

"Good."

"Edward said she looks like Julia."

I hadn't mentioned Julia's name for years.

"So you and Sloane were talking it over?" I said to Meriwether, who didn't reply.

"Can I see your cell phone?" I continued.

Meriwether took his phone out of his pocket.

"No service, right?" I said.

"Yours?" he asked.

I shook my head.

"Edward's?"

I shook my head again.

"Somebody's jamming them," he said.

"That's what I thought."

"I'll unjam them."

"So what's wrong with the *Gwinnett*?" I asked.

"Gas line's cut."

"Shit," I said. "Can you fix it?"

"Probably."

"How long?"

"Then you'll take her off the barge?" he asked.

"I have to," I said.

"To where Nick?"

"I don't know yet," I said. "Anywhere but here."

As a rule, Meriwether's face does not belie his feelings. However, in the last few hours aboard the *Dumb Luck*, a lot of rules had been suspended. Meriwether looked uneasy, and his expression said he didn't want to speed the dancer's departure by repairing the gas line.

"OK, I'll fix it," he said but didn't move. When I said nothing, he finally started to walk across the deck. I remember thinking, Great, now both of us want her to stay.

What happened next was a perfect illustration of being careful what you wish for, because Meriwether hadn't gone more than twenty feet when we heard the first gunshot.

10

As the next three shots exploded, I pulled my gun and ran back to the mudroom door. Meriwether followed with whatever lethal weapon I was certain he had on him.

I reached the kitchen in about five seconds, where almost everything looked the same. The kettle was still on the hot plate, the tins of tea were still lined up in a row, and the bottle of tupelo honey was still open next to the dancer's cup. But the stool she had been sitting on was flipped on its back, and the dancer was gone.

"Hey," I started yelling. I didn't know her name. Goddammit. "Hey, where are you?"

I automatically scanned the butcher block, the table, and the floor for anything different—like blood—and saw nothing.

"Nick," said Meriwether, who had been right behind me, "the shots came from there."

He was pointing in the direction of Sloane's quarters. The gunfire had stopped, and the direction he pointed out would not have been my guess, but sound, especially on the water, can be deceptive. We headed for Sloane's rooms because Meriwether, with his uncanny sense of distance, is rarely deceived.

Almost there, we slowed down, and after Meriwether flattened his back against the wall, I threw the door open.

I waited, listening; there was no one in the sitting room and no sound except rain hitting the roof of the cabin. I ran for Sloane's bedroom and pushed open the door.

What I saw stopped my heart.

Sloane's bed was empty. His bedside lamp was on the carpet, its shade at a crazy angle, broken in half. His books and magazines were scattered.

Dim light came from the far side of the room, where one of the blackout curtains had been ripped down by whoever smashed the window from the outside, spraying glass all over the floor.

When Meriwether came through the door, I saw the glint of a knife in his hand.

"You take the deck," I said, and he was through the broken glass an instant before I heard the sound behind me.

I swiveled, ready to fire. Vowing to hurt the man who hurt Sloane.

"Don't shoot, for God's sake!"

That was Edward Sloane walking out of his bathroom, one sleeve of his white silk pajamas soaked with blood.

"Edward," I said, running toward him. "What the fuck—what happened—where did he hit you?"

"Just my forearm, it's nothing much," Sloane said. "Do you have the girl?"

"No," I said. "She's missing. Could the shooter have her?"

"He couldn't," said Sloane. "There was no time—he never got past me."

"Why not?" I asked.

"He changed his mind," said Sloane. "He went back out the window onto the deck and dove into the river."

"Changed his mind?" I demanded. "Are you sure he went into the river?"

Sloane's lips tightened.

"Go find the girl," he said.

Trying to figure out where she could have gone in such a short time, and why she didn't hear our calls, I ran, pumped by the fear that she was hurt. Or worse. On my watch.

I checked Meriwether's knife room, computer room, living room, bedroom, and bathroom. Nothing. Nothing in the large closet next to the mudroom.

I ran past a locked door that led to the panic room and the depths of the barge, then through the living room and the library to the guest room and to my room, where I found nothing. Same with my weight room and office. Nothing.

There was no way off the barge except down the ramp, down the ladder to the *Gwinnett*, which was pulled up or over the side. There was no reason for the dancer to jump, and without light she'd hardly know her way through the mudroom to the deck. If she did get on the deck she wouldn't know which way to turn to reach the long ramp leading to the beach.

When we heard the gunshots, she knew I was just seconds away. She must have known I'd come.

With blood pounding in my head and spikes of pain driving into my leg, I went back to the kitchen to try and retrace what might have been her steps from the beginning.

I had no ideas, so I did the smart thing. I yanked a chair away from the table and kicked it across the room, where it crashed into the wall.

"Goddammit," I said. "*Where are you?*"

Then I heard a sound. Faint but definite.

"I'm here."

11

Her voice came from a small closet where Meriwether keeps staples. Next to where the chair hit the wall. I jerked the door open and saw her uncurling from behind some big jugs of rice vinegar. She was pale but calm.

"I'm so sorry," I said hoarsely, and held out my hand.

"Nick," she said as I pulled her up.

"Didn't you hear us?" I said.

"I heard the gunshots," she said. "Or that's what I thought they were, so I ran into the closet and hit my head on the bottom shelf. I guess I passed out, because the next thing was you, now. What happened?"

"Somebody got on the barge," I said.

There was blood on her forehead, and when she touched it, her hand came away red.

"Let's get Sloane," I went on. "He'll fix you up. I'm very, very sorry about this—"

"No need," she said.

She stood on tiptoes and put her arms around my neck; her head just reached my shoulder. She leaned into me and brushed her hand across my cheek.

"I'm all right," she whispered. "I'm better than before."

Did she mean before the attack or before the intruder? It didn't matter. I couldn't wrap my arms around her because if I did, it wouldn't be the beginning of a love story. It would be the end of something. It would be the end of Rue. And the end of the separate peace I'd made with myself.

Carefully, I pushed her away. But even in doing it, I knew I would always remember how her body fit against me, her warm hand on my cheek, her violet eyes, and her long tangled hair. There would never be another perfume like the scent of her hair that morning.

I got a towel from a drawer next to the sink, ran it under cold water, and was dabbing at the blood on her forehead when Sloane and Meriwether walked in.

"You're hurt!" said the unalarmable Meriwether.

"I'm OK Meriwether," said the dancer. "I was hiding."

"My dear girl," said Sloane, "what happened? Let me take a look."

The sleeve of his dressing gown—which is what he calls his bathrobe—was rolled up, revealing a bandage.

"Really I'm fine," the dancer said. "But what about you? What happened to your arm?"

"Let's sit down," Sloane said, suddenly sounding weary.

He went over and sat heavily in one of the chairs by the Shaker table custom-made in Canterbury, New Hampshire, for Sloane's great-grandfather. Because it was on loan to a museum in Virginia at the time, it escaped the fire that destroyed Sloane's townhouse.

When the show at the museum was over, Sloane ordered the table delivered to Weehawken. I said I didn't want it because it was too valuable for the barge, but he insisted on putting it in the kitchen.

One night a couple of weeks after the table arrived, I was sitting there with him, drinking a bottle of his Château Mouton Rothschild Bordeaux.

I don't argue with Sloane, so I'll say we were discussing my not wanting the table.

In the middle of the conversation, Sloane casually knocked his wine over. He then cleaned it up casually. He said the table was meant to be used, so I might as well start using it now since I was going to inherit it anyway, along with everything else in his estate. Because, he explained quietly, I was as close to a son as he would ever have.

It was quite a moment, since neither one of us is sentimental and, although Sloane has no family, I never expected anything. He is on the boards of so many charitable foundations, if I ever thought of it, I'd imagine his money would go to those hospitals and research centers, and something for the Sisters.

"Well, Edward," I'd said, "I appreciate the thought, but I'm sure you'll outlive me."

"Quite so," he said. "It's a distinct possibility. And in that case, the table will go to Memorial Sloan-Kettering. To avoid additional paperwork, that's already in my will. Who knows, I might be a demented invalid when you predecease me."

"You put that in your will?" I said. "You actually think I'll go before you?"

"No Nick, not really," Sloane had said. "But you're still reckless. Very reckless. You drink too much, and you put yourself in the line of fire. And it's not because you think you're bulletproof. Entirely the reverse, in fact."

"A death wish Edward," I'd said. "That's sitcom psychoanalysis— it's below your dignity."

"Which doesn't necessarily make it untrue," he said, "does it? You're too old to keep pushing the envelope—or whatever it is you're doing."

"It's not true," I said. And I was getting angry. We'd been in this part of the forest before and I didn't like it.

"You've got to say good-bye to Julia," he continued. "You can't expect to have any peace until you let her go."

"Fuck you Edward—I let her go the day she died."

It was obvious he had blasted a nerve because I'd never spoken to him like that before. I immediately made an apology and he accepted it. The table stayed, and he didn't mention Julia again until the night of the storm when he met the dancer.

"Tell me what happened to you," said Sloane when he got a closer look at the new cut on the dancer's forehead and the lump that had formed around it.

She explained hearing the gunshots, finding the closet, hitting her head, and losing consciousness.

Sloane shot me a scorching look, then said he needed astringent and a bandage and it was a damn good thing the cut didn't require stitches. Plus, he added, he wasn't willing to discuss the recent incident while he treated the dancer. He wanted calm. When he finished he said he was ready.

"Did you get a look at the guy?" I asked.

"I couldn't see the man's face because he had a hat on—a baseball cap. It was pulled down low and he was wearing a long raincoat—I think it was dark green or brown."

"How big was he?" I asked.

"He wasn't big," said Sloane. "He seemed fairly average, on the thin side—and I imagine he was young and fit because he moved very fast; he vaulted easily over the rail into the river."

"Could you go back to the beginning?"

"It's a short story," said Sloane. "I went back to sleep after you left, and the sound of smashing glass woke me."

"That's when you saw him?" I said.

"Yes," said Sloane. "And he saw me."

"When did he fire at you?"

"Immediately. The first bullet missed. He was not much of a marksman."

Meriwether and I exchanged a glance, and Meriwether pushed away from the table.

"I'll dig the slug out of the wall," he said.

"It's so awful he got into your bedroom," the dancer said.

"He didn't get far," said Sloane, who paused for a moment and gingerly moved his bandaged arm.

"Dr. Sloane, are you in much pain?" asked the dancer.

She put her hand lightly on his, and he smiled.

"No, no," he said. "Don't worry."

"We heard three more shots," I said.

"And one of them grazed my arm," he said.

"Then what?" I asked.

"He left," Sloane said.

"Just turned around and left," I said. "Why?"

"Obviously he changed his mind," said Sloane.

"Why do you think he changed his mind?" I asked, trying not to sound as impatient as I felt.

"Maybe he didn't want me to shoot him," said Sloane.

"What're you talking about Edward?" I said. "You don't have a gun."

"That's right," said Sloane. "I don't have a gun. I have two guns."

"Are they loaded?" I asked.

"Well, Nicky," he said, "what damn good would they be if they weren't loaded? Rue and I, unlike you and Albert, have been unarmed until recently."

"Rue has a gun?" That really surprised me.

"Rue?" said the dancer.

"I didn't say that," answered Sloane.

"We have to talk about your guns," I said, "but not now."

"Dr. Sloane," said the dancer, "could it have been a woman?"

The thought hadn't occurred to me—and I wondered why it had to her.

"Yes," said Sloane. "I suppose it could have been."

"What made you think of that?" I asked.

"I don't know," said the dancer. "Just a feeling."

"A memory?" I asked.

She clasped her hands and put them under her chin.

"Something—I'm not sure," she said and turned to Sloane again. "You saw him—or her—actually go over the side?"

"Yes, definitely," said Sloane. "He's gone. Or she."

Sometimes, when Meriwether and I traveled on a job, Rue would go to her own place, leaving Sloane alone on the *Dumb Luck*, which was a very big place without an alarm system. The old man was not faint of heart, but he knew about Chenvenko, Olivier, and a few other people who should have been in jail. That's no doubt why he got the guns. Or maybe there was another reason.

I hadn't thought until then that the target might not have been the dancer or me.

Sloane had been a psychiatrist for many years. Besides his private practice, he did a lot of pro bono clinic work. And as an expert witness, he'd given testimony that put a few very dangerous people in prison.

Also, after Sloane's townhouse was destroyed, I talked to a couple of Arson/Explosion guys who had not been able to pin down the cause of the fire. They thought there was something hinky about it, but the squad had not found a single piece of evidence to support that theory.

Anything was possible, including the chance it was the dancer's attacker who cut our lines and broke into Sloane's room.

"I'm going to check with the Boat Basin," I said, focusing on the attacker and for want of a better idea. "Maybe they noticed something unusual. The guy didn't fly across the river, and they don't have too many motorboats over there, so if one's gone they'll know."

"What's the Boat Basin?" asked the dancer.

If she came from the city, her question might not necessarily reflect the amnesia—it wasn't such a well-known spot. And if she came from somewhere else, she was even less likely to know.

"It's a place where boats can stop to refuel or dock on a long-term basis," I said. "Some people live there all the time on houseboats."

"It's a floating trailer park," said Sloane, who maybe forgot he was living on a barge that once was a bunker sludge recycling site. "Did you consider that he could have driven through the tunnel?"

Sloane was referring to the Lincoln Tunnel, and, of course, I'd considered it because it is one of the three ways to get across the river—unless you're traveling by seaplane or have a boat from somewhere besides the Basin.

The Weehawken Ferry was the third way after the Boat Basin and the tunnel. But it didn't run in the middle of the night.

"One thing at a time," I said, answering Sloane's question.

To be more accurate I could have said: the only thing at this time. The Boat Basin was specific, contained. I knew people there. An unknown car coming through the tunnel, at an unknown time, wending its way across Weehawken to the shore, was another story.

My cell phone rang just then and scared the dancer, who started to rise out of her seat. The rings she remembered from twenty or more years back sounded different. With Meriwether around, there are always tech surprises. And it is not mine to question why—or in this case how or when—he had time to unjam the phones.

I checked caller ID and recognized the number of a client who phoned about five times a day, every day. I let the call go to voice mail; she could wait a couple of hours. The next call was signaled by barks. This started when Rue found out different ringtones could be assigned to different people and she asked if she could program my phone. Since the sound is never on when I'm working, I told her to go ahead. Fallon's ring was a bark.

"Are you alone?" he asked.

"No," I said.

"Go somewhere alone."

"OK," I said and started walking to my office.

"What's up?" I continued. "You already find out who she is?"

"No," he said. "No reports of any missing person matching the description you gave me. It's something else."

"What something else?"

"The kid you were telling me about from the hospital," he said. "The intern."

"Yes," I said. "Justin Greenburg. Did he call you?"

"No," said Fallon. "He ain't gonna be making no calls."

"What does that mean?"

"What's a matter with you Nick?" said Fallon. "It means he's dead."

12

I couldn't respond. I looked out at the rain, down at my desk, then noticed that the front of my jeans and gray T-shirt were covered in white powder. White flour. It must have rubbed off on the dancer from one of the big sacks in the storage closet. I put my hand on my heart, felt the smooth flour, and tried to feel where she had been.

"Hey, you still there?" Fallon asked.

"Yes," I said. "I'm here."

"He was the guy who called you, right?"

I remembered Greenburg anxiously saying he could get in a lot of trouble for helping the dancer leave the hospital...

"Nick," Fallon went on, "are you fuckin' listening to me?"

I knew that Bellevue was under his jurisdiction. Manhattan South.

"Yes, he was the guy," I said. "What happened?"

"I'll tell you when I see you. I want you to come in."

"Why?"

"Because there's more. A lot more. And bring the girl."

"She can't remember anything," I said.

"Maybe something will jog her memory."

"I doubt it."

"Look," he said, "this homicide is going to kick up a shit storm. We think your dancer is connected to more than the mugging— and to more than the kid who got killed."

"I'm listening," I said.

"Just do me a favor and bring her in," said Fallon. "How long will it take?"

"The *Gwinnett*'s fucked up—I'll have to drive."

"So?" he said. "When will you get here?"

"I don't know," I said and clicked off.

Fallon and I usually operate on a system of reciprocity. When a case takes me to the NYPD, he is not only my contact and sometime unofficial backup, but he also puts me on the fast track to information not available to the public, or to private investigators.

Ironically, I do the same for him—with information not available to most police officers. It's hard to believe the NYPD doesn't have the same resources that I have. Obviously they don't have Meriwether. They also do not have access (as we do through a gift from Sloane) to some of the vast searchable archives to which law firms, magazine publishers, and universities subscribe. Deep Web databases are expensive, but if you think the NYPD—except for the elite Puzzle Palace—would be the first in line with need and budget allotment, you'd be wrong. Fallon says the department doesn't trust most of the cops with certain sensitive information—like credit card numbers.

Before I returned to the sleep deprived and the wounded, I went to my room and took a three-minute shower. Even though I didn't feel better, a shower, a shave, and clean clothes made me look better, which was a good trick.

Meriwether, the dancer, and Sloane were in the kitchen at the Shaker table where Sloane's bandaged right arm was resting on a rolled-up towel. He'd put his good arm around the dancer's shoulders. And Meriwether—who could be counted on to vanish from any room to avoid even the briefest obligatory handshake from a new client or a guest—was holding her hand.

I didn't say why I was going to the city because I didn't want to tell the dancer about Greenburg—at least not yet—and I had no intention of taking her to Manhattan South. Fallon would just have to make do with me. It was hard to gauge how pissed off he'd be. His temper was as unpredictable as everything else about him—except getting the job done. Which he always did, and that's why he wasn't kicked out of the police force years ago.

Meriwether gave me the bullet he'd dug out of Sloane's wall. In spite of his almost superhuman ability for multitasking, there had been no time to fix the gas line in the *Gwinnett*.

I asked Sloane if I could borrow the Mercedes, and he barely hesitated before saying yes.

"By the way, I expect you to replace my pajamas," he added, obviously assuming the intruder was after me, a bet smart money would have taken with pleasure. "They came from Asprey. I'll get you the address."

The dancer followed me out of the room,

"Could we talk for a minute?" she asked.

"Sure," I said and led the way to the library.

I turned my back to the still-burning embers in the fireplace; she perched across from me on an arm of the couch.

"Where are you going?" she asked.

"I have to take care of some business."

"May I come with you?"

"No," I said. "You'll be fine with Meriwether."

"Doesn't he ever sleep?"

"Not like other people," I said.

"Do you understand that I am really sorry?" she said.

"Trust me," I said, "he never does anything he doesn't want to do."

"I wasn't talking about Meriwether," she said. "Although I am sorry to put him out too. I was apologizing to you. I didn't mean to drag you into whatever this is—"

"You didn't drag me into anything," I said, flashing on an image of Justin Greenburg wringing his small, nervous hands outside the Emergency Room at Bellevue. "And there's no reason to think anything that's happened here is about you."

"Just coincidental?" she said.

This wasn't the moment to tell her that now there was little doubt. That Greenburg's death was about her. That Fallon was waiting to interview her.

"When you came to my hospital room," she said, "you were sure we'd never met. Everything happened so fast after that, I haven't asked what made you decide to help me."

She moved off the arm of the sofa to the edge of the coffee table. Closer to me.

I wasn't going to tell her the reason, but I needed to start giving her some version of the truth, so I explained about the Jane Doe vagrant designation, about the Thorazine, about the psych ward. I told her how Greenburg waylaid the nurse and orderly pushing the gurney.

"Oh God," she said. "I wonder if they figured out what he did when they found me gone. Let's call him. It shouldn't be hard to find him."

"Not now," I said and looked at my watch. "Now's not a good time because I have to get going."

"Why aren't you taking your boat?" she asked.

"The boat's out of commission."

"But when Meriwether brought it back he didn't say anything."

"He didn't say anything to you," I told her.

I couldn't stop looking into her eyes. I always meant to ask Julia what color she put down on her driver's license. I'd have to check sometime what colors were on the DMV list. After brown, blue, green, hazel.

"It was because you have enough going on," I continued.

"Nick, please, tell me, I need to know."

"We didn't want you to worry about anything more. But the fact is the *Gwinnett* didn't come loose. Somebody cut her loose and also cut the gas line."

"Oh no," she said.

"You are not in danger," I said. "We weren't counting on trouble, and whoever it was caught us off guard. I don't expect him back—but if he tries to come back, he'll regret it."

"Thanks," she said weakly, crossing her arms in front of her chest as though she were cold. "You told me you didn't know if he was coming after me. And I'm not worried that he's coming back. It's just…if it's about me…I don't feel like a woman who would make somebody want to attack her…personally."

"Whoever attacked you took off. A cabdriver brought you to Bellevue. The attacker didn't know you were there, and he doesn't know where you are now. What happened here was about me."

"Why?" she asked.

We were facing each other, and I put my hands on her shoulders, marveling again at how fast the art of lying could come back.

"I'm not sure," I said. "But there are a few people who wouldn't mind hurting me."

"Who would want to hurt you?" she asked.

I laughed. The mood broke.

"The bad guys," I said.

"Seriously?"

"Yeah," I said. "Seriously bad guys."

"What about the bad girls?" she asked.

"Those would be the good girls."

I think she smiled before she turned away and stared out the windows, where a strong wind was blowing the rain horizontal.

"I think you should stay until the rain stops," she said.

"It's not going to stop."

"You mean never?"

"No," I said. "I mean it's not going to stop anytime soon."

"Please stay with me," she said.

I told her she'd be fine with Meriwether and Sloane, and within five minutes I was out in the storm again. I didn't like the heavy hits of cold rain on the beach. I didn't like the slushy mud on the way to Pauline Prochevsky's garage. I didn't like the way I felt when I tried to remember exactly where it started: in the hospital, on the *Gwinnett*, or when the lights went out. The niggling feather of fear in my head about the dancer.

So far, one moody savant and one homosexual psychiatrist were under her spell, the *Dumb Luck* was under attack, and Justin Greenburg was dead.

Luckily, Pauline didn't see me coming to the house, so there was no need for small talk. And I'd bring her another copy of the plastic-wrapped *New York Post* I swiped from her front porch steps.

Sloane's half of the garage was impeccable and held nothing but his perfectly maintained chocolate-brown Mercedes sedan. It wasn't as old as he was, but it was old, and I hoped the brakes would hold going through deep puddles of water and all the roads that needed repair before and after the Lincoln Tunnel.

I backed the Mercedes out of the garage and called Meriwether to say where I was going.

"I'll tell Edward," he said. "He's still with her in the kitchen. They're finishing their tea. I'll be outside her door as soon as she goes back to the guest room."

"Are you trying to find out who she is?" I asked.

"Not yet."

"Could you do it now?" I said and waited. "Meriwether?"

"Sure."

"She's got to go," I said.

"I know."

13

Traffic in and around New York City gets bad when it's hot, bad when it's cold, and worse when it's raining, especially during rush hour. Which is when I reached the Lincoln Tunnel and found the cars there first at a crawl, then at a standstill.

Time to catch up on the latest rejiggered news capsules. As I was tearing the plastic off the *Post*, I decided I better bring Pauline a box of candy to make up for the pilfering.

A photograph of the mayor and the police commissioner shaking hands filled the entire front page. The cute headline read NUMBER ONE WITHOUT A BULLET, and, according to the article, New York was now the safest city in America.

Portland, Oregon, would probably have something to say about that, but there was no definition of *city* and there was nothing more specific to back up the claim than "recent polls" and "latest surveys." Why not print whatever sounded good? This stuff was designed for short attention spans, which grew even shorter as the temperature rose.

And New York in fact had gotten a lot safer in recent years. But tell that to someone who would always carry an ugly number 44 scar on her back.

I began regretting my decision to ignore Fallon's order. I was letting all that hard-heart capital I'd built up in ten years be eroded by a little waif with violet eyes and a quirky smile.

After another ten minutes, I checked in with Meriwether again, who said none too gently that nothing had changed since the last time I called. He was outside the guest room door with his laptop. The dancer was resting and Sloane was asleep.

I'm not good at sitting around. That's when things creep up on me; and because I like to run my thoughts, not the other way around, I wasn't ready to deal with remembering the twists in my life that led to the dancer.

It's an old story about what happens when an arrogant little punk thinks he's bulletproof. He becomes more and more brazen until, if he's lucky, he gets busted before he gets killed.

I guess I got a break from Lady Luck when three cops nailed me in the men's room of a Rivington Street bar. I had made a big sale about half an hour earlier, so I wasn't holding enough cocaine to be charged as a dealer. Just a user, which was bad enough.

The nuns were shocked by the news of my arrest and needed an explanation from God, so they all went into full prayer mode.

All except Sister Mary A. She had let me give God a run for his money because she was sure He would always win. She didn't expect an arrest to be in His plan, and she was furious at both of us. She skipped deep prayer and called Sloane. He'd already been disappointed when I refused to go to college even if he paid my way. Now this. He was just as furious as Sister Mary A, but nevertheless hired a lawyer, who I fired because I was too ashamed to take anything from him.

The judge gave me a choice between going to jail or joining the service. Either way I would be a prisoner. At least in the marines there was fresh air.

Three days after the court ruling, Don King, the boxing pro-moter with the famous hair and the million-dollar deals, showed up at the gym to see one of his boys who worked out there.

I was hitting the speed bag and didn't notice him until he was in my face.

"I watched you before," he said. "In the ring."

"I didn't know," I said.

"Yeah, I got my ways," he said. "And you seen the kind of fighter I handle? It ain't about if he knocks a guy out. It's about how he knocks the guy out. It's the style, the improvisation. So I'm looking at you. I ain't seen a left hook like that since Basilio. And I ain't seen blue eyes like that since Cooney." He patted me on the cheek. "Too bad you got shit for brains."

He wasn't talking about getting busted. He meant I wouldn't have served more than six months if I'd been smart enough to find somebody who could work the system. He should know; he only did four years after his lawyer got a murder charge reduced to manslaughter.

"Get in touch if you're still in one piece when you get back. I'll be here."

I went into the marines hanging on to the hope of going pro when I got out. I'd only be a couple of years older. Stronger. And ready to start small like a lot of other good boxers. King would take me on because a left hand as good as mine aced shit for brains any day.

That hope, which had kept me going, died along with two guys from my fire squad in a Saudi border town called Khafji. Everybody said I was lucky to escape with only a shattered leg.

And I was lucky, but the leg would never be the same. Boxing was going to be my future. Bad leg, no future. Nowhere to go.

I would never turn to the nuns, who had their own problems. They were all getting older, and because they had been excommu-nicated they had lost any benefits from the church. Only Sloane, who was in Africa with Médecins Sans Frontières when I got home, stood between them and poverty.

I was lost, and that thing about if you look into the abyss long enough it will look back at you got it wrong. Nothing looks back at you. I took the first job I could get, and after five years at Owen Security Inc. I was chained to the abyss.

14

My cell phone ringing was a welcome relief from the memory until I heard the voice of Fallon's partner, Linda Goode.

"I'm waiting for you," she said.

"Let me speak to Fallon," I said.

"He's not here."

I said nothing, waiting for her to elaborate. When she didn't, I asked where he was.

"Not. Here."

For a woman as unattractive looking as Goode, she could get along better if she acted nicer, which I said once to Rue, who shot back that I wouldn't make a comment like that about a man (which was true) and that it was Goode's defense mechanism. I told Rue she should go into business with Sloane, and after that our conversation went south.

"I heard you, Linda," I said. "But he asked me to get my ass into the city and now my ass is stuck in the Lincoln Tunnel—so where is he?"

She obviously didn't like my tone and let me wait.

"Come on Linda," I said. "I'm about to shoot my way out of the tunnel. You don't want blood on your hands, do you?"

"Such a tough guy."

"Fine," I said. "You can be the tough guy and I can turn around, go back home, eat some fried eggs, and get some sleep."

"You've got the assault victim with you, right?"

"Yeah," I lied. "But Fallon called and I want to know why he's not there."

"He's at Bellevue," she said. "I stayed here to start questioning the victim—"

"Did you get a hit on her? Do you know who she is?"

"Not yet," said Linda Goode.

"She can't remember anything about the attack," I said. "What's the point of dragging her in for questioning?"

"There's a point," she said.

Sister Mary Alphonsus would be saying: Count to ten.

…*eight, nine, ten.*

"What is that point?" I said calmly.

"I'm not on speakerphone, am I?" said Goode.

"No."

"We think the woman may be involved in something bigger than the assault."

"I can't guess what you're talking about," I said. "But you're hot when you're mysterious."

"You're not the least bit funny Sayler," she said. "We'll lay it out for you when you get here. Please put your passenger on the phone. I want to talk to her…Nick?" Goode spoke louder, "Nick can you hear me—"

"You're breaking up," I told her. It was a lie she might believe since I was in the tunnel.

"Nick—darn it," Goode said and clicked off when she heard nothing.

I finally got out of the tunnel about ten minutes later and went via Ninth Avenue to West Thirty-Fourth Street, where once more I found the traffic moving not at all. So I opened the *Post* again, but I couldn't focus because all I could see at that point was Justin Greenburg's earnest turtle face.

I called Meriwether, who greeted me with: "She's still resting. I'm still outside the door."

Then I told him what Goode said about the dancer being part of something bigger.

"Vague," said Meriwether.

"She said she'd elaborate when I got to the precinct."

"Maybe it's about 44," said Meriwether.

"Maybe." I hadn't seen the dancer's cut-up back, and I didn't want to.

"I'll think," said Meriwether.

"I'll let you know what they have," I said. "And will you ask her to call me later?"

"OK," he said. "And don't worry. Nothing's going to happen to her."

Before I hung up I asked Meriwether about the rain, and he told me it wasn't going to stop for at least another thirty-six to forty-eight hours because yet another storm was coming in. It didn't matter whether he divined the information through one of his mysterious neural pathways or from the Weather Underground. He was always right.

I turned to the back of the newspaper to see the results from yesterday's races at Belmont. Then I checked the stock market. Then the ads. Anything was better than thinking about Greenburg or the dancer.

Or thinking about Julia, who would have done anything to avoid haunting me. But there was only one thing she could have done to manage that. And as far as I know, no one, including Jesus Christ, ever came back from the dead.

I found a parking garage on First Avenue and Twenty-Seventh Street. If Sloane's car got a scratch or a dent, there'd be all hell to pay, so I gave twenty bucks to one of the attendants, a skinny

Dominican kid with attitude. Told him to make sure the Mercedes came out the same as it went in.

I had only about six blocks to walk, but distances stretch out in the rain, even in August. It made me think that maybe in a few years when I turn forty I'll buy an umbrella. And remember to get haircuts. And quit smoking altogether. And be nicer to Rue. But I was always nice to Rue—so I was already wanting to make up for something I hadn't done.

And already jumping ahead to forty. Obviously, you can't stop the clock and sometimes things get better. What's better for me is now I expect to reach the age of forty.

Without the NYPD Emergency Service trucks in front and the police department medallion by the door, the beige brick precinct house would be indistinguishable from the places around it. On the other hand, if you know what it is, it stands out like neon.

I'll never lose my aversion to police stations and don't go to them very willingly, and the only reason I ran up to the door so fast that morning was the rain.

15

Inside, I nodded to the desk sergeant, who knew me, then took the stairs up to the second floor. I passed an interrogation room and a conference room before I reached the big square office where Fallon spent as little time as possible. It was a space shared by over a dozen cops, who were drinking coffee, talking on the phone, doing their paperwork, and bullshitting.

I headed to the far corner, where Fallon and Goode work facing each other across an old-fashioned partner's desk that looks like a valuable item. And probably is.

Every April or May when high-ticket residential neighborhoods do their spring cleaning, if you have some time and a pickup truck, you can furnish an apartment with what they throw out in the street. Goode found the desk on Central Park West and Seventy-First Street a few doors down from the Dakota.

She arranged to have it delivered, and I guess she thought Fallon would be pleasantly surprised. She settled for his not getting mad about the disruption of his space. In fact, her entire relationship with Fallon is about compromise. And eventually capitulation. Sometimes they fight, but he always wins.

Fallon's my friend, and whenever one of my cases takes me to the NYPD I spend time with Goode because she's his partner, and whatever floats her boat is fine. All I want is peace.

I pulled Fallon's chair away from his side of the desk, and as I sat down I spotted Goode marching toward me across the big square room. She's thirty-five years old, a squat woman with a face only her mother could love. She has a hard head, a hard heart, and deadly aim with a revolver. If you care to make the effort—and most people don't because it takes a long time to get used to her brusque manner—you'll find a soft core somewhere in that petrified heart.

"Get another chair," she said.

"Good morning to you too, Detective Goode," I said.

"Use this one," she said, pointing to a folding chair.

"OK," I said. "Take it easy."

"Where's the victim?"

"She still can't remember anything, so she decided to stay on the barge."

"What is wrong with you?" Goode said.

"I told you she couldn't remember anything," I said.

"You also told me she was in the car."

"I know."

"Why did you lie?"

"Because I didn't feel like having this conversation," I said.

"Sayler, you are such a pain in the ass."

"But you still like me."

"I don't like you," she said.

"You like me a little."

"Did you ever hear about interfering with a police investigation?" she said. "I mean it. You know how important these first hours are."

"If you're talking about Greenburg's death," I replied, "yes I do understand, but the woman cannot remember anything, like I said. So no lectures, OK? There's too much shit going down, and I haven't slept in a week."

"I don't care about your sleep deprivation."

"Tell me what happened to Greenburg," I said. "And what did you mean about the dancer being part of something bigger?"

"Fallon's going to lay it out," she said.

"I thought we didn't have any time to lose," I said. "You've never been shy before."

I got nothing from her but tight lips.

"When's he coming back?" I went on. "Where is he?"

"He's at Bellevue," she said. "He'll be here. You want some coffee?"

"OK," I said. "Thanks."

"What do you take in your coffee?" she asked, not able to drop the attitude since she knew I always drink black coffee.

Goode had been gone to get the coffee about two minutes when Thomas Fallon finally came in out of the rain and saw me waiting at his desk. It was barely nine thirty, but his dark-brown eyes were bleary and he was wearing a white shirt that looked like he'd slept in it. He had pulled his tie completely apart so the two ends were hanging on either side of his collar like a scarf.

Although Fallon is one of the best—maybe the best—homicide detectives on the entire police force, he's not a poster boy for New York's finest. He's about five ten and skinny and tends to slouch. When Sister Mary A met him, she said it looks like he combs his hair with the leg of a chair. As far as I know, he never works out. But appearances deceive. He's as tough as they come. And when he's not depressed he's got a certain offbeat charm. It helps during interrogations because, every now and then, a suspect is more interested in Fallon than he is in lying, and that allows Fallon to get the answers without even asking the questions.

Fallon greeted me in a subdued way I didn't like, then looked around and said, "You didn't bring her, did you?"

As I shook my head, he sat down and slowly swiveled his chair around a couple of times.

"So she still can't remember fuck-all anyway—is that it?"

"Not exactly," I said.

"Not exactly?" he asked.

"I mean Sloane checked her," I replied. "He couldn't say when she'll get her memory back, but it's coming back some because she's remembered a few things—"

"Like *what*?" said Goode, who materialized in time to hear the part about the dancer remembering a few things. "Why didn't you tell us?"

"Relax, Linda," said Fallon. "He's gonna tell us."

"Like Ronald Reagan is president," I said.

"Is that how it's going to come back?" said Fallon. "From when she was a kid?"

"Sloane couldn't predict the time frame and neither could Greenburg," I said. "So what happened to him?"

"I'm gonna tell you," he said, checking his watch. "Here's what we know, and it ain't much. When the shift changed at the hospital, a nurse's aide found his body laid out on your dancer's bed—the bed she'd been in."

"Stabbed?"

"Strangled."

"With what?"

"Hands—Linda, we got any tomato juice around here?"

Goode replied that she'd look and glanced my way defiantly lest I think she was doing this because she was female and/or subservient. We'd been through this kind of thing many times before, and I suppose it was a tribute to her self-esteem that she failed to understand I didn't care if she sprouted wings, turned into a parakeet, and perched on Fallon's shoulder.

"This murder's already kicked up a shit storm," said Fallon.

"Like you told me," I said.

"Looks bad for everybody when a doctor gets killed inside his own hospital. Everybody's going to have it tomorrow," he said. "Fucking Internet. They'll have it in the middle of the goddamn fucking Sahara desert."

"So much for safest city without a bullet," I said.

"Yeah," said Fallon, "no shit."

"You're sure Greenburg's death had to do with the dancer?"

"I'm still reserving judgment," said Fallon.

"Did anybody see anything?" I asked.

"Nope," said Fallon. "So far, nobody saw nothing and nobody heard nothing."

"How the hell could somebody kill Greenburg and nobody saw anything?"

"You spent much time around hospitals lately?" asked Fallon.

"No time at all," I said. "Except last night."

"Well," said Fallon, "they got no staff."

And now, I was thinking, the understaffed workforce at Bellevue had been reduced by one.

"People yell bloody murder all the time," Fallon went on, "and nothing happens unless maybe they're hooked up to monitoring machines. Even then. Usually it's the crazies making all the noise. The aides call them screamers."

"I thought that meant something else."

"It means that too," said Fallon.

"What about the old lady in the other bed?"

"I questioned her," said Fallon. "Told me she was asleep."

"She wasn't asleep when we left."

"She meant later. Said she remembered the girl. And you."

"Yeah, she thought I was a bartender—she was calling for a drink."

"Did you give her one?" asked Fallon.

"We were all out of scotch," I said.

"How the hell could you run out of scotch?"

"You tell me," I said. "You're the detective."

"So are you," said Fallon.

"We don't have time for these stupid little games," said Goode, who was back with a big can of tomato juice. She put it down hard in front of Fallon.

"You think the old lady was telling the truth?" I asked. "About sleeping through the whole thing with Greenburg?"

"I don't know," said Fallon. "But I talked to her twice and her story didn't change. You think she's lying?"

"Maybe she's scared," I said.

"She didn't act scared," Fallon said.

"What about the cabdriver?" I said. "The one who brought the dancer in?"

"Nobody remembers what he looked like, but we're going to review the security videos," Fallon said.

"How soon can you get them?" I asked.

"There's a problem," said Goode.

Fallon closed his eyes and shook his head.

"What?" he asked, eyes still closed.

"Bellevue Security called back a little while ago—" said Goode.

"And you were going to tell me when, Christmas?"

"He was here," Goode said, pointing at me.

"Just tell us, for Christ's sake," said Fallon.

"They said the rain was so heavy it blurred the images."

"But the rain wasn't consistent," I said.

"They're running the videos—that's all they can do," said Goode.

"What about the interior cameras?" I asked. "Don't they have them on every floor?"

"Yes," said Goode, "but the ones on eight weren't working—they'd been down for a few days. Also six and seven."

"What about the lobby?" I asked. "They've got cameras in the lobby, don't they?"

"Some of them were out too," said Goode. "They're checking as fast as they can—it's a big place."

"Shit," said Fallon, who'd been slowly swiveling in his chair. "Shit, shit, shit. What about state-of-the-art technology? The cameras inside are no good—the fucking cameras outside don't work in the rain—"

"They work," said Goode.

"Except they can't see anything," I said.

"Sykes—he's the head of security at Bellevue," said Goode for my benefit, "he said maybe one of their techs could recover something. But he doubted it. And so do I."

"Always looking on the bright side, ain't you?" said Fallon. "How am I supposed to drink this?" He was pointing to the can of juice.

After Goode left again to look for a glass, I asked Fallon if anybody had an idea about who sprang the dancer or where she went.

"Only Greenburg," he replied and tilted his chair back as far as it would go.

A few minutes later, Goode returned with a glass and an opener, which she placed in front of Fallon.

"Here," she said. "I'm not opening the can."

16

"Let's go over this fast," said Fallon, checking a little notebook he took out of his pocket.

"Couldn't be fast enough for me," I said.

"Nobody knows who brought the dancer in. Maybe a cab-driver, maybe not."

"The guy who brought her in wasn't the perp—" said Goode.

"Because if the perp had a change of heart he would've called 911—not risk showing up carrying the vic," said Fallon, who always got mad when I needled him about how he and Goode finished each other's sentences like a married couple.

"OK," I said. "Let's say something happened during the attack. Some interruption or maybe she fought him off. Maybe she got herself into a cab. Let's say the guy who attacked her followed them to Bellevue."

"Then the guy hid at the hospital, killed the doc, and went across the river," said Goode. "Cut the power, cut your boat loose, jammed the cell phones, and tried to get into Dr. Sloane's bedroom, then disappeared—sounds like Batman."

"I was thinking Hellboy," I said.

"The perp had to have a car," said Fallon.

"Maybe he got a cab too," said Goode.

"Not in the rain, with blood on him, right behind her," said Fallon. "No—he'd have to have a car to follow her to the hospital and get there in time to know where she went—the ER is an obvious call. But after that—the place is a maze. If he wasn't following close, he would've lost her."

"You're right," I said. "The guy did get there fast. Greenburg told me the dancer was only in the ER for about twenty-five minutes before they sent her up to the neuro floor."

"That can't be right. They keep everybody waiting for hours," said Goode. "Even bullet wounds get held up. She was conscious—so how did she manage to get out of the ER that fast?"

"I don't know," I said.

But I did know. Even cut and bruised and bleeding, her kind of beauty opens doors everywhere.

"Where do you think he parked…" said Goode.

"Bingo," said Fallon, and Goode blushed, her face going from white to pink to red in about two seconds. In spite of myself I felt sorry for her.

"So he got a parking ticket," I said, remembering stopped traffic around the hospital. "How fast can you get a printout of last night's tickets?"

"We can't," said Fallon. "There're not entered into a computer yet—they're all downstairs in the summons box."

"Seriously?" I asked.

"Seriously," said Fallon.

"Quaint," I said.

"I'll go through them when we're finished here," said Goode. "I'll make copies of the ones that fall in the right window of time—"

"Just pull them Linda," said Fallon, "and you can read the numbers off to Meriwether. He can run the plates faster than us—and he can also tell us the names of the drivers' grandmas and what they had for dinner, isn't that right Nick?"

"The sooner the better," I said, looking at my watch.

Goode glared at me.

"Linda, I don't give a shit," I said. "I'll read the numbers to Meriwether."

"Or I'll read the numbers and you drive," said Fallon. "It don't matter."

"I didn't say anything," Goode said.

"OK," said Fallon, "so the perp follows the cab from the scene, leaves his car somewhere near the hospital, tracks the girl to the room on the eighth floor."

"If he could hide close enough to watch us leave," I said, "he either couldn't risk being seen chasing us out the fire door—or couldn't catch up with us. We were zigzagging between the fire stairs and the service stairs, because I didn't want security on my ass—"

"Always thinking," said Goode.

"She must've been fast—with a head injury," said Fallon.

"She was the one who wanted to run," I said.

"So he waits till the coast is clear," Fallon said, "and he grabs Greenburg—"

Fallon's cell phone rang, and he silenced it.

"He forces Greenburg to say who I was," I said, "and where we went—and he strangles him so Greenburg can't identify him."

Fallon swiveled his chair around a few times.

"You're right," Goode said evenly to me. "He killed Greenburg because the doc got a look at him. There's no other reason."

"Since when do they need a reason?" Fallon said. "Besides being a psycho serial killer."

"Yeah," said Goode, "but usually the psycho serial killer does have a reason. A pattern—Sayler, give me that."

She was looking at her pen, which I'd picked up and was rolling over and under my fingers like a half-dollar. When her cell phone rang, she ignored it the way Fallon had.

"Obviously I'm missing something here," I said, handing her back the pen. "All of a sudden you're talking about a serial killer. I thought

Greenburg's murder was connected to the dancer—now you're saying there's a guy killing doctors—what doctors besides Greenburg?"

"It's not doctors," said Goode. "We think Greenburg was an ancillary victim of circumstance."

"It's women," said Fallon. "Dancers."

New York has not had to deal with too many serial killers. Any cop knows—and is grateful—that the real thing's a rare bird. Fallon and Goode would never use the term casually.

When Fallon's cell phone rang again, he answered.

"Yeah, Sykes," he said. "I was in a meeting. Yes, she was too. What's up?"

He listened for a couple of beats.

"Well, we're in luck," he said.

One beat.

"I mean I found the guy who sprang the patient." Fallon pointed at me.

Another beat.

"I'm a detective—that's what I get paid for. I'm going to bring him over, but I got no time for the hospital to hassle him about protocol."

He clicked off.

"You're fucking unbelievable, Tom," I said, getting out of my chair. "I'm not going to Bellevue because this is not my fucking problem. I don't want them to know my name, my face—nothing. If this is a trade like I give you Bellevue, you give me the pattern— you can keep the fucking pattern. Maybe the girl's a target—but it's not my problem. I'll bring her in as soon as she feels better. She's not my fucking problem."

"So Nick," Fallon said, "you wanna tell me she's not your problem one more time?"

Years earlier, Fallon was the only cop who was sure I wasn't a murderer. He risked his career by publicly disagreeing with the district attorney. Later, when I asked him how he knew, his only answer was tapping his temple with his forefinger.

I sat back down, and Goode, who'd been pretending she was otherwise engaged with some notes and paper clips, turned to Fallon.

"So what exactly did Sykes say?" she asked.

"The old lady in the other bed just changed her story," said Fallon. "Said she would talk, but only to the guy who took the girl out of the room. Said he was a sailor."

"I suppose she expected us to find him by magic," said Goode.

"Isn't that what you do?" I said to Goode and threw my arm around her shoulder. She shook it off so fast I almost got an elbow in the eye.

Fallon took a long swig of tomato juice from the glass into which Goode had poured it after opening the can. Then he took three manila folders out of the top drawer in his desk and gave them to Goode. They were marked in his big loopy handwriting: *Staten Island, Bronx, Manhattan.* As soon as she had them she headed for the door.

"Let's go," Fallon said, looking at me. "Nobody in the hospital will know your name. That'll be my deal with Sykes. Talking to the old lady won't take too much time, and your dancer's safe with Meriwether."

"Enough," I said. "She's not my dancer."

"Your guest, what the fuck—come on," he said, walking toward the door.

"All right," I said because Fallon and I didn't ask each other for favors very often. "In and out and no hassles."

"None," said Fallon. "Let's go."

Goode was waiting in the hall.

"Thomas," she said, "you should take an umbrella."

People who grow vegetables in Jersey or lawns in Greenwich must have been happy with the rain. Since the only thing that grows in Manhattan is money—in a good year—the downpour had already gotten very old for me.

Luckily Fallon and Goode's black Impala was parked across the street from the precinct house.

Fallon got in and assumed his usual slouch behind the wheel, and a few minutes later Goode, who'd stopped to get the parking tickets out of the summons box, joined me in the backseat so she could show me the crime scene photographs in the manila folders.

Fallon pulled away from the curb, slid neatly into the traffic, and cleared his throat.

"About a year ago," he said, "me and Abe Hirsh and a couple of other people—"

"Women," interrupted Goode.

"It don't matter whether it was girls or geese," said Fallon. "The point is I was with Abe."

Goode didn't comment.

"Me and Abe—I know him since the academy," Fallon continued, "we both got this Saturday night off and we were eating dinner at an Italian place on Staten Island—"

"Staten Island?" I said.

"Yeah, that's where he worked out of the 113th. He usually comes to the city on his night off, but he had to get home early to the wife—"

"The wife wasn't one of the geese at the restaurant," said Goode.

"Linda, what the hell's wrong with you?" asked Fallon.

"Nothing," she said. "Why don't you just tell him about the homicide?"

"I remember I was having chicken parmesan and Abe was eating manicotti—"

"All *right* Thomas," said Goode.

"So Abe gets a call there's a 187," Fallon continued. "He's the squad commander so he's gotta be there, and I go with him because it was a homicide and what else was I gonna do. Takes us about two minutes to get over there. The CSU guys were already at the scene, but they couldn't do nothing because they had to wait for the ME's office. And you know they're always short-staffed, yada yada, and it was the weekend. The vic was African American. Female, twenty-seven years old. About a hundred and fifteen pounds. Somebody beat the shit out of her and broke her neck, which was the cause of death. No sexual assault. No robbery. She was pretty. Not then. But pictures we saw later. She was local. Lived with her two kids. Safe neighborhood."

"They say most neighborhoods in Staten Island are supposed to be safe," I said.

"Yeah, that's what they say—I guess they got good public relations—but you know," said Fallon. "So this girl's walking back from the convenience store with a carton of milk and some cat food. The ME put the time of death about an hour before we get there."

"What am I waiting to hear?" I asked.

"When you called last night," said Fallon, "you told me she was a ballet dancer who had a concussion, was beat up and cut. What kind of cuts did she have?"

"Do you already know?"

"Number 44 on her back," he said. "Very artfully carved—goddamn—hey—"

A car had tried to pull in front of him. The black Impala is unmarked, so people don't know any better. It probably wouldn't matter anyway—New Yorkers don't even pull over for ambulances anymore.

Fallon was yelling out the window, venting, so Goode picked up the story.

"Six months after the Staten Island vic, who was a dance teacher—"

"You buried the lede," I said.

"Yes, well I was getting to it. She was a dancer," Goode said. "She taught dancing to little kids."

"Then Hirsch moved to the 231 in the Bronx," said Fallon, back in the conversation.

"Why did Hirsch go to the Bronx?" I asked. "Who'd he piss off?"

"Nobody," Fallon said. "Not Hirsch. I don't think he ever pissed off nobody in his life. They wanted him because the projects are such a bad mess and getting worse—it was a last-minute thing, and he went because they put him on the Captain's List."

Nobody would ever voluntarily move from Staten Island to the Bronx unless there was an incentive, like a promotion in the near future, which was what being on the Captain's List meant.

"His first night on duty," Fallon continued, "a young Dominican woman turned up dead with the number 44 sliced into her back. She danced at a strip club. Whole thing was same MO as Staten Island. No robbery. No sexual assault, which was unusual in both of these two homicides. Also no witnesses. Nothing. Hirsch called me from the scene…"

Fallon stopped talking, and the silence in the car was almost tangible.

"And?" I asked.

"Yes," said Goode, "well…"

More silence.

"Go ahead," said Fallon. "Tell him what happened."

"It's hard," she said quietly, looking down at her hands.

Then I saw something I'd never expected from her. Tears.

17

"Hirsch got killed that night," said Fallon. "He went by a Rite Aid on his way home to pick up some cough medicine for his kid and walked into a robbery. Tried to stop it and a crank case shot him dead for his trouble."

"In Queens," I remembered. "I heard about it. You never said anything."

"What's to say?" Fallon rasped.

He was right. What's to say.

"So," Fallon continued, "the paperwork on the homicide got fucked up. I don't know what happened, but nobody put the two girls together."

"Even with the 44s," I said.

"Even with them," Fallon said. "And neither one of the girls were in our jurisdiction, so me and Linda decided to keep the connection to ourselves for a little while. And see what we could find."

"On our own time," said Goode.

"I don't care," I said.

"We knew as soon as the 44s got on the record—which would be when they got an anonymous tip from us—the news would get picked up, and in five minutes there's 44 hysteria going down. Serial killers, yada yada."

"The cops wouldn't keep quiet," I said.

"No," said Goode. "Because there would be confusion about who knew what when and why nobody put it together earlier since it was so obvious."

"Fuckin' up on evidence like this is bad enough, but it's even worse because everybody's scared shitless about making their numbers," Fallon added.

By numbers, Fallon was talking about CompStat, a computerized accountability system. At mandatory weekly meetings, all seventy-six precincts, plus transit precincts and service areas, are required to report every summons, complaint, and arrest. The stats are fed to the computer, and the information is tracked. No one can drop the ball because Big Brother is watching.

"So if you give them an anonymous tip about the dead girls and the dancer and they put the pieces together, which is the point," I said, "won't they notice that Hirsch was in both places?"

"Well that's the good news about being dead," said Fallon.

Goode handed me the three manila folders. The Manhattan folder was empty except for a single sheet of paper with three words scrawled on it: *Talk to Sayler.* The two others contained crime scene photographs.

I've looked at a lot of dead vics and pictures of dead vics, but I've never got used to them.

I could see even in black and white how the spilled milk had diluted part of the wide circle of blood around the Staten Island girl's head. The Dominican girl's short skirt was ripped up the back, showing a pair of underpants. Not bikinis or a thong. Just plain old white ones, which on a stripper made the whole thing particularly sad.

Fallon, who'd started up again with the offending car, pulled his head—now wet from rain—back inside.

"Can you believe that shit?" he said, powering up the window.

He meant the traffic.

18

"I'm missing how you made the connection between those two victims and the girl on the barge," I said. "I didn't tell you anything. Greenburg didn't know what was on her back because he didn't dress the wound. She didn't know either. She still doesn't know. Sloane's the one who saw it and told me."

"The hospital's required to call in an assault," said Fallon. "And somebody—one of the attendings—told a beat cop from the Thirteenth. I don't know why Greenburg didn't see the paperwork. Maybe he saw it but didn't tell you because he thought it would scare you off—who the hell knows."

"All right. The dancer got to the ER before midnight," I said. "They didn't find Greenburg till after seven. So you put it together after you got my call."

"What—did I forget to thank you?"

The traffic was stalled, and Fallon, who wasn't interested in drawing attention to his authority unless it was for a good reason, did not like to turn on his siren. Which didn't keep him from leaning on his horn like a civilian.

"God fucking dammit—"

"Your blood pressure's going up," said Goode.

"Worry about your own blood pressure," said Fallon.

"Tell me what your thinking was," I said.

"One murdered girl," said Goode, "is bad enough. Two with a signature like this might be a gang thing."

"Yeah," said Fallon, "I thought it might be MS-13. Maybe another initiation rite."

"Could have been," I said, because he was referring to Mara Salvatrucha, the most vicious gang extant. "Except they would have done more to the girls than cut their backs."

"OK," said Fallon. "I agree. So it don't look like our girls were victims of a gang hazing or a turf war."

"It could be about the collective unconscious," said Goode.

"Collective unconscious," muttered Fallon. "That's about everybody buying Hush Puppies at the same time, not about homicide."

"You never know," said Goode.

"This is what I know," said Fallon. "As soon as everybody finds out there are *three* girls—even if one of them didn't get killed—there's gonna be fallout like you never seen. Because we're in the middle of this friggin' campaign about how we're so friggin' safe in this city."

"And we're in this officially now," said Goode, "because Bellevue's in our precinct."

"I expect a call from the C of D any minute, and the clock is ticking so loud it's giving me a migraine."

"Take an aspirin," I said. "I want to get on with this, and we're sitting in the car not moving."

"You're welcome to walk," said Goode.

The car was at a dead halt again, and I was tempted. Strongly.

"We haven't had a real good serial killer since Rifkin on Long Island," mused Fallon. "With the prostitutes. All buried in the backyard at his mom's house. The old bag claimed she didn't know jack about the corpses and the ladies' undies all over her son's room. I guess Shawcross holds the record—but my favorite is the Sunday Sadist."

"A lot of people wouldn't care for your choice of words," said Goode. "And how many women have to get killed before you call somebody a real good serial killer?"

Fallon ignored her and said, "Nick, you know about Emil Kane?"

"Sure," I said. "The Sunday Sadist. Before my time—but I've heard of him."

"Tell me what you've heard about him," said Fallon.

"Why?" I asked.

"Just indulge me," said Fallon. "You'll get my point in a minute."

"Is this really necessary?" said Goode.

"No," said Fallon, "but we're stuck in this goddamn shit traffic and Sayler's gonna like it."

"The only thing I'm going to like is getting the hell out of this car. I told you I'd talk to the old lady, but I meant today, not tomorrow."

"We're almost there," said Fallon in a rare display of patience given that we hadn't moved two blocks in ten minutes.

"All right," I said. "What I know about the Sunday Sadist is he always killed redheads and always on Sunday."

"Is that all?" griped Fallon. "What're you, Sayler, twelve?"

"You know where he's going with this?" I asked.

"I think so," said Goode.

"Maybe, Tom," I said, "I just didn't share your fascination with rape and homicide. I think he sliced off their—what was it, ring finger?"

"Yeah," said Fallon. "Anything else?"

The car had gotten rank since Fallon closed the windows against the heavy rain.

"No, that's it, that's all I got," I said. "Except claustrophobia."

I reached for the door handle, but Goode grabbed my hand.

"They were all dancers," she said. "Not prostitutes, just dancers, including one ballet dancer."

"You're kidding," I said.

"Nope," said Fallon. "Nice respectable redheaded dancers. Not a hooker in the bunch. And he did six all told. Our guy almost did three so far."

"Why dancers?" I asked.

"Why not?" asked Fallon.

"That's really not funny, Thomas," Goode said and turned to me. "The redhead thing was about his mother—classic. Sunday was the only day he had off work. He never gave up why he wanted dancers, but it didn't matter. The DA made his case, and Kane got life without parole."

"Morgenthau was the DA?" I asked. He had been Manhattan DA for my entire lifetime. Finally left office when he was about ninety."

"No," said Goode. "It was longer ago than that. Nick Hogan was DA—those court transcripts are on microfilm—RTCC doesn't have them because they haven't been entered into the system."

"Can you get him down here?" I asked. "Pick his brain."

"What's left of his brain," said Fallon. "He's been up in Ossining for the last forty years."

"What," I said, "has he got Alzheimer's?"

"I don't know," said Fallon. "But we couldn't get him out anyway if we sent an armored truck."

"How about going up there?" I said.

"Goode, you want to go?" asked Fallon. "I ain't going."

"No thank you," said Goode. "Besides, there isn't enough of a parallel to make that kind of effort. For one thing, there's been no sexual assault in the 44 attacks."

"Are you sure?" I asked.

"There was no evidence in the first two cases," said Goode, then cleared her throat. "And we would know if there was rape or any sexual assault on your friend. According to the hospital there was none."

My friend.

Finally we got a break in the traffic as we approached the hospital, where Fallon could park anywhere.

"OK Nick," said Goode, "are you ready?"

"Yeah," I said. "But this is not good for me. The only person who knew I got the dancer out of the hospital is dead. Now Sykes knows."

"He don't know your name," said Fallon. "He needs us, so his hands are tied. He's got to cover his ass—because he's already in big trouble."

"It'll be hard to cover his ass with his hands tied," said Goode.

Fallon chuckled, and Goode could not control the smile that softened her tight lips.

She rarely got that kind of response from Fallon. But then again, she rarely said anything funny.

"Just be sure there's no link to me," I said.

"Didn't I keep you out of it when we took down Chenvenko's guy?" said Fallon, almost gleeful. It was true; he never mentioned my name. But he didn't mention his either. Since he was on suspension at the time, it was in his vital interest to make sure no one knew he was within fifty miles of Brighton Beach.

The NYPD got an anonymous tip from Fallon about where to look for a stash of homemade hand grenades. After finding them, the cops announced that the death of Chenvenko's man was a result of internecine battling. The investigation would die a quiet death. They were never going to knock themselves out over another dead thug, unless they could get a line on Chenvenko, who was so untouchable no one even had a picture of him.

"I need a promise from you," I said.

"I'll do the best I can," said Fallon.

"That's not good enough," I said.

"Well it's all we have to offer," snapped Goode. "Maybe you should've thought twice before you hooked up with some strange girl—when Rue's out of town."

19

"So when're you calling in your tip about the 44s?" I asked Fallon.

"Today," he said as he double-parked the Impala across the street from Bellevue.

Then the three of us ran for the main entrance. That is, Fallon and I ran. Goode opened her umbrella and walked.

We slip-slid our way across the rain-slicked floor through the crowded lobby toward a bank of elevators and jumped in.

When the elevator doors opened onto the eighth floor, I saw four uniforms stationed about thirty feet apart down the corridor and one guy in a suit fast-walking toward us. He was Sykes, head of Bellevue security, and he was waving, like maybe we wouldn't recognize who he was.

This would have been impossible since he looked exactly like a retired FBI agent, which he was. Heavyset, red-faced, white-haired, and dressed in a suit, he wore an American flag pin on his lapel and his tie tack was also an American flag. There was a green silk square in his breast pocket, a different touch.

Fallon introduced me as a civilian observer.

"You told me you had the sailor," said Sykes sourly as he checked me out. "A handsome young sailor according to the old lady. This guy's no sailor—so who are you, pal?"

"Like I told you," said Fallon. "I got the sailor right here and he's my civilian observer."

"I never heard of a civilian observer before," said Sykes.

"We often enlist their help," said Goode, as Fallon cackled to me in a whisper: "Young and handsome, that's a good one."

"What did you say, Detective?" asked Sykes.

"I said let's proceed, Mr. Sykes."

"Look," said Sykes, "I got the hospital administrators on their way up, and TV cameras circling like jackals, and I got a hospital with thirteen hundred beds and sixteen hundred patients—gridlock in the ER—"

"Yeah, life's a bitch," said Fallon. "Where's the old lady at?"

The four of us headed down the hall past room 848, which was now a crime scene, where there were two more uniforms.

Soon we reached the closed door of room 822.

"Listen, I am appealing to you," said Sykes, who was beginning to sweat and had to use his silk square to mop his face. "The whole hospital is up my ass. So is the deputy commissioner because the commissioner is up his ass, because the mayor has already scheduled a meeting with the doc's parents and the media is going crazy to have a press conference here."

"Yes," said Goode, wrinkling her nose—probably at the image of the deputy commissioner climbing up into Sykes's ass—"we sympathize."

Hospital security had been hustling the Channel Five crew out the door as we were going in.

"And you understand," Sykes said to me, "whatever this patient says can be impactful, so it's very important that you stay here to review with us."

I was counting on Fallon, and he came through.

"Like I told you," he said, "we'll take care of everything with him."

Then he motioned to the uniformed NYPD cop standing guard outside room 822 to open the door.

The guard stepped aside as I entered, and I heard Sykes tell him to leave the door open. I pulled it shut behind me, and Fallon obviously prevailed again because it stayed shut.

Murder had upgraded the old lady to a private room with a bigger TV, but when she saw me, she put QVC on mute. I hadn't got ten a good look at her in room 848. In 822, morning light filtered through the rain and dirty windows and joined in a very depressing combination with the fluorescent light above her bed.

She was probably about seventy-five, smaller than I remembered, now wearing an old-fashioned quilted bed jacket and red lipstick. She had short gray hair cut like bubbles around her face, and her bony fingers were badly twisted by arthritis. When she saw me, she started blinking her eyes as if that action would summon up a picture from the night before. Then she pointed to a folding chair.

"Pull that chair up where I can see you," she said.

I moved the chair closer to the bed and sat down.

"It's nice to meet you Mrs.—?"

She took her glasses from her tray, put them on, and leaned forward.

"It's Mrs. Newell. But you can call me Margaret," she said.

"OK, Margaret," I said. "I'm Keyser."

"How'd they find you?"

"I turned myself in."

"Your girlfriend too?" she asked.

"No," I said. "I paid the bill. She didn't have to come back."

"How is she?"

"She's good." I smiled. "I'll tell her you asked."

"She was beautiful," Margaret Newell said. "Even though she was banged up pretty good. But because of her, everybody ignored me. I asked for ginger ale and they brought me apple juice."

"She'd be sorry to hear that, but getting back to what happened—"

"Why aren't you in uniform today?"

"I'm on shore leave," I said. "So last night you wanted a drink, remember?"

"I was waking up from a dream," she said. "I don't even drink. Well maybe a glass of wine once in a while—"

"What made you realize I was a sailor if you were asleep?" I asked.

"I wasn't asleep when I heard the doctor and the girl talking about a sailor."

"You told Detective Fallon that you didn't remember anything after my...girlfriend and I left because you went back to sleep," I said. "But now you remember something?"

"I didn't go back to sleep. How could I sleep?" she said. "I rang for the nurse to give me a pill, but they don't pay attention...and I didn't forget anything. I just didn't want to tell it to the police."

"Why not?" I asked.

"I don't like cops," she said.

"I see," I said and waited.

"I had some problems with them a long time ago. I think they just wanted an excuse to talk to me. I wasn't born old you know. They accused me of stealing a bottle of brandy. I just put it in my pocketbook because it was heavy—then I forgot it was there."

"Margaret, I'm sure you were a very pretty girl—you still are," I said. "I mean a pretty woman—and sometimes a bad cop will hassle a good-looking girl."

"It happened more than once," she said. "But I was forgetful back then. I'd forget to pick up a shopping basket..."

"Lovely and forgetful," I said. "Happens all the time. But now you're more sophisticated and you remember more."

"That's exactly right," she said.

"So you were actually awake after we left," I said. "Do you know how Dr. Greenburg died?"

"You're very handsome, Keyser," Mrs. Newell said. "You probably would have liked me when I was younger."

"I would have," I said.

"Pull your chair up a little more," she said, and when I did she whispered, "I think he must have been dead before. What I saw was a man putting the doctor on the girl's bed. He believed I was asleep too. He didn't think twice about how shocked I could've been. How I might have a heart attack."

"But you didn't call for anyone after he left?" I asked.

"No," she said. "He put the person down very gently. I didn't know anything was wrong—besides, I could've rung till I was blue in the face and they never come. I couldn't even get a glass of ginger ale out of them to save my life."

"Did you see what he looked like?"

"The man who carried the doctor?" she said, and I waited. "I did."

"Was he tall?"

"Medium. Not tall. Not short."

"Was he heavyset? Or skinny?"

"Medium," she said.

"Was he white? Black? Latino?"

"I couldn't tell," she said. "He was wearing a baseball cap. And a long coat. It's raining out, isn't it? And gloves. In August."

"Did you get any sense of his face?" I asked.

"It was dark," she said. "I mean the room was dark. His hat was pulled down over his face."

"How did he get the doctor in the room?" I asked. "Was he carrying him?"

"No," she said. "In a wheelchair. Then he picked him up and put him on the bed. He could have been one of the stupid orderlies who pretend not to hear you."

"But this guy had a coat and hat on," I said. "Orderlies wear uniforms."

"I thought he was probably on his way home—or out to a bar or I don't know where they go," she said.

"Can you remember anything else?" I asked.

"Isn't that enough?" she said and pulled the inevitable Kleenex out of her sleeve to blow her nose.

"Margaret," I said, "you're a very important witness. And this is a homicide investigation. I think you should tell the police what you know."

"I don't want to talk to them," she said with a pout that would have been more appropriate coming from a teenager. "Why don't you tell them they should send an artist over here and I can describe the man."

Fat chance. The NYPD doesn't keep even one artist on the force, and if they did they wouldn't send him out to draw the generic man.

"I don't know about that," I said. "You can take it up with the detectives. I—and my girlfriend—would appreciate it if you would let them debrief you. If you don't feel like talking to Detective Fallon again you could talk to his partner, Detective Goode."

"I suppose so. What's he like?"

"She's a woman. Linda Goode."

"I'll take Fallon," Mrs. Newell said. "But he looks like a drinker."

Fallon, Goode, Sykes, and the uniformed cop were standing outside the door to 822.

"She remembers a guy," I said. "Medium height, weight, build. She thinks Greenburg was already dead when the guy brought him in the room in a wheelchair."

"Nothing else?" said Goode.

"Zip," I said. "Except strong enough to overpower a guy who weighed about a hundred and thirty pounds, then drop him into a wheelchair and lift him onto the bed."

"I could do that," said Goode.

"You could do better than that," said Fallon.

Goode smiled a little. To her those might as well have been words of love.

"I'll go in and see her," said Goode.

"She wants Fallon," I said.

"Great," Fallon said. "Like I have time for this."

"Bring her a glass of ginger ale."

2 0

I checked my watch and figured by now Meriwether was sure to know who the dancer was, so I ducked into an empty waiting room around the corner from 822 and speed-dialed.

"What's happening?" I asked.

"Status quo," Meriwether said.

"So who is she?"

"I don't know," he said.

"How can you not know?" I asked.

"The power's not up yet and my laptop ran out of juice."

"And the rest of your stuff?"

"Everything's dead."

Meriwether, who works Goldbach's conjecture the way other people work a crossword puzzle, is suddenly paralyzed by a power outage?

"That's fucking unbelievable," I said. "You must have a spare battery. What about the boat—can't you get some juice there? You don't need the gas line for that."

"I promised not to leave her," he said, "and I didn't. And I won't. And you sound wired."

"Yeah," I said. "I'm fried."

"No shit," said Meriwether. And we both clicked off.

Although I never said Meriwether and I were a perfect team, we're usually in better sync than this on a case, but since I've been insisting this wasn't a case I imagine he still didn't feel like he had to help send the dancer on her way.

A few times a year, Meriwether goes to a *zendō* in upstate New York by the Beaverkill River. He likes the dreamy Asian girls he sometimes meets there, and now and then he invites one to the barge.

None of them ever speaks a word of English, which seems to be a prerequisite. He talks to them in Mandarin or Japanese or Vietnamese. One word he must know well in all languages is *good-bye*, because I've never seen any of the girls more than once.

Meriwether's only female friend is Rue, who's charming and kind; nevertheless, it took her a couple of years to win him over.

Apparently, the dancer had done it in less than a day.

When I left the waiting room on the eighth floor my leg was cramping up again, and as I went slowly down the hall toward the elevators, I saw three men and a woman wearing dark suits, in spite of the weather. They were walking briskly, all four abreast, with a gloomy sense of purpose that prophesied trouble for Fallon and Goode. And me.

When I passed them, I had the feeling I was getting away with something.

But my split second of euphoria vanished in another elevator carrying another load of fat, damp people.

Then out the revolving door and back into a heavy drizzle with the cliché of the day from Sister Mary A: It could be worse. Sure, I'd say, it could be raining locusts. And she'd get mad at me, but not that mad because at least I remembered something from the Bible.

When I got to the First Avenue garage and retrieved the undented, unscratched Mercedes, I gave the Dominican kid a soggy ten and drove out into the miserable fucking traffic. And since Sloane had sent his Blaupunkt radio out for repair, I had nothing to listen to but the noise inside my head.

The way I work I'm rarely prepared to take a bullet, but I'm always prepared to fire one. And although he had cheated me by dying before I could get to him, whenever I fired, I was firing at the man who took away the one thing I could never replace.

It's no coincidence that when I turned myself into a legitimate person, I became a legitimate person with a license to kill. I've noticed that a lot of legitimate people confuse permission to carry a gun with encouragement to use it. I'm not one of them because I don't need any encouragement. Or restraint. Only no choice. Which hasn't happened yet. Except once, and it was a guy who tortured and raped children so it doesn't count.

I'd just run a red light when my phone started playing a Chopin nocturne, which meant Sloane was calling.

"Nick," he said. "Go to the Boat Basin. Albert patched up the gas line in the *Gwinnett*. He's staying with the young lady and I'm coming to get you. It'll be faster."

"Why?" I asked. "I'd have to leave your car on this side of the river."

"That's fine," said Sloane. "I can pick it up later—it will take two hours to get back if you drive because there's been a big accident in the Lincoln Tunnel so traffic is halted going in both directions—"

"That's no good," I said. "But I don't want you to come out in this weather to pick me up—what's going on?"

"We know who she is."

PART TWO

You often meet destiny on the road you take to avoid it.
— French Proverb

21

The Goddess Good Luck frowns on lying, so she picked that moment to pay me back for all the times I lied about cell phone signals breaking up.

Before I could learn the dancer's name, Sloane's voice started to crackle and then we lost the connection. Calling him back resulted in nothing except that incredibly annoying busy signal sound. So I gave it up and concentrated on weaving through the choked traffic, cross town to the Seventy-Ninth Street Boat Basin, where I keep a parking space and a slip for the *Gwinnett*.

The Boat Basin, located where West Seventy-Ninth Street meets the Hudson River, floats off five docks tethered close to the Riverside Park Promenade. In spite of being just a few blocks from Zabar's and the Gap, the Boat Basin is an anomaly. A place, through many decades and several iterations, where polished yachts live in harmony with dumpy houseboats and dirty trawlers.

My friend Mandell Goodhue, the longtime dockmaster, looks like Captain Ahab and acts like Karl Marx. He's meant to collect dock fees and vehicle fees from everyone who uses the Boat Basin for tying up a boat or parking a car. And he carries out his responsibilities by taking from each according to their ability—and giving to each according to their need. Which means the yachts pay a lot and the poor people pay a lot less and the couple with the sick baby and the leaky boat pay nothing. As long as the city bureaucracy stays wrapped in red tape, the dockmaster can support his ragged utopia.

In a classic case of hurry up and wait, I parked the Mercedes and looked out to the river, trying to catch sight of the *Gwinnett*. From where I was, the gray of the sky and the gray of the river merged, and I put visibility on my list of things to learn about—from Meriwether, who would know. How visibility was calculated: 12 percent visibility versus 10 percent versus nil.

The old man, who hated wasting time, would be forced to slow down when maneuvering a boat in such bad weather. I didn't mind waiting another twenty minutes, since maybe I wasn't so eager to put the dancer in a slot like everybody else with her own name, her own address, and her own list of sins.

"Her name is Hadley Fielding," Sloane said as soon as I took over the wheel and pointed the *Gwinnett* back toward the New Jersey shore.

"She was with the New York City Ballet. And you were right: for a while she was their prima ballerina."

"And then what?" I asked.

"She retired a few years ago," Sloane said.

"Do you know why?"

"Personal reasons," said Sloane. "All the accounts I saw were vague. Then I came to get you."

"How did you find out who she was—did she remember something?"

"No," he said. "It was Albert. He took a shortcut. He wanted to see the business card that led her to us."

"So?" I said.

"Apparently you never took a good look at the card," Sloane said.

"That's right," I said. "There was no time—and there was no point. I didn't recognize her. A lot of people have my card."

"And the young man, Dr. Greenburg," Sloane said, "he didn't notice anything?"

"Edward, I don't know what he noticed," I said. "It doesn't matter. What did *Meriwether* notice?"

"It was a seven-digit number scrawled on the back of the card in phone number format, three hyphen four," said Sloane.

"So Meriwether figured out whose number it was?"

"Do you want to hear his process?" asked Sloane.

"Not really," I said.

"What else are you doing on this boat ride?" asked Sloane maddeningly.

"Besides driving the boat?" I said.

"You can listen and drive can't you?"

"OK," I said. "I'm listening."

"If you know very well where the person is, whose number you're writing down, you often just skip noting the area code. And you might even skip the name, for your own reasons, for example—"

"You're the shrink, Edward," I said, many decibels above normal, "but I get the idea. So then what?"

I didn't care how Meriwether figured it out. I was sure he got it right, but I resigned myself to hearing this information from Sloane instead of Meriwether, who spoke my language.

"Meriwether," Sloane continued, "compiled a list of all the area codes in the tri-states within a hundred-and-fifty-mile radius of the city. Then he compiled a list of cell phone area codes, which was more complicated, but luckily he started with the regional area codes."

"Makes sense," I said to indicate I was paying attention.

Thankfully, at that point Sloane cut to the chase.

"You know Meriwether," he said. "Still, sometimes he amazes me. Within a short time he found the right number and the right name, which was Margo Holderness. Who lives in Stonington, Connecticut."

Sloane had made the call, and Margo Holderness told him she was Hadley's best friend. They were dancers together. He didn't know much more because Hadley took the phone, and when she got off, she either chose not to say anything or had nothing to say.

Not too long after our conversation was put on hold by constant explosions of thunder and a lightning strike that missed us by inches, I was relieved to see the *Dumb Luck* outlined in the foggy distance. Solid as ever, undisturbed by wind or rain or the human condition.

When we finally reached the barge, after Sloane disembarked and I secured the *Gwinnett*, I knew it was not quite now or never with Hadley Fielding. Only now or later.

I wanted to meet the prima ballerina. But I would miss the no-name dancer.

Waiting for us just inside the mudroom door was the same person. She hadn't shape-shifted into another body and taken on another persona or affect. She greeted Sloane and didn't speak to me until he was gone.

"Nick," she said. "Do I look different?"

"I was just thinking you look the same."

"And I feel the same. Except now I'm responsible for Hadley Fielding—do you understand what I mean?"

"I understand," I said.

"And I'm afraid to remember what happened," she said. "Do you think it was the man who attacked me who broke in last night?"

"I don't know."

"But it could have been," she said.

"And Godzilla could come," I said.

She took a sip of water from a glass she'd been holding with her left hand. There was no sign she'd worn a wedding ring, and if she had been wearing one when she was attacked, it was obviously gone.

The other victims were found with their rings and chains and watches. Hadley's jewelry would have been better—but serial killers don't usually collect trinkets even if they're valuable. They take more grisly souvenirs or leave them. Like the number 44.

"Did Edward tell you about Margo Holderness?" the dancer asked. "I talked to her again after he left to get you."

"He told me she was your best friend," I said.

"Yes," said Hadley. "That's what she said. The number I wrote on the back of your card was a new number for a phone in her house. She said her husband believes in landlines, but keeps changing the phone numbers and they're always unlisted."

"What else did she say?"

"She said she'd been expecting me and she was worried to death…it must be true."

"That she was worried?"

"No," said Hadley. "I mean it must be true that she's my best friend."

"If she was so worried, why didn't she call the police?"

"I didn't ask her that question," said Hadley, "but she answered it anyway. She said sometimes I didn't show up when I said I would. That I didn't always say where I was…"

"What other questions did you ask her?"

"None," replied Hadley. "She said she'd tell me everything when she saw me."

Meriwether probably knew as much as there was to know already. But the Internet had existed for Hadley for only a few hours, and she didn't ask. And Meriwether rarely offers; it doesn't occur to him.

When Hadley paused I saw her wince in pain. I didn't say anything, but I couldn't avoid thinking about the wounds on her back, the number of stitches she had, and the inevitable scars she'd be left with.

"Margo Holderness lives in Stonington, Connecticut," she went on. "I can get there in a few hours."

"You're ready to leave the barge?" I asked evenly.

"Edward is expecting me to leave," she said just as evenly.

"No," I said. "I'm sure you misunderstood him."

"I didn't misunderstand," she said. "He told me it would be a good idea to be with my friend. Much better than staying on the *Dumb Luck*. He said you really were very busy…"

It wasn't the first time Sloane had tried to protect me from myself, and now he'd gone too far, but there was no point in getting angry since this time he was right.

"Margo said she'd send a car," Hadley continued, "and I—"

"Call her back," I interrupted. "Tell her I'll drive you up there."

Hadley didn't respond.

"What is it?" I asked.

"I already told her."

2 2

Hadley asked if I could give her something to write on, because she wanted to make some notes. She wanted to put down some thoughts.

I found a yellow pad and a couple of number 2 pencils, appropriate for her time frame, and left her in my office while I went to my bedroom to fish out one of those musty cigarettes.

I was committing the Eighth Sin.

Pride, Covetousness, Lust, Anger, Envy, Gluttony, Sloth, and Smoking.

I called Pauline to ask if I could borrow her Buick and promised that Sloane would take her anywhere she needed to go.

Two smokes neither helped nor hindered my very strong feeling that we were dealing with the same guy who killed the other two girls. One evil guy who—in less than twenty-four hours—attacked Hadley, killed Greenburg, and shot Sloane, and whose tracking and vanishing skills made him quicker than anyone I knew except maybe Meriwether.

But Meriwether was missing a big piece of himself, and although we never discussed it, I knew he'd give up all his other powers in exchange for that one piece.

I wondered what piece was missing from the man who'd carved a number 44 into Hadley Fielding's back.

The underbrush bordering the beach is dense, and the heavy rain that day stayed warm. There was a good chance the guy was near us, hiding, waiting. He wasn't going to pack it in now because he was on a roll; plus people who don't sleep are usually stoked on drugs. And for all I knew he could be a tracking, vanishing sniper too.

I could have kept Hadley on the barge, but she was already scared and I didn't feel like trying to outlast the guy when all I had to do was outsmart him.

By now he knew that besides jumping into the Hudson River, there were only two routes away from the barge. One was accessed from the *Gwinnett*; the other was down the ramp and up the embankment to the cul-de-sac where we keep our cars, except for the brown Mercedes.

The *Gwinnett* was tied up in plain sight.

There was nothing parked in the cul-de-sac. One of my cars was with Rue; the other, my old Porsche with the cracked block, had been out of commission for a year. The bike I usually use needed a new tire, and Meriwether's truck was in the shop.

The killer couldn't have eyes on everything. Watching the *Gwinnett* and the ramp to the barge at the same time would be impossible even for him; but there was no way to know which way he was looking and I couldn't afford to guess.

Since past performance is the best predictor of future performance, I was sure the killer had a plan.

But I had a better one.

I'd owned the *Dumb Luck* about six months when I discovered a hidden path. It started about two hundred yards north of the barge with an opening in the bushes on the embankment. On the other side of the narrow entrance there were paving stones separated by lush green moss in a specimen tree arboretum with vine-covered arches creating the effect of a fragrant green tunnel.

The only person stupid enough and rich enough to spend a shitload of money building a secret path out of a citadel into the backyard of an old lady in Weehawken would be the person stupid enough and rich enough to lose a barge in a poker game.

When I told Pauline I'd discovered the path she said she was worried about violating some zoning law and asked me not to mention it, which I haven't.

Once in a while I'd walk through the trees, hacking away at overgrowth, then forget about it for a couple of years.

Just before Hadley and I left for Connecticut, I said that although I still doubted she was in danger I'd decided to err on the side of caution and follow a more secure route away from the barge.

"How is it more secure?"

"Just in case someone is watching," I said, "he won't be able to see where we go."

"You've really changed your mind about my not being in danger," she said.

"The path is pretty," I said. "It'll be...fun."

Christ, I thought, I'm decompensating.

"*Fun*," she repeated. "You don't seem like the fun type."

"I'm not a type," I said.

"Well, that makes two of us," she said. "Doesn't it?"

A few minutes later, Hadley and I strolled down the ramp from the barge in the ongoing rain. Hadley was wearing the fisherman's hat with the flaps down and looked like a teenager. I was wearing a cap and we were both wearing slickers as we headed toward the secret path.

In spite of my leg, I try to be in shape. I also try to believe the running and the working out mitigates the drinking, smoking, and crap food I like to eat. I know my reflexes are slowing down, but they haven't failed me yet.

Nevertheless, I'd learned never to underestimate the enemy, who in this case was an anonymous killer probably younger and faster with the cunning of an obsessed psychotic.

"This is gorgeous," said Hadley as we walked under the tunnel. She stopped to examine some green-and-white ivy curling around a low-hanging branch.

"We don't have time for this," I said.

"Why not—we can't be seen in here."

"You can admire this stuff next time," I said.

"Next time?"

She smiled, and I tried to look away from her eyes.

"Come on Hadley," I said, finally turning away. "Let's go."

Yes Sayler you asshole, let go.

Pauline's lawn started where the tunnel ended, and we ran through the grass to the garage, both of us eager to get out of the rain and into the car.

Even though it did seem unlikely for the guy to have seen us leaving Pauline's, I drove around the back streets of Weehawken for a while before I was satisfied no one was following.

The trip to Stonington, Connecticut, where Margo Holderness lived, would be under three hours, mostly going north on Interstate 95, the biggest and busiest corridor along the Eastern Seaboard.

The speed limit on I-95 is sixty-five. And that's where I kept the Buick, mostly in the middle lane. It wasn't as old as Sloane's Mercedes, but it wasn't a Mercedes either, so I didn't want to push it in the downpour. I was no longer in a hurry.

We'd been driving for about thirty minutes without conversation. Hadley's eyes were closed, and I thought she'd fallen asleep until I felt her touch my arm.

"Nick," she said. "I want to ask you something."

"OK," I said.

"And I don't want you to misunderstand—"

"I'll let you know," I said.

"What's the real reason you've done so much for me?" she asked.

"I told you before—I was raised by nuns."

"That's the answer?" she asked.

"Isn't that the right answer?"

"Maybe it's the right answer," she said. "I just don't think it's the true answer."

"You've lost your memory, Hadley," I said, taking it on faith that she wasn't being coy. "Otherwise I'm sure you'd remember that there's a long list of men in your life who are always fighting for a place in line to help you—if you need help."

That embarrassed her. She was staring down at her tightly clasped hands.

"You're a very lovely woman," I went on.

"And that's why you're helping me," she said, putting a hand to the bruise on her cheek. "Because you think I'm lovely?"

"Well," I said, "I've always been a sucker for a pretty face."

"I see…" she said.

We drove along in silence for another fifteen minutes.

"There's something else," she said, picking up the conversation as if no time had elapsed.

"Something else you want to ask me," I said.

"No," she said. "Something else you didn't tell me."

"There are a lot of things I didn't tell you."

She was quiet, and as we rolled on for another few miles the silence grew uncomfortable.

Finally I said, "Yes, there's something else."

After I was arrested, when forced to, I laid out the facts about Julia and me. I never discussed my feelings for her. Not with Fallon, at first to defend myself. Or later to explain. Not with Sloane, who had met Julia once and knew most of the story. And not with Rue except for a quick history, which I owed her. She got the point and didn't press for details, another reason I like her.

But suddenly, in the private bubble of Pauline Prochevsky's Buick with the windshield wipers rhythmically sweeping away the heavy rain, I felt like talking about Julia.

23

One Sunday night in August, ten years ago, somebody wearing a Nixon mask tried to kill William Carteret, president and CEO of the private equity firm Silverstone, where his area of expertise was leveraged buyouts.

Carteret was a big man, and although fit had gone to fat, he was strong and managed to fight off his attacker.

The second attempt on his life was more deadly—but not for him. A new driver, alone in Carteret's limo, was killed when a hidden bomb exploded.

As a natural-born bully and an early architect of the hostile takeover, Carteret was regularly responsible for hundreds of people losing their jobs, severance, health insurance, and pensions. Any one of those people could have sent the series of death threats that culminated in the attack on Carteret and the death of his driver.

Carteret might have thought he was bulletproof, but he wasn't brave, and that's why he decided to seek 24-7 protection for himself and all his valuable possessions—the most priceless of which was his beautiful wife.

Silverstone could afford first-tier bodyguards, and shortly after the explosion, they called Owen Security Inc., which immediately dispatched their best men to guard William Carteret's life.

When he was at the office, Mrs. Carteret would need her own bodyguard, and Owen Security sent me.

Carteret said he didn't like a revolving staff in and out of his house, so to maintain continuity, Owen offered each bodyguard a seven-day workweek, which paid double time on weekends. I needed the extra money to keep a step ahead of my gambling debts. But after one hour with Julia, I would have worked for nothing.

From the first day, Julia and I shared a recognition that linked us in a way far more intimate than sex. We trusted each other with the private thoughts that ordinarily make you grateful no one can read your mind. We shared secrets and confessed sins and talked about the burdens of anger we both carried coiled in our minds.

She had a worse time of being abandoned, because she knew who her parents were. She knew there was no need to give her up; they simply didn't want her.

They were teenagers having a good time. Later, they married other people, had other children, moved to other states, and left no forwarding addresses. They disappeared, deliberately.

Julia was kept in the Northern Missouri Department of Social Service system until she was nine years old, when she was farmed out to some relatives who suddenly appeared to claim her.

She'd seen other children being rescued by aunts or grandfathers who materialized out of nowhere. When she got the same surprise, the miracle she thought it was turned out to be just the opposite.

In the DSS, there were few laws to protect the children and few social workers who cared about them. Some social workers learned how to snake through the loose bureaucracy. It was easy and lucrative. All they had to do was accept bogus documents proving a blood relationship, then lose the paperwork. Those who made these arrangements defended themselves in court some years later by saying the kids were never sold into prostitution.

The people who took Julia wanted another pair of hands to work their failing Jackson County farm. What they didn't want was another mouth to feed and told Julia she was lucky to get anything.

They couldn't hide her, so they were forced to send her to school, where she was regularly expelled for being a troublemaker.

After one of those episodes—she stole the teacher's lunch when she was thirteen—the adoptive father dragged her out to the barn to teach her a lesson. But when he unfastened his belt, it wasn't with the idea of giving her a lashing as usual. That time he threw her on the floor and raped her. Then called for his oldest son to have a go. Then the father again, then the son. Then the second son. Until she was bleeding, bruised, and unconscious.

The next morning, she ran away for the first time. She lived in the woods for five days before the Missouri State Patrol found her and brought her back to the farmers. Although she'd said nothing, one of the state troopers threatened to bring charges if anything happened again.

The family found other ways to torture her, but she was stubborn, and three years later, they didn't call the state patrol or the sheriff as they had done the other times. They let her go. She wasn't worth the trouble.

Julia worked as a chambermaid in a motel, a waitress in a diner, and a hostess at a busy strip club, where many patrons dropped by for lunch-hour lap dances.

One of these was Mr. Gerald Wilson, a tall, thin, polite man who came in every Wednesday and Friday and paid a girl to simply sit next to him, where the only thing he did was hold her hand.

One Friday half the girls were out with a stomach flu, and Julia agreed to sit next to him and while holding his hand learned that his wife of thirty-five years had died and he was lonely.

He was the manager of the best hotel in St. Louis, and a few weeks after he met her, he hired Julia to work in the office. Less than two years later, Mr. Wilson married a lady he met at church and moved to Austin, but not before seeing that Julia was promoted to the front desk.

Julia spent her spare time reading and working in the hotel garden. She wore a wedding ring to keep men away. The thought of being touched repelled her, and if she wanted friends she found them in books.

Then she met William Carteret.

He was on a business trip, and Julia was the one who checked him into the hotel. He was no more struck by her beauty than everyone else, but something as inconsequential as a wedding ring—or a husband if there had been one—would not deter Carteret.

Almost twenty years Julia's senior, he was still young at thirty-nine. And rich. And persuasive. He wanted to take care of her. No one had ever taken care of her, and she was exhausted from the constant vigilance that informed her life, so she married Carteret in St. Louis and he took her back to New York, where he made it clear very soon that he owned her.

She was a quick study and learned the social rituals that were part of his life. Her life was books. He didn't like her to have friends, and she told me she didn't care. She had spent most of her life crammed into rooms with other people. Solitude had been her salvation.

When she realized that something was very wrong with Carteret, wrong with his emotions, she embraced solitude again and accepted living in his bell jar. He rarely touched his precious specimen. He preferred to look at her or take her out to show her off. The only thing he demanded was obedience, which would have been unacceptable to another woman. But Julia wasn't like other women.

At thirteen, dragging herself up off the floor of the barn in Jackson County, she accepted that in her heart, she was and would always be alone. She taught herself how to be wary, how to fight and run, hide and disappear.

In Carteret's house, she was safe, she wasn't locked in or locked out; she had money, however much she wanted, and she was content—relieved—to be a person apart.

She and her husband were members of no group, entertained elegantly but rarely, and appeared only at very lavish events, ten-thousand-dollar-a-plate benefits. People gossiped incessantly about the strange life of the Carterets.

I eventually learned from Edward Sloane's friend, Constance Cohen that in the minds of social, moneyed New Yorkers who had any connection to Silverstone or wished they did, the stunning and mysterious Julia Carteret had become, over only one decade, an almost mythic figure. Ironically, it took the circumstances of her death to prove that she was human.

24

"Go on," said Hadley, when I stopped talking.

"Not right now," I said. "I want to figure out what's happening on this road."

We were barely into Connecticut when the traffic started to slow down, then became slower, and finally stopped entirely. Nothing was moving on either side of the highway for as far as I could see.

Calling Meriwether with his police scanners and all his other equipment—primarily what ran in his brain—would be the fastest and most accurate way to get information.

I stayed on hold for about two minutes, and when he came back on the line he explained that two big rigs had collided in the heavy rain, sending cars across the meridian and creating a massive traffic jam.

Ambulances and fire trucks were having a hard time getting through, and there were no helicopters because of the storm.

Meriwether estimated that we wouldn't move for at least another hour. Said he'd get back to me if anything changed.

Hadley took an apple from a bag of fruit Meriwether had packed for her.

"You have very nice friends," she said, not realizing she had already met most of them.

"You sound surprised," I said.

"Yes," she said. "I don't know why. Maybe I don't have nice friends."

"I'm sure you have fine friends," I said, although I wasn't sure about that at all.

We listened to the rain for a few minutes.

"You should eat that apple," I said.

"Nick," she said, "how did Julia die?"

Julia passed her time with her books and her music and her garden. Townhouses as grand as theirs always came with outdoor space, some of which was very lush with landscaping. Twice a month, Julia worked for an unfashionable charity trying to place older children for adoption. From her house on West Tenth Street, she walked fifty or sixty blocks north almost every day to Central Park, where she ran when it was warm and skated when it was cold.

When I asked the obvious question—why she hadn't left Carteret—she said it was destiny. It was her good luck. She had stayed with him so she would be there to meet me.

What I call luck is different. It happens; you don't wait for it. You don't depend on it because you know how easily it can turn its back on you. But I didn't say that to her.

I didn't ask why destiny hadn't put us together earlier, in a bar or on a street corner. Nothing mattered except being with her.

Carteret's untraceable death threats continued, and so my job as Julia's bodyguard continued.

She and I went to Central Park, to hotel rooms, and to the rat studio I was subletting from another guy at Owen Security, who was in Pennsylvania recovering from gunshot wounds.

The room was small, the refrigerator hummed, and there was a huge empty birdcage in one corner. The overhead fan was broken, and the only furniture was a card table and chair and a single bed where in the afternoon we would lie on the white linen sheets Julia bought at a ridiculously expensive store in SoHo.

She brought music on CDs, and when I heard Ravel's Bolero *for the first time and realized it was written to parallel a long, perfect, explosive fuck, Julia laughed. But then we listened to it every time we went to the studio.*

Sometimes I try, but I can't forget how she covered my closed eyes with kisses and how she cried the first time she saw the scars on my leg. I said the fucked-up leg got me Owen, which got me to her. We liked making up our own story, and we liked that pretty soon we wouldn't have to edit any more chapters.

I don't know how Carteret found us out. At home the house-keeper and the cleaning ladies were around all the time, so we kept our distance, but maybe we got careless. Or he had us followed. Maybe he noticed a change in Julia. Maybe he didn't know until that last afternoon.

Mrs. Bendell, the housekeeper, left on her vacation at seven thirty in the morning. At eight, there was the usual changing of the guard. The night man and I met at the front door, where he told me as always that it had been an uneventful twelve hours.

At one minute after eight, Carteret went down the front steps to his limo, which was driven by Owen's longest-serving employee, Jerry Deutsche, who stayed with Carteret until eight in the evening.

On Sundays the schedule was more flexible maybe by half an hour one way or the other, but the Carterets never left the city. No house in the country, no weekend trips.

The plan never varied. Monday through Friday at eight Carteret left for work, and at six thirty he came home. On Saturday he came home at two thirty. All the shifts changed at midnight and eight except mine. Which meant I was responsible for Julia only ten and a half hours weekdays and six and a half hours on Saturday. Often the same on Sunday. Not ever enough time.

That day, a Wednesday, was our first time alone in the house, and as soon as the door closed behind the night guy, we went upstairs, cut the air-conditioning, and opened all the windows. Julia took off her pink shirt and threw it out the third-floor window. Although she hated my gun, I told her I couldn't throw it out the window, so I took it off and put it on her dressing table. Then she slipped a disk into the CD player and Bolero *began to play. It started, as always, low and slow and unrelenting. Making its promise.*

We drank champagne for breakfast, and later Julia decided we would have lunch outside on the terrace.

As with everything else, Carteret controlled the kitchen. His blood pressure had gone through the roof after his car blew up, and the doctor put him on a strict diet. So, true to form, when the menu changed he wouldn't allow any food in the house that wasn't part of his diet.

What Julia ordered for us from a nearby restaurant was a box of sandwiches. Big fat ones, I remember. Corned beef, smoked turkey, ham and cheese. The opposite of the fish, salads, and steamed vegetables served every night to Carteret and her.

She had been in a fugue state for so long, it didn't matter if he expected her to eat what he ate, drink what he drank, and be there whenever he wanted her. He was the center of the universe, and she was a star who could leave his orbit only if she were prepared to fall.

The traffic began to pick up, and after a while, in spite of the rain and the sixty-five-mile-per-hour speed limit, a lot of trucks and cars powered along doing seventy-five. I normally would have been one of them, except normally I wouldn't have been driving to Stonington, Connecticut, in an old Buick with an injured ballerina.

"Maybe you should call your friend and tell her that we'll be late," I said.

"I don't really want to talk to her right now," said Hadley. "I didn't tell her exactly when we were going to arrive."

"OK," I said. "It's your schedule. I'm your driver."

Hadley was looking straight ahead as she spoke. "Will you tell me the rest of the story?"

I remember perfectly the shape, weight, and the feel of the big white box the guy from the restaurant delivered. It was tied with red string, which I carefully untied to take a quick look. I saw there was enough to feed four hungry people, not two who had lost their appetites for food. Then I closed the box and retied the red string.

When I imagined Julia up on the third floor lying on the bright-yellow chaise in her dressing room wearing nothing but her gold earrings, I doubted that we'd open the box at all.

But it wouldn't be just playtime during these next few summer afternoons because we were going to make our plan. When she would tell Carteret she was leaving. How she would deal with him. Where we would go. It didn't matter that I'd lose my job when she walked out of her marriage. It didn't matter that she was a dozen years older or that we had no money. We'd be together for the rest of our lives, and we'd figure things out like everyone else.

After I tipped the deliveryman and he left, I locked the door behind him.

To augment the beefed-up security system in the house, all locks had been changed. A new, very elaborate lock had been installed on the front door a few weeks earlier. Only four keys were made, which by design and by law were impossible to copy. If they were lost, a new lock would have to be put in.

The first key belonged to William Carteret, who was in his office. Another key was held by the manager of Owen Security, who kept it in the company safe with other client keys. The third one was issued to Mrs. Bendell the housekeeper, who was en route to Orlando. And the fourth key—Julia's—was in my pocket.

But the sound I heard coming from the front door was the sound of the lock disengaging. I was carrying the big white box on an upturned hand like a waiter would carry a tray. My other hand was empty because for the first time in all the time I had worked at the townhouse, I was unarmed.

25

For an instant the man in the doorway was backlit by the blinding midday sun and I couldn't see who he was until he closed the door behind him.

"Mr. Carteret," I said.

He pointed to the box I was holding.

"What's that?"

"It's Mrs. Carteret's lunch. I was just about to unpack it for her."

"Looks like a lot of food," he said.

I wasn't going to agree, disagree, or shrug my shoulders. I said nothing. Finally he pointed to the box again.

"Leave it," he said. "I'll bring it up to her. And you can take the rest of the day off."

"OK," I said. "My phone's in the kitchen—I'll call the office, tell them I'm going."

"It isn't necessary for you to call," he said.

"It's just policy," I said.

"Pick up your phone tomorrow," he said. "You can leave now."

I put the box down on a side table, as he stood next to the door. His body language signaled I had no choice.

I went through the door, and because he didn't move, it was obvious he was waiting to see me walk down the short flight of steps that led to the sidewalk.

I stopped on the bottom step.

"I don't see Deutsche," I said.

Jerry Deutsche, the Owen driver, should have been parked in front of the house. He was meant to be with Carteret at all times.

"I'm not concerned about my safety today. I gave him time off too," Carteret said. "It's such excellent weather. I decided to spend some time with my wife. Alone. I'm sure you can understand that, Sayler, can't you?"

"Yes," I said. "I understand—but you don't want me to stay outside and keep an eye on the house? You shouldn't be without protection."

"We'll be fine, Sayler," he said and closed the door.

I walked a few paces away before looking back. There was no point looking up—Julia was on the other side of the house, the quiet side, with a view of the garden. Now I hoped to God she was wearing more than her jewelry.

He said to pick up my phone tomorrow. So I was still working for him. Or did that mean pick up the phone before you leave because you're fired? He said he wanted to spend some time with his wife. Maybe that meant he would be going back to the office. Maybe he wasn't home for the rest of the day. Maybe I could see her for a few minutes before tomorrow.

I waited a couple of beats before I started walking, twenty blocks north, twenty blocks back. A block west. A couple of blocks east, where I went into a Tasti D-Lite and ordered a chocolate cone. I'd never been in one of those places before, so I didn't know they made the stuff out of air and cardboard. I threw the cone away and bought a pretzel off a vendor a couple of minutes too late to discover I couldn't eat anything.

My leg was starting to hurt; I hadn't walked for very long and the weather was hot and dry, so there was no reason for the pain.

Sloane and Sister Mary A are a perfect couple. Pop and Mom and the errant boy. No matter what trouble I stirred up, no matter what happened, she would say there is always a reason, and God knows the reason.

There is always a reason, Sloane would agree, and Nick knows what it is. On some level.

Yes, she would then say, because God has given him the ability to reflect. And Sloane would then say yes dear, however you want to describe it.

I walked another block and watched people coming out of Dunkin' Donuts with big cups of iced coffee, which gave me the idea to get one myself. Then I went across the street to a liquor store where I got two airplane-size bottles of Jameson and poured them into the coffee. The guy behind the counter said it looked like a good idea. Such a hot afternoon. Maybe he'd try it after work.

I killed a couple of hours, walking, replaying every word Carteret said. *Pick up your phone tomorrow. I want to spend some time with my wife. You can understand that.*

I spotted a deli with a bank of flowers outside. Carnations, mums, sunflowers, and roses. Lilies of the valley were Julia's favorite, but you couldn't find them except for a very short time at the end of spring, and we were far from it. The white roses looked nice, so I bought a bunch and kept walking.

I stopped at a newsstand, bought a copy of the Post, threw it away, smoked a few cigarettes, then finally went back down to the corner of Fifth Avenue and West Tenth Street, half a block away but with a good view of the townhouse.

Carteret had arrived around 12:20. How much time is some time? Some time is not all day.

Spend some time with my wife. Then he'd go back to the office, so maybe Deutsche would be coming to pick him up. How much time off did he give Deutsche? Would Deutsche be back for the rest of his shift, which went into the evening? I looked around to see if Carteret's black Bentley was parked anywhere on the street, which it wasn't.

I couldn't call the house and I couldn't leave. All I wanted was to see Julia for a few minutes. Just see her. I knew I'd be back there in the morning, but it wasn't soon enough.

BOLERO

There were still pay phones on the street then, so I called Jerry Deutsche because even though he was off, he should know Carteret's schedule.

"What's up?" said Deutsche when he answered my call. He was the most senior operative at Owen and did everything by the book.

"Not much," I said. "I was wondering if Carteret was still at the house?"

"What are you talking about, Sayler?" said Deutsche. "He's in the office. I picked him up half an hour after I left him there."

"I thought he gave you the afternoon off," I said.

"Then he called and said he changed his mind," he said. "Where are you?"

"I'm on the street," I said. "When he got home he gave me the rest of the day off."

When Jerry Deutsche didn't say anything, I went on, "Is something wrong?"

"Yeah," said Deutsche. "Something's hinky here. Mr. Carteret told me you were at the house. You were helping Mrs. Carteret plant some stuff up on the terrace."

I dropped the phone and started to run.

2 6

I opened the door with Julia's key, and as I sprinted for the stairs I caught sight of the box from the restaurant on the front hall table. Still tied in red string.

As I ran up three flights of stairs, I could hear Bolero *playing. The door to the master bedroom was closed, so I knocked. And knocked again.*

"Julia," I said.

Nothing.

"Julia," I said louder, knocking harder, finally opening the door. "Hey," I said. "I'm back. Where are you?"

Nothing.

The door to the terrace was ajar. And the first thing I saw was the round glass table where we were going to eat. It was upended, the silverware, broken plates, two napkins still in their silver rings, all mixed up in the shattered glass.

By the time I got to her dressing room my heart was pounding, and if hearts explode, it would have happened then.

"Julia," I said and opened the door.

She was on the floor next to the bright-yellow chaise. She had an ugly bruise on her face, a split lip, and there was a tear in her blue silk robe. Not a tear, a rip. A hole. A place covered in blood.

There was so much bright-red blood. Fresh blood. But she was still breathing, and she opened her eyes as I knelt beside her and put my hand flat on her chest.

"I'll kill him, Julia," I said. "I swear to God I'll kill him."

"Nick…" she said and tried to move.

"Don't move, don't talk," I said. "I'm calling 911. Just hang on."

"Don't call," she whispered.

I was sure she had a chance. Or maybe I couldn't think anything else. The phone was in reach, and I made the call.

"An ambulance'll be here in a few minutes," I said. "You're going to be OK."

"No," she said. "I'm not. I'm dying."

My hand was still on her chest.

"You're not dying," I whispered as my throat tightened up. "I won't let you die."

"Nick," she said.

"Be quiet, Julia, save your strength, don't talk," I said.

"Listen to me," she whispered. "I have never loved anybody but you and I will always love you…take care of yourself please…and… don't forget me…"

Her eyes were so bright, violet, before she closed them for the last time, and the black lashes were so stark against the skin that had become completely pale. She took a small breath and then another and then nothing. Her face changed and there was no pulse in her neck. Everything stopped and there was no reason to breathe air into her lungs because it wasn't her lungs. It was her heart. I knew she was gone.

I put my arms around Julia and felt her warm blood soaking into my shirt. From where I lay with her on the floor I could see sudden rain falling on the terrace and I could hear sirens screaming toward the townhouse.

The police are always the first responders to a 911, and almost immediately after the sirens stopped, people were pounding up the stairs.

Four uniforms came into the room with their guns drawn, and two of them dragged me away from Julia. Their voices seemed distant, and I didn't care what they were saying. I didn't protest when somebody pushed me back down on the floor and told me to put my arms straight out so they could frisk me. After they were sure I didn't have a weapon, they pulled my arms behind me and snapped a pair of handcuffs on my wrists. There were so many voices.

I heard one guy say, "She's beautiful. What a beautiful woman."

"What's a matter with you, Beecher?" from another voice. "She's dead. Ain't beautiful no more."

By then there were more cops in the room, a herd. One of them was a sergeant in plainclothes, kneeling next to Julia.

"The body's warm," he said. "Who's the guy?"

"Hey," said one of the uniforms to another one who had picked up one of the white roses scattered on the floor. "Don't touch anything—you know that for Christ's sake. You're fucking up a crime scene. Everybody out now."

All but that cop and the sergeant left the room.

"Call crime scene," said the sergeant.

"I already did," the cop said. "They're coming."

The uniform and the sergeant walked out of earshot and conferred. They looked blurry, and I closed my eyes. I could hear Julia's voice. I could see her in the park, in the conservatory garden where we used to go and sit by a fountain where three young girls danced in bronze.

27

An hour later I was in a precinct house interrogation room being questioned by NYPD homicide detective Thomas Fallon. Wearing wrinkled clothes and scuffed shoes, he was a thin, wiry guy, with a raspy voice. His hair kept falling in his face, and he'd throw his head back to get it out of the way. He paced slowly, playing with a rubber band.

He wanted to know how long I'd been working for Owen Security, how long I'd been working for the Carterets. And what had happened starting when I walked in the door to begin my shift that morning. I told him everything except about Julia and me.

"So she ordered lunch," said Fallon. "Did she usually order out?"

"No," I said. "The housekeeper usually makes lunch, but the housekeeper went on vacation early this morning."

"Pretty convenient," said Fallon.

When I refused to take the bait, he went on, "What did she order?"

"What difference does it make?" I asked.

"Maybe I'm testing your memory," he said. "So what was it?"

"Sandwiches," I said. "A few different kinds. Where's this going? You've got the box, right?"

JOANIE MCDONELL

"*The lady had an appetite,*" *said Fallon.* "*That's a lot of food—who else was coming to lunch?*"

"*Nobody,*" *I said.*

"*So she wasn't expecting her husband,*" *Fallon said.*

"*Like I already told you,*" *I said.*

"*There was a broken table out on the terrace,*" *he said.* "*Set up for two people. Was that you and her?*"

"*Yes.*"

"*Did you usually eat with her?*"

"*Usually,*" *I said.* "*Yes.*"

"*What else did you do with her?*"

Finally he was getting to me.

"*I was her bodyguard,*" *I said.* "*I did what she did. You must know the drill.*"

"*OK,*" *he said.* "*Getting back to the husband. Carteret came home around twelve thirty. I guess he wasn't expected since that table was for her and you. Or maybe you got it wrong, maybe it was for her and him.*"

"*He never comes home before six,*" *I said.*

"*Except today,*" *said Fallon.* "*That's interesting. What happened after he came home?*"

"*I already told you,*" *I said.*

"*Tell me again,*" *said Fallon, who never stopped walking and playing with the rubber band.*

"*He told me to take the rest of the day off,*" *I said.*

"*But you didn't,*" *said Fallon, whose raspy voice was already getting hoarse.*

"*I left and came back.*"

"*Why did you go back?*" *asked Fallon.*

"*Mrs. Carteret wasn't supposed to be alone,*" *I said.*

"*But that was her husband's call, right?*"

"*I wanted to see if she was OK.*"

"*But you found her dead.*"

"*Dying,*" *I said.*

152

"And you didn't kill her."

When he got no response, Fallon continued, "OK. You already said you didn't do it."

The rubber band he was playing with was stretched out, so he got a new one out of his pocket.

"What kind of gun do you carry?" he went on.

"The kind Owen Security issues to everybody," I said. "A .38 Smith & Wesson Airweight."

"Where is it? It wasn't at the scene."

"I don't know."

"Where do you think it is?" Fallon asked.

"I don't know."

"Why didn't you have it on you?"

"I left it in the house," I said.

"Where in the house?" asked Fallon. He stopped pacing. "Sayler—OK, what was going on with you and Mrs. Carteret?"

I didn't answer, and Fallon kept on talking.

"She was what—thirty-seven, thirty-eight, great looking but a little strange I heard."

"How did you hear that?" I was furious at the invasion.

"How's this for an idea," said Fallon. "You were banging Mrs. Carteret. She broke it off. You killed her."

"I didn't kill her," I said.

"Who did?" asked Fallon.

"Who the fuck do you think, you fucking asshole—"

He did a quick sidestep when I lunged at him. I lost my balance, crashed into the wall, and slipped down to the floor. When I want to hit somebody I hit him. Not that day though. I felt weak and slow, and sick. Fallon pulled me up, shoved me back into a chair.

"I'll let that go," he said. "But you gotta cooperate. Are you gonna cooperate?"

I nodded.

"How's this for another idea—you were banging Mrs. Carteret. Her husband finds out and he kills her."

"I should have gotten her out of that fucking house."

"She could walk out herself," said Fallon, "if she wanted out."

"No..." I said.

And then I realized how it had been. She hadn't been afraid of him before I met her. Now she was afraid of what he would do if she left. She was afraid of what he'd do to me.

"So let me take a guess here," said Fallon. "Carteret gets suspicious, but maybe he isn't sure. He comes home, but he doesn't fire you. He just tells you to leave. For the day. He goes up to see the wife, and maybe he sees the table with all the fancy stuff on it. And he confronts her. Then he shoots her...? With what?"

"How should I know?" I said.

"We questioned Mr. Carteret. He's broken up—you can imagine. Said he doesn't own a gun. Told me his wife—Julia—was scared of you and wanted you out."

When I didn't say anything, he made a little slingshot out of the rubber band and sent it flying.

"OK," he went on, getting ready to leave. "I'll be seeing you."

"I left my gun in Mrs. Carteret's bedroom."

"Uh-huh," said Fallon. "If it's there, which as far as I know nobody saw it, we'll find it. They did find a pink shirt out in the garden—how do you think it got there?"

"I don't know," I said.

"They found a CD on the bed," he said. "Broke in half. Name was Ravel's *Bolero*. Does that mean anything to you?"

"No," I said.

Fallon waited maybe a full minute before he spoke again.

"Oh yeah, another thing," he said. "The crime scene unit picked up a book out on the patio. Must've been on the table that got turned over. Love poems by Emily Dickens."

"Dickinson," I said. Because Julia had told me about her.

"Did you ever see that book?" said Fallon.

"No," I said. "I don't know what book you're talking about."

"There was an inscription," said Fallon. "'To my best beloved Nick.'" He stopped pacing and looked at me.

"What did you say the husband's first name was?" he asked.

"You know his name," I said.

"I forgot," said Fallon. "So help me out here—is his first name Nick?"

"No," I said. "It's William. William fucking Carteret."

"What happened out there on the patio?"

"What do you think," I said.

"I'm going to ask the questions," he said. "But to answer that, it looks like you and her were having an argument. What were you fighting about?"

"We weren't fighting," I said. "I wasn't there. It was her husband."

"How do you know if you weren't there?"

"I know," I said. "But there's no point talking. Because I'm fucked anyway."

"Why's that if you didn't kill her?"

"Because she's dead."

28

It was his call about what would happen next—which was a trip to the Tombs, the prison down by city hall.

After seventy-two hours, the DA decided to charge me with murder two and set bail at a hundred thousand dollars. Since Carteret could get anyone on the phone in one call, I was surprised it wasn't more.

Guilty or not, I was the last person Owen Security wanted to be associated with, and they stayed as far away from me as possible. The Sisters of Perpetual Grace didn't know how to find Sloane, who was somewhere in India, trekking with his partner, Lafcadio Voll.

Because there was no one else in my life who could post the 10 percent of bail money I needed to get out, I went directly to Rikers Island, a place worse than anything that's been written about it.

The reason I was only there a week was because somebody posted bail. When I got out of Rikers I didn't know who did it or where to find out. I called Fallon, who didn't know either and told me to call the DA's office, which I wasn't going to do.

I went back to my sublet, where I found a letter obviously hand-delivered stuck under the door.

I opened the heavy envelope and read the brief note.

Nick,

My son tells me you are a good friend of his. The newspapers are painting a dark picture of you, but I would always believe my son first.

He's traveling and can't be reached, but he asked me to post your bail on his behalf and I have done so. You owe us nothing.

I am very sorry about Mrs. Carteret. We saw her socially over the years, and I must say she was unforgettable.

Good luck,

Michael Teak, Sr.

There was a knot in my throat thinking about Mike Teak. What a thing to do. I'd heard he was working for the State Department. Maybe in the CIA. If his father said he was unreachable, I was sure it was true and all I could do was be grateful and hope my friend stayed safe.

I packed the letter with everything else I owned into a duffel bag, left the sublet, and moved in with the nuns. They had tracked down Sloane, who was en route back from India.

I had introduced Julia to Sloane a few days before he left on his trip. We met for a drink at the boathouse restaurant in Central Park, and I was sure he would see in her what I saw.

At the table he said think clearly and be very careful. Then explained to Julia he was senior enough to tell me what to do, but I was still too young to listen. Julia told him not to worry, she was old enough to understand.

In spite of what we were talking about, we laughed, finished a bottle of wine, and then I took Julia home.

Sloane didn't try to warn me away from her because she was older. Or married. Or damaged. He did repeat that I was in a dangerous position.

And he was right; I didn't listen.

When Sloane and Lafcadio Voll got back from India, Sloane and I went to see his attorney, who was a partner in a big firm that, it turned out, did business with Carteret. Because of the conflict of interest, and self-interest, the attorney sent us to see a well-known criminal lawyer from another firm. Within minutes, the guy started talking about a plea.

Owen Security at least sent me my last paycheck, which I never expected. I gave it to the nuns and continued to stay in my old room, sleeping most of the day and some of the night.

The grand jury was scheduled to consider my case, and the papers wouldn't leave it alone. Low-rent celebrity-sucking television was just starting in those days, and they loved it. TV always geared up in the fall—like the flu—but in summer, particularly August, when nothing happens, a good love triangle culminating in murder was the perfect story.

They called Julia a socialite and ran pictures of her in evening gowns from when Carteret showed her off at charity balls. The only times she was photographed. Carteret the grieving husband, who had been regularly characterized in the business pages as a greedy bastard who took no prisoners, was suddenly heroic.

They dug up an old picture of me in boxing trunks. It was in a minor Golden Gloves event. I was seventeen and never got beyond the quarterfinals, which didn't stop reports of my being vicious in the ring. And since I was eighteen when I got busted for selling dope, the records weren't sealed. So it was "the respected businessman," "the stunning socialite," and "the bodyguard whose good looks belie the vicious drug-dealing criminal he really is."

They never mentioned the Bronze Star. Maybe the dumb fucks thought the V on it stood for vegetable. Fine by me. There was no valor in saving two and losing two.

The guy at the liquor store remembered me, and Deutsche told the cops what time I called him and the call could be traced to the pay phone on the corner of West Tenth Street. But neither the visit to the liquor store nor the call to Deutsche could help me since the exact time of death was imprecise. It was somewhere between when Deutsche dropped off Carteret and when I called 911.

When asked why he had a change of heart about spending the afternoon with his wife, Carteret said he'd forgotten some important papers and ordered Deutsche to take him back to the office.

It looked bad for me; I could have killed Julia after he left, gone out for an hour, disposed of the murder weapon, returned, and called 911. There was no proof I was in the townhouse when Carteret left except Carteret's word. There was no proof I wasn't except mine.

Before the marines, when I went up to visit Teak in Cambridge, Massachusetts, was the only time I'd even been out of New York State.

After the Middle East, I could survive anywhere. Except jail.

The border between Canada and the US stretches for more than five thousand miles. The longest unpatrolled area lies between Washington State and British Columbia, and that is where I would run. If they found me, they could kill me.

The day before the grand jury was scheduled to meet, I was mapping a route into the Northwest Territories when Tom Fallon called to give me the news that whoever had been threatening William Carteret's life finally caught up with him.

After Julia died, Carteret moved into the Four Seasons Hotel and stayed there while the third floor of the townhouse was being redecorated. The hotel bar was famous for the hot working girls who showed up at cocktail hour trolling for big fat assholes like Carteret.

The last time anyone saw him alive was when he got into an elevator to take one of the girls upstairs. A few hours later an anonymous tip sent hotel managers to his suite, where they found him dead of a single gunshot to the back of the head.

Going through his things, the cops found my .38 and a handwritten letter to Julia dated the day before her death. He had obviously changed his mind about sending it and decided to deliver the message in person.

He told her he'd hired a private detective—not from Owen— who took pictures of Julia and me. He said she was a cunt and a whore who had disgraced him, that she deserved to die and he was going to kill her. He signed it William Carteret.

I've never gone to Julia's grave.

Because she had no family to step in and fight the terms of Carteret's will, she and the man who murdered her lie side by side under a huge marble headstone in Northeast Harbor, Maine. She wouldn't have expected me to visit. Early on we agreed that dust went to dust and ashes to ashes. She was gone.

29

The rain seemed worse, or maybe I was more tired than I thought.

Hadley didn't say anything at first. And she didn't cry, which I appreciated because I didn't feel like comforting her just then.

"Nick, you never said what Julia looked like."

I kept my eyes on the road. I didn't want to see the dancer's face.

"She was beautiful."

Three big trucks in succession, in the fast lane, passed me, sending up a wave of water the windshield wipers could not do battle with. I kept checking the side mirrors, trying to stay in the lane, when I spotted the white pickup behind us.

It stayed on my tail for the next thirty miles. Not a very good way to follow someone—but I was dealing with one arrogant fucking psychopath. After thirty-five miles, I slowed down, and the white truck slowed down; I went faster, it went faster; I changed lanes, and it changed lanes. This cat and mouse carried on for another twenty miles until the pickup drew parallel to the Buick, attempting to edge me into the slow lane. I could have avoided it, if the traffic hadn't slowed down.

I started pulling away, hoping the driver I was cutting in front of was fast enough to hit the brakes when I made my move. That driver did hit his brakes, but the truck stayed with me, close enough for me to see its front license plate was missing and its windows were tinted black, a feature you don't see in many pickups.

The Buick was not up to any innovative driving, so I stayed in the slow lane with the pickup truck inches away on my left. There was a narrow emergency lane on my right that went as far as a four-foot steel railing. On the other side of the railing a steep, craggy stone cliff left nowhere to go except straight down. Not far, but far enough.

The railing stopped where the danger of going over the cliff ended, where the emergency lane was wider and flanked by a big stretch of grass.

That's where the pickup ran me off the rain-slicked road. All I could do was handle the steering wheel because putting my foot on the brake would spin the car as it skidded and I'd have no control at all. It seemed a lot longer than a few seconds before I finally slid to a halt, leaving deep tire tracks of mud in the grass.

The white pickup had also stopped. It had been under control and deliberately went horizontal in front of the Buick, blocking it.

"Get down," I said and pulled Hadley off the seat.

"What's happening?" she said, crouching on the floor.

"I'm going to find out." I reached across her empty seat for the Beretta I'd surreptitiously stowed in the glove box.

I waited.

"Who is it?" said Hadley from the floor.

"I don't know yet," I said. "Just stay where you are."

The tinted window on the passenger side of the pickup powered down. And I still waited.

Then a bare white ass stuck itself out the window.

"God fucking dammit," I said, yanking my door handle.

The driver of the white pickup was trying to get the truck off the grass. His wheels kept spinning in the mud, but he was going nowhere, especially after I shot out his two back tires.

Almost instantly, the driver's window descended a few inches and I heard a voice cracking adolescently from fear.

"Stop shooting," he yelled. "Please—it was only a joke."

I glanced at the dented and scraped Buick; Hadley hadn't gotten up off the floor. Obviously she was still terrified and that was enough. I walked around to the front of the truck and shot the left front tire—then the right one.

Until a few minutes earlier, I thought I'd been up against a shape-shifting killer who magically resurfaced in spite of my best efforts. I suppose it was better being soaked to the skin again because of some bare-ass assholes. I didn't need to get the merry pranksters out of the truck because I didn't care who they were.

But maybe I wanted to hit somebody.

"Get the fuck out of the truck," I said.

As three preppy-looking boys jumped out with their hands up, I heard a car door slam and then Hadley was beside me in the rain.

"OK," I said. "What's the fucking joke?"

The kid on the right, who must have been the one who mooned us, started to lower his hands.

"Oh no," I said, pointing the Beretta at him.

"What the *hell* were you doing?" Hadley said to the boys.

"School starts like in three weeks," said Bare Ass, "but the fraternity looks for pledges now."

"And the fraternity we want to get into," the driver said, "gives out assignments to see like if you have what it takes."

"And what's that?" I said.

"Like you know," said the driver, who was the tallest of the three, with a head way too big for his body. "Like whatever."

"Yeah," said the scrawny, nervous middle kid. "Every day for a week we have to like moon a car on I-95 and take pictures you know like to prove it. Wednesday was Corvettes, yesterday, it was like Cadillacs. Today is Friday which means Buicks. And there are like no Buicks and like tomorrow it's just Honda Accords."

"Oh there's not going to be any tomorrow," said Hadley.

All three boys, who had been staring at her since she arrived at my side, backed up a step or two, although she hadn't moved.

"Like what do you mean?" asked the driver.

"What part of the sentence did you fail to understand?" she asked, walking slowly, almost floating, toward the boys while the rain beat down on all of us.

"Like I mean what do you mean?" said Bare Ass.

When she was nearly nose to nose with the boys, Hadley turned toward me.

"Are you going to kill them?" she asked.

"I'm trying to decide," I said.

"Well it's Friday," she said as the boys stood shivering. "What do we do on Fridays?"

"Friday is for busting kneecaps," I said.

"That's right," she said. "But I don't want to spend any more time in the rain—my hair's already ruined."

"It won't take long," I said. "You can wait in the car."

"No," she said. "We're late already."

The boys started to lower their hands and turn toward the shelter of the truck. I was ready to leave too.

"We didn't say you could go," Hadley told the boys, stopping them. "There's one more thing."

"What?" asked the middle kid weakly.

"I want your, um, mobile telephones and your wallets," she said.

The boys looked at me and saw that I had put away the Beretta, but they kept their mouths shut and handed over the things she asked for. Hadley put the phones in her pockets, removed the driver's license from each wallet, and returned the wallets. Then she gave me the licenses. I liked that she saw us as a team, and I studied each kid's license as I dreamed up the last item of misery I was about to hand them.

"Oh, by the way," I said. "Now that we know your names, we're going to make you pay for the inconvenience you caused us."

"How?" mumbled Bare Ass.

I looked at Hadley.

"The usual?" I asked her.

"Definitely," she said. "You better warn your parents—so they'll be prepared."

Heading back to the car, Hadley said, "What was going to be the usual?"

"I have no idea," I said, and she laughed.

Humor. Greenburg. Poor Greenburg. Thinking of the little turtle strangled and laid out on that bed in the hospital wiped away anything funny about the ridiculous frat boys.

The Buick got off pretty light—dings and scratches. I went to the trunk to see if Pauline had anything in there we could use as towels, like towels. All I found was a spare tire, a shiny jack, and an antique edition of *101 Common Mistakes in Etiquette and How to Avoid Them* by Emily Post.

Back on the highway, I decided to push the Buick because Hadley's teeth were chattering. And my leg had been pounding far past the time someone else would break out the real painkillers. I never touch any kind of drug and haven't for years. But sometimes I need to concentrate on the reasons why. So from the start of the trip to Stonington, when I wasn't talking about the past or dealing with idiots in the white truck, I was concentrating on how good it was not to be a drug addict.

And maybe that's why I never saw the black BMW that had been with us since Weehawken.

30

Margo Holderness would have clothes for Hadley. And unless Margo's husband was a giant or a midget, I could borrow something of his. So instead of stopping at a service plaza to buy oversize, overpriced *I* ♥ *NY* T-shirts, we pressed on to Stonington, a pretty little seaside community, which was, according to a sign at the town line, home of the last commercial fishing fleet in the state of Connecticut.

We drove on for about three miles until we reached a narrow two-lane causeway leading up to the private peninsula where Margo and her husband lived on a high point of land overlooking Narragansett Bay.

The final leg of our trip was along a dirt road through a forest of evergreens. The road ended at a locked gate between two square granite pillars, which in turn stood between privet hedges that looked one or two stories high. On the right-hand pillar a bronze plaque read:

> *But some assert, on certain grounds,*
> *(Beside the damage and the wounds),*
> *It cost the king ten thousand pounds*
> *To have a dash at Stonington.*

On the left pillar there was a gray steel keypad in a recessed niche, where I punched in the code Margo had given me.

The gate swung open to let us through, then clanged shut behind us. The dirt road had become a long, curving driveway made of white and gray gravel shining in the rain and lined by huge elm trees. Flaring out behind the elm trees were nothing but rolling green lawns, where not a single blade of grass had the nerve to turn brown and no errant dandelion reared its little yellow head.

To our left the grass rolled down to a seawall, with a dock below it. The rest of the lawn apparently went on forever.

A gigantic oak tree stood solidly to one side of the huge Holderness house, which was built in a quasi–Greek Revival style, pristine and evenly white. There wasn't a spot of dirt even in the ridges of the fluted columns that supported a second-floor balcony above the eccentric portico.

No doubt some undocumented Mexican, who might have walked across the Rio Bravo in the middle of the night, regularly took his life in his hands, again, getting on a ladder or hanging off the roof to clean the uppermost reaches of those columns. Detailing, after the power wash.

Far off through the rain I made out a guesthouse, a pool house, and a tennis court. And I wondered where the money came from.

"Look," said Hadley, pointing toward the main house. The higher branches of the oak tree swept out almost far enough to touch the balcony onto which a woman, oblivious to the rain, had just run. The woman waved madly and then ran back inside.

"Was that your friend?" I asked.

"I don't know," said Hadley. "I still can't remember my own name. And I can't recognize my best friend. If she is my best friend."

"What do you mean *if*?" I said. "The numbers on the back of that card led straight to her—and when you called she said she'd been expecting you. She couldn't lie because she didn't know you'd lost your memory."

"Maybe she knew," said Hadley.

"How could she?" I asked. But Hadley didn't answer.

"I guess she couldn't," Hadley finally said. "But after what happened, how am I supposed to trust…someone I don't know?"

"You trusted us," I said.

"I had no choice," she said, smiling as her violet eyes picked up light from some mysterious source in the gloomy afternoon.

We reached the house just then and watched the front door fly open. A tall redhead with a gorgeous body, wearing skintight blue jeans and an all but transparent white T-shirt, came bounding toward us, repeating *Oh my God* over and over. A big golden retriever with a wildly wagging tail followed at a gallop.

As soon as we got out of the Buick, he reared up on his hind legs and knocked Hadley back against the car door trying to lick her face.

"Down, Buddy, down," cried the redhead, and when I went to grab the dog Hadley waved me off, pushed him down, and held his collar.

The dog's enthusiasm took the edge off what would have been an awkward first moment.

"Bad boy, Buddy," said the redhead. "Bad boy."

"That's OK," said Hadley, and the dog ran beside her as the three of us hurried out of the rain and into the house. "I guess he likes me."

"Of course he likes you Hadley," said the redhead. "He's your dog."

When the heavy door closed behind us, the redhead threw her arms around her friend but immediately let go when Hadley went stiff.

Hadley didn't recognize her best friend. To her, the woman was a total stranger.

We stood in a round entrance gallery on a black-and-white marble floor done in checkerboard style from which a dramatic staircase curved around and up to a second and third floor.

Whatever style the inside of the house was, it was not related to the outside. The dull, pearlescent light coming through domed glass high above our heads made me feel, without benefit of hallucinogens, like I was in a giant conch shell.

The gallery was designed like a wheel with rooms off equidistant, invisible spokes. I could see a living room, dining room, and a library. The other rooms were behind closed doors.

"Come on," said the redhead. "We'll all get pneumonia. And that would be a disaster."

As we followed Margo Holderness I whispered to Hadley, "Anything look familiar?"

"Nothing," she said. "I can't believe I ever set foot in this house before."

31

Straight ahead, a set of double doors opened onto a solarium done in white wicker with pink-and-green geometric patterns on the chaises and the couch. There was a bank of orchids on one side and a little upright piano; a nice touch if you didn't care about the humidity keeping it permanently out of tune.

"I'm going to get you some dry clothes—both of you—you must have been walking in the rain," said Margo as she grabbed Buddy's collar. "I'm freezing cold myself. Be right back. Come on Buddy."

It was easy to see that Margo was cold, and after she and her breasts left the room, I watched Hadley walk from window to window.

"God," Hadley said, "how can it keep raining like this?"

We talked awhile about storms from the northeast and hurricanes. We moved on to cyclones, earthquakes, and tsunamis. And volcanoes. Safe territory.

When Margo came back, she gave us towels and clothes and pointed us toward two bathrooms.

Luckily, the husband and I wore about the same size. But the similarity stopped there. My pants, shirts, and jackets come from Secaucus, where I stock up every couple of years. I buy the rest of my stuff in Weehawken. The husband's white shirt was from Barneys and his pants were Armani.

In the bathroom, I tried without success to reach Fallon, then Goode. I didn't expect that they'd get caught screwing around with CompStat because they both, especially Fallon, had been in tight spots before, and they both—especially, it turned out, Linda Goode— were slippery.

She proved how quick she was with concocting bullshit a year earlier when she saved Fallon's ass from a third suspension. He was one of the only people in the history of the department who had been awarded two service crosses, so they'd never kick him out, but they would make him suffer. They'd take him off the street.

It's not that Fallon doesn't think, it's just that he doesn't think when he's with some blonde girl drinking himself past the place of no return. He forgets or doesn't care that certain violations mean suspension. Whether or not they sound serious to a civilian is irrelevant. The department has its own set of rules, and Fallon has broken most of them.

This last episode got out of control when a snitch reported, accurately, that Fallon, who was on duty, had been knocking back shots at a bar called the County Kerry, only three blocks away from the Thirteenth Precinct.

This was not only a serious violation; it also carried the subtext of defiance for which Thomas Fallon was so well known. He had made enemies along the way. They took his behavior as an embarrassing personal affront. Despite his heroics, which must have stirred up a lot of jealousy, his getting away with so much incensed certain higher-ups. They were always waiting for one more fuckup serious enough to give them a reason for chaining him to a desk.

Fallon wouldn't have asked her to do it, but Goode immediately stepped up. She said neither she nor Fallon was drinking when they were together at the County Kerry investigating some suspicious activity, which she documented with a well-written report. Nobody doubted the stolid detective because they knew Fallon couldn't stand her and thought the feeling was mutual.

What she got as a reward for putting her career in jeopardy was Fallon's grudging appreciation. To her it was like winning the lottery.

Rue didn't say anything to me, nor did Fallon or Goode. And I didn't say anything to them either, although I did know that at the time the two detectives were supposed to be conducting their investigation, my girlfriend had been eating a sandwich in the park with her unlikely friend, Detective Linda Goode.

On the way back to the solarium I heard music, and when I got to the door, I saw the dancer, dressed in white pants and a white shirt at the piano.

She stopped playing when she saw me.

"Procedural memory," she said.

"Where's your friend?" I asked.

"Right here," said Margo, who'd come up behind me. "Hadley! I heard you playing. You remembered the music—that's awesome!"

"I remembered how to play," said Hadley, "I just don't know what I was playing."

"That was from act one," said Margo, startled. "From *Giselle*."

The two women looked at each other silently. But silence was not Margo's style.

"Well never mind—don't worry," Margo began chattering. "You look beautiful anyway. She always looks beautiful—thank God you're all right. You are all right, aren't you? I mean look at your face—at least the cut didn't need stitches. That bruise will go away, but it must hurt. Do you want some ice? No? Hadley's tough. Did you know that? OK, let's all relax. What happened—" Margo stopped herself to take a breath.

"Oh I'm sorry," she went on, looking at me. "We haven't even been introduced—well I mean, you know what I mean. You're Nick Sayler, right? Here's a sweater for you. And this one belongs to you Hadley—it even smells like you."

Hadley clearly found that comment distasteful, but she finally took the sweater and then slowly brought it up to her nose. After a couple of beats she put it on.

They say smell is the keenest sense. I'd say it's a fucking odd way to remember yourself.

"Thank you very much," said Hadley.

"Thank you very much?" said Margo. "Please Hadley, don't thank me. I love you—you're my best friend. We're like sisters."

"Do I have a real sister?" asked Hadley.

A wing of pain flitted briefly across Margo's face.

"Nope," she said. "Just you and me babe—are you guys hungry? Let's go in the kitchen. Mildred's there. She can give you something to eat. Then you can tell me what happened. I don't want to know. Well yes I do. Was it horrible?"

As we made our way to the other side of the house, Margo rattled on to Hadley about her French lessons, her trip to Petra, her dressmaker, her landscaper.

She said nothing about the past. And Hadley didn't ask. Margo seemed to be waiting for something, waiting for the other shoe to drop. She didn't grab the phone and start making calls to announce Hadley's return. Where were all the people in their lives—the friends, the family—or where at least were the stories about their lives?

The huge kitchen looked like it came off the cover of *Perfect Kitchen* magazine.

A woman, probably in her sixties with graying hair in a ponytail and black button eyes, was at the island in the middle of the room chopping onions in the rat-a-tat-tat way of experienced cooks. She was wearing baggy blue jeans and a T-shirt with a Universal Pictures logo on it.

"Hadley, honey, I was sending up prayers for you when I heard," she said in an accent from somewhere south of South Carolina. "I can't kiss you 'cause I smell like onion."

Good, I thought. The dancer doesn't have to endure another kiss from a person she doesn't recognize.

"Tell me what you want to eat," the woman continued. "I can make anything."

"Hadley," said Margo, "you like Mildred's Cobb salad or salad Niçoise—"

"Whatever's easy," said Hadley. "A sandwich."

"What about you, sugar?" the woman said to me.

"I'm good," I said.

"Oh please eat something Nick," said Margo. "We've got cold steak—we can make a baked potato in the microwave."

"Fine," I said. Margo figured men eat steak and potatoes; in my case she was right.

"OK, go on now," said Mildred. "I got to work here."

3 2

"This room is better for a nasty day," said Margo.

Which was true. The study she led us to smelled like cedar, and, given the scale of the house, it was small. There were bookshelves with sets of leather-bound books, all looking suspiciously new. Heavy, decorative coffee-table books fulfilled their job description. There was a big flat-screen TV and doors like the ones leading into the solarium. These doors opened onto a rose garden, where the color of the reds and oranges and pinks popped in spite of the rain.

Except for Jameson there was a fairly well-stocked bar. Ketel One rocks for Margo, Hadley wanted Perrier, and I settled for a double shot of Patrón Añejo.

You don't get a hangover from mixing drinks; you get a hangover from mixing a lot of drinks.

Mildred buzzed over the intercom, and when Margo took a call from Prada and talked to her personal shopper using words like *chicorée* and *batiste*, Hadley picked up one of the art books and I looked around the room.

The mantel above the fireplace was given over to photographs. Mostly in silver frames shining like they came out of the Tiffany boxes yesterday.

A picture of three beautiful dancers caught my eye. They were wearing tights and leg warmers, leaning against a barre in front of a mirrored wall. It was a younger Hadley and Margo and a third girl with long blonde hair. Hadley and Margo were smiling for the camera; the third dancer looked straight ahead, wistful or somber.

"Who's this other girl?" I asked Margo just after she finished telling Mildred not to put through any more calls.

"That's Victorine," said Margo. "They used to call us the triplets."

"Are you all still close?" I asked.

"No…" Margo thought better of whatever she was about to say and pointed to another photograph. "That's my husband."

It was a head shot. A money shot of a man with a few laugh lines around bright-blue eyes, a mop of sun-streaked hair, and dimples on either side of a famous signature smile.

"You didn't mention your husband was Billy Holderness," I said.

A TV actor who happened into a fantastically successful movie franchise that made him a major star. Three films so far, which opened in the summer, always going straight to the top of box office sales.

"I didn't think about it," Margo replied. "The thing is most people just know."

"He's an actor Hadley," I said. "Very famous—one of the most successful movie stars in the country."

"In the world," said Margo. "His movies get sold everywhere because a lot of the dialogue is *uggh, ahh, pow*." She accompanied the sounds with a couple of karate slices into the air. "Translates well."

"Very well," I said.

"Yeah," said Margo. "Look around."

"I have been," I said.

"McKenzie Black bought all this," Margo said, referring to Holderness's character. "But Billy played some other roles before McKenzie changed our lives…"

"McKenzie Black is a soldier of fortune," I said to Hadley. "He always saves the world."

"And gets the girl," Margo said, turning to Hadley. "You knew him first, babe. You introduced me to him."

There was a photograph of Hadley as the doomed Giselle, wearing white, executing a grand jeté, head turned slightly away from the camera, caught forever in midair.

Margo showed us more pictures of McKenzie Black jumping out of planes, and Billy in real life, such as it was, driving a Ferrari. In a snapshot of Billy bareback on a white horse, the laughing girl behind him with her arms around his waist was Hadley.

I walked over to an étagère in a corner, with glass shelves and glass doors. Locked. I recognized a few of the items, because they looked like the ones Meriwether owned.

"I make him keep them locked up," Margo said. "But it's kind of useless. He's always coming home with a new one and doesn't even close the doors."

"I can see he's a serious collector," I said.

"Yeah," said Margo. "I hate them, but there's nothing I can do about it. Billy has always loved knives."

3 3

When the intercom buzzed, Margo marched over to the phone and said, "I don't care who it is. No more calls unless it's Billy. Take messages from now on. How long till we have some food?"

"*Re*lax girl," said Mildred over the intercom. "You'll get it when I bring it."

Hadley was staring hard at the photographs as if looking long enough might bring back a memory.

"All these kids," Hadley said, pointing toward sparkling children at birthday parties or wedding parties. "Are any of them yours?"

"No," said Margo, "they belong to friends. Billy and I don't have children."

"Where is Billy?" I asked. "Is he going to be here later?"

"The movie he was shooting wrapped last week," Margo said. "*Black Night IV*. He dies in this one—but not really."

"He's got to return for number five," I said.

"He wants to buy an island," Margo said.

"Manhattan?" said Hadley.

"There's the old Hadley," said Margo. "I knew you'd come back."

"You didn't mention where he is," I said.

"He's in Alaska," said Margo.

"What's he doing in Alaska?" asked Hadley, whose memory maybe included the information that Alaska wasn't a first choice for postproduction R & R.

"Fishing," said Margo. "I don't know—whatever—trekking, looking for polar bears. He likes to be alone. His managers aren't happy about that. There are always insurance issues. So he took a guide, I think. And a SAT phone, which seems not to be working. I thought the point was those phones are supposed to work anywhere—Alaska, you know, or the South Pole."

"Aren't you worried about him?" asked Hadley.

"What—are you kidding?" Margo said. "You know Billy. He thinks he's McKenzie Black."

For the next twenty minutes, Margo identified every person in every photo, hoping that a face or a place might ring a bell with Hadley. I thought it was kind of generous for Margo to do that since earlier she'd been obviously hurt by Hadley's not recognizing her face.

This was taking some kind of emotional toll on Hadley, and she seemed relieved when the dog came prancing into the room followed by Mildred carrying a tray heavy with wine and sandwiches and a plate of steak and potatoes as promised.

"Buddy!" Mildred yelled. "Buddy come on over here—Buddy sit! I'm sorry—Buddy sit."

Buddy had no intention of coming, sitting, or stopping. He trotted over to Hadley, and all hundred pounds of him tried to jump into her lap.

"Buddy down!" cried Margo.

Buddy wasn't listening. He was wagging his tail, making little yelps of pleasure. Hadley stroked his gold-colored head and then said, "OK Buddy, lie down."

And down he went, to the floor at her feet and put his head between his paws so he could watch his mistress.

"Hadley," said Mildred, "I made a nice tuna sandwich for you—try it."

"Thank you Mildred. I'll eat in a little while."

"Whenever you want baby," said Mildred as she set down the food.

"Margo," said Hadley, pointing to a snapshot on the desk. It was a child with her arms around a dog who looked very much like the big dog at her feet. "Is that Buddy?"

"Yes," said Margo, "that's him."

"And who's the little girl?"

Margo glanced toward Mildred, who was heading for the door.

"Mildred," Margo said. It was an entreaty.

"I'll be in the kitchen," Mildred replied. She shook her head very slightly from side to side meaning, *Not me, I ain't saying nothing.*

"Wait a second Mildred," Hadley said. "Margo?"

"She's my godchild," said Margo.

"What's her name?" asked Hadley.

"Gemma," said Margo, whose face was suddenly flushed.

"She's a pretty little thing," said Hadley. "Do I know her?"

Margo for once couldn't speak.

"Margo," Hadley repeated, "do I know her?"

"Honey," said Mildred, "precious little Gemma was your daughter. She passed coming on three years ago."

"Isn't this fucking rain ever going to stop?" Margo sobbed.

Mildred slipped out the door, and Hadley went over to put her arm around Margo. She smoothed Margo's red hair back from her wet cheeks.

"Thank you," Margo said, composing herself.

Hadley looked unsettled when she heard Gemma was dead. But no more so, I imagine, than she would have when she heard about the death of any child she'd never met or even heard of before. Whose family she didn't know. Hadley Fielding was still a stranger to the dancer.

"Margo," I said, "who was Gemma's father?"

"Nile, of course," said Margo. "Hadley?"

Hadley shook her head. It wasn't coming back to her.

"He's Nile Sutro," Margo said to me. "Her husband."

What had I expected? Parthenogenesis?

"Yeah," I said, although nobody asked me. "I've heard the name." A violinist. A cellist. Something like that.

"Tell me," said Hadley.

"He's a concert pianist," said Margo. "A virtuoso. Since he was a kid—like you were—and here's the thing, he's really the only person in his generation who crossed the line between classical and everything else. He plays concerts around the world. He composes for the movies—"

"Right." I muttered.

"What did you say?" asked Margo.

"Nothing," I said.

"Well, Nile is a big star," said Margo. "Not as big as Billy—but Billy would probably say Nile was more successful."

"Why's that?" I asked.

"Nile won first prize," said Margo, and I had a feeling I knew what was coming.

"What do you mean?" asked Hadley.

"You, babe," said Margo. Suspicion confirmed. "Nile got you. I was the consolation prize."

"Well I'm sure that's not true," said Hadley.

By now, a normal person would have asked about the child. But Hadley was not a normal person. I wanted the reason to be because she was suffering from amnesia.

"Why don't you tell Hadley about the other things in her life?" I said.

If Margo didn't start soon, we'd be in that room forever. And three's a crowd.

"Well OK," she said with a sigh so deep she must have learned it in a yoga class. "You were born in Boston."

She told Hadley about her father, the Princeton football player who later became a successful banker. And about her mother—always in frail health, too frail to pursue a promising career in the ballet—who died when Hadley was ten.

Her final request was that Hadley be allowed to dance. She knew her husband would promote only tennis—to learn in boarding school, refine at college, and use as a social tool for the rest of her life.

But the mother had seen in Hadley what she herself, even at her best, never possessed. And that was magic.

34

Hadley's father honored his deathbed promise by taking Hadley for an audition, after which she was invited to become a student at the School of American Ballet. Founded by the legendary choreographer George Balanchine, the school is part of the New York City Ballet, and except for the Kirov in Moscow, it is the most famous training academy in the world.

Margo and Hadley met there as eleven-year-olds, and although Hadley could remember nothing about the school or her career, she knew who Balanchine was. She and Margo seemed impressed that I too recognized his name. My friend Allegra Trent would have been proud.

That first year of Hadley's training was the last year of Balanchine's life. During what would be his final visit to the school he looked in on the youngest students.

He was not well, his hearing and eyesight had gotten weak, but he was still Balanchine and his opinion was still more important than anyone else's.

"When he saw Hadley," said Margo, "he stopped the class in progress and asked her to do a series of fouettés, jetés, and entrechats—you know what all those are?"

"Yeah," I said. Sure I did. "Go on, it's a good story."

"It's a *true* story. So Balanchine kept her going for another ten minutes, and when she finished, he called her over. They say he leaned on a cane with one hand and put the other hand on her head like he was anointing her.

"God creates," Margo said in a Russian accent. "I do not create. I only know who was born to dance. You will be the next *prima ballerina assoluta*."

She explained there had been so few *assolutas* in the history of the ballet, it was a stunning thing to hear from the man whose disciples were among the best ballerinas ever. Alexandra Danilova, who lived with him, Maria Tallchief, who married him, Suzanne Farrell, who broke his heart.

And finally Hadley Fielding, whom he never lived to see realize his prophesy and become, if only very briefly, the greatest of them all.

"I can't remember how to dance," said Hadley, looking past Margo through the window at the heavy gray sheets of rain.

"Yes you can," I said. "You did. Last night. When we were at the barge."

"Barge?" said Margo.

"He lives there," said Hadley.

"Who lives on a barge?" Margo asked, no more or less incredulous than most other people who heard about the barge for the first time, or saw it.

"Never mind about that Margo," said Hadley. "I'll tell you later."

Margo picked up a plate of small round cookies that Mildred had left and offered them to us.

"They're strong," she said.

"What do you mean, strong?" asked Hadley. Making me wonder whether she had forgotten or just didn't know.

"Hash?" I asked.

"The best," said Margo.

"I'll pass," I said, and after Hadley passed too, she calmly asked Margo to tell her what happened to her child.

Margo wolfed down a cookie and half a glass of wine and took a couple of deep breaths.

"You were performing *Giselle* at Lincoln Center the night Gemma died," she said. "It was the opening gala, sold out at five grand a pop to people who were dying to see Hadley Fielding because the critics agreed that you owned Giselle. Baryshnikov was in the audience, as were the Clintons, who expected to meet you."

"Did you dance that night?" Hadley asked Margo.

"Oh no, I washed out years earlier—I was good, but I mean look at me. I was way too big."

Margo said she was in bed with a migraine the night of the gala. Sutro was in Russia nearing the end of a long tour. Holderness was in the audience, and little Gemma was with Lolek, the Polish nanny, at the Sutro house in Sneden's Landing, a place up the Hudson where you couldn't buy a toolshed for under $4 million.

Mildred had been lobbying Hadley to get rid of Lolek. Said she was a gypsy and not to be trusted. But Lolek came with excellent references from the best agency in New York and had been the perfect nanny. She'd studied ballet for years in Poland, Gemma loved her, and she'd learned to stay out of Nile's way when he threw a tantrum.

The nanny said she left urgent messages for Hadley during the performance. Not a surprise when no one backstage could remember taking the calls.

Lolek was phoning because she was taking Gemma to the ER. The child had suddenly come down with a mysterious illness and was running a high fever.

When Hadley finally learned what was happening, Billy drove her to the hospital, but by the time they arrived it was too late.

No one knew what killed little Gemma. The hospital kept Hadley waiting an hour before letting her see the body, at which point she became hysterical. She demanded to see every person who was involved with her child during the few hours before Gemma died.

Even Billy's star power did not make the hospital administration move any faster; no doubt they were getting their ducks in order for an inevitable lawsuit.

That day and thereafter the hospital stood by its claim that there had been too little time before Gemma died to learn what was wrong with her.

And Hadley refused, irrationally, to permit an autopsy.

Later, Nile Sutro for once did not argue with his wife.

Well after dawn Billy insisted on taking Hadley home, but when they reached the road that led into Sneden's Landing, Hadley said she couldn't bear to go to her house, didn't feel up to talking to Lolek. She directed Billy to a nearby cottage that belonged to her friend Katie Allen. Katie and her husband were in East Hampton visiting Katie's mother, and Hadley knew where the spare key was hidden.

As Hadley lay on the bed in Katie Allen's guest room, Billy explained that Margo was on her way to Sneden's and he was going back to the hospital to deal with the unfinished details.

The night of Gemma's death, Sutro canceled the rest of his tour and flew back to New York on a Gulfstream GIII loaned to him by a former Russian gunrunner trying to reinvent himself as a patron of the arts.

When he landed, his driver took him directly to the hospital and then to Sneden's Landing, where he confronted Lolek, and during the angry fight that followed she left deep scratches across his face. Sutro's driver tried to break up the argument and got fired for his trouble.

Hadley and Margo were at the funeral home during the argument, and when they returned the nanny and the driver had already left.

Nobody could understand why Hadley didn't insist on interrogating Lolek—who'd gone to parts unknown with the driver—until Hadley said she believed the story. It had been an idiopathic event. And the point was, her baby was dead.

Hadley and Sutro separated less than a year later. He stayed in the Sneden's Landing house; she rented a place in the Chelsea section of Manhattan.

"Moving to the city didn't help," Margo said, "because you couldn't work. Then you hoped if you got out of New York...you went to London to the Royal Ballet, but you couldn't practice—you couldn't rehearse. So you returned. You thought you could take another year off and still be young enough to go back to performing. But you didn't go back."

Margo turned to me and said, "She's never danced again."

That news, like Sloane's observations about her not being in condition for the ballet, had as little impact on Hadley as the account of Gemma's death. She just couldn't regret experiences she didn't remember, and I admired her for not pretending.

Margo went on to say that recently Sutro had been begging Hadley for another go at their marriage. Amazingly, Hadley agreed. She'd been packing up her things the night of the attack. The next day she'd planned to come to Stonington and spend some time with Margo before Sutro returned from his tour.

After a second hash cookie, Margo decided to tell us it was a good thing Billy wasn't in Stonington. He'd been fed up with Sutro for years—now he was pissed off at Hadley too for getting ready to make the same mistake twice.

"Because we know Nile still blames you for Gemma's death babe," Margo went on to say. "He's still furious that Billy was with you at the hospital. He was always a pain in the ass, but now he's turned into a total prick."

"But you're all still friends?" I said.

"No," said Margo. "Billy's finished with Nile. He even made me take away his pictures and get rid of the knife Nile gave him for his twenty-fifth birthday. His favorite one. It belonged to John Wilkes Booth. I guess I'm more easygoing. And Nile's a real artist."

And a prick. John Wilkes Booth. Jesus.

"Why would I want to go back to this man?" asked Hadley.

"Because, babe," said Margo, picking up another cookie, "you love him."

"Where's he now?" I asked.

"San Francisco tonight, two nights in LA—then Houston and home. Hadley, do you want to call him?"

"Not now," said Hadley.

"OK," said Margo. "Later then. You have to call him."

"Margo," Hadley said quietly, "I don't want to be rude. But the truth is, I don't have to do anything."

35

If Margo's feelings were hurt, she didn't let on, and I was relieved that the wine-and-cookie combo had calmed her down. Listening to her early chatter was like being attacked by a pellet gun.

"I have an idea," she said. "Let's do something different. We've got this archivist in New York who put everything together, all our clippings and—"

"No please," said Hadley. "It'll be easy to read about our good times. I just need to know if there was anything else…bad."

Margo sat down on the floor and talked to me.

"There was something else," said Margo.

What the fuck else, I thought. The girl's father and husband were both dicks; her child died. Her career was over, and she'd been attacked by a sick fuck who hadn't given up yet.

"Go ahead," I said.

"It goes back a lot of years."

"Tell me," said Hadley.

But Margo turned to me, which seemed to make it easier for her.

"It happened after Hadley made a guest appearance at the Kennedy Center to raise money for the Washington Ballet. She was with Billy then. Nile was with Victorine."

"Your friend the other ballerina," I said.

"Yes. She was wild about him. They went to Washington to watch Hadley dance and bring her home."

"Where were you?"

"In the city," Margo said. "I was odd man out at the time, but here's the thing: I could have gone, but Nile had a small car—an old Jaguar convertible, yellow—and there wasn't any room. Isn't that funny? I don't mean funny—I mean—"

"Ironic," I said.

"Yeah, I was too big. So they were fifty miles out of New York on the Jersey Turnpike—it was winter, snowing, icy, middle of the night. Nile was tired—but nobody could blame him. A bus skidded, there was a pileup, and the car was totaled."

Margo rose from the floor and slowly paced the room as she spoke.

"After the wreck, everything changed."

"Hadley was with Nile," I said. "You hooked up with Billy. What about Victorine?"

"She must have hated me," said Hadley, "if she was that much in love with…Nile."

"Oh, she would have gone apeshit…" said Margo.

"But?" I said.

"The EMTs told us she died on impact," said Margo, her eyes filling with tears again.

"You don't have to go on," said Hadley.

"I'm OK," said Margo, wiping her eyes with a tissue. "Let me just tell you the rest. Even though we were 'the triplets,' and all that, Hadley and Victorine were rivals. Big-time. Since we were kids.

"There could only be one prima ballerina. Victorine was stronger, more driven, more competitive—technically brilliant. But Hadley was…astonishing. And then there was Balanchine's prediction. Everybody in the ballet is so superstitious."

"So," said Hadley, "I got her place and her boyfriend by default."

"No," said Margo, "you earned the place. And Nile claimed he'd been about to break up with Victorine because he'd always loved you."

"He had to say that? He couldn't just let her rest in peace," said Hadley.

"Well," said Margo, "yeah. It would have been nice. Poor Victorine, her life was messed up from the beginning—we just didn't know how bad it was until after she was dead."

The phone rang again. A couple of times. A moment later, Mildred came on the intercom.

"Margo—"

Margo went over and smacked the intercom button.

"Mildred," she said as her voice rose, "what is it?"

Her question was met with silence.

"Oh come on, I didn't mean to yell at you. Everybody's upset today."

"You can say that again," said Mildred. "Including me. Your brother's on the phone."

"Which one?" Margo asked.

"Both," said Mildred. "I told them what happened, and they want to talk to Hadley."

"Well they can't," said Margo. "We'll call them later."

She clicked off the intercom.

"You know the boys," Margo continued, looking at Hadley, who was shaking her head. "They're identical twins…maybe they'll jog your memory. They were just babies when you met them. You used to play with them all the time when you were at my house. They both were in love with you."

"Did I have a favorite?" asked Hadley.

"Andy thought it was Chip, and Chip thought it was Andy— but no, you didn't have a favorite, did you?"

"When I get my memory back," said Hadley, "I'll let you know."

Margo went and sat on the edge of the coffee table, close enough to pick up Hadley's hands in her own.

"I already know everything," she said. "Look at me babe. It's me, Margo. Mildred's in the kitchen. Victorine was our best friend. Nile is your husband. Billy is my husband. Look at me Hadley. You're not fucking with me are you?"

Hadley pulled her hands away.

"*Fucking* with you?" she said, standing up. "I don't even know you. Nick, I'd like to leave now."

36

I said I wanted to wait half an hour, said I was hoping the rain would let up.

Hadley grabbed Buddy, who apparently remembered a lot more than she did, and went out for a walk. In the downpour.

Margo sighed again so deeply she could have lifted off. Then the phone rang. Stopped for a few seconds. Then rang again followed by Mildred's voice on the intercom: "Sorry to bother you—"

"Mildred," said Margo, hitting the intercom button, *"Please. Don't keep doing this.* I don't want to know about any more calls unless it's Billy. *OK*? Whoever it is get rid of them."

After a moment of silence, Mildred said, "It's for Nick Sayler. The man says it's urgent."

"Well who is it?"

"I don't know—he wouldn't give his name."

"I don't care who it's for," said Margo. "We never take those no-name calls. What's gotten into you—"

"First he called on the main number and I didn't put him through—but this call came in on the new private line."

Margo looked down at the flashing light on the phone.

"Sorry Mildred, I didn't notice," said Margo.

I held out my hand, and Margo clicked off the intercom and gave me the receiver.

"This is Sayler. Who am I talking to?"

There was no response except heavy breathing. Classic anonymous heavy breathing. The kind you read about, but can't really imagine how ugly it is until you actually hear it.

"What are you saying?" I said. "I can't hear you."

Then the heavy breathing turned into heavy panting, faster and faster, until there was a yelp of release and a broken connection.

"Who was it?" Margo asked.

"My office."

"Well please don't give out our private number again," said Margo. "Billy will get really pissed off."

"Margo, I'm sorry," said Hadley, who had saved me the trouble of looking for her by returning on her own. "I know best friends trust each other—and you wouldn't have asked me that if you didn't have a reason."

Margo jumped up and embraced her.

"I'm sorry too," said Margo. "I didn't mean to offend you—I don't know why I said it. There was no reason."

Margo was looking at me over Hadley's shoulder, and her face sent the message she still thought there was a reason.

"Oh hey," said Margo, letting go of Hadley and checking her watch. "Look what time it is—let's watch the news. Billy and I never miss the news."

I was getting slow on my feet because I couldn't think of a legitimate reason for asking her not to turn on the TV.

The anchorman announced flash-flood warnings for coastal Connecticut. Then there was a story about someone falling off the Fishers Island Ferry, news about a drive-by shooting in Hartford, and after a commercial for Big Bob's car dealership, the focus shifted live to New York City, where the mayor had called a press conference in front of Bellevue Hospital.

This was how Hadley was going to learn about Greenburg.

"Hadley," I said. "I want to talk to you."

"The news will be over in a minute," said Margo.

"That's where I was," said Hadley. "Bellevue. Why do you think they're there?"

"It's bad Hadley," I said.

"Shhh," said Margo, who was half in the bag. "We're about to find out."

"Hadley," I said. "I want to tell you something."

"God," said Margo. "Please be quiet for a sec—Billy might want to know what happened. We always watch the news."

"Tell me after the news," whispered Hadley.

I can't think how many times I've seen a mayor—Koch, Dinkins, Giuliani, Bloomberg—standing before a phalanx of reporters with a police commissioner by his side, most notably Bill Bratton, whose star outshined Giuliani's. Bernie Kerik disgraced and jailed for corruption and fraud, and Ray Kelly, who stepped up to the plate twice and seemed set to stay there for life.

Standing under an umbrella held by an aide, the mayor was wearing a dark suit with an American flag on one lapel and a white shirt with a subdued blue striped tie. I was glad he appeared to be showing respect for the late Justin Greenburg.

To the mayor's right was the police commissioner, holding his own umbrella, also in a suit and tie. His head was entirely bald, his shoulders at attention, and his lips pinched so hard they nearly disappeared. I recognized the man on the mayor's left as one of the hospital administrators I passed walking to the eighth-floor elevator after I talked to Mrs. Newell, who'd briefly been Hadley's roommate.

In the tight scrum behind the microphones, half-hidden by the hospital administrator, I saw Fallon's familiar slouch and unkempt hair. Linda Goode, who was next to Fallon, appeared to be wearing lipstick.

"First, I want to say that our hearts and prayers go out to the family and friends of Dr. Justin Greenburg," intoned the mayor.

"Oh no," whispered Hadley.

"While we don't yet know the details of the homicide," the mayor went on, "we do know that Dr. Greenburg's death was a tragedy. Rest assured that I am putting the full force of my office behind our effort to apprehend the perpetrator and make certain this will never happen again. Thank you."

"Nick, what happened?" asked Hadley. "How did you know?"

The police commissioner handed off his umbrella, adjusted his microphone, and cleared his throat.

"Know *what*?" said Margo.

"Thank you Mr. Mayor," the commissioner said. "Let me underscore the mayor's dedication to finding the perpetrator of this heinous act. I have appointed a task force to investigate the crime, and I can promise the task force will get results. Thank you."

All the reporters started shouting questions at the same time, waving hands and microphones. The mayor took a step forward.

"That's it," he said.

They always appoint a task force. So many they've become meaningless.

As the news cut away to a commercial for Big Bob's Discount Stores, my cell phone started barking.

"Nick," cried Hadley, "please tell me what *happened*."

"Excuse me, Hadley," I said. Candy-ass. "We'll talk in a few minutes—but I've got to take this now."

"You know I could have you arrested," said Fallon by way of greeting when I answered my phone out in the gallery. "Where the fuck are you?"

"I called you three times," I said.

"Don't try to get on my good side," he said.

"You haven't got a good side."

"Yeah, look who's talkin'."

"Listen, Tommy," I said, "Greenburg alone wouldn't rate a press conference. Obviously everybody knows about all three attacks now. But I suppose you and Goode didn't exactly go to the head of the class when you announced now there were three women attacked with the same signature."

"That's exactly right," he said. "But at least you can thank me. I went back to neuro and established nobody seen nothing. Covering your ass for the moment."

"For the moment?"

"Then I ran down the ER doc who stitched up your dancer, and he corroborated she had the memory loss Greenburg wrote on her chart. He gave me that 44 was cut into her back. I was just double-checking."

"I know," I said, "because you haven't seen her yet."

"So now we got a task force, two dead girls, a dead doctor, and a Jane Doe vagrant supposedly wandering around the city."

"And you're getting shit-on-a-stick instead of a lollipop."

"You can't run out on me like this. You gotta bring her back."

"I will," I said.

"Now," he said.

"Tomorrow," I said. "Just don't forget, she's the victim."

"And a witness."

"With no memory," I said.

"Did you see me on TV?" he said, giving it up for a minute.

"I saw you," I said. "Behind the police commissioner. You look bad."

"Yeah," said Fallon. "I feel bad. Think I must've ate something. I couldn't answer you all day because they make us turn off our cell phones if we're with the mayor."

When Fallon says he ate something it means he drank something. A lot of something.

"That's smart," I said. "Make the homicide detectives unavailable."

"Tell me where the fuck you are," he said.

"Stonington, Connecticut."

"We could go get her," he said.

"Yeah," I said. "Two hours up, two hours back, and you can't force her to go with you. Or maybe you want to get hold of a judge."

"Don't be an asshole, Nick," he said. "She got a name?"

"Hadley Fielding," I said. "She was a ballerina."

"And what? She lives in Stonyville?"

"No, I took her to her friend Margo Holderness."

"Holderness," he said. "Please don't tell me that's connected to McKenzie Black."

"Tommy Fallon," I said. "I didn't know you went to the movies."

"What do you mean?" said Fallon. "I'm a normal person."

"Yeah," I said. "And I'm Jack Reacher."

"Who?"

"Forget it," I said.

"OK," he said. "Is this woman any relation to Billy Holderness? And I hope not, because then I'll have the media people so far up my ass—"

"Mrs. McKenzie Black," I interrupted.

"Shit," said Fallon.

"So McKenzie Black just changed his unpublished number to another unpublished number…" I said and went on to tell Fallon everything, including the phone call from the pervert.

"Well fuck me," said Fallon. "Just get her back here tomorrow. Nick—"

"I heard you," I said.

"Where the fuck is Stonyville anyway? He coulda called from anywhere."

I stopped talking when Margo passed by me and gave me a small wave. I waited until she ran up the stairs.

"*Stonington*, Connecticut," I said. "And he's here," I said. "Or near here. I really think he is."

"Lucky you're a one-man SWAT team," said Fallon.

"This isn't funny Tom."

"Yeah, but right now there's nothing I can do," said Fallon. "Or tell nobody else to do. We ain't got the manpower, and I doubt Stonyville's got the brainpower."

"Speaking of which," I said, "where's Goode?"

"She's down at the Puzzle Palace," said Fallon. "And I'm talking to people about serial killers who we think our guy ain't. He's some other kind of psycho. Watch your back buddy. I'll see you tomorrow when you come in, her and you."

37

The Puzzle Palace is One Police Plaza, where the hyper-teched-up Real Time Crime Center is located on the eighth floor.

The first of its kind anywhere—the RTCC pulls together and gives detectives and field officers, in an instant, as much all-encompassing information that's available. Though it isn't in the same league as Quantico, it's very effective, and Goode has gotten better at her job because she's learned how to use its resources.

In terms of investigative technique it's no surprise that Fallon and Goode are as different as they are in every other way. He believes in instinct; she believes in data. He has his gut. She has CART, the Computer Analysis Response Team; NIBRS, the New Incident Based Reporting System; and UCR, the Uniform Crime Reports.

She also has, out of Quantico, FBI Special Agent Betty Murphy, a woman she met at one of the law enforcement seminars detectives are required to attend every six months. Agent Murphy, who was lecturing at the seminar and who subsequently became Goode's friend, reminded me, the one time I met her, of a bird. A tough little beady-eyed, beaky-nosed bird.

I remember the first time Goode described her all in one breath as a senior-officer-at-NCAVC-the-National-Center-for-the-Analysis-of-Violent-Crime-which-advises-federal-state-and-local-law-enforcement-on-threat-assessment-and-major-case-management.

CIAP—which Fallon invariably writes as CRAP—the Criminal Investigative Analysis Program, exists under NCAVC's umbrella, as does the FBI's best-known and least-understood service, the Violent Criminal Apprehension Program, ViCAP.

The only profiler in ViCAP is a software system programmed to gather and distill information about serial criminals. There is no one anywhere in the Bureau whose job description or title is profiler. Or supreme profiler. But if there were, Betty Murphy would be it. Her PhD in behavioral science and many years spent delving into the minds of pathological murderers informed all her comments. In a perfect world, there'd be a seamless exchange of information between the FBI and other law enforcement agencies. But the cops like to call the FBI Fancy But Ineffective and the real world is ragged. Access to NCAVC isn't granted automatically to the NYPD or any other police department.

Linda Goode and Betty Murphy manage to outmaneuver barriers. The two of them look like improbable friends, but so do Goode and Rue. I suppose it's because women have a lot of friends. At least more than men. Definitely more than me.

When I returned to the library to tell Hadley the facts about Greenburg's death, we'd both already passed the point of pretending she and the barge break-in were unrelated.

"We should celebrate," said Margo, bubbling back into the library carrying a bottle of Cristal rosé and a big scrapbook.

Hadley looked at me with eyes now navy blue in the shadowy room.

"Celebrate," said Hadley. "I don't think so."

"Why not? You're here, you're in one piece," Margo said, popping the cork. "We have a new friend—a cute one. And here's the thing—truth be told, sometimes I wouldn't mind losing *my* memory for a few days."

Hadley didn't say anything. She just picked up a glass of champagne and so did I.

Margo opened the scrapbook, but Hadley said she didn't want to see it. She was exhausted from trying to pull up memories. Undaunted, Margo suggested they go upstairs to her bedroom and watch the first McKenzie Black movie, and Hadley agreed.

Outside the window, dark clouds locked out the sky, and I had a feeling I'd never see her in the sun.

"I'll come with you," I said.

"No," Margo said. "Just girls."

"OK," I said, "just girls."

"See you after the movie," said Hadley, accommodating her friend.

"Help yourself to whatever," Margo said to me as she put her arm through Hadley's, pretending that they were back in the good old days. Or at least the old days.

It was a strange deal though, the way Margo cheerfully reported that Billy had preferred Hadley—hinting that he still might feel the same way.

Sutro claims he wants her back, but maybe he wants her dead because of the little girl. Maybe Billy thinks if he can't have her, nobody can. Both of these guys live on another planet where people have been kissing their asses for so long, they really believe they live by different rules. Both of them had the means to get fake IDs, alter their appearances, and hire private jets, or better yet hire assassins. I couldn't think of why either one would maim and murder two other women except to prevent focusing an investigation on Hadley Fielding's killer.

Or more importantly why either one would actually want to kill Hadley Fielding. These two would rather kill each other. And I was so burnt that afternoon I knew I wasn't even grasping at straws. I was grasping at smoke. When I crossed Sutro and Holderness off the list, there was no list.

38

Outside, the grass beyond the driveway swept down toward the seawall. Fog covered the bay like a puffy gray quilt and a thin mist swirled around where I stood under the portico sheltered from the rain. It was peaceful there. But it was the Beretta still firmly wedged into the small of my back that gave me comfort.

After that phone call from 44, a few steps from the front door was as far as I'd be away from the dancer.

When I started to feel the odd greasiness in the air you get by the sea on stormy days, I decided it was time to go back inside and have a talk with Mildred.

I found her still in the kitchen, sitting on a stool, smoking a thin brown cigarette.

"You got another one of those?" I asked.

She pulled a tin out of a drawer and handed it over.

"Thanks," I said, lighting up with the wooden match she gave me.

"You look like you're hurting," said Mildred. "What is it?"

"My leg," I said. "In bad weather."

"You want Tylenol?"

I thought about my old pal oxycodone. A lot of people claim a junkie never comes back. And a lot of people are right. But not all.

"You got aspirin?" I asked.

"Extra strength," she said. "Nothing else though."

I didn't respond.

"I'll go get it," she said and disappeared, like a black Alice through a door I hadn't noticed before. And I was like the Caterpillar, who was the first addict I ever met. Sister Mary Alphonsus obliviously introduced him, smoking his hookah and sitting on his mushroom, as she read chapters of *Alice in Wonderland*.

"You want some water?" asked Mildred, returning with a bottle of Bayer Back & Body in her hand.

"Have you got Jameson in here?"

"Got everything," she replied, and we both decided to have Jameson rocks. She put the ice in the glasses and I poured.

"You got a heavy hand sugar," she said.

"Tell me about Hadley," I said.

"Well what do you already know about her?" she asked.

"Exactly what she knows about herself—nothing."

"Aren't they waiting for you in the study?" asked Mildred.

"No, they're upstairs," I said. "Don't you want to talk to me?"

"No baby," said Mildred. "I want to talk to you. But maybe it ain't my place."

No longer a bossy family member, all of a sudden she was a discreet servant.

"I don't think she'd mind," I said.

"Well what part of her life do you want to hear about?"

"You decide."

"I like you," Mildred said.

"Thanks."

"Hadley's still married," she said.

"I know."

"And that don't matter to you?"

"Who would want to hurt her?" I asked, ignoring what she said since it was more of a challenge than a question and she knew it.

Mildred lit up a fresh cigarette, inhaled, exhaled, and stubbed it out.

"Nobody," said Mildred. "That girl's an angel from heaven. She might be a little…complicated, and if some folks don't understand her, I say that's their problem."

"I don't have a problem," I said.

"Her mama died. Her daddy took her to the ballet school…he got married, had more kids, and the wife cut her off…they never came to see her dance…she spent every Christmas with Margo's folks…her and Victorine…poor Victorine, she was a strange one with the two brothers run off to the circus and the sister went bad…she didn't have nobody up north except Hadley and Margo and the boys…"

"The boys," I said. "You mean Holderness and Sutro."

"Yeah, all them went down to Mississippi…after the wreck…"

"I heard about the wreck," I said. "Sutro was driving. Tell me about him."

"OK, but I'm gonna tell you one other thing just for the record, got nothing to do with nothing."

"OK," I said.

"Margo was never as good as Hadley, no one is, but she was better than Victorine—it's just that she grew. She's a big girl."

"She looks more like a chorus girl," I said.

"Yeah, and talks like one, I know. She made up a new Margo when they told her she couldn't be a ballerina."

"She's good with all that now?"

"Yes she is," said Mildred. "She's just fine."

"And Sutro?" I asked again.

"A selfish, selfish man. He ain't a patch on Billy Holderness… Billy, he'd do anything for Hadley starting way back when—you know who was with Hadley at the hospital the night baby Gemma passed? Billy. He took care of everything. Signed papers, calmed down that hysterical nanny—I didn't care for that girl, Lola or some name. Too big for her britches. What I am meanin' to say is Billy always looking out for Hadley."

"And for Margo," I said.

"Yeah, of course," said Mildred. "And for me."

"So what about you Mildred? How do you fit in?"

"Oh, I know them girls since they was babies." Mildred said. "I was an assistant to the wardrobe mistress at the ballet."

Mildred topped off our whiskey and went on, "I think we should call Billy."

"They haven't called Sutro yet," I said. "And Margo's been trying to reach Billy. She doesn't know where he is."

"Yeah," said Mildred. "She don't, but I do."

39

Before I could pry anything more out of Mildred, Margo twirled in carrying an empty bottle.

"I spilled the champagne Milly," said Margo. "Could you get me another one?"

Last time I looked Cristal rosé, depending on the vintage, was going for four, five, six hundred dollars a pop.

"Come on Milly," said Margo. "And Nick Sayler. Let's lighten up around here. It's such a shitty day. Milly, where do you keep the cookies?"

Mildred dropped her eyes and didn't respond.

"I'm not a cop," I said.

"I know," said Margo, giggling. "You're a private dick. How private is your dick, Nick? Milly, please get the damn cookies."

"Margo," said Hadley, "may I borrow your car?"

I hadn't seen or heard her slip into the kitchen.

"But it's pouring out," said Margo. "And it's late and you've been drinking. And the movie isn't over."

"No," said Hadley evenly. "I haven't been drinking, you have. And I don't mind the rain. And we can finish the movie when I get back."

"Where do you want to go?" Margo asked. "I mean you don't remember where you are."

"I know where I am now," Hadley said. "And you can give me directions."

"You don't have your driver's license with you," Margo said.

"Why would I get stopped?" said Hadley. "I just want to go to a gas station or a drugstore."

"For what?" said Margo.

"Cigarettes," she said.

"You don't smoke anymore," said Margo.

"Listen," said Hadley. "Am I a prisoner here? I mean I don't know when I'll remember anything. Driving is part of procedural memory. So you either trust me or not. It's that simple."

When Margo looked my way, I didn't engage.

"Sure," said Margo. "I trust you. Take a car. I'll give you money and directions. Do you still have a headache? You're not going to pass out are you?"

"No, I am not going to pass out, and I'll take Buddy for protection."

"From what?" asked Margo.

"From the night," Hadley intoned ominously. And Margo laughed.

The three of us went through the house to a spotless five-car garage, where Margo suggested her friend take the Land Rover, which looked like it hadn't been used since it arrived from the showroom.

As soon as Hadley had backed onto the driveway, I said, "OK, give me the keys to another car."

"Are you going to follow her?" asked Margo.

"No Margo," I said. "I just thought I'd take a spin in your husband's Lamborghini."

"Sorry," she said, got a set of keys off a nearby hook on the wall, and threw them to me. There was the Lamborghini charging bull on the key ring. Too late to say I didn't mean it.

"I'll come with you," she said, opening the passenger side door.

"That's not a good idea," I said.

"OK," she said reluctantly. "Don't lose her."

I waited for Hadley to get through the gates before I started, slowly, after her. She wouldn't recognize the Lamborghini on the highway and in any case wouldn't be looking for a tail.

After fifteen miles with few other cars on the road, she pulled into a 7-Eleven.

I parked under a broken light at the far side of the gas pumps and watched Hadley in the store with Buddy on a bright-green leash. She slowly walked the perimeter of the place, looking at everything. Ice cream, shaving cream, coffee machines, magazines. She circled the place one more time before she got in the checkout line to buy a pack of cigarettes.

I'd kept track of the action in front of the 7-Eleven, scanned the parking lots of the adjacent McDonald's and the King Kullen across the road. Nothing going on. Two pickup truck drivers, young with nose rings and old with tattoos. A middle-aged lady wearing a raincoat with sleeves turned up to reveal the plaid.

The only person who interested me got out of a MINI Cooper. The medium-size figure had black rain gear on reaching to the ground and head covered with an oversize hood, which did a good job of hiding the face. The person, without looking at anything in the store, slipped into place behind Hadley, turned so the face was still not visible. Whoever it was started talking to Hadley, and I opened the car door.

I was already heading toward the store when the hood came off, showing the face of a young blonde girl. Probably no more than sixteen years of age. You never know.

Hadley ran out of the 7-Eleven through the rain, Buddy by her side, jumped back in the red Land Rover, and pulled out to the road. I waited a minute to see if there was any action, which there was not.

As I gunned the Lamborghini onto Route 1, I eyed the speedometer—which read up to a tempting 210 miles per hour. A shame not to try it out. Maybe another time.

I stayed a conservative fifteen car lengths behind Hadley for about five miles. A little bit into mile six, after a violent crack of thunder and half a dozen jagged lines of lightning, the moderate rain exploded into a hammering downpour, which threw a blinding gray curtain across the windshield. I decreased the speed to thirty miles an hour—which is way too fast when you can't see—until the deluge let up about two minutes later.

I should have spotted her immediately because there were no cars on the road ahead. I ramped up to seventy-five, eighty-five, and with a little more pressure the speedometer read ninety. Then I slowed down because at that speed I would blow past her.

If she had been on the road.

40

My cell phone vibrated and barked.

"*What?*" I yelled.

"We got the last Bellevue videos," Fallon said over a crackling connection. "They—"

His next words cut and in out—I couldn't hear him, and I was trying to see through the rain.

"Later," I said and dropped the phone.

Nobody could have grabbed her, and at least I didn't see a pileup. She couldn't take a wrong turn because Route 1 was almost a clear shot back to within a mile of the private causeway leading to the Holderness place.

The phone barked again, and I let it go.

Where the fuck was she?

Skidding the Lamborghini into a reckless U-turn, my hands tightened on the steering wheel and I drove back to check a service road off Route 1 that Hadley could have turned onto by mistake. But even in the rain she wouldn't have mistakenly drifted onto a road that was at a right angle to the highway.

Having lost time, I fishtailed into another U-turn. Sixty, eighty, ninety-five. A hundred and fifteen miles per hour. I didn't know what I was prevailing against, but prevail is what keeps me going.

He must have been on the road…or the causeway…watching her leave Margo's…waiting for her to return…

My cell phone buzzed and rang. A normal ring.

"What?" I said into the phone.

"Hi," she said, "it's Hadley."

"Hadley, where are you?"

"I'm back at Margo's," she said. "There's a shortcut to the causeway over a back road—I must have remembered it because I just went into autopilot. Margo said you followed me—and I'm calling because I didn't want you to think anything was wrong. Where are you—"

I cut her off, pulled over to the side of the road, and leaned back in my seat. I took a deep breath, exhaled, and then drove Billy Holderness's Lamborghini at a respectable seventy-five miles per hour across the causeway and back home to its dry, climate-controlled garage.

And for the second time in one day, I didn't pick up on the black BMW sedan that somehow from far behind followed Hadley to the 7-Eleven and back through the storm to the Holderness estate.

A wall of smoke greeted me when I walked into the study. Ballerinas aren't quite like jockeys who weigh in before a race—but they might as well be. To keep their weight down, Allegra Trent and all her friends popped speed and chain-smoked. Apparently Hadley and Margo had reverted to form.

"Hadley," I said, "that was a bad move. I didn't know what the fuck happened to you."

Sitting on the sofa, she stubbed out her cigarette and lifted her eyes.

"I wanted you to know that I can take care of myself," she said.

"I know you can take care of yourself," I said. "You were the one who was leaving the hospital with or without me. You don't have to prove anything."

I walked out of the study unlike a brat kid only because I didn't slam the door behind me.

When I answered Fallon's call, I was again standing on that black-and-white checkerboard floor, which was beginning to take on psychedelic qualities without even one hash cookie to make it fun.

"So what do you got Tom?" I asked.

"We got bubkes," Fallon said, and I heard him switch to speakerphone to include Goode in the conversation.

"What about those last Bellevue videos?" I said.

"They sent them over," said Goode, "and we were hoping to salvage something—but, as they said, the images are very blurred—from the rain and from moisture getting inside the cameras. We haven't reviewed all of them though—maybe we'll still see something—"

"Yeah, good luck with that Linda," interrupted Fallon.

"We're going to be late for the meeting," said Goode.

"Yes ma'am," said Fallon. "Nick, they've already called another meeting for that ad hoc task force—and I have go sit there while they dick around. So I'll see you tomorrow, at the office. Her and you."

No way, my friend.

A little later when Margo was turning off lights in the study, Buddy started to growl. It was a low rolling growl, fiercer than ought to be coming from a clown like him. He ran over to the doors, ears on alert.

"What's the matter boy?" said Hadley, trying to pat his head. He moved away.

"It's probably a rabbit—a wild rabbit," said Margo, stoned, suppressing a giggle. "I'll let him out."

As soon as she opened the doors Buddy flung himself out and vanished across the lawn.

"Does he usually take off like that?" I asked.

"No," said Margo. "Yes. I don't know, maybe."

"How's he getting back in?" I asked.

"I'll leave the door open," said Margo, yawning. She took one of the little hash cookies out of her pocket and bit into it.

"Don't leave any doors open," I said. "And put your alarm on. Buddy can sleep outside tonight. It'll put hair on his chest."

"It's raining," said Hadley.

"He's a dog," I said.

"Buddy," called Hadley. "Margo, will he come back?"

"He always comes back," said Margo. "Close the damn door, the rain's getting in."

I felt like I'd been cooped up in that house for a week when we finally went up to the second floor, where Margo led us into Hadley's room at the end of the hall. Big and square and everything was white on white. Or cream or egg or whatever they call it. Taupe. The curtains, the armoire, the little desk.

"This is the room you always stay in," Margo said.

"Nile and me?" asked Hadley. She was looking at an old-fashioned four-poster bed standing high off the floor with a soft white canopy.

"Yes," said Margo. "You and Nile."

"Nile," said Hadley. "What kind of name is Nile?"

And Margo said, "What kind of name is Hadley?"

We all laughed. Then Hadley went across the room and opened a set of twin doors made with heavy glass panes separated by twisted lengths of wrought iron. Beyond the doors, the bowed balcony, where we first saw Margo, seemed to disappear like the sides of an infinity pool, and when Hadley walked outside it looked like there was nothing between her and the night except a narrow white rail blurred silver by the rain.

"Hadley, Jesus," said Margo. "What's with you and the open doors? Come back in. You want to get pneumonia? And look, there's water all over the floor."

"Sorry," said Hadley, pulling the doors shut. "I'm keeping everyone up. Thank you for everything Margo. And Nick..."

She walked into her bathroom and closed the door. A moment later we heard the sound of water rushing into the tub.

"Margo," I said. "Did you turn on your alarm system?"

"Not yet," said Margo. "As soon as everybody gets settled, Milly will turn it on."

"Are you sure?" I asked.

"Pretty sure," Margo said. "What's the problem?"

"Nothing," I said. "But why not use the alarm if you have it."

"We have you," said Margo.

41

In the guest room across the hall from Hadley's room, everything matched. Blue-and-white-striped curtains, blue-and-white quilt on the bed. And squared-off corners. Unisex.

"If you don't like this I can put you in another room," said Margo.

She bounced up and down on the bed a few times.

"It's very nice," I said.

"Do you need anything else?"

"I want to talk to you for a few minutes," I said.

"OK—if I can ask you one thing first," she said, suddenly not so stoned.

"Go ahead."

"Why did Hadley have your card in the first place?"

"I don't know."

"Why do you *think* she had your card?"

"That's two things," I said. "But same answer. I don't know."

"Your turn," she said. "And if you turn out to be a reporter, Billy will kill me. Kill. Me. We have a policy. Billy likes to control his publicity. That's impossible, of course—but we never help the paparazzi and all those kind of people. I mean don't take this the wrong way, but maybe I should Google you to see if you're who you say you are."

"Be my guest," I said.

"OK, if you don't mind," Margo said. "I'll be right back." She bounced off the bed, went out the door, and closed it behind her.

When she looked me up she'd see I'm licensed in New York, New Jersey, California, and Florida. Not Connecticut. Which didn't matter because I wasn't working.

She'd also see the articles about Julia's murder and the photographs of Julia. It would be impossible to miss the resemblance to Hadley. Even in grainy black and white it would be impossible not to sense the violet eyes.

Ten seconds later Margo was back.

"Oh, forget it—I believe you, but there's one more thing."

She was nibbling on another hash cookie. Maybe Mildred went light on the hash—or Margo had developed a high tolerance.

"That's three things," I said.

"Just let me see your gun—reporters don't carry guns."

"PIs don't necessarily carry them either."

"Come on Nick," she said, and I pulled the Beretta from where it was hidden in the small of my back.

"Can I hold it?" she asked, smiling.

"No," I said.

She pouted for a couple of beats before she came around.

"So what do you want to know?" she asked.

"Was there ever a Nile–Margo configuration?"

"Of course not," she snapped, instantly losing her good humor.

"I'm just trying to get the backstory right," I said.

"Why do you need the backstory?"

"Maybe there's something that will help jog her memory—some detail will ring a bell."

"OK."

"First there were the triplets Hadley, Victorine, and you."

"Yeah," said Margo. "And always in that order."

"And Nile Sutro and Billy Holderness were friends. Anybody else in that inner circle?"

"No, just us."

"And the next degree of separation," I said, "was your family, your twin brothers, Hadley's father, stepmother, and little siblings, and Victorine's grandmother, plus the two brothers who ran off with the carnival and the sister who went bad."

"The sister who went bad." Margo smiled a little. "That sounds like Mildred. She's the only other person who knows everything."

Which includes where Billy Holderness is.

"So what's everything?"

"I meant about Victorine's life," said Margo. "It turned out to be so depressing we decided we'd keep our mouths shut—out of respect for her memory. I'll make it brief."

"You never know what might shed some light."

"Probably not this," said Margo.

"Probably not," I said. "But go ahead."

"Victorine was a blue blood from a Mississippi plantation, and there was always some reason why the family didn't come up. We never knew exactly what the story was. But we knew Victorine had secrets."

"So she was the descendent of slaves," I said, "not of the plantation owners."

"It's not very nice to talk like that," Margo said.

"Was she?"

"No," said Margo. "She was poor."

"Even worse."

"Ha ha," said Margo. "We called her grandmother to ask if we could cremate Victorine and scatter her ashes at River Hill, the family plantation. Turned out the only River Hill was the local elementary school. We found her grandmother in a smelly one-room apartment. And she was very pissed off. She said the other siblings had as much talent as Victorine. Her sister wanted to be a ballerina too and the boys were both nationally ranked in track, which she said was a big deal."

"It is," I said.

"She told us they wanted to try out for the Olympics."

"Well that's over the top," I said.

"But it was Victorine who won a place at the ballet school in New York. Her grandmother sold the family house in order to establish Victorine and support the others. Then the money just ran out. And the grandmother was furious."

"She bet the farm on the wrong kid," I said.

"Yeah," Margo said. "The one who died. It was a bad investment. Everybody lost."

"Except Hadley."

"That's a shitty thing to say," said Margo.

Margo had moved off the bed to the floor and was lying flat on her back. She'd broken up a cookie and was dropping it into her mouth. Getting to be a less reliable reporter crumb by crumb.

"What about Hadley's family?"

"Oh, they've got plenty of money," said Margo. "Not that it matters. It's a good thing Hadley never needed any money except for school. I already told you, Mr. Fielding married a real bitch."

"The wicked stepmother walked in and locked Hadley out," I said.

"Here's the thing," Margo said. "Hadley's father was too weak to stand up for her. Fucking asshole."

"And the new children?"

"Two snotty boys," said Margo. "Really snotty."

"What's the stepmother's name?" I asked.

"Phillipa," said Margo. "Phillipa Forrest. We think she made it up. In fact, we think she's a total fraud and a liar. Apparently nobody knew exactly where she came from or anything about her. This was way pre-Google. She just slithered into Mr. Fielding's life one day—and that was that."

"There must have been more to it."

"Probably," said Margo. "Hadley never asked because she was afraid she'd find out something sordid."

"Sordid?"

"Yeah," said Margo with no further explanation. "Hadley figured she couldn't change anything, so it would be easier not to know. Do you think this so-called amnesia is more of that—like to the max?"

"What do you mean *so-called*?" I said. "Downstairs you asked her if she was faking it. Why would she do that? Look at her face. Somebody hurt her."

"Oh, nothing against her, Nick," said Margo. "But Hadley's always been a little…detached. She's had a lot of sad stuff happen—so I was thinking maybe she saw a chance to erase everything. If everyone believed that her memory was gone, maybe she got to try and make it be gone."

"That's a theory," I said, "but the amnesia is for real. It happens to a lot of people who get cracked on the head."

Margo pulled a cigarette and lighter out of the cookie pocket and lit up.

"Yeah," she said. "Maybe."

"Tell me about your brothers," I said. "Andy and Chip."

"They are self-explanatory," said Margo.

"Are they?"

"Of course they are." Now Margo was getting annoyed again. "My brothers have nothing to do with anything. So forget about them."

"OK," I said. Why argue? Weed makes you paranoid, and hash makes you more paranoid.

"Maybe Hadley had your card because she was planning to hire you," said Margo.

"Why would she need an investigator?" I asked.

"I don't know," said Margo.

"You brought it up," I said. "Was it something about Sutro?"

"No, it would have been about those letters," said Margo.

"She was getting anonymous letters?"

"No, not anonymous," said Margo. "Every public person gets letters from crazies—they still like regular mail—I guess e-mail is so easy to trash without reading it. Hadley got some mean stuff, everybody does—but the letters I'm talking about were from that stupid bitch Lolek, the nanny who was with Gemma when she died. It was like Lolek was the mother and everything was Hadley's fault. And Hadley wasn't even the one who threw her out…Do you think a woman could have attacked Hadley?"

"I doubt it," I said.

"Women are strong," said Margo, flexing a bicep. Not bad.

"One more thing," I said. "Does the number 44 mean anything to you?"

"Forty-four bottles of beer on the wall," Margo sang, "forty-four bottles of beer—take one down and pass it all around—"

"Anything else?"

"McKenzie Black carries a .44 Magnum. Why?"

"Roulette," I said.

"Oh."

Margo stood up and flicked an ash into a nearby wastepaper basket. A live spark fell on the polished wood floor, where it glowed bright orange, and when she stamped it out I remarked that the whole house was wood.

"It sure is," she said, heading for the bathroom, where she doused the cigarette. "Every bit of it, old dry wood; it could go up—poof—in a minute. But not tonight." She waved at the windows in my room. "The rain. It's so wet. And Billy's got us insured up the wazoo anyway. Night. Sleep tight."

I watched Margo walk up the hall with exaggerated steps, one foot lined up in front of the other, like on a catwalk—and I was hoping she didn't smoke in bed, because while the vast outside of the house was battered by rain, the vast inside of the house was perfectly dry. And it probably could go up—poof.

42

When I called Meriwether from the Lamborghini, he had agreed to come up and replace me. And he likes to get on the road early. Hadley would probably still be sleeping when I left. No good night tonight. No good-bye tomorrow.

Across the hall, the light was off and the door was closed. I'd leave mine—and the door to the bathroom—open when I took a shower. All I needed was a short time in the hot water. Then cold and I'm good to stay awake till morning.

I put the Beretta on the tiled counter by the sink and took off Billy's shirt and pants. And his green–and-purple boxers. I stepped into a shower with good water pressure for a change and picked up a fresh bar of soap with squared-off corners that smelled like lemon.

Ten minutes later, I was clean, dry, barefoot, and wearing another pair of Billy's skivvies. Mildred had laid them out on the love seat in the corner along with the rest of a change of clothes.

I picked up a book called *The Third Brother*. Margo had two brothers, Victorine had two brothers, and so did Hadley. Half brothers. Two plus two equals four…

A piano has eighty-eight keys. Half that…

I hadn't asked the date Sutro's tour ended.

Thankfully there was no computer screen staring at me, so I didn't have to find out, although there was always my phone. Fuck it. I leaned back against the blue-and-white upholstered headboard, laid the Beretta on the bedside table, and started reading about a kid with a real brother and an imaginary one.

I looked up now and then to see the closed door across the hall bathed in the dim-colored light coming from the nearest of half a dozen little chandeliers, which were spaced evenly along the hall ceiling.

Faraway barking got closer. When I walked out of the guest room to see what was up, I almost collided with Hadley running out her door.

We both saw Buddy at the same time as he loped up the stairs from the first floor, dripping water on the rug, smelling like what he was.

He barreled over and leapt at Hadley, who hugged him so hard the front of her long white nightgown turned transparent.

"Look at this," she said. What, was she kidding? "Nick see, it's blood."

She was right, there was a streak of blood on the nightgown.

"Must have been a savage rabbit he got mixed up with," I said. I didn't know jack about dogs, but I could recognize a knife wound or a bullet wound. "I'll take a look."

I wasn't going to let her be daunted. And what was I thinking? Some apparition with a silencer on his gun had nicked a galloping dog—in the dark. Plus the big golden retriever didn't seem to be in a lot of pain.

"No," she said, "I'll look." Then she realized she was standing there as good as naked. "I've got to get a robe."

She ran back to her room, Buddy following. I sat on the top step, trying to think about boxing stats.

The stats were useless when she came back wearing a man's shirt instead of a robe and carrying a couple of morbidly heavy bath towels to rub down Buddy.

"It looks like he has a cut on his shoulder," she said.

"Hadley," I said quietly, "how the fuck did the dog get back in the house?"

"I left the study door open—a little," she said.

"You went down there when I was in the shower," I said. "Didn't you?"

"I couldn't let him sleep outside."

"Did you turn the alarm back on?"

"I never turned it off, because I don't know where it is. But now the door's still open. I better go down and lock it."

I shouldn't have been surprised when she was up in one effortless motion and running down the hall to the stairs, Buddy at her heels.

The girl had a dancer's timing and an athlete's instincts—and she was so very beautiful. Or maybe when I looked at her I saw Julia.

The dog was barking again, but by the time I decided to go down and have a look, Hadley and Buddy were on their way back up. I couldn't know Buddy's habits, and there was no point in walking outside to take a look around the vast lawn and enormous trees. I wasn't going to see a phantom killer out for a midnight stroll. And sometimes a bark is just a bark.

"Locked the door," said Hadley. "I still don't know where the alarm is—but Mildred said she closes up and sets the alarm every night."

"Good," I said. Right. Maybe Mildred hadn't had as many drinks and as much weed as I suspected.

When Hadley and I sat back down at the top of the stairs she said, "Buddy's better than an alarm." She was right about that. A big dog is better than any alarm system. "And," she continued, "I have you." The tone of her voice was neutral, and her face was in shadow so I couldn't see her eyes.

Some women call me insensitive because I don't like long conversations about nothing. I don't care. Call me a bastard. At least that would be true. Maybe sometimes I skip the sensitive part because it's too hard, like when I told Hadley Meriwether would be coming in the morning, and he'd stay with her after I left.

"I didn't realize you were going," she said.

"You like Meriwether."

"Yes, but I thought you said I wasn't in danger."

"Just to be on the safe side," I said.

Sister Mary A would like that.

"I imagine it'll be all right with Margo," I continued. "I mean Meriwether being here. What do you think?"

"I don't think anything, because I don't know Margo. I don't remember her or Mildred or my husband or my child—and I don't remember who attacked me, but I'm afraid of him."

"We'll find him," I said. "I'll find him."

"But you won't stay with me," she said.

"I can't."

"Let's go back," she said, standing.

She led the way down the hall and barely paused before following Buddy into her bedroom.

"Good night, Nick," she said. And after she closed her door, I heard the key turn in the old-fashioned lock.

I got the message. This lady, even with no past, knew she was not one to be rejected. No one got a second chance.

Hadley couldn't know how ironic it was to make a point of locking me out. There were other men who wanted to protect her. Nile Sutro, Billy Holderness, Justin Greenburg. But I was different because I was the only one ready to take a bullet. I'd been ready for ten years.

43

I went back to the book, and when I looked up there was maybe a hint of dawn in the sodden sky over Stonington. We had made it through the night.

I wouldn't sleep until the household cranked up. Until Meriwether arrived. Then I'd leave. Sleep in Pauline Prochevsky's car for a couple of hours. Anywhere except across the hall from Hadley.

I lay back, looked at the ceiling, and forced myself to think about boxing.

The best fighter ever, pound for pound, was Sugar Ray Robinson, who started his career at eighteen by winning the Golden Gloves. When I was boxing, Sugar Ray was long gone. He died broke and alone, which was a lesson I should not have ignored.

I knew the stats on every champion in every weight class starting with the early guys—Tunney, Louis, Schmeling, LaMotta. I knew endless trivia like Rocky Marciano at five eight was the shortest heavyweight champion. Mike Tyson was the youngest at age twenty.

Nobody respects anything about Mike Tyson now. People tend to forget that for a guy with a pimp for a father and Fairy Boy for a street name, Iron Mike came pretty far before he went crazy.

I met him once in Atlantic City and he acted sane enough, but he did sound like a girl.

Sugar Ray's famous Valentine's Day fight with Jake LaMotta was playing in my head. In Chicago. Thirteen rounds. He donated the entire purse to charity.

I closed my eyes.

A thunderstorm raged outside the Chicago Stadium and inside the crowd was screaming…

Not cracks of thunder…not the crowd. I was up and across the hall before I was fully awake. I threw myself against the locked door and slammed into it three times before it gave.

Hadley was kneeling on the bed holding a gun straight out in front of her. A gun that at a split-second glance looked exactly like the Beretta I had in my hand.

Buddy was on the floor, bleeding, struggling to get on his feet.

"There," Hadley screamed, pointing to the open doors. "He jumped off the balcony—do you see him—is he on the ground?"

I saw him, but not on the ground.

He was hanging on to a heavy branch on the giant oak off to the right side of the balcony. His feet were braced against the tree, and his cap was pulled low so it obscured his face even when he looked up at me for an instant before he plunged downward. He hit the ground rolling and got up running.

I dropped my gun and dove for the tree. The branch I caught bent under my weight, and the slippery bark sliced my hand. I lunged to a lower branch, which gave me time to spot a sturdier one.

The wind changed then, blowing in my eyes. I could still make out a branch that was in the right place and I went for it. Grabbed it just in time. And then it snapped. A big, strong-looking branch snapped. And I fell.

My bad leg took a hit, my hands were bleeding, and I recognized the pain that stabbed my side. Broken ribs hurt like hell. Not serious though, unless they puncture a lung, which hadn't happened or I'd know it.

I took off after the man, who was running across the wet grass, downhill toward the locked gate between the hedges. It was a race I didn't like because he had a big head start, but life is usually four to one against anyway.

If he got past the gates into the woods, I knew I'd lose him again.

My friend Mike Teak always cleared his head when he ran, and it worked for him. Up at Rucker Park they used to say he was the second fastest white kid in the city. Don't think, he told me, just run. And I told him, no worries, man. A smart drug dealer never has to run.

No worries.

The killer reached the bottom of the hill but didn't head into the woods after he vaulted over the gate. By the time I got to the gate all I saw was a black BMW sedan kicking up showers of mud as it swerved down the dirt road toward the causeway.

When Margo, Mildred, and Hadley barreled up in the red Land Rover to haul me back to the house, the police were already on their way.

Not soon enough though. That fuck in the BMW had probably breezed past them on Route 1, driving in the opposite direction.

44

During the fast ride away from the gate, we exchanged what little information we had. The intruder came up the tree and onto the balcony and through a door that Hadley hadn't locked after she went out on the balcony a second time. He never touched her.

Buddy went for him, getting in the way of the bullet he fired.

Hadley fired at the same time, but didn't think she hit the guy, and I didn't either judging from the way he got down the oak tree, across the lawn, and over the gate.

I wouldn't have been a match for him even if I was the one with the head start.

When we reached the house, Hadley flew up the stairs to see about the dog. Margo raced after her, heading for her room to shower away the lingering effects of too many hash cookies before the police arrived, and Mildred went to phone the veterinarian.

I grabbed one of the landlines in the kitchen to call Meriwether and fill him in on every detail I could remember, which didn't include the BMW's license plate numbers because they were deliberately caked with mud. I did think I saw something that looked like a tower on the back plate—but it was dark and maybe I imagined it.

I asked Meriwether to contact Fallon and Goode so I could get back to Hadley.

I ran up the back stairs from the kitchen to the second floor and down to the big white room at the end of the hall. Hadley was there, sitting next to the bed with her arms around Buddy, who was dazed and bleeding.

Rain blew in from the balcony and was beading into little puddles on the highly polished wood floor. The curtains looked like white bellows filled up by the wind, deflated, and filled again, and Buddy growled when I went near Hadley.

"Quiet Buddy," she said and reached up to touch one of my bloody hands.

"Let me clean those cuts," she said.

"We don't have time for that," I said though my hands were burning with splinters from the tree. "The cops'll be here in two minutes, and we're standing in the middle of a crime scene. And I want to know where you got the gun."

"The gun…"

"Yeah," I said and went over to the bed where she had left it. "This Beretta right here. Notice the left-handed safety. Last time I saw it, it was in my desk at the barge."

"I took it when I was in your office…making notes," she said. "I'm sorry, I should have asked you."

"And what do you think I'd say?"

"Nick, you don't know the reason I took the gun."

"All right," I said wearily.

"It was because I was sure even before we left the barge that you wouldn't sleep in my room. And if I couldn't have you right next to me—"

"Hadley," I said and lifted her off the floor and up against my dirty, bloody chest.

"They here," said Mildred, whom we hadn't seen in the doorway. As Hadley slid away from me, I grabbed the Beretta and handed it to Mildred.

"Put this somewhere."

As if it were an apple, she dropped it into the pocket of her blue jean jacket and slipped into Hadley's bathroom maybe one second before two Stonington cops came marching down the hall under the little multicolored crystal chandeliers.

Since they missed the housekeeper carrying a concealed weapon, all they saw was a big dog on the floor and a dirty, bloody guy in borrowed shorts standing next to a beautiful woman wearing nothing but a man's bloodstained dress shirt.

The older of the two had suspiciously black hair and was squeezed like a sausage into his uniform. The younger one, who looked no more than twenty-one or two, was a string bean with freckles whose mouth dropped open when he saw us.

"I'm Sergeant Coleman," said the older man. "This is Officer McNamara, and you are—?"

"I'm Nick Sayler," I said, "and this is Hadley Fielding."

"You're Hadley Fielding," McNamara said with awe.

"McNamara," snapped the senior officer.

"Yes," said Hadley, smiling. "Have we met?"

I was impressed by how smoothly she tried to defuse the tension.

"No," said McNamara. "But my girlfriend is in *love* with you. I mean she really loves you. You were her idol. You—"

"Get some clothes on," said the sergeant. "We'll be downstairs."

I didn't like his tone, and a few years back I would have said something. Done something.

It wasn't worth it. Every minute that passed, the killer was getting farther away.

After the cops left, I retrieved the Beretta I'd dropped on the balcony before my high dive. I took the other one back from Mildred, who'd come out of hiding in the bathroom.

"God, Mildred," said Hadley, "what if they looked in there?"

"I'm just the maid, baby," she said, exaggerating her Southern accent. "Come up to leave some mo' towels."

She nodded at me, and I nodded back then left her to help Hadley.

Back in the blue room across the hall I called Fallon, who said he'd heard from Meriwether and they were already on their way.

The pain was intense in my side, and as I showered the dirt and blood off my body, I wondered just how many ribs were broken. I'd ask Sloane to take a look, although I knew there was nothing to do about them. No painkillers for me, and doctors didn't wrap you up like they used to because—as Sloane told me last time I broke a rib—wrapping compresses your lungs, which get less air, which can lead to pneumonia, etc.

There's always a silver lining, Sister Mary A would say—and she'd be right this time—because the good news was that my ribs hurt so much, the throbbing in my leg was strictly second tier.

As I was slowly pulling on another set of Billy Holderness's clothes, which Mildred somehow found time to lay out on the bed, I saw out the window two more cops emerging from another squad car and heading for the house.

I had both the Berettas now and stuck one of them into the waistband of Billy's skintight black jeans—definitely not my style—and stashed the other one in the back of a drawer in the bathroom. Unlikely the cops would be looking there, and I had a license. If the one bullet Hadley fired at the intruder had lodged in the balcony, I'd deal with that later.

Showered, dressed, armed, and remembering the bottle of Jameson in the pantry, I was ready to deal with the day. Outside there was very low visibility. Just enough to catch sight of a familiar chocolate-brown Mercedes pulling up and parking behind the most recent police car.

Meriwether got out of the driver's side and, unlike the cops, did not run toward the house. He knows the danger has passed and the elements do not daunt him.

I stuck my feet into Billy's million-dollar deerskin moccasins and—since Meriwether, who looks menacing and doesn't like to speak, was about to reach the house—ran downstairs. I passed McNamara stationed at the wide-open front door and met Meriwether as he came in.

"Excuse me, sir," said McNamara. "I need to know your name."

Meriwether ignored him.

"Sir," said McNamara, lowering his voice like a little kid who's trying to sound older, "your name and ID."

"He's my associate," I said. Not that it should matter. However, McNamara looked relieved. And didn't press Meriwether. Although it was one, the house hadn't been officially declared a crime scene yet.

"Which way did he go?" Meriwether asked when I led him back under the portico.

"Down to the gate," I pointed. "And over. If there was blood, it was probably mine—but it's been raining nonstop—nothing to see."

"OK," said Meriwether.

He headed down the hill. I don't know what he thought he'd find. I don't question his methods.

I don't question Rue either when she claims he's a secret sorcerer priest, a *houngan*—because although she's a smart girl, she was brought up in Martinique, where there are people who still practice vodou. And why not a sorcerer savant? No big deal on the *Dumb Luck*.

Meriwether hadn't bothered to waste time asking about the bullet that grazed the dog. Since the slug was evidence, it was the property of the state of Connecticut. Just as the bullets from Sloane's bedroom wall would be the property of the state of New York.

Meriwether came back with nothing and stayed nearby while the police questioned me. I answered different versions of the same questions again and again. And again. Upstairs, downstairs, and outside. So did Hadley, Margo, and Mildred.

I had given Fallon the code to open the gates, and it was two long hours before they used it. Meriwether and I were back under the portico when we finally saw their car coming out of the fog, heading toward the house.

Ignoring parking protocol as always, Fallon pulled up on the lawn. Goode got out with her umbrella. Fallon refused to share it.

"Fuckin' A" was the first thing Fallon said. "The soldier of fortune business is doing pretty good. Is McKenzie Black home yet?"

"Not only is he not home," I said, "nobody knows where he is."

"Except the paparazzi," said Fallon.

"Not even them," I said.

"Do you have notes on the last twenty-four hours?" Goode interjected.

"Hello Linda," I said. "Nice to see you too."

"Hello Sayler," said Goode. "What about those notes?"

"I don't take fucking notes, and I don't work for you—and there's nothing I didn't say in those voice mails I left you."

"Jesus Nick," said Fallon, looking me up and down, checking out the black pants and the black shirt, "you look like shit."

"These clothes are my new style," I said and watched Goode roll her eyes.

"Yeah, them too," said Fallon. "But I meant what's going on with you—the leg acting up?"

"Yeah," I said. "The leg, and a couple of ribs. And my hands."

"Nothing new," said Fallon.

"You didn't take anything, did you?" said Goode.

"He don't take nothing," Fallon said.

"Linda," I said. "You want me to pee in a cup?"

Such an irritating fucking woman. I should whip out my dick and pee on her foot.

4 5

Sergeant Coleman appeared and asked Fallon and Goode who they were. It's unusual for New York detectives to be out of state working a case, but not unheard of.

After Coleman shook hands with both of them he said, "We've just declared this a crime scene. You understand."

"Of course," said Goode.

Civilians would assume the crime scene was Hadley's room and the balcony. Fallon and Goode understood that Coleman was referring to the entire house, and following the letter of the law, he could have meant the property too. This time it was just the main house.

No one was allowed to come in while they conducted a preliminary investigation. A civilian might also think he should have extended the courtesy to Fallon and Goode of saying it was all right for them to enter because they were police. Not so. Sergeant Congeniality did not need to make a point; he was following procedure.

Procedure was not one of Fallon's strong suits.

"So what the fuck have you done so far, runnin' around the house?" Fallon asked. "The guy came in, went out, and got away. He ain't hidin' under the piano in the sunroom."

Coleman's fists clenched, and he sucked in his stuffed-sausage gut so hard his shoulders rose. Then he turned his back, strode into the house, and slammed the door behind him. Goode looked at Fallon and said, "Congratulations."

"You're a nut job," said Fallon, then pointing his chin at the driveway, "more fun seekers."

An old green Mustang came charging through the rain and stopped short, half an inch away from a Stonington police car.

The two red-haired guys who emerged from the car were identical in every way except for the white Notre Dame football T-shirt on one and the blue Notre Dame football T-shirt on the other one.

Who else but Margo's brothers, Andy and Chip. Margo told them to stay away. Obviously the twins didn't take orders from their sister.

The boys nodded to us as they sprinted to the house, where they were stopped by another duo of Stonington cops.

Because the episode on the balcony came under their heading of Unusual Occurrences, Coleman had called in two more officers, bringing the total up to six from Stonington—maybe the whole force.

By my count there were now fifteen people in and around the house. More than enough to destroy any real evidence.

The boys were getting belligerent, saying they were family, but the cops didn't care—and the noise brought Margo and Coleman to the door.

Unless they started throwing punches or bottles, Fallon wasn't interested. Particularly because he was looking at a long gray limo speeding up the driveway doing maybe sixty, then fishtailing to a stop to avoid the Mustang. Finally parking on the grass next to Fallon's Impala.

"What do you think we got now?" said Fallon, watching the man who unfolded out of the backseat.

He was wearing a long black coat with a half cape in the back—probably like the ones favored by Jesse James and Cole Younger. But featherweight, not oilskin. No black Stetson and no sidekick on a paint horse. Just the limo driver, who jumped out of the car, popping open an umbrella.

The man waved him away and headed toward the house, looking in our direction.

"Hey, who the fuck are you?" he called.

The rain matted his blond hair, and his blue eyes were bloodshot. But there was no mistaking the famous face.

Within seconds, Hadley, dressed in blue jeans and a lavender shirt, raced barefoot past Coleman and the cops at the door, past the twins, who were still arguing with Margo. She was going to greet Billy Holderness I thought. So did he—and pivoted around as she passed him.

She was running to meet another vehicle making its way up the long drive over the wet white stones. The driver stopped; Hadley got into the passenger side and slammed the door behind her.

Then the black BMW made a U-turn.

Fallon, Goode, and I pulled our guns and started running toward the car, as did Billy, minus the gun. Margo's brothers blew out from under the portico like twin cannonballs. Behind them Margo and Mildred ran into the rain, each calling to Billy, who couldn't be bothered. He was trying to open the passenger side door.

"Get away from the car," said Fallon.

"I thought she didn't remember anything," said Goode as we ran, positioning ourselves on the driver's side. "It looks like she recognized that car."

"I don't know," I said.

"Get out of the car with your hands up," ordered Fallon.

The pain in my side was finally taking over and everything was blurry. Too blurry to make out the face of the driver who emerged from the sedan.

"Do you recognize the guy?" asked Goode in a low, tight voice. She was still standing next to me, but she sounded far away.

"I can't tell—" I said.

"Nick," said Goode, reaching out her arm.

"No," I said. "I'm OK."

The car and the sky started spinning, and Goode's brown shoes were the last things I remember before I went down.

PART THREE

Beauty is merciless. You do not look at it.
It looks at you and it does not forgive.
— Nikos Kazantzakis

46

Yale–New Haven Hospital would ordinarily be about an hour from Stonington, but not if McKenzie Black was at the wheel of his Porsche SUV with a police escort.

When I came to in the recovery room, Sloane was standing over me, which probably meant I was dying.

"Where am I?" I asked in an unfamiliar hoarse voice.

"New Haven," Sloane said. "Yale–New Haven Hospital."

"What happened?" I said.

"You broke some ribs, and one of them punctured your spleen," said Sloane. "Part of your spleen had to be removed. I approved the surgeon—who was able to deal with it laparoscopically. Later they want to give you a CAT scan because you lost consciousness. You're on antibiotics because you were cut up. You've got a lot of bruising—and I imagine you're exhausted."

He was right about that; every part of my body ached. Pain shot through me in every direction. There were bandages around the palms of both hands, and I felt a bandage on my left side.

"I told the surgeon that you did not take opiates," said Sloane. "She left an order for ibuprofen."

"That'll be a big help," I said. "Can you get me some Jameson?"

Another fierce wave of pain seared through me.

"Certainly," he said. "And caviar. And a Russian serving girl in a French maid's outfit."

Ignoring his comment, I asked, "Where's Hadley?"

"In Stonington with her friends," said Sloane, who then hesitated for a moment as if weighing his next sentence. "She was here. She waited through the surgery and through two hours when you were in recovery. Meriwether was here too and Billy Holderness and Linda Goode. Tom Fallon went back to the city to meet with the mayor's task force."

"Why did Hadley leave?" I asked.

"When she heard you were recovering well, it was time to go," he said.

"You didn't tell her to go, did you?"

"No, I didn't," said Sloane. "Holderness was waiting for her and was getting impatient. He wanted her to drive with him, not Meriwether. But Meriwether is back with her at the Holderness house."

I could just see Margo trying to make conversation with him.

"Meriwether said until you decided what the next step was, he'd stay with her."

"I can't believe Billy Holderness was up for that idea," I said.

"He wasn't," said Sloane. "Hadley overruled him."

"Did Fallon and Goode question her?" I asked.

"Yes, and there was nothing new. She still couldn't remember anything," said Sloane. "She insisted that Meriwether be present."

Good for her.

The pain caught me again.

"What does a spleen do?" I asked.

"Not much," said Sloane. "It's an organ you can live without, and you only lost part of yours."

"So I should be happy?"

"I'm going to see about that ibuprofen," he said.

Not too much gets past Sloane, who suddenly looked older and smaller in his perfectly tailored navy blue blazer.

"Wait a minute, Edward," I said. "There's something else I have to know."

"Fine," he said. "I'll be right back."

That was the first time I thought about how I'd feel on the day Sloane didn't come back.

A few minutes later, a reedy, gray-haired nurse preceded Sloane into the room. Her colorless eyes were magnified by round, wire-rimmed glasses. She wore a classic white uniform with what looked like a battle ribbon on her chest pocket just above the nameplate, "Gerta Schmitt." She also wore thick-soled, white lace-up shoes and one of those weird nurse hats from yesteryear.

"Here we are," she said in a voice that immediately makes you want to commit murder. "We'll feel a lot better very soon."

Don't they ever hear the jokes?

She placed two pills and a small cup of water on the table beside the bed and tried to lift my head.

"Let's take our pills," she said.

I twisted away from her bony grip and sat up.

"Let's not," I said. "Let's wait a minute. Edward, who was the man in the black car?"

"Well I'll get some applesauce," said the nurse, backing toward the door. "We can put the pills in the applesauce. The cart's just outside in the hall. I'll only be a jiffy."

"Right before I passed out," I said, "Hadley got in a black BMW—on the driveway going up to the house."

"Lie down Nick," said Sloane. "Just rest. You can hear about all that later."

"No," I said as I tried to kick the blanket off me.

"We've got some nice applesauce," said the nurse, who'd returned so fast she must have had the applesauce in her hip pocket. "What are you doing?" Her voice rose. "We can't get out of bed."

"Move away Edward," I said.

I yanked the blanket away and swung my legs over the side of the bed. I stood up unsteadily, and the needles from the IVs burned as they pulled out of my arm.

"Nick," said Sloane, "for God's sake—"

"Tell me who was driving the BMW—"

"Get back in there," the nurse commanded, and I grabbed the side of my bed because I knew my knees couldn't hold me. And I was right about that.

47

It didn't take long for Apple Sauce to haul me back into bed and hook up the IVs again. Saline and antibiotics.

I slept for I don't know how long, but it was night when I woke and noticed that instead of regulation blinds, the room had curtains, which were pulled back. What I saw through the large window was rain falling into the pale, mustard-colored glow rising up from New Haven, Connecticut.

Sloane was sitting in an upholstered armchair, his feet on an upholstered footstool, under a small spot of light reading something on his iPad. There was a bottle of wine and a glass on the table next to him and a big basket of roses on the chest of drawers across the room.

"Edward," I said.

"I'm here," said Sloane.

"I can see that," I snapped ungratefully. "Who was the man in that black car?"

"I told you," he said. "And it was navy blue."

"I appreciate your attention to detail," I said. "But apparently I was unconscious when you told me. So who was he?"

"The *veterinarian*," he said.

"Veterinarian…"

"Yes. I heard the whole story on the phone from the house-keeper. Smart woman. She told me Hadley had suddenly become entirely focused on the dog's injuries. Almost fixated. Very, very upset about the dog. I would call her behavior displacement anxiety, which probably denotes her concern about you."

"I doubt that's true," I said.

"I don't know, Nick," said Sloane, pampering me. "You're probably right."

"So how'd it work out with the dog?" I asked.

"All I know is that they've moved the veterinarian into the house for the duration."

I wasn't sure and shouldn't care if Buddy had eclipsed me in Hadley's mind, but I wouldn't bet against him. What I thought, though, was the guy who said you can always depend on two things, an old dog and a pocketful of money, got it wrong. He should have said: The one thing an old dog can depend on is a pocketful of money.

"I've got to get out of here," I said to Sloane, "and you shouldn't have put me in this room—it must be fifteen hundred bucks a day."

"I believe it's actually eighteen hundred," said Sloane. "And I'm not the one who's paying for it. Billy Holderness said he owed you for your services. He said he's paying for everything."

"The hell he is," I said.

My services.

"He can well afford it Nick, and I don't want you going anywhere for at least another twenty-four hours," said Sloane. "You could get an infection, tear the stitches, you could—"

"I heard you," I said. "Do you have my phone?"

Nurse Apple Sauce walked in with a tray in her hands.

"Dr. Sloane, you can leave," she said. "I'm sure we'll be all right."

"You remember Miss Schmitt," said Sloane. "She's one of your private nurses."

"Yes," said Nurse Gerta Schmitt, "there are three of us. Eight hours each. So how are we feeling now? We should be feeling better."

"We feel like shit," I said. "And we would like some privacy from our private nurse. Because we would like to make some private calls."

Sloane took my cell phone out of his pocket and put it down on the table next to my bed with a little more force than necessary.

"Come along with me Miss Schmitt," he said. "I'll buy you a cup of coffee. I'll take responsibility for your absence."

"Edward," I said, "wait a minute—why did the veterinarian make a U-turn in the driveway?"

"Apparently he was parking," Sloane said. "He wanted to back up. He was very sorry about the commotion."

When Sloane and the nurse left, I checked my phone for messages. The most recent—in the last two hours—were from Mildred. Voice and text. All virtually the same: "Nick, call me," she'd said. "It's very urgent. I don't want to leave no voice or text because I don't know who might have your phone. Must talk to you."

I got Mildred on the first ring.

"Nick," she said. "Thank the Lord I got hold of you. I didn't think I could even talk about this to Meriwether or nobody—because I don't know who knows and what it means. Oh, how do you feel? Sorry 'bout the operation and the ribs and all."

"Mildred," I said. "I'm good. No problem here. What's going on?"

"Well," she said, "this morning—a couple of hours ago, after Hadley took a shower—"

I didn't want her to find out this way.

"—and she asked me to help her change her bandage on her back."

"Mildred, did she see it?"

"No," said Mildred. "And I didn't tell her nothing, and thank Jesus she didn't want to see it or ask for no mirror. It's the number 44. It's healing—but she's gonna have a scar. What does it mean?"

"OK Mildred," I said. "Are you calm?"

"Are you?" she said.

"I'm going to tell you the whole story now," I said. "Meriwether knows, also Fallon and Goode—the cops from New York. But Hadley doesn't know and neither does Margo or Holderness—and you can't say anything yet."

"I can keep my mouth shut," said Mildred. "Just because Billy tells me everything don't mean I tell him everything."

I explained about the other girls, the connection with the doctor at Bellevue, and about the breather who called on the unlisted number.

"You're the only one who's heard his voice," I said. "Do you remember anything special?"

"No," said Mildred. "White man, that's all."

"Does 44 mean anything to you?" I asked.

"Nothing," she said. "Nothing from the past with the girls or the boys. Or not nothing I can remember—you tried the Scriptures yet? Lotta nutcases likes the Bible."

"You want to look through the Bible for things that have 44?"

"Why not, sugar?" Mildred said. "I got to do something to help besides cook."

I was sure by then Meriwether had exhausted everything from the King James Bible to the *Bhagavad Gita*, but why not let her give it a try. She was already in the loop.

"Keep your eyes on Hadley," I said.

"Don't fret, baby, she safe with us."

My next call was to Rue, who was with a friend from Martinique in a little town on the Bayou Teche. I gave an edited account of how I wound up in the hospital. She is the rare woman who doesn't always demand details. All she said was she'd come right back—leave the car, take the next flight—and I told her that Sloane was already giving me more attention than I needed or wanted and that she should stay in Louisiana for another week as planned because I was fine.

There's a reason the word *whole* is included in the witness oath. *I swear to tell the truth, and nothing but the truth* doesn't quite cover the waterfront.

Fallon texted that he was at the mayor's official residence: *fking gracie mansion & goode was back at the fking puzzle palace & no news on fking 44.*

Goode texted that she was making headway but didn't elaborate.

I got voice mail when I tried Meriwether, who didn't eat meals with people. He texted back that he was having breakfast with Hadley.

I didn't call Hadley. And she didn't call me.

Just as I was trying to bribe an orderly to run out and get me a pint of anything, Nurse Second Shift swept in and scared the poor guy out of the room.

This nurse, whom Sister Mary A would call pleasantly plump, was an obese young woman with short blonde hair and a silently sullen attitude—which beats hysterical cheerfulness any day of the year.

I watched reruns of *Law & Order* through the night, and not long after what I knew was dawn by looking at the TV time and temperature, my surgeon, Dr. Linda Ferrari, arrived.

Still somewhat rare in the boys' club of surgery, she was about five eight, with a white lab coat over a tight black dress. High heels with ankle straps and a lot of jangly gold jewelry. She led a group of residents into the room, and, after saying hello, she discussed the finer points of a splenectomy with them. Then she focused her kohl-lined eyes on me and smiled as though she meant it.

"How're you feeling today Mr. Sayler?" she asked.

"I'm feeling like I want to get out of the hospital," I said.

"Done," said the very pretty Dr. Ferrari.

My kind of doctor.

48

The unique sound of a knife being pulled across a whetstone signaled a call from Meriwether.

"Hadley wants to leave," he said.

"Where does she want to go?"

"Away from Stonington."

"She's a free agent," I said. "We can't tell her what to do and Fallon can't either."

"I told her I'd take her," said Meriwether, "except I told her I didn't like to drive in the rain."

I laughed.

"She didn't believe that," I said.

"Probably not—but she doesn't want to leave alone. And she thinks you're in the hospital for another two days."

"Who told her that?"

"Edward," he said.

"It's better for her to stay there with you," I said. "And the palace guard. We don't have shit on the guy, and I think he's around. I think he's going to try again."

"I do too," said Meriwether.

"What about this rain?" I asked.

"It rained in New York City for seventeen days straight in 1943. From Thursday, May 6, to Saturday, May 22."

"Do you think we'll beat that?"

"No."

"Match it?"

"No."

"Good. So how long is this rain going to last?"

"I don't know," he said and clicked off.

When we got back to Weehawken, Sloane said he'd take Pauline out to lunch, and I gratefully left him and his car at her house and then went by foot to the barge.

Since Meriwether was in Connecticut, the cupboard was bare. Not a big deal. I poured some Jameson over a cube of ice and got a couple of cigarettes out of my hidden stash.

The whiskey seemed more powerful than usual, and the smokes made me light-headed as I caught up on messages and returned a few calls.

There was nothing crucially time-sensitive going on, and luckily my clients were willing to cut me some slack as I milked my visit to Yale–New Haven Hospital for all it was worth.

After a few cups of coffee with some more Jameson, I felt stoked enough to head across the river.

I'd been told by the lovely Dr. Ferrari not to exert myself, and although I rarely do what I'm told, I decided against the ferry, since a cab could take me only to the top of about a hundred and fifty stone steps, down which I'd have to walk to catch a ride across the river from Weehawken to Manhattan.

Climbing down the ladder to the *Gwinnett* and fighting the wind and rain to cross the Hudson was not in the cards either.

My last choice was to call the Palisades Rapid Taxi Service and hope they'd live up to their name for once. I had already wasted three days.

49

When people are questioned by someone with a badge and a gun, they talk too much or they talk too little—they feel guilty when they've never stolen so much as a pack of chewing gum or cheated on their wife even once.

Private investigators are not so intimidating; no badge, no gun, or no gun in sight, and most importantly no authority. As a private investigator not hindered by police departmental protocols, I could ask whatever questions of whoever, whenever, wherever I wanted.

The problem was, after I walked into Bellevue Hospital for the third time through the Emergency Room entrance, which was looking unpleasantly familiar, I didn't know what those questions would be.

I headed over toward a desk under the sign "Information" to see if Mrs. Newell was still a patient on the eighth floor. She had so much fun the last time I saw her, she probably was trying to stretch her fifteen minutes of fame as far as possible.

"Excuse me," said a young woman who'd come up behind me and tapped my shoulder.

I turned around to see a girl of East Indian descent. Pretty in the way that any young girl is pretty. In middle age, she'd be invisible. At twentysomething she had energy and was wearing a cute little yellow-and-white dress.

"Yes," I said. "What's up?"

"It's still raining out, isn't it?" she said as she fussed with a straw purse, trying to protect it with a plastic bag.

"It was when I came in," I said.

"Five days now," she said.

"And no end in sight," I said. "What can I do for you?"

"I saw you." She paused. "With Justin. Me and him were kind of friends—well acquaintances. I volunteer a few nights a week."

"I'm sorry about Justin," I said as she kept looking at me.

"I wasn't going to mention this," she said. "I didn't expect to see you. I don't even know who you are."

"I was an acquaintance of Justin's too," I said.

"I remember something."

I waited. It's usually better to wait.

"I mean I saw something," she went on, "but I didn't tell the police."

The beleaguered NYPD was not trusted by many, including myself, Mrs. Newell, and according to the plastic pin on her chest, Jenny Bajpai.

I waited.

"The police," she continued, "asked everybody if they remembered anything about that woman, the one who came in with the concussion. Or if they remembered anything about the cabdriver who brought her in."

"Yes," I said. "Did you see them?"

"I figured the security cameras would get everything," she said. "Then I heard the rain screwed them up."

So much for the security of hospital information.

"That's what I heard too," I said.

"I remember the cabdriver," she said.

"And you haven't talked to the cops because…?" I asked.

"Do you ever see any Indian cops?" she asked. "Or Pakistani or Afghan?"

"No," I said, figuring there must be a few in the department, though I'd never seen one.

"What do you think that's about?" she asked.

"You tell me," I said.

"This is a mistake," she said. "I shouldn't be talking to you. I don't know who you are."

"My name's Nick Sayler," I said like a nice, easygoing guy. "I came to Bellevue that night because Justin asked me to. He wanted me to talk to the woman with the concussion."

"Why?" she asked.

"Because she had my business card on her."

"Uh-huh," she said.

"Listen," I said, "I've got to go. Here's my card. Call me if you change your mind. Or call Detective Fallon or Detective Goode at the Thirteenth Precinct."

"OK," said Jenny, looking at the card. "What does '*Security*' mean—Sayler Security?"

"Got to go, Jenny, take care," I said as I turned away.

It still amazes me that in business, romance, and dealing with witnesses, the announcement of departure as a ploy works so often. What an easy, no-maintenance tool. You'd think everybody would be onto it.

"Wait a minute," she said and fidgeted around some more with her straw bag. "Don't you want to know why I don't trust the police?"

I really didn't give a shit.

"I thought you already told me," I said. "But go ahead."

Whatever it was might translate into trusting me. And I didn't have another witness in mind.

"Look," she said, "I was born here, and people sometimes ask me where I'm from—like what foreign terrorist country or something. After 9/11 cops look at my brother like he's a criminal just because he's a young guy with dark skin. I mean our uncle died in the North Tower."

"My brother died there too," I said. A seriously bad lie considering all the people whose brothers did die. I silently apologized to Sister Mary A. It was a means to a righteous end.

"Oh no," she said. "How terrible, I'm so sorry."

"I still can't talk about it," I said.

"You should probably go to a grief counselor," she said. "Even now it might help."

"I did," I said. "I can't talk about it, really."

"I'm sorry," she said. "I'll tell you about the driver, OK? But don't say you heard it from me."

A nice girl, but not smart.

"I won't," I said.

"Like I said, me and my friends volunteer here usually a few nights a week," she continued, "because we thought maybe we'd meet some doctors—like Indian doctors. But we found out they'd rather be with, you know, the white nurses. Even the really fat ones."

"Men can be stupid," I said.

"Seriously," she said. "But I'm a realist. If not a doctor, then somebody else. I'm twenty-six."

"You look a lot younger," I said.

"Thanks," she said, touching her hair and pausing. "The guy who brought that girl in was an Indian cabdriver. Very cute. He was in a hurry to get out of here, so I didn't get a chance to meet him—but I got the phone number of the cab company because the car was parked right outside the entrance, where you met Justin. I figured maybe I could call for a cab…"

I couldn't fucking believe it.

"Did you call?" I asked.

She shook her head.

"Not yet," she said. "Because I have to figure out how to get him without mentioning he came to the hospital. But I can give you the number. It's a good thing he wasn't a gypsy."

She rooted around in the straw purse until she found a scrap of paper with a phone number.

I punched the number into my contacts and then hit the speakerphone button as I called, so Jenny could also hear the recorded message: "This is Big Y Taxi and Limousine Service. If you are—" I clicked off and wished her good luck finding what she was looking for.

"You too," she said before heading out into the rain.

Right. Me too.

50

If you want to track down a driver of any kind of cab, for any kind of reason, you will have a problem. Gypsy cabs are unregulated, and unless you memorized the license plate you would be shit out of luck. And the yellow-cab drivers, in spite of posted registration numbers and photo IDs, are notoriously hard to find.

They like to stay under the radar because outraged passengers have been known to beat the crap out of them for a real or imagined incident.

I figured for me it wouldn't be hard to find the guy—but it wasn't going to be that afternoon.

I've slept on park benches, under Dumpsters, on subway trains, and at the end of an empty aisle behind a hair dryer display at Walgreens. That's easy.

What's hard is getting any rest. Especially while not sleeping more than two hours without interruption. Which had become my problem between springing Hadley and meeting Jenny Bajpai.

I knew I was on my way from terminal crankiness through half-speed reflexes to bad-trip hallucinations. Maybe the perp, who had little in common with other humans, didn't ever sleep, but if I couldn't close my eyes and shut down my brain for at least six hours, I'd be useless.

When I got back to the *Dumb Luck* and checked my e-mail, there was a message from Meriwether with a lot of information about the number 44, which he warned me was random.

I printed out the pages and took them into my bedroom, stripped off my clothes, and lay down. I remember the first lines swimming across the paper just before I dove into a dreamless sleep.

Twelve hours later, I woke up not a new man—just a man who could look in the bathroom mirror without seeing double.

With no black spots floating in front of my eyes, I lay back down on my bed and read Meriwether's notes on the number 44.

Nick:

Giving you the obvious. Possibilities countably infinite. Sent copies to Fallon & Goode. Am working up some algorithms.
**

Math: 44 is octahedral number, can be partitioned 63,261 ways
**

Chemistry: Chemical element ruthenium is atomic number 44
**

Numerology: 44 is a master number; represents self-discipline, endurance
**

Bible (new St. James)
Genesis 44: Joseph's cup
Isaiah 44: God's blessing on Israel
Jeremiah 44: Disaster because of idolatry
Ezekiel 44: The prince, the Levites, the priests
Psalm 44: To the Chief Musician. Contemplation
**

Wyoming 44th state
**

Obama 44th president
**

Colt .44 Magnum .44 Ruger rifle .44 Henry rifle
**

UK country code 44, Royal Ballet box office 44 (x) xxxxx 44 xxx
**

44 Laws of Spiritual Development, *by Cayce*
Forty-Four Turkish Fairy Tales, *by Kunos*
Forty-Four Years of the Life of a Hunter, *by Browning*
**

44 AD St. James apostle witnessed Transfiguration, was executed by Agrippa I
**

Deaths: Age 44
St. Victor (wrote about Dionysius)
Irwin (crocodiles)
Reeve (widow)
Escobar (coke)
And others
**

Births: 1944
Joe Frazier
Rudy Giuliani
Sirhan Sirhan
Kinky Friedman
And others
**

Nostradamus: Centuries 1–6 & 8–10 have a quatrain 44
**

United States Code 44 governs public printing & documents
**

Twin Towers: Express elevators at each building stopped on the 44th floor

*

Chapter 44 Kabbalah: The teacher must know the outer cir-cumstances & inner soul of the student
*

I Ching: Hexagram 44 represents intercourse, social & sexual
*

ALSO:
There is at least one BMW dealership in every state.
License plate possible tower motif:
Kansas—2001–2002 State capitol lightly sketched
Mississippi—Biloxi Lighthouse 2007–present
New York—Last Statue of Liberty plate issued in 2002
Oregon—Douglas fir 1988–present
Tennessee—State capitol lightly sketched

Sent the slug I got out of Dr. Sloane's wall to Fallon. It was a .44.
Stonington cops have the .44 from Hadley's room.

I found the coincidence at the Twin Towers chilling, but nothing rang a bell, and I had no time to think about the infinite con-figurations of a number that could be somebody's coat size or the number of kittens he'd killed.

If Hadley knew what 44 meant, it was still locked in her memory.

51

Raja Jang was the name of the cabdriver who picked me up in Manhattan on West Thirty-Fourth Street where the Palisades Taxi again dropped me. Ignoring the law which prohibited cabbies from talking on their cell phones while driving, Jang spoke Urdu nonstop into his Android during the ride to the Bushwick area of Brooklyn and ungraciously agreed to wait.

The Big Y garage was actually a huge asphalt parking lot etched with long, crisscrossing cracks where the tar had given way.

There was a chain-link fence around the lot and, beyond it, the rusted remnants of an industrial site. I couldn't guess what kind of factory might have been there originally—one that manufactured actual stuff.

The rain gathered force and beat down on about eighty yellow cabs parked neatly between faded lines on the cracked tarmac, all ready to go when the shift changed. The cars all looked in pretty good shape.

A dilapidated little building that housed the dispatch office was another story. It was situated in the northeast corner of the lot, and with most of its windows boarded up, I doubted it could meet even the least stringent fire code in Brooklyn. If it did, someone was way paying off a fire inspector.

I knocked on the sooty door, and a female voice from inside yelled, "Yeah?"

"I want to talk to the dispatcher," I said.

"What for?"

"I'd like to come in," I said. "It's raining."

"Who're you?"

"Nick Sayler," I said. "I'm a private investigator." Sometimes the truth works.

"I didn't have nothing to do with them people." The voice grew louder because the person inside had approached the door.

"I just want a little information," I said. "Not about you."

She didn't respond.

"I'll pay," I said.

"How much?" she said.

"I'll give you twenty to get me in out of the rain."

I knew she was looking out the peephole, and a moment later she opened the door.

She was a young woman, obviously the only dispatcher at a desk so littered there could be a box or two of actual cat litter hidden under the piles of papers and empty coffee cups and candy wrappers.

Stuffed into clothes a few sizes too small, she must have outweighed me by thirty pounds. Even the gold chain around her neck with the gold letters spelling out *Latrisha* looked too tight. Her hands though were surprisingly pretty except for the iridescent green fingernails, which looked like lethal weapons.

She threw me a roll of paper towels, and I wiped the water off my face and neck. I'd already resigned myself to walking around in a wet shirt and was trying to reach some Zen state to transcend the pain in my leg, which had met and married the pain in my side.

"OK," Latrisha said and held out her hand, into which I placed a soggy twenty-dollar bill.

She was wearing an earpiece and microphone, and when the phone rang three times in a row, I was impressed at how quickly she took the calls and efficiently dispatched the drivers. I knew she was dealing with the fleet's limos—meaning black sedans—because yellow cabs couldn't be reserved.

She listened to the fourth caller for half a minute before saying, "What—you crazy? Call 911." She punched the Off button on her desk console and looked at me.

"Some dude's having a heart attack and they call a car service," she said. "So what you want?"

I told her, and she said she didn't think she could get that information.

I dropped a fifty onto the rubble on her desk, and she said she *maybe* could find out who drove that cab to Bellevue.

I knew the information was about five computer keystrokes away thanks to the GPS system recently installed in all Big Y vehicles. My source was very last century: the yellow pages.

I was in a hurry, so I dropped another fifty bucks into the mess on her desk. It bought me the name of the driver who took Hadley to the hospital, but Latrisha said she didn't know his schedule.

"Have you got a number for him?" I asked.

"What's that worth?"

"I'm almost tapped out," I said, and it was almost true.

"What you got left?" she asked.

I put down two tens and a couple of quarters and waited while she took three more calls in a row and sent a car to pick up a passenger at LaGuardia's Delta terminal, another at the corner of Prince and Mercer, and a third at the Lexington Avenue entrance to Bloomingdale's.

"That all?" she said as she picked up the bills with her green talons, generously leaving the change.

"Latrisha," I said, "why would I lie to you—do you want me to turn my pockets inside out?"

"OK," she said, tapped the keyboard of her computer, and came up with Narinder Singh's cell phone number.

"What about his address?" I asked.

"It ain't in here," she said. "You sure you ain't got no more money?"

"I'm sure," I said. That is, I had no more money for Latrisha. And Meriwether could get the address. "Thanks for your help."

"Maybe I'll give you a freebie," Latrisha said as I started for the door.

"What's that?" I asked.

"I know where the driver's at right now..." she said.

She paused, trying to stare me down. She had all the time in the world to dick around.

"I really don't have any money," I said.

"You lying," she said.

I opened the door.

"Khyber Pass," she said. "That's where all them ragheads hang."

"He wears a turban?" I asked.

"No," said Latrisha. "But he's a raghead."

5 2

Raja Jang was parked on the corner waiting. He was still speaking warp-speed Urdu on his cell phone—maybe the same call—and didn't seem to register when I got back into the taxi.

The tab was up to ninety-five dollars. I couldn't remember how long it had been since I took a case without a per diem, but since I hired myself this time, at least there was no paperwork.

The address Latrisha gave me was on Blanchard Street where, tucked between a dry cleaner and a furniture store, I would find the Khyber Pass Restaurant and Bar.

The place had no air-conditioning, and since it was already very dim in the early evening, it was probably always dim. Probably for a good reason.

There were stock pictures on the wall, the Taj Mahal, Shiva, Buddha, and an orange, green, and white Indian flag—same colors as Ireland—pinned up next to a map of Rajasthan.

Booths and little round tables were mostly empty, except for a couple of small groups in the back. Two girls and a guy in a booth and three guys at a table.

A short, square-shaped man wearing a black jacket over his white shirt, in spite of the heat, greeted me with a menu and asked whether I'd prefer a table or a booth.

"Thanks," I said. "But I'm not staying—I'm just looking for somebody."

"I don't know," said the man.

"I heard he and his friends are always here—I heard it was a great place."

The man smiled a little.

"His name is Narinder," I said.

The man glanced toward the back of the room and said, "That's a common name."

"Narinder Singh," I said.

"I don't think so," said the man, who apparently wasn't accustomed to lying. He glanced toward the back of the room again.

"I'm going to just go ask those guys," I said, and the man shrugged. No point in arguing.

I decided to try the boys' table first, where three people in their twenties were eating what looked like tandoori chicken or something close. They were all dark-skinned and wearing T-shirts. One guy had a Yankees cap on and two pierced earrings in each ear.

The second one wore very thick, tinted glasses, which must have made it hard to see in the semidarkness.

The third guy was very skinny with a scraggly beard; his T-shirt read: Burniators Kickball Champions.

"I'm looking for Narinder Singh," I said.

"I told you," said the kid in the glasses to the Burniator.

"We both told you," said the kid with the earrings.

"I'm him," said the Burniator guy. "What do you want?"

"What do you think?" said the kid with the glasses.

"Who are you?" asked Narinder Singh. "You're a cop, right?"

"Wrong," I said. "My name is Nick Sayler. The woman you brought to Bellevue a few nights ago is a friend of mine."

"Shit," he said.

"We knew it dude," Earrings said.

"They've got video cameras everywhere," said Thick Glasses.

"I shouldn't have done it," said Narinder. "I can't afford to get in any trouble—my father just leased a taxi for me."

"He'll kill you," said the guy with glasses.

"Definitely," said the guy with the earrings.

"I know, I know," Narinder said and paused. "But I couldn't leave her there."

"Where?" I asked.

"Who are you?" he asked.

"I told you," I said. "I'm not a cop. I'm a private investigator."

"Do you have ID?"

I needed him, so I produced it. Licensed in the states of New York, New Jersey, California, and Florida.

"That good enough?" I said.

"How did you find me?" he asked. "How did you get to see the video?"

"It doesn't matter," I said, letting him believe the videos existed. "But listen Narinder, you did the right thing. You probably saved her life. I want to find out who hurt her."

"What about the cops?" asked the earrings guy.

"I'm a couple of steps ahead of them," I said. "And to tell you the truth, I'm more interested than they are. They get a lot of assaults—for me this is personal."

"Is she your girlfriend?" asked the glasses guy.

"Yes," I said. "We're engaged."

"It was around ten," said Narinder. "You want to sit down?"

I pulled a chair away from one of the nearby tables and sat.

"You want a beer?" asked Earrings.

"I'm good," I said. "Go on."

"I dropped a fare off on West Twenty-Sixth and Tenth. I wasn't expecting to get anybody there—it's pretty deserted—and the rain, you know. I figured I'd head downtown…"

"And?" I said.

"And I saw her lying on the ground and two black guys were hunched over her," he said. "They were more like young kids it looked like, and when they saw me they took off on skateboards."

"What alley's that?" I asked.

"I don't know. There's a lot of renovation on hold around there; they have a few alleys left in between the buildings—believe me, it's not a place you want to stop at night."

"Do you think you could recognize the kids?"

"No," said Narinder. "And I'm not saying that because I don't want to be involved, which I do not."

"Can you remember anything?"

Narinder leaned forward, sighed, and shook his head slowly back and forth, which probably meant he was imagining how pissed off his father would be when he found out about all this.

"Not much," he said. "It was dark, it was raining, and they took off as soon as I slowed down."

"Can you remember anything—even a little detail?" I said. "How tall they were—what they were wearing—did you see their sneakers?"

"I didn't see anything man, I mean it," said Narinder.

"Just try to think for a minute," I said. "Are you sure they were both black? Nobody was Latino or just with dark skin?"

He shook his head.

"Do you remember how tall they were?"

"One of them was, you know, sort of average, but the other one was a little guy, and…he was wearing red sneakers—definitely, I'm pretty sure they were red. My lights caught the color—and red skateboard."

"And you're sure about the street—a lot of streets look the same over there by Ninth, Tenth, Eleventh Avenue," I said.

"I'm pretty sure," said Narinder.

"Is it in the car's GPS history?"

"No," he said.

"You're sure about that?" I said.

"Totally," he said.

I didn't bother asking how or why he disabled the device. There was no reason to lie about what he saw unless he was the guy who attacked Hadley, which I didn't think he was.

"Thanks," I said, standing up. "If I found you, the cops probably will too. I suggest you go to them first."

"You have nothing to hide," said Thick Glasses.

"I thought she might die," said Narinder. "I didn't want it on my conscience. That's what happened—but I don't have to go to the police because I didn't do anything."

I took a card out of my damp wallet, wrote Fallon's name and number on the back, and gave it to Narinder.

"Call this guy," I said.

"You said you weren't a cop," said Narinder angrily, smacking his hand down on the table in his first display of emotion that must have been building.

"I'm not," I said. "I showed you my ID. Now look on the other side of the card. Sayler Security—that's me. And, oh yeah, you guys got girlfriends?" I asked.

There was a brief silence as they wondered what the hell kind of question that was.

"I'm married," said the guy with the earrings.

"I'm gay," said the guy in the glasses matter-of-factly.

"I don't," said Narinder. "What's that got to do with anything? You said you believed me—I didn't attack her."

"Relax, I know you didn't," I said. "You helped me out just now—so I'm going to return the favor. There are some very pretty girls working preadmissions at Bellevue. Next time you're over that way, look for the one named Jenny—tell her I sent you."

53

Back in the cab Raja Jang bitched that all this waiting around was costing him money. He was correct because picking up and dropping off fares during the time he clocked waiting would have been more lucrative. Especially because it was raining. Too fucking bad.

Instead of telling him to shut the fuck up, it was a city law he couldn't throw me out unless I was disorderly, threatening, or drunk, I told him there was another forty in it over the tip to keep going. Why rock my little boat in the middle of an epic downpour?

Shooting to break my two-hundred-dollar cab fare record, I told Raja Jang we were going back to Manhattan.

I called Meriwether in Connecticut and asked him to put Hadley on the phone.

"Nick," she said. "Are you all right?"

What a funny girl.

"I'm good," I said. "I'm always good."

"Oh, of course," she said. "I forgot. But your surgery—"

"I'm OK," I said. "How're you feeling?"

"The same," she said. "I'm in a house full of people who think they know me, and sometimes they're annoyed that I can't remember them—as if it's my fault—"

"Blame the victim."

"Not Billy though," she said. "He's been very kind. He hasn't reminded me once about what good friends we were. Which makes me think we were."

"Yeah," I said, "good old Billy."

She let that go and continued, "Nile Sutro keeps calling, and I'm not ready to talk to him. He still doesn't know about the attack. Margo keeps making excuses for me—I lost my phone, I can't remember the password for messages, I was walking Buddy, having a manicure in town. He's always too busy to press her. I sent him some…text messages. But I haven't called except during performances. Now he finally thinks something is up because we haven't talked in days, and he asked Margo if I changed my mind about going back with him."

"What did she say?"

"She said I hadn't changed my mind. She thinks I should call him now—and tell him what happened."

"What do you think?" I asked.

"I'm going to wait," she said. "At least another day. They say he's completely absorbed with his concerts."

And I would say not. I would say the genius could be absorbed with his work and his wife at the same time.

"Meriwether and I have been watching the news," she went on. "We haven't seen anything about the mayor's task force. About Justin. Or about me. And Thomas Fallon called, just to check in he said."

"Hadley," I said, "I found the cabdriver who took you to Bellevue."

"Why didn't you tell me?"

"I'm telling you now."

"Do you think he was the one—"

"No, I'm sure he wasn't," I said, hoping she wouldn't ask why I was sure, because "I'm just sure" is not a very satisfying answer. "He told me where he picked you up—on West Twenty-Sixth Street. In Chelsea. Near your apartment."

"Does he know what happened?" she asked, her voice dropping almost to a whisper.

"No," I said.

"He must know something."

"Hadley," I said, "I have another call. I've got to go."

"When will I see you?" she was asking when I clicked into the next call.

What a chickenshit motherfucker I was.

"Betty Murphy and I got a couple of hits," said Linda Goode as she skipped any greeting—a habit she must have picked up from Fallon. "Betty decided which was the likeliest."

"With so little information," I said.

"That's what we do," Goode said with more than a hint of self-congratulation. "And I trust her reasoning. It's just the bare bones so far. She's working up the psychological profile, and I'm at the Puzzle Palace again. I'm looking for more possibles."

"Could you send what you've got to Meriwether?"

"One of these days, I'm going to have to tell Betty about Meriwether."

"Fine," I said. "You do that. Meriwether doesn't care—he leaves no tracks. So you can fuck up Fallon's career—and if he lives long enough to get his pension, it's revocable. And you're not so innocent yourself. But we're all sacrificing the good for the greater good, aren't we?"

"What do you mean if he lives long enough?"

"Figure it out, Linda."

"I'm going to send a note on Murphy's hit to your phone," she said.

"Just read it to me," I said. "I don't know how to do the phone stuff."

"That's a lie," she said. "I need you—"

"Linda," I said, "I've been waiting my whole life to hear those words."

"Shut up Nick," she said. "I need you to be up to speed on the information since you've seen the guy."

"In the dark," I said. "At a distance. I told you everything Sloane and Hadley and I saw. It doesn't amount to much."

"Get back to us," she said.

"Have a nice day," I said.

5 4

Goode was right; I do know how to use my phone for more than calls. I don't know as much as the average eleven-year-old kid, but I can open a document. I just didn't want to, because it was a pain in the ass reading on the little screen.

Nevertheless I went to mail, downloaded Goode's document, and opened it the fuck up. Murphy's main hit was: Aristophanes Mallekmaddani Komodoppolete Dillon (a total of forty-four letters), né Aristophanes Dillon, DOB April 4, 1974, Miami, Florida. Aliases Ari Dillon, Joseph Dillon.

Class C felony promoting prostitution, Class E felony unlawful imprisonment, Class D felony use of a child in a sexual performance, three felony assault arrests, misdemeanor arrest possession marijuana, last known addresses Forty-Fourth Street Jersey City, Forty-Fourth Street Far Rockaway, 2 East 169th Street Bronx Forty-Fourth Police Precinct.

Meriwether's call interrupted my squinting.

"You got the sheet," I said.

"Just now," Meriwether said.

"And?" I asked.

"I already had that information."

"For how long?"

"Does it matter?"

"Why were you waiting?"

"Motive," said Meriwether.

"Yeah," I said. "We'll have to find out."

"I'm working on more," he said. "I'll call you later."

"Sooner than later."

I never would have said that in the past—but Meriwether had never been distracted by a woman in the past.

As soon as I clicked off I heard my phone's tritone. Fallon had sent a one-word message, which read: *Nothing.*

My last stop with Raja Jang was Eleventh Avenue and West Twenty-Sixth Street, where I paid him the fare, plus tip, plus forty, and let him go, wishing I knew a couple of choice words in Urdu.

On the best day in August, West Twenty-Sixth Street between Tenth and Eleventh Avenues wouldn't be a welcoming place, with its construction-site walls of corrugated metal covered with graffiti and its deserted buildings. Not welcoming unless you were a kid with a skateboard.

Narinder was right; ambitious building had been started in a few places, and now if it was not abandoned, it was suspended. I counted three alleys on the north side of the street—narrow and unlit. Dark in the day—darker at night. Good places to hide.

It didn't look like anyone was working down toward Eleventh Avenue. Just a few pedestrians hurrying along, fighting the wind for control of their umbrellas.

I checked the alleys that were closer to Tenth Avenue running north to south on each side of the street. I could only see daylight at the end of one of them: between West Twenty-Sixth and West Twenty-Seventh.

The attacker couldn't have been on foot, or he wouldn't have known where Narinder took Hadley after he put her in his cab.

So what happened?

He changed his mind.

He was interrupted, ran to his conveniently parked car.

He wasn't ever going to kill her.

It really didn't matter. That was then.

Walking around in the lashing rain, I had gone from wet to water-logged. And just as I made up my mind I wasn't going to see any skateboarders until the storm calmed down, four of them, all white kids, materialized. Coming from four different directions, they were heading straight toward me like animals with eyes on their prey. As a bystander, I would have laughed; they looked like something out of the old movie *West Side Story*—a choreographed cliché.

It got less funny when they came at me fast and very close, but they all flew past me in a crisscross pattern. Then gathered, figuring they'd watch me run. They'd probably played this game many times before. Perfected it.

I needed to talk to them and didn't want to dick around. The quickest way to get their attention was to set up a new version of chicken.

I didn't move. Just made a sign that meant *bring it, you little fuckers.*

And they did—one kid in a black tracksuit and a black turned-around baseball cap with a skull and crossbones on it snapped the tail of his board and jumped over my left shoulder. The next one wearing some kind of cowboy clothes, spurs on his skate shoes, did the same, only came at me backward and flipped over my right shoulder. The other two, dressed for the weather, with their Windbreakers flapping, headed directly toward me. That's when I thought I would actually take a direct hit and pop my recent stitches—but each one veered off, spraying water, jumping their boards into the air and grabbing them as they spun going down.

All four started again, but when the cowboy hit a pothole under a small pond of rainwater and was unceremoniously parted from his board, I called the game.

The kid in the black tracksuit skated up and stopped an inch away from my face.

"Dude, are you crazy—or what?" he asked.

"I want to talk to you," I said.

"Me," he said. "I didn't do nothing."

"I know," I said. "I want to talk to you and your friends over there."

The three other kids had parked themselves about twenty feet away.

"You don't look like no cop," he said.

For one thing, cops probably don't go to work with bandaged hands, but I'd accept his opinion as a more insightful observation.

"Thank you," I said.

"Are you from reality TV?" the kid asked. "We got some good stuff."

"No," I said. "Sorry. Just a few questions. I'll pay."

"We ain't fags," he said.

"Just a few questions," I said.

"'Bout what?" he said.

"Go get your friends and I'll tell you."

"Dude, let's see the cash," he said.

I didn't reply.

"OK," he said and skated over to his friends.

After a couple of words, the two in the Windbreakers took off, and the skateboard rodeo rider came back over with his friend.

"Where'd they go?" I asked.

"They thought you was a cop," said Tracksuit.

"And what are they, felons?"

Cowboy laughed and Tracksuit shrugged.

"You a movie scout?" he asked.

"No," I said. "I'm a private investigator."

They looked at each other in surprise. The only detectives they were likely to meet would be the ones who arrested them.

"That's a nice watch," I said, noticing the Rolex the cowboy was wearing. So big it was hard to miss. "Looks like a good fake. Where'd you get it, Canal Street?"

"It ain't no fake," said the kid. He got a shut-the-fuck-up look from the other kid and stopped talking.

Two minutes and two twenties got me the names of the kids Narinder Singh had described. At least the board names of the small kid in the red skate shoes and his buddy. The two of them were always together. The regular-size kid was Po.

"What's Po for?"

"I don't know," said Cowboy and laughed. "Rhymes with ho."

"If you got another twenty," said Tracksuit, "I know his real name."

"I got ten," I said.

"His real name is Digger."

"Digger what?"

"That's his real last name," said Cowboy.

"It'll be easy for me to find out if you're lying," I said.

"He ain't lying," said Cowboy, and with such a good character reference I handed over the ten.

It turned out that the little one with the red skate shoes was actually fifteen. Everybody called him Red Hawk after some old guy they watched on YouTube.

I learned that he was pretty much a star, best of the boarders who hung around those streets in Chelsea. He was shredding at all the parks and was set to compete at Shields Skatepark someplace in New Jersey over Labor Day.

They didn't know Red Hawk's real name—and apparently in this group, except for Digger, nobody had a last name. Or an address. Or a school. And they didn't exchange phone numbers. They just knew Red Hawk and Po didn't live around there. And they were both black.

"But I ain't prejudice," said the cowboy.

"I need to talk to them," I said. "It's urgent. And there's cash in it for you and for them—so if you're holding out, it ain't worth it."

"What do you want them for dude?" asked Tracksuit.

"You know what *confidential* means?" I said.

"Yeah, I know," said Cowboy, not the sharpest tack in the toolbox. "It means secret. Right? Oh, I get it."

"They ain't been around the last couple of days," said Tracksuit.

I bet they haven't.

"It's been raining," I said.

"We don't care," said Cowboy.

"Just give them the message," I said and gave each boy two of my cards. "Or you can call me."

Then Tracksuit stuck out his hand to shake hands, which we did like two businessmen ending a conference. It was an oddly touching gesture that still sticks in my mind.

55

I walked a block and ducked under the first awning I saw. A vacuum repair store where the vacuums in the window looked vintage, as did the old man playing solitaire on the counter by the cash register.

After I sent Meriwether a text describing the two boys, I called Shields Skatepark, which turned out to be in Flemington, New Jersey. There I was put on indefinite hold by a teenage girl working in the manager's office.

Red Hawk must be a serious competitor to go to Flemington. Most kids like Tracksuit and Cowboy and probably—at least at one time—Red Hawk had never been outside New York City.

Plus they didn't skate at official places which required wrist guards and helmets. For that reason they'd probably never go to the fanciest park around at Pier 62. Too many rules.

Shields had rules too, one of which, I was certain, required signed waivers from anyone over eighteen or the custodian of anyone under eighteen who so much as touched a board or thought about doing a nosegrind.

I had identified myself as Detective Thomas Fallon of Manhattan South in New York City and asked for the roster of entrants in competitions over Labor Day, and when the girl came back on the line, she told me the manager would call me. I reminded her that this call was police business.

"Where is the manager now?" I asked.

After a few beats, the girl said she didn't actually know, but had left a message on his voice mail.

"Give me his number," I said, and she did after I reminded her again that I was a policeman.

My call to him also went to voice mail, which is infuriating since it treats all men as equals. This is the president of the United States calling; I need your help to avoid a nuclear incident...

After my second call, which included an order to e-mail copies of all Labor Day entrant information to Albert Meriwether—who then would know everything I knew—it was time for a drink.

I decided on the Standard Hotel, and since I didn't see a cab anywhere, I started to walk, favoring my bad side and bum leg. Good luck the incision and the metal rods were both on my right.

I'd been in the rain since I got out of the cab from Brooklyn, so continuing down that slippery slope to middle age, I gave in and bought an umbrella from a guy on the corner just before I crossed into a neighborhood officially called Gansevoort Market, which is its official name. As far as I know nobody has ever used that name.

It's still called the Meatpacking District because about a hundred years ago, this little piece of Manhattan, which runs from Sixteenth Street down to Gansevoort, east to Hudson Street and west to the river, was once filled with slaughterhouses and packing plants.

Decades later the neighborhood was the site of notorious sex clubs like the Mineshaft, the Anvil, and the Hellfire Club, which carried the motto: *Fais ce que tu voudras*, Do what thou wilt. And they did, never knowing about the vicious disease that would cut so many down so young.

The S&M, B&D playground was then taken over by fancy little boutiques selling eight-hundred-dollar shoes—Rue likes the ones with the red soles—and four-hundred-dollar scarves.

None of the buildings around there were more than a few stories high, which made the twenty-floor Standard Hotel where I was heading stand out like a huge glass book opened in the middle, or a giant bent wing.

A couple of years ago I was working a case that took me to the hotel about a dozen times, so I got familiar with it, and although it's not my usual kind of place, I go by now and then when I'm in the area.

After I stopped in the men's room to towel off my hair and dump the umbrella, I walked out to the nearly deserted rooftop lounge, found myself a little table under an awning, and asked for a Benediction, which is about as close to a state of grace as I ever get.

It's a girl's drink, but I like it, and when I told Meriwether about it, he added orange bitters to the champagne and Benedictine, making it even more excellent. I might not know how to fry an egg, but I know what goes into my drinks.

As I lifted my glass, my cell phone barked. I'd taken Fallon to the Standard a couple of times. He hated girls' drinks but he loved girls, and each one was usually better looking than the last at the rooftop lounge. Or got better looking with more drinks. It didn't matter to Fallon.

His liking the Standard was about as strange as my liking Benedictions. But predictable people are the ones who get killed.

"Guess where I am?" I said.

"Yeah," said Fallon, "it don't matter. Wherever you're at it's better than where I'm at."

"All right," I said.

"We got another homicide."

A chill rippled across my neck.

"Another dancer?" I asked.

"I don't think so," he said. "It's a boy—a skateboarder kid. Strangled. The number 44 carved in his back."

"Where?"

"The High Line."

"What's he look like?" I asked.

"Dead," said Fallon.

I waited.

"Black. Maybe thirteen, fourteen," Fallon continued. "Little. Easy to take down."

"What was he wearing?"

"Wearing," said Fallon. "Where's this going?"

"Tell me what he was wearing," I said.

"Baggy red shorts, white stripe down the side," said Fallon. "Torn-up red T-shirt says Got Dank on it."

"What about his shoes?" I asked.

"Yeah, what about his shoes?" said Fallon suspiciously. "Do you know something?"

"Tom," I said. "How could I know anything? I'm just picking up any detail about 44 I can and sending everything to Meriwether. As usual."

"Seems like more than usual," said Fallon.

"I've never worked a case like this before," I said.

"This ain't your case," he said.

I waited a few long beats until Fallon finally said, "He's wearing red shoes. Red skateboarding shoes."

The High Line Park is just above the Standard, a few minutes by skateboard from Twenty-Sixth Street.

East of Tenth Avenue running parallel to the Hudson River, built thirty feet above the ground on a stretch of what used to be the West Side Line's elevated freight railroad, the High Line is the newest, cleanest, and strangest park in the city.

Sloane likes it because he says it reminds him of the Promenade Plantée in Paris. I don't know much about Paris, but I do know that for a long time after train traffic stopped thirty years ago, trees and tall grass grew wild along the abandoned railway and any kid including me who ever wandered into the place was sure he'd found his own secret paradise. And since not very many people knew about this urban Eden, it was an excellent place to sell drugs to my regular customers.

I hadn't deliberately avoided the High Line in its new incarnation, but I suppose I didn't want to see how it had changed—especially after I heard someone say they were trying to retain the romance of the ruin.

I climbed the stairs from the Fourteenth Street entrance and saw the place wasn't as bad as I thought.

They'd designed a nice green landscape over the big steel deck supported by those huge steel columns. A fountain here, a fountain there, concrete slabs somebody must've thought echoed the old railroad ties. Tall grass that looked the same as ever and a lot of pretty flowers carefully planted so they wouldn't look carefully planted.

Because they didn't have any tall trees, there was a 360 degree vista of the city. And an open view of most of the park made the first murder at the High Line a very bold one done by a very insolent killer.

I leaned against a bench, called Meriwether, and told him not to let the dancer out of his sight. Then I promised myself a long visit to the Kalahari Desert because I'd deserve it after going through this rain that never quit.

There was a bigger than usual group of cops standing on the other side of the rain-slicked yellow crime scene tape. Off to one side I saw Linda Goode watching me approach from under her big black umbrella.

She waved me past a couple of cops who'd started heading my way, and I followed her to where Fallon was in a debate with a prematurely bald man in a seersucker suit too tailored, even damp from the rain, to belong to a plainclothes detective.

Maybe somebody should tell him there's no more bald. Unhappy balding men are now happy hipsters with shaved heads. Whoever my parents were, they handed down the good hair genes—or at least that's what Rue claims. So thanks folks, wherever you are.

The man in the seersucker suit was switching his navy blue umbrella from hand to hand as he talked and looking more agitated by the second.

"From the commissioner's office," said Goode in a whisper. "Henry Kuzon. Spokesman for the task force. They don't trust us to say anything."

"And you, Detective Goode," said the spokesman, stepping away from Fallon.

"Yes," said Goode calmly.

"You will contact us with anything new. And I mean anything at all. Who's this?"

"I'm Nick Sayler," I said.

"And who authorized him to be here?"

"He's our civilian observer," said Fallon.

"Civilian observer," said the spokesman sourly. "I've never heard of a civilian observer, and I know all the programs."

"Well you need to do some homework," said Goode. "The department instituted this about five years ago. It's aimed at law enforcement professionals and concerned—"

"All right Detective, fine, I heard you," said Kuzon, who then glared at me and waved Fallon to his side.

The two of them moved out of earshot, where Kuzon talked angrily and Fallon nodded.

Having finished his tirade, Kuzon nodded curtly to us and speed-walked away through the muddy grass in his moderately expensive tassel loafers.

"What did he say?" asked Goode.

"Said fuck civilian observers. Get rid of Sayler."

Ordinarily Goode would have said something like that's a great idea. Not then.

Compared with his usual blatant disregard of regulations, Fallon's calling me his civilian observer twice in one week was small-time. Because if Kuzon remembered to check, he'd learn that there were only two categories of civilian observer: first, the concerned citizens who patrolled their blocks in bright-orange jackets attempting to discourage crime. The second kind was anyone over eighteen with a valid photo ID who wanted to ride along in a patrol car for two hours.

"O-K," said Fallon to Kuzon's departing back. "C'mere, Linda."

Goode went to join Fallon and confer in private, which was fine by me.

Looking in the other direction about thirty yards away, I saw, covered by a heavy tarp, what I knew were the earthly remains of a boy called Red Hawk, acknowledged by everyone as the very best skateboarder in all of Chelsea.

56

"Let's go for a walk," said Fallon. "I got something to show you."

Goode's brow beetled up and she looked around, as if to see who was watching.

"Give it a break," Fallon growled to Goode. "Nothing's gonna happen."

The three of us walked away from the crime scene, a hundred yards, two hundred yards, three. We went behind a copse of trees, with our backs toward the distant police.

"I got this," said Fallon. He pulled on a latex glove and took a gold bracelet out of his back pocket, a simple bangle.

"Go ahead," said Goode, "have a look."

"Where'd this come from?" I asked.

"Must've fell out of the kid's pocket," Fallon said and held the bangle tilted at my eye level.

Lying to a deputy from the commissioner's office was nothing compared to the very serious offense of moving evidence at a crime scene.

"Yeah," I said. "I can see it's engraved—all the way around. What does it say?"

Goode intoned: "*To Hadley, my* assoluta, *love forever, Nile.* What do you think?"

"I think what you think," I said. "The dead skateboarding kid was killed by 44, and the bracelet links him to Hadley."

287

"Anything else?" asked Fallon.

"No," I said.

"Why did you ask me about his shoes?" asked Fallon.

"Tommy," I said, "what do you want to hear?"

"I don't know," Fallon said. "We got a lot of nothing substantial. A lot of pieces."

"They'll come together," said Goode, who was able to blow off her glum outlook on every aspect of life if she thought Fallon needed to be cheered up.

"What about the videotapes at the hospital?" I asked.

"All shit," said Fallon.

"Betty Murphy?" I asked Goode.

"What I told you before," said Goode. "She's staying on it. What about Meriwether?"

"He's still in Stonington with Hadley," I said. "And his computer."

"Did you run checks on all the parking tickets from that night?" I asked.

"No black BMWs," said Goode. "No BMWs at all. I am keeping Murphy and Meriwether up to speed."

"I want the ballet dancer to come in, Nick," said Fallon. "I'm serious this time. Make that happen—because nobody's really got nothing new except another homicide. I know she still don't remember nothing—but I want her to look at pictures."

He ran his hands through his unruly hair and went on, "I gotta take a break from this shit. Let's get some coffee."

The police had closed the park and called for more backup to keep away reporters, all of whom had scanners and knew police codes. When the department changed the codes, the reporters learned the new codes.

Fallon and Goode didn't have to stay with the body. Nothing official could be determined until the medical examiner arrived, and since there were only a couple of medical examiners available in Manhattan, there would be a wait.

"Let's go to that place across from the Fourteenth Street entrance," said Goode as she and Fallon started walking.

"You coming with us?" asked Goode.

"I'll walk out with you," I said. "Then I'm heading back to the barge."

"How's the side?" asked Fallon as we neared the steps going down to street level. "How're you feeling?"

"Not good," I said.

That was the whole truth.

I was still on the stairs when the tritone sounded with a text from Meriwether giving me Po's full name, which was Harpo Digger, his mother's name, Mary Digger, and their Harlem address I recognized from when Mike Teak and I learned our way around up there. Black people are in the minority now, but years ago the streets could be dicey for white faces. Unless the white faces belonged to two guys with friends at Rucker Park.

I was heading to central Harlem, a big part of which was once controlled by a gang called the Preacher Crew. An innocent name for a vicious pack of gangbangers. Killers who used to stash their victims under rotting floorboards near where Mary Digger was living thirty years later.

There were still some rotting floorboards in the neighborhood, but if there were any corpses underneath, I hoped none of them was her son.

The Digger residence was in a building ten floors high. The front door to the tiny lobby was open, the lock broken. The elevator was also out of commission. The place was dirty, smelled like shit, and the hot weather made it worse.

By the time I'd climbed the stairs to the tenth floor and found 10 F, my leg felt like it was ready to give out. All the music from all the boom boxes and newer speakers in the street and in the building came together in one long rap cacophony, and for a minute I considered walking away.

The doorbell had been ripped out of 10 F's door frame and replaced with a wad of once pink calcified bubblegum. I knocked. I could hear the drone of a TV and a baby crying, but no one came to let me in. The peephole in the door had been smashed and then covered with dirty gray duct tape.

I knocked again. And again.

Finally a girl's voice came from the other side of the door.

"We don't want nothing," the voice said.

"It's the police."

57

Right here I'll say that a lot of crimes, including murder, go unsolved in the city. Primarily because they are undetected. I wasn't worried about being charged with impersonating an officer. I'd done it before, most recently over the phone when I called the skate park in New Jersey. It worked well in the right circumstances. Way downscale like this where most of the people were afraid and way upscale where some of the people were surprisingly clueless.

If anybody wanted to see a badge, I had one. An excellent fake. Expensive, made in Montreal, the go-to place for a counterfeit ID, which I also had: John Gibgniew.

If anyone wanted to check up on me, when they discovered Officer Gibgniew didn't exist they'd think they didn't get the spelling right and lose interest before going through every *Gi*, *Ge*, and *Ga* in the police roster. Fallon probably suspected I used a fake ID but never said anything. I didn't want to tell him, and he didn't want to know.

"Wait a minute," said the voice. It seemed she went back in the room, probably for a consultation.

"Hey," I said, knocking on the door. "I don't want to open the door myself."

I never knew what level of bullshit was going to work until I tried it out. Almost all of it worked.

The girl inside the apartment twisted two locks; the door opened a couple of inches, held by a chain. I showed her the badge.

"How I know it's real?" said the girl, who looked like she was sixteen or seventeen.

"Well, because I say it's real," I said pleasantly. "I can show you my ID and my gun if you want. But it's getting pretty hot in this hall."

"OK," she said and opened the door. "You don't have no uniform."

"That's right."

"Because you a plainclothes cop, right?" she asked.

"That's right," I said. "May I come in?"

"Yeah," she said. "Come in."

She was a skinny girl, all bones and a high skinny ass wearing crotch-length shorts, platform heels, and a little blouse with incongruous ruffles. Her hair looked like it was between jobs, and she was holding a naked baby—maybe a year old.

"There's my mom," the girl said. "She don't feel like talking."

Behind her, Mary Digger sat on a couch so dilapidated that she was almost touching the floor. The big flat-screen TV, late model, was a few feet away. A beautiful blonde on the screen was hawking a new face cream that studies showed decreased wrinkles by at least 40 percent within six weeks.

Mrs. Digger was wearing a version of the outfit her daughter had on. She was probably no more than thirty-five—but she looked old. Tired. Not a junkie though. Just done hoping for anything more than maybe a magical face cream or a bigger TV. She had a beer in one hand and a cigarette in the other. An ashtray filled with butts was balanced on the arm of the couch.

I introduced myself—John Gibgniew.

"I don't want to take up your time, Mrs. Digger," I said.

"I don't have no choice," she said, "do I?"

"Well I have one question," I said.

"Which is…" she said warily.

"Where is Po?"

"I don't know," she said, putting one Kool Menthol in the chipped ashtray and lighting another while it still smoldered.

"He's not in trouble," I said. "We just need to talk to him."

"If he ain't in no trouble with the cops," she said, "he in some other kinda trouble. He scared. He gone."

Just then another baby, older but still crawling, made his way into the room dragging a dirty diaper along the floor. A third child, a little girl, naked, followed and gave him a good kick in the butt apparently just for the hell of it.

"What the fuck you doing?" the teenage mom yelled.

And the little girl began wailing—so now there were three screaming children in a hot room that stank of smells I didn't want to identify. The mom, maybe she was seventeen not fifteen, herded them out of the room.

A few minutes later—during which time Mary Digger repeated that she had no idea where her son was—the skinny girl returned without the kids, who were disturbingly quiet.

"Go ahead," Mary Digger said. "Ask Sherice—we don't know where Harpo's at—he could've went anywhere."

"My name's Beyoncé," said Sherice. "I changed it."

"Well, Beyoncé," I said, "if you were going to guess where your brother's at, what would you say?"

She glanced at her mother and shook her head.

"We don't know," said Mary Digger.

"You haven't asked me why I want to talk to him," I said.

"We know why," said Sherice.

"OK," I said. Patient. Kind.

"We know something happened this week," said Sherice. "Scared the shit out him—I told him it was stupid to hang with them skateboarder kids, them white boys don't want him—him or even Jamal."

293

Finally Red Hawk's name, Jamal.

"What happened?" I asked.

"Don't know," said Sherice.

"Look ladies, I've got some very bad news."

"Oh no no no," cried Mary Digger. "What happened to him?"

"Nothing happened to your son as far as I know. But one of the skateboarder kids is dead. The one they call Red Hawk. Po's friend. Jamal."

"Them fuckin' assholes," said Sherice. "They think they can do all their shit jumpin' over cars with them skateboards—they play chicken in the street. I always tell Po somebody's gonna run him down."

"This boy who died was not run over in a traffic accident. He was murdered at the High Line. And we're not looking at Po for any of this—but we think he might know something—might have said something to you."

"Like what?" asked Sherice.

"Like what happened," I said. "Or where he might be right now."

"Sherice," said Mary Digger, "shut."

"It's Beyoncé," Sherice retorted. "How many times I got to tell you?"

"Oh Jesus," said Mary Digger. "Po's going to get hisself killed too. He the onliest thing I got—he the best thing in my life—" Suddenly she began sobbing.

Apparently Sherice had not made the cut—and this was not lost on her.

"I'd say if I knew where he's at," Mary Digger said, wiping the back of her hand across her face.

"She's lying," said Sherice. "Po knows something about something."

"You shut," yelled Mary from the couch, where she tried to heave herself up from the sagging cushion. It was too hard though, and she fell back. "Just shut, Sherice."

"Beyoncé," Sherice screamed. "Beyoncé Beyoncé Beyoncé!"

"What do you think he knows?" I asked. "It's important. We think whoever killed Jamal will go after Po too. We don't want anything to happen to him. That's why I have to know where he is."

Mary Digger closed her eyes for a few beats, weighing her choices.

"What time is it?" she said, now looking at the TV. "Go on and tell him, Beyoncé, there ain't much time."

58

The Port Authority Bus Terminal used to be famously dangerous and so depressing you wouldn't even want to sell drugs there.

After the city cleaned it up they tried to change the name of the neighborhood, from Hell's Kitchen, where I grew up, to Clinton. Named after the Republican governor George Clinton, not the Democratic president Bill Clinton. Nobody ever knew which was which, so everybody had a gripe and the name didn't stick. Now a lot of people like the old name. Sounds romantic—like romance of the ruins. Maybe that's why my address is New Jersey.

The Port Authority subway station, where I got off the E train, has four tracks and two platforms—three if you count the one that's been abandoned so long nobody knows why they built it. It's a tiny hamlet compared to the bus terminal megalopolis that sprawls across two vast city blocks above it.

All the terminal levels are connected by a labyrinth of stairs, ramps, and escalators, leading toward the gates that service over three dozen bus lines.

Growing up in Hell's Kitchen, you had to know every means of transportation since you were usually running away from someone. So I still knew my way around because even after gentrification, the gateways were still pretty much in the same spots as always. Which was lucky because I only had twelve minutes to find one squirrelly kid in a place that handles two hundred thousand people on any given day.

Panting, with sweat dripping off my face and soaking into my shirt, I tried to stay focused and kept running until I reached gate 14, where the Peter Pan bus to Washington, DC, was scheduled to leave in one minute.

I got to the bus before it completed the arc it needed to get into the street. When the driver ignored my pounding at the door, I flashed my phony badge. On city property with building security and transit cops around, this impersonation was trickier, but I had no choice because Harpo Digger was my only lead.

"John Gibgniew," I said when the door opened. "NYPD. We believe there's a runaway on this bus. A minor. We need to question him."

"OK," said the driver, who wore his long gray hair in a ponytail. He was slumping in his seat, drumming his fingers on the big steering wheel. "Don't make me late—you'll ruin my record. There's a competition for best driver on the Eastern Corridor. And I could win unless you screw it up. I mean you know Officer. I'm sorry."

"Where's your microphone?" I asked.

"Just push that button," he said.

"Po Digger," I said into the mic, "please come to the front of the bus."

"Now," the driver chimed in.

Nobody moved.

"Po," I said.

Still no one came forward. I motioned to the driver to close the doors.

"OK," I said and started moving down the aisle. I knew what the kid looked like because there were a couple of pictures of him on his skateboard taped to the wall in his mother's place.

"Let's go," I said when I spotted him in the right aisle, last window seat at the back.

"I didn't do nothing," said Po angrily as he got his backpack out of the overhead compartment and yanked his skateboard from under his seat.

Since the days when I had to face a line of stone-faced nuns who looked nothing like friendly penguins, up until the last few days, I hadn't heard the familiar litany so many times: I didn't do nothing.

As soon as our feet hit the ground, the driver screeched away from the loading platform and I led Po over to a bench against the wall.

"You a cop, right?" said Po.

"Yeah," I said. "Who else would get you off that bus?"

"I don't know," said Po. "Maybe somebody lookin' for me."

"Who?" I asked.

"Forget it," he said belligerently. "What you want me for?"

"Dump that backpack," I said.

"You got a warrant?" he said.

"Do you know what a warrant is?"

"You know what I mean."

"Dump the bag," I said.

He dumped the contents of his small backpack on the bench. A bunch of T-shirts, shorts, a pair of brand-new Nike skate shoes, a dozen candy bars, *Skateboarding* magazine.

"Unzip that," I said, pointing to the side of the backpack.

"Ain't nothing in there," said Po.

I unzipped the pocket, felt inside, and found, on a gold chain, a plain round gold locket with no engraving. In the locket, which was made for two pictures, one side was empty. The other side held a tiny photo of a laughing child. It was Gemma, Hadley's daughter.

"Here's your warrant, you little cocksucker," I said, holding the locket in front of his face.

"You got to read me my rights," said Po.

"Yeah, what else you got in the bag?"

"Nothing."

"Unzip that outside pocket."

"Nothing in there," he said.

I unzipped it.

"And here's your rights," I said, pulling out a Smith & Wesson .38, street value about forty dollars.

"It ain't mine," he said.

"Illegal possession of a firearm gets you automatic one year in jail. You want to go to jail?"

The kid looked scared. He wasn't a gangbanger. He was a skateboarder. A cold-blooded little fuck of a skateboarder.

"No," he mumbled.

"Maybe they'll send you to Tryon."

The kid immediately drew back, shoulders up, scared. Tryon is a juvenile detention center in Fulton County, notorious for killings, beatings, rape, and suicides.

"No," said Po. "Not Tryon. I heard about Tryon."

"So you're going to talk to me, right?"

"Yeah."

"And I'm going to talk to you. Move," I said, pushing him toward the escalator.

When we got to the main floor, I took him into a coffee shop, thankfully air-conditioned. I sat him down, ordered a couple of cheeseburgers, and told him about his friend. Po turned his face away as far as his neck would let it turn. I imagine he didn't want me to see him cry. Maybe he was just crying for himself.

59

Thursday night, he told me, they were hanging in Chelsea even though it was raining hard, hoping it would stop so Red Hawk could practice for the competition. But the rain got worse, so they decided to go to an alley they knew to smoke some weed.

That's when they saw a guy with a knife in the alley; looked like he was trying to kill a woman who was on the ground. They scared him off just by showing up. Then they grabbed the woman's purse and jewelry.

"We would've called 911," he said.

"Yeah," I said. "So why didn't you?"

"Because a cabdriver saw us—in his headlights."

"Didn't you see she was bleeding?"

"It was dark."

I was an instant away from killing this kid.

"So when the cab pulled up you took off."

"We figured he'd call 911."

"What about the attacker—did you get a look at him?"

"Sort of," he said reluctantly.

"What did he look like?" I asked.

"Just a regular-looking white guy," Po said. "Had a baseball cap. We seen him jump in a black car and take off."

"What kind of car?"

"I don't know," he said.

Changing the subject was worth a shot.

"What were you doing at the High Line?" I asked. "I saw a sign up there that said no skateboards."

"We was just checkin' it out dude," said Po. "We was afraid to go back around Twenty-Sixth Street. Then we seen him up there at the High Line and we ran. I dropped my board, but Red would never drop his—so I got ahead of him, and when I turned around he was gone and the dude was too. Me and Red, we fast, but that dude was fast as us."

I already knew the guy was fast, and he was white and he was medium looking in every way. Po had seen him twice and maybe knew how all the medium, average pieces came together.

"So you think you could identify him?" I said. "Try to remember everything you saw—and don't lie."

"Maybe I could," said Po. "We got a better look at him at the park, but we only seen the other one for a second because he was in the car—"

"The other one?"

"Yeah," said Po. "The one who was drivin'."

Five investigators, including one certified genius and one hot shit from Quantico, never thought there might be two of them. We just believed we were dealing with a perp who could outrun Secretariat and fly without wings, not to mention be in two places at once.

No one could have been that fast, could have seen everything. And never dropped the ball. Meriwether and Murphy, Fallon and Goode missed it—and worst: I missed it.

Serial killing is not usually a team sport, though tandem killers are not totally unknown. Sloane followed the case of two psychiatrists in Stockholm who killed and cannibalized twenty prostitutes, went to trial, and were acquitted on a technicality. The Washington sniper...

"You didn't know they was two of them?" asked Po.

"Are you sure?"

"Sure I sure," said Po. "Can I have some ice cream?"

I ordered ice cream and asked him about the driver.

"So how'd you see the other guy?"

"How do you think I seen him?"

"This is not the time to be a wiseass," I said and reached across the table to squeeze his arm very hard. "Are you hearing me?"

"OK," he said. "Dude, that really hurts."

"What're you going to do," I said, "call the police? Just answer the questions or I'll twist that arm until I hear it break."

Then I dropped his arm.

"When the dude with the knife opened the door, the light come on—and I only seen the other dude for a second. Man, you know, I don't know, they was both white."

"How about the car?"

"Black," he said. "Black windows. Looked fancy."

"Do you know what make?" I asked.

"What make?"

"What kind of car?" I said.

"I don't know."

A lot of city kids weren't into cars. They didn't learn how to drive. They didn't care. They could get around on the train, and there was no place to go outside the city anyway.

"Did you get a look at the plates?"

"Yeah," Po said. "When they went past the streetlight. They was covered with mud—I didn't see no numbers—but in the middle I seen—you know one of them things they have on castles. Where the princess lives."

"A tower," I said.

"Yeah," Po said. "A tower…"

"What else?"

"Nothing."

"You know who makes license plates?" I asked the kid.

"Yeah," said the kid, "I know—up in Attica and Sing Sing."

"You got it," I said. "So maybe you can remember some more stuff."

"I can't," said the kid. "I ain't been in trouble before."

"I don't believe you," I said.

"Maybe once…or two times."

"Well you're in big trouble now," I said.

"Fuck man," Po said, "I tol' you everythin' I remember. Where's Red Hawk at?"

"I'm not sure," I said. "The police have him for now—he'll go to the medical examiner's office—then his family can take him."

Po put his arms on the table and then buried his head in his arms and started sobbing.

"I should've not ran," he cried. "I should've went back and saved him. He's a little guy. This was my fault. He dead and I'm going to juvie. And that dude's gonna kill me. Red Hawk would've won at Shields…"

"Come on Po," I said because people were looking at us. "Get it together. Nobody's going to kill you."

60

My text to Meriwether, Fallon, and Goode: *I got the other kid from the scene. He claims there were two perps.*

Text back from Goode: *Bring him in. Don't call Tom. He's with the Commiss.*

Meriwether didn't have to tell me he was on it since I know his mind started rejiggering the instant he got my message.

And I started rejiggering mine. Three sets of men came to mind. They were all young, therefore at least reasonably fast. They were all brothers, so the tandem idea was already in place. Unfortunately, they were all very remote possibilities because motive was basically nonexistent, but they were all I had so far.

Margo's twin brothers. They loved Hadley. She rejected them. They were too big.

Victorine's two brothers. Too far-fetched.

Hadley's two younger half brothers. Too ridiculous. Their slippery mother would make sure they were the only heirs.

And what about the two other murdered girls?

After I took Po to Goode at Manhattan South, her reaction to the latest information was predictable:

How did I find the kid?

Where did I find the kid?

Is the kid telling the truth?

How did I determine that?

The new information—if it's true—changes everything.

How come you didn't think there were two of them?

Et cetera…

"Are you sure you gave me everything you know?"

"Yes, Linda," I said. "I gave you everything."

Almost everything.

By the time I got out of the precinct house, it was dark, the heavy drizzle had died down to a light drizzle, and I was thinking somebody should give me the big shiny gold star I deserved for not engaging with Goode. Or calling Hadley.

But the only prize I got that night was an eventless trip to the *Dumb Luck*.

When I got there I was so burnt, I swallowed three aspirin with a little Jameson, dropped my clothes on the floor, and went immediately into a deep, dark sleep.

Early the next morning, when I woke up, the rain had stopped, the sun was out, and everything was not all right with the world, but at least the weather had improved.

I checked my voice mail and found nothing from Meriwether or the detectives, which was a bad sign. There were calls from a couple of clients. And a message from Rue, who speaks English with a French accent. I always like listening to her voice—even if sometimes I don't like what she's saying. Which wasn't the case this time as she described what she was going to do to make me feel better when she got back.

The last message came from a blocked number: "Nick, I'll be in New York day after tomorrow and I must see you. It's very important, but I can't talk on the phone. I'll call when I get to the city. Good-bye until then."

The caller didn't identify herself, but she didn't need to because I recognized the husky voice. It was Allegra Trent.

The night I brought the dancer aboard the *Dumb Luck*, I thought about trying to reach Allegra, but decided against it since she was probably in some remote opium den where she never had to leave the couch to see the yeti. Too stoned to think.

I was very surprised to hear from her just then, and I wondered if it was anything more than an odd coincidence.

In the meantime, I was out of leads except for one. Which was more of an idea than a lead. Not even a hunch. Just a thought.

I sent Meriwether what I knew about the Polish girl who had been little Gemma's nanny. The nanny who'd become unglued enough to send threatening letters to Hadley.

Within half an hour he had tracked down Lolek Petrofi via the Polish consulate in New York. That is, he had tracked her to where she was meant to be. Officially. But not in fact.

According to Margo, Hadley never saw the woman again after meeting her at the hospital in Nyack. When Sutro arrived the morning after Gemma died, he grilled the woman, got in a fight with her, and fired her.

In her angry, crazy letters she blamed Hadley and Nile for ruining her life. And threatened to destroy Hadley.

The attending doctors on duty at the Hudson Hospital when the child died explained again that the illness was idiopathic and mysterious, but it was not a poison nor could it have been deliberately engineered and controlled.

Hadley usually threw away the letters, often unread. She didn't blame Lolek for Gemma's death; she blamed herself. Margo said Hadley had only remembered a devoted young nanny—a shy, pretty girl whom she hired in part because the girl had studied ballet for years before she came to the United States.

Hadley received one letter every six months or so—however, in the last year there had been more. And she said she was going to do something about them. After she and Sutro got back together.

61

Now that we knew there were two presumably male perps, the thought of this Lolek being behind all the killings was even more remote than before. Fallon wouldn't let me near the Staten Island and Bronx cases, so I proceeded down to the penultimate item on my punch list, which now had been expanded to include talking to Allegra Trent and a couple of other bullshit possibilities.

The weather had turned perfect, and after taking a lot of courses in Sloane 101, I knew why the bright sun made me feel worse than the relentless rain had done.

The Fielding-Sutros hired their nanny through the Bascombe Agency in Manhattan, which is the place to go if you want an actual baby nurse or a high-ticket nanny from England. British accents are very expensive, thus valued by the hyper-rich who'd taken to accessorizing a family of four with at least one additional child. In a city where first grade in private school could cost thirty grand, these kids were big status symbols.

The Bascombe Agency vetted their girls—and a few boys— of many nationalities to within an inch of their lives. Any misdemeanor took the offender off the roster permanently. And a woman who'd been present at a child's death might as well have been a leper carrying a new strain of the disease.

I'd worked with Bascombe once when a man ran off with the French au pair the agency had placed, and took the kids along. The wife didn't want to deal with the police, who would be investigating a kidnapping, and that's how I got into it. Sayler Security is nothing if not discreet. Laura Bascombe was very cooperative since she didn't want the police involved any more than the abandoned wife did.

It wasn't a complicated deal, and after I found the runaways at Casa de Campo in the Dominican Republic, I took Mrs. Bascombe to a celebratory lunch at the Russian Tea Room, where the old girl kept up with me vodka for vodka. That case ended with everybody living happily ever after. The mom got $40 million and the kids, the dad got $40 million and the French girl, I got a big bonus, and Laura Bascombe got off the hook.

August is a busy time for employment agencies that place domestic staff, as people scramble for help before the school year starts. But when I told Laura Bascombe I was working on an important case and this girl Lolek was a missing link, she said she'd make time for me.

The Bascombe Agency occupied the second floor of a brownstone on West Eighty-Fourth Street. I had only been there in winter when the heat was suffocating. In August the air-conditioning was freezing. Otherwise, almost nothing had changed except the faces of the three young women waiting for their interviews. They'd have to wait a little longer.

"Nick Sayler, Nick Sayler, Nick Sayler," said Mrs. Bascombe, entering the reception area.

She was a big, tall, white-haired woman with a very large bosom. That would be the word. Even in February she wore flowery dresses—always the same style and pattern, but the color of the flowers was different with the day of the week. And sturdy brown shoes. Nothing had changed here either, except, I noticed, it being August, the sturdy shoes were white.

"What a nice surprise—in a way," she said. "Let's go and talk."

Before she led me to her office she told the girls who were waiting to see her that patience was a virtue.

Sister Mary A often proclaimed the same about that virtue, though she was no example, for sure.

In her office, sun bounced off the glass-covered photographs of London Bridge, Buckingham Palace, and the Queen Mum with a couple of King Charles spaniels. After her third vodka at the Tea Room, Laura Bascombe confided that she herself had come from Canton, Ohio.

She got right to the point.

"Lolek was a lovely young woman," she said. "She attended a ballet school in Warsaw and came to work in New York because her family lived somewhere on a farm and needed money."

"Do you know what happened with Hadley Fielding's child?" I asked.

"What a tragedy," Mrs. Bascombe said. "A terrible tragedy. I was an admirer of Ms. Fielding long before I placed a nanny with her. I thought Lolek would be a good fit because of the ballet connection. Ms. Fielding was happy about that."

"What about Nile Sutro?"

"I never met him," said Mrs. Bascombe. "And I never talked to him. Lolek led me to believe that he wasn't very much involved with day-to-day life at home—until, of course, the end."

"Why do you think he fired her like that?" I asked.

"I imagine he was overcome with grief and lashed out."

"Where do suppose Lolek is now?"

"You are aware we had to drop her," said Mrs. Bascombe, "so why would I know that?"

"Because, Laura," I said, "you know everything, and this is important. Trust me. I'll tell you the whole story—when it's over."

"And my name will never be mentioned."

"You have my word."

We stared at each other.

"Russian Tea Room?" she asked.

"Absolutely."

6 2

With full disclosure from a small agency in Newark that took a chance on her, Lolek was working for a family in Alpine, New Jersey.

My methods don't need to pass any test except the one that determines whether I've broken a law. Decorum and good manners are discretionary. So my calling Mrs. Eve Heller, Lolek's employer, instead of Lolek is what it is. Or was. I gave her some bullshit about Lolek being the beneficiary of an insurance policy and told her to check me out online. Licensed in New York, New Jersey, California, and Florida.

She got back to me a few minutes later and said Lolek would return from errands in an hour and a half.

New Jersey has a bad name, so places like Alpine always surprise people. It's not quite as beautiful or pricey as Sneden's Landing, but nothing is.

I parked in front of a Tudor-style house and saw a couple of little kids chasing each other around in a crazy circle, fighting over a yellow Frisbee.

"Hey," I said. "Is this where the Hellers live? I don't see any street numbers."

A little girl with a T-shirt that read Alpine All-Stars came over and said, "We're not allowed to talk to strangers."

"Well you're talking now," I said.

She did an eight-year-old's impression of a theatrical pout, putting one leg out as though she were posing for a fashion shoot.

"You're right," she said. "OK, it's the Hellers'. I'm Natalie Heller."

"I bet your friends call you Nat," I said.

"Anybody would know that," she said, twisting her hips in a way that made me hope her parents would send her to boarding school on a mountaintop with armed guards.

"Is your mother in?" I asked.

The mother answered my question by trotting out the door and across the lawn, waving the child away.

"Natalie," she said, "what do I always tell you?"

"To wash my hands after I go to the bathroom?" And the kid was a wiseass too. I smiled. A two-second break from the business that took me to her house.

As I was chatting with Mrs. Heller, Lolek drove up in the Hellers' SUV. When she got out and I was introduced, I asked her to take a walk with me.

It was hard to imagine her as a shy, pretty girl just a few years ago. The woman by my side was overweight and dour.

"You're not from insurance," she said as we walked away from the kids on the lawn.

"How do you know?" I asked.

"Easy," she said. "I never be lucky to inherit money. I got nobody. So are you from police?"

"Did you do something to warrant the police coming?"

"I don't have to talk to you," she said.

"No," I said. "I wanted to ask you about Gemma…"

She shook her head angrily, and tears immediately welled in her eyes.

"Who are you?" she asked. "I'm not scared. Mrs. Heller trust me. I didn't do nothing and she knows it."

"Does she know about the letters?"

"So now the bitch want to ruin my life again?" She spat on the ground. "Bitch."

"You thought you wouldn't get in trouble for those letters to Hadley Fielding?"

This woman was no longer young or pretty and obviously had never been bright.

"Why get in trouble?" she said. "I had right. How you find me?"

"I'm a detective."

"The bitch sent you."

"Lolek," I said, "her daughter was the one who died. Why do you keep accusing her of doing something wrong? Do you think she did something?"

She set her lips closed hard, as if trying to keep herself from speaking.

"Yes," Lolek finally said.

I put my arm around her. And she seemed to feel comforted, which was the idea. No more defensiveness. We stopped and I rubbed her back in an avuncular way. I'm not in a contest for nicest PI of the year. Of any year.

"You can tell me," I said.

"I hate her," she said.

"You wouldn't hurt her though," I said. "I mean hit her or something."

"I would kill her," she said and spat on the ground again.

"Really?"

"I wish she was dead. I would kill her with my hands."

Maybe this style of nannying worked with the smartass Heller kid.

"Lolek," I said, "what did she do to Gemma?"

"Nothing," she said. "She done it to me."

I waited and was rewarded by a fresh torrent of tears and coughing sobs.

"You haven't talked about this," I said soothingly, using a cheap tactic Sloane would definitely not approve of. "You need to get it out."

"Nile," she sobbed. "He loved me. He said he was going to marry me."

So the nanny was not part of a tandem killing team and was not a liar trying to cover up her crimes. She was simply a victim of the same virtuoso who, I remembered, bad-mouthed the other ballerina, Victorine, after she died.

Nile Sutro and Lolek Petrofi, I thought, driving away from Alpine. When pigs fly.

6 3

At the sound of a familiar bark, I answered my phone.

"I'm coming out to the barge," said Fallon.

"What's up?" I said.

"You there?" he asked.

"On my way."

"I'll see you soon."

The next sound I heard from the phone was a tritone signaling a text from Meriwether: *Holderness wants me out. Hadley asked me to stay.*

I returned the text: *Stay.*

His response was: *I am.*

I wrote: *What about Sutro?*

Meriwether wrote: *She talked to him.*

I wrote: *And?*

Meriwether wrote: *He's coming back.*

I wrote: *When?*

Meriwether wrote: *?*

I got back to the *Dumb Luck* about five minutes before Fallon, and when he arrived, I didn't bother to ask how he snagged a ride across the river on a Marine Patrol boat. They're strictly prohibited from taking any passenger unless it's part of a rescue operation. But Fallon's a hero to a lot of law enforcement guys.

When he walked into the kitchen he looked tired. Not just tired from drinking all night. It was a different kind of exhaustion.

There was a secret optimism living somewhere inside the dark-tempered, foulmouthed Fallon. Without it, he never could have committed himself for such a long time to identifying the problems, patiently tracking the bad guys, and facing them down, hardly ever enjoying much more than a silent, righteous satisfaction. He's cheated death so many times in his optimistic pursuit of justice that he's not on the side of the angels. They're on the side of him.

"You got a beer?" he asked.

"You know where they are."

"Meriwether still in Stonyville?"

"For now," I said.

"You know we don't do protective custody except for a witness—so that's why I didn't offer nothing."

"Get your beer, Tommy," I said. "If you were her, wouldn't you rather be up there with movie stars than locked into some second-rate hotel with a fat matron cop?"

"Some people like fat girls," he said.

"What happened with the kid? Po Digger?"

Fallon pulled a Red Stripe out of the refrigerator.

"He couldn't tell us no more than he told you," Fallon said. "He looked at a lot of pictures, didn't see nobody. Goode put him and the mom and the sister and her kids on a bus for North Carolina," he said. "To the mom's sister. A little summer vacation. He'll come back when we need him."

"What makes you think he'll come back?"

"You scared the shit out of him with them stories about Tryon. And we told him you personally would go down there and drag his ass back if he tried to run."

"So did you come out here for any reason other than my great company?"

"Naw," he said. "That was it, and I couldn't take no more over there with Goode and the task force and the fucking commissioner and the fucking mayor at Gracie Mansion. So I'm off duty. Practicing for permanent off duty."

"You serious?"

"I always wanted to learn how to fish," he said. "So I could put up one of them signs, you know, Gone Fishing. And I want to retire before they kick me out. Me being on this investigation just reminded them I was still there."

"What about Goode?" I asked.

"She don't like fishing," he said. "She don't like the sun."

"Maybe she can take up tennis somewhere. Like Ottawa," I said. "At night."

"She'll stick around. Make twenty years."

"So what do they have against you now?" I asked.

"Nothing new," he said. "You know they've been wanting me out for a long time—and now they can nail me for whatever."

"Whatever, like what?"

"I don't know," he said. "Like not showing up for a meeting with the commissioner and the mayor at Gracie Mansion today."

"What'd you tell them?"

"I was sick."

"They can't kick you off the job for that," I said.

"No, they're just biding their time," he said. "Let me put it this way: The piano player, Sutro, he's coming back tomorrow from his tour. Sometimes if somebody's a VIP or, you know, involved in some traumatic case, whatever, the department sends a cop to meet them as a courtesy. But they don't send no homicide detectives. I'm the chauffeur tomorrow. What does that tell you?"

"I don't know," I said. "Gone fishing."

After about ten minutes of silence, Fallon asked, "You got any ideas?"

"Yeah," I said. "My idea is to take these beers outside."

On the way there, he Frisbee'd a CD into the trash by the mudroom.

"What's that?"

"Video transcript," he said. "The weather was good, so I took a ride up to Ossining."

"I don't believe it."

"Got a buddy up there works for Warden Osborne Lewis, and he fixed me up with Emil Kane. No paperwork."

"The Sunday Sadist—that was my idea," I said.

"Well you can thank Jesus you didn't go," he said.

"You learned a lot, huh."

"He gave up why he chose dancers," Fallon said. "But it don't mean nothing. Nobody gives a shit. I don't give a shit."

"So why did he kill them?" I asked.

"The big secret was he chose dancers because you could always count on them to have a good body. He said he just wanted a nice girl with a good shape, and he wasn't no pervert. But it never worked out with these girls because after he locked them in the car they always saw his great big, huge, prizewinning boner and got scared. That made him have premature ejaction and the girls saw, so he had to kill them."

"Premature ejaction," I said.

"Right," said Fallon. "But he did say one thing that struck me…"

"Here I am Tom, all ears," I said.

"You're a pal," Fallon said. "When I described our guys, he said even with the 44 shit, if they don't stick their cocks nowhere that means they don't really want to hurt the girls. They just want to kill them. Which is what Goode and Murphy think too. I mean no sex. It's different."

"So?"

"Yeah, so crap," said Fallon.

"What'd you give Kane to get him to talk?"

"Said he could watch the play-offs and the World Series."

"You going to make that happen?" I asked.

"What do you think?" he asked.

"I think the guy raped and murdered six women."

"Bingo," said Fallon. "The joke's on him."

Having taken our beers out on deck, Fallon and I watched the sun set into a sky that held no surprises. Going down, it left behind a mix of picture-postcard colors. Gold, purple, rose, and pink. And violet.

When it got dark we walked over to Pauline's for dinner and afterward back to the *Dumb Luck*, where we finished a bottle of Rémy. I put Fallon in the guest room and went to bed myself, hoping I was too wasted to dream.

At least Hadley was safe with Meriwether, Holderness, and Holderness's private guards. The veterinarian was probably still there, and maybe they invited a few of Buddy's friends over to round out the security team.

"Rue," I said, with my head still buried in the pillow the next morning. I tried to take her hand that she had laid on my shoulder, but she pulled away.

"Don't go," I mumbled from my half sleep.

"I'll see you later," she said.

"Hey wait a minute," I said. "Shit."

I sat up, completely awake now.

"I'm sorry. I shouldn't have come into your room."

"Hadley," I said. "Jesus, what are you doing here?"

"I know Rue's your girlfriend," she said. "I didn't think—"

"Forget it," I said. "I was asleep. This is not about my girlfriend. What time is it? I thought you'd get here around eleven."

"I'm early," she said. "I should have waited for you to wake up."

I didn't have anything on, so I wasn't getting out of bed.

"Come back here," I said. "Sit down."

"You're angry," she said.

"I'll get over it," I said. "But if I'm protecting somebody, I like to stick to the schedule. I don't like stunts like this. Like the Beretta."

"I asked Meriwether to bring me here. And he did. I wanted to be with you for a few more hours. I didn't think I was a client."

She was trying to keep hold of her composure. All I wanted to do was touch her. Put my arm around her. Pull her into my bed. But I didn't. Instead I played a more familiar role. Just acted like a prick.

"You told Holderness and Margo you were going, I hope," I said.

"I left them a note," she said.

"Oh Christ," I said. "What time is it?"

"It's seven. We left around four thirty."

I was computing how long it would be before I had McKenzie Black shouting into my phone or calling the cops.

"Nile Sutro is coming back today," she went on. "I said I'd go home with him. I have to get it over with."

"Margo told me," I said. "You're going through with the reconciliation you planned before…the accident."

"There's no reason to stay here, is there?" she asked, looking down at her hands.

"I'm sure your husband will hire security," I said, and she knew I was answering a different question. "Until we get the person."

"It's all right," said Hadley. "Meriwether told me there were two men. It does make it worse somehow. But I still don't remember."

"We'll get them," I said.

But it wasn't true, or at least the "we" part, because no matter how she made me feel, I never really had a dog in this fight. And it's a good thing I don't believe in the soul, unless it pertains to Lady Day, because my soul was not getting saved. I kept this woman safe for a few days and that's all. I looked into Hadley's eyes. How could anyone else have eyes that color?

"Nick," she said, looking straight back at me—but whatever more she might have said was cut off by my cell phone ringing. A Cajun song: "*J'ai Passé Devant Ta Porte.*" I Passed by Your Door. Rue's tone, programmed in there months earlier. Maybe it was she, not Meriwether, who had the vodou going on. Or maybe she never trusted me.

Calling from Virginia, she said she figured she'd reach Weehawken sometime late in the evening.

After Rue and I rang off, there was nothing I could say to Hadley. She was a smart girl. Nile Sutro's wife.

"What the hell," rasped Fallon, bleary-eyed at the open door to my room. Carrying his phone in one hand, he was barefoot, wearing only shorts, more disheveled than ever, but no longer exhausted.

"Good morning, Detective," said Hadley, moving past Fallon. "I'll be with Meriwether."

"I didn't expect her for a couple of hours," I said before Fallon could ask. "I guess she wanted to get a jump on the day. Meriwether drove her down."

"Yeah, maybe she wants to come out to the airport with me and we can both greet her husband," said Fallon.

"A welcoming committee," I said.

"Yeah," said Fallon, sitting in the chair across from my bed.

"Gone fishing," I said.

"Yup," he said.

"So where's the official investigation now?"

"I'd say it's gonna be held up by everybody scrambling just to keep a lid on their own part of it. I mean you wanna turn on the news? It's everyplace. Where's your computer?"

"I can wait," I said.

"They call him 44," intoned Fallon. "Vicious serial killer stalking New York City has hit three boroughs. Where will he strike next? Who is the mystery victim? Will Jane Doe surface? NYPD under heavy scrutiny—"

"Maybe you can have a second career in the news."

"You think?" said Fallon.

"How's the commissioner handling this?" I asked. "Who's going to be explaining?"

"It ain't gonna be on me's all I know," said Fallon, wandering into my bathroom, coming out with an empty glass. "It'll be that asshole from the task force, Kuzon, and it'll have to be the truth for a change. Up to a point. You got anything to drink?"

"Up to what point?" I asked and pointed to a half-full bottle of Jameson on one of the windowsills.

"Up to nothing's on the record after Bellevue," said Fallon, pouring himself a generous shot.

"Did the anonymous tip give them the connection between the girls and Greenburg and the skateboarder kid? And what about you and Goode in Connecticut?"

"Yeah, the tip gave up that information, but Connecticut ain't in no report. We were on our own time. Just looking at trees or birds or whatever the hell they got up there." Fallon was still holding the bottle. "You want a drink?"

"No," I said, putting up a hand. "I'm good."

"So what're you gonna do?" Fallon asked. "You gonna come forward and talk about Sloane getting shot on the barge and about Stonington?"

"I'll speak to Hadley. It's her decision. She knows the perps are still out there. How's talking about it going to help the investigation? You're not going to force her to go in, are you?"

"I ain't forcing nobody," Fallon said. "I'm trying to stay out of the way. In fact, if she comes in the story will blow up even more. Because not only is she white, she's sort of famous and the other two were colored girls."

"Jesus Fallon," I said. "What century are you in?"

"Women of color," he said.

"Like Rue," I said.

"Just jerking your chain," he said. "You been bent out of shape since you met Mrs. Sutro."

"Having a good time with that?"

"Yes," said Fallon. "No. Not really."

"Why don't you go get some clothes on," I said. "Take the bottle."

Half an hour later, I put Hadley in the library for a nap, and was in the kitchen drinking orange juice with a little vodka when Fallon came to say good-bye.

I walked out beside him.

"Did you talk to Goode?" I asked before he climbed into the *Gwinnett* with Meriwether.

"Yeah," he said. "She got nothing."

I didn't have anything either I thought as I watched the *Gwinnett* move across calm water toward Manhattan.

Anything except the return of wrenching, angry memories.

What I lost was half a spleen and a sense of stability.

I didn't figure it was two guys.

I didn't see the BMW.

Sayler Security was based in a location with no security.

Sloane was wounded. Even a flesh wound could be serious at his age.

Two minutes more of my dream about the Valentine's Day fight in Chicago and Hadley could have been dead, the same as Greenburg and Red Hawk.

My cases usually ended neatly. Questions answered. Problems resolved. Client, if not happy, at least satisfied. They rarely ended with a bang, but they never ended with a whimper. Like this.

65

The Lady Luck had abandoned me before. And I knew better than to ask any favors. I refused to hear Sister Mary A chanting: It was for your own good, Nicholas. She never acknowledged any other Lady except Mary, Mother of God. But who the fuck knows, maybe all of them got together to get me off the case and send the dancer home to her husband.

Around eleven, Hadley and I went out to the deck of the *Dumb Luck*, ready for a last trip across the river. Meriwether, back from ferrying Fallon, brought the *Gwinnett* around, tied up, and joined us.

"Do you want me to come with you?" asked Meriwether.

"I'll be all right," I said.

"Backup?" he asked.

"No," I said. "Not this time. Everything's OK."

I knew it was a dangerous thing to say. There was no way to know everything was any more OK than it was the day we went to Stonington. But this was the last day on my watch, and I wanted to be alone with the dancer.

"Fallon told me that later he was going over to JFK to meet Sutro because the police wanted to give him a courtesy escort home," said Meriwether, dragging out the conversation.

"They do it once in a while for people who are going through some trauma," I said.

"Or are important," said Meriwether.

"I didn't ask for it," said Hadley.

"We know that," I said. "Fallon got the order from the task force spokesman."

"What about Goode?" asked Meriwether.

"I'll say this for her. She hasn't let up. Those leads, every one smoked out. But she and her friend Murphy have been working their asses off, crunching numbers. Yesterday they tracked down two sick weirdos both forty-four years old. Spent twenty years as cell mates in Attica, block forty-four."

"I had that," said Meriwether.

"So you know both of them had solid alibis for last Thursday."

"I do," he said.

"And you were going to tell us—"

"Now," he said.

"Goode also got a couple of guys to walk around Foxwoods and a few of the casinos in Atlantic City to see if anybody was betting big on number 44."

"She told me—but it was like grasping at straws," said Meriwether. The ultimate mathematician, who had done nothing to help Hadley go back to her life. I didn't need Sloane to figure that one out.

"Good-bye Meriwether, and thank you for everything," Hadley said, standing on tiptoes to hug him. And kiss his cheek. Then, even knowing how he felt, I was pretty much blown away to see Meriwether raise one of her small hands to his lips.

"Good-bye Hadley," he said. "Be well."

Meriwether helped Hadley into the *Gwinnett*, but before I got aboard I asked him quietly if he thought there were any other suspects at all—anyone at all on the radar.

"Not that I can see right now," he said. "But you've still got to watch out for her."

If Meriwether wasn't the best friend I'd ever have, his comment would have pissed me off quite a lot.

"Don't worry," I said. "I'm taking her to castle Cohen. The security is so tight over there they probably have snipers on the roof of the Metropolitan Club. But after Sutro shows up, it's not my call anymore."

Had Sloane been with us he would have said there were a lot of buildings near Constance's place, but the Metropolitan Club was the only one designed by Stanford White, who was murdered by a man called Harry Thaw, husband of the woman Stanford White was screwing.

Crossing the river was easy and fast. And I didn't see any craft near us, which didn't preclude our being watched through binoculars.

We tied up at the Boat Basin, walked up to Seventy-Ninth Street, and hailed a cab. Fortunately the driver didn't question me about my choice to make a big loopty-loop, twice, from the West Side to the East Side. Finally, having taken particularly special care—after my nearly lethal errors—to be satisfied no one was following us, I told the cab to pull over at Fifty-Eighth Street and Fifth Avenue where Central Park begins, so we'd have a little time to walk.

There was a festive vibe in the air because the Madison Avenue Summer Fair was going on. To accommodate the pedestrian crowds, many of the side streets between Fifth Avenue and Park Avenue from Fifty-Ninth Street to Seventy-Ninth Street were closed, as well as the vehicle entrances to Central Park. So vehicle traffic was at a crawl.

We walked past street vendors at their stations; the guy who sold frozen ices looked like the favorite. There were lots of kids fooling around, girls in short-shorts running, and people pushing strollers with so many bells and whistles they could probably navigate on autopilot. A couple of skateboarders blew past us, and there were some kids practicing *parkour*. This latest craze is a kind of extreme gymnastics where people looked like human pogo sticks bouncing off benches and walls. It was also something that reminded me of my age. There was no comfort in thinking it would be hard to do even without the titanium pins in my leg.

A few paces away a guy was walking a big golden retriever.

"How's Buddy doing?" I asked.

"He's recovering," said Hadley.

"Did Margo ever say why you gave him to her?"

"Nile didn't want him. He said he reminded him too much of Gemma. But Margo said he didn't like dogs anyway."

Sister Mary A would commend me for keeping my mouth shut.

We walked on, not touching. She didn't take my arm; I didn't put my hand on her back as we crossed the street. It felt unnatural. The few inches between us would glow like crazy if there were a forensic light-source test for awkwardness.

"Are you OK?" asked Hadley.

"Never better."

"Really?" she said.

"I'll miss you," I said.

"I'll miss you too," she said and hesitated. "You know I don't want to leave. Nick, you know that, right?"

You don't win the lottery if you don't buy a ticket—and you don't win the lottery if you do buy a ticket. That's where I was. I had nothing to say.

And I was thinking about the time Mike Teak made his way over to Ninth Avenue and gave me his lucky basketball. He was in trouble with his parents for sneaking off to Harlem.

Not that his parents had a problem with Harlem or sneaking. It was that Rucker Park sent a lot of guys to the NBA—a nightmare for the Teaks. I don't know if Mike Teak had a shot or not—and I don't like organized sports, so my opinion wasn't informed anyway.

I didn't want to accept the ball, but Teak said take it for luck. Then he went to Africa on a safari with his family and I went to the gym where I was trying to train for the Golden Gloves.

I kept the basketball in my locker, and every time I was there I took it out to bounce a couple of times. All fighters have amulets, and it became mine.

I liked to think of myself as a boxer. The truth was, at that moment I wasn't anything but a wannabe with a lot of wasted potential. Between being a minor league street hustler selling drugs and taking exams for other kids, there wasn't enough time to train. Still, that didn't keep me from fighting—it only kept me from winning.

The first bout of the season, in September, did not have a happy outcome. And the next time I saw Teak, I told him what happened. The ball was bad luck, I said, because the guy broke my nose, knocked me out, almost killed me. Teak laughed, pointing out that I was still alive—and that was the good luck.

Hadley was alive and no less well than when we left Bellevue. That was lucky. I'd make serious trouble for myself if she stayed. So ultimately, it was lucky she was leaving. It just didn't feel that way as we strolled up Fifth Avenue with some of Manhattan's grandest buildings on our right and Central Park to our left. We could have been a happy couple on the way to lunch or to stop by and see the polar bears at the zoo.

Meriwether texted a message that Nile Sutro had hired the Rivers-Davis Agency to provide security for Hadley and for him, and two men were already at the house in Sneden's Landing.

In three and a half hours, Sutro's plane was scheduled to set down at JFK. It would take about fifty minutes from landing to Constance Cohen's, so Hadley and I were at under four hours and counting.

After Sloane reached Constance at her summer house in Roquebrune-Cap-Martin in the South of France she called to alert the building that Hadley and I were her guests and to give us the keys to her apartment. The doorman was of the old school; he knew our names before we gave them, tipped his hat to Hadley, and asked if we needed anything.

I said we were fine and that in about three hours Mr. Sutro would be arriving. I told the doorman to send him to the elevator, then ring us. I wanted Sutro to come to me and get Hadley instead of my taking her down to give her to him. Macho bullshit, but only I would know. Maybe he would too. That was the point.

There are few elevator operators left in the city, because of automation and expense. Automation and expense, however, are not serious considerations in this particular co-op, where the cheapest apartment goes for $12 million.

In Constance's building that day, the elevator operator was an old fellow who'd probably been working there for two or three hundred years. He'd been trained not to speak unless spoken to, and therefore we rode in silence as we ascended to the fifteenth floor, where the door opened directly into Constance's vestibule.

Her duplex occupied the entire fifteenth and sixteenth floors of the building. Because her husband had died a few years earlier and her children and grandchildren didn't visit much, she often said she should sell the place and move to something smaller. Yet she never did because the penthouse on Fifth Avenue with its view over Central Park's treetops was still too breathtaking to give up. And her memories too happy.

Hadley and I walked around the first floor, admiring Constance's eclectic paintings. After a few minutes of concentration, Hadley started remembering and identifying the artists. There was a beautiful Monet. A few William Merritt Chase landscapes, two large Chagalls, a series of six pictures that looked like feathers by Cy Twombly—I never heard of him—but I was sure she knew what she was talking about. After we went down the hallway leading to the dining room and stopped in front of three Degas ballerina drawings, Hadley began blinking back tears. With everything that happened I only saw her cry once before, briefly in the hospital when she thought she was trapped.

"You'll dance again, if you want," I said with no authority.

"It's not that," she said.

"Do you feel like telling me what it is?" I asked.

She said nothing. She was drawing uneven breaths trying to stop the tears, but it wasn't working. That was the moment to put my arms around her, and I don't know how I kept myself from doing it.

After a while she stopped and raised her eyes. When she spoke, she was entirely composed. Which made it worse.

"I was crying," she said, "because Constance Cohen collects Degas drawings, and I will never meet her. And I will never meet Sister Mary Alphonsus or your friend Teak or anybody else in your life…you don't have to say anything."

That was true. I couldn't say what I thought and I couldn't lie to her, so I was silent.

66

Constance and her husband had been great supporters of the Metropolitan Museum, where they'd donated a room to hold Greek antiquities. When we walked through the dining room, Hadley told me the two large statues there were Greek kouros, which were always nude, as opposed to Egyptian statues, which were always partially clothed. That didn't make it any easier to understand why Constance kept a couple of naked guys standing near the head of the table or to know how Hadley could summon up their provenance.

I also didn't understand if her memories came with a context. In whatever way they were coming back, I was glad she still wasn't up to date.

She would probably be spared the thoughts and images of her brutal attack because even when she recovered it was unlikely that she would remember.

I didn't know any victims of attacks who suffered total amnesia except her—but I do know a lot of victims. Almost all of them permanently block out the event. And if they remember anything, everyone knows eyewitnesses give inaccurate descriptions. Someday I'll have to ask Fallon what percentage of perps in lineups are actually identified.

Hadley and I wound up in the kitchen, which was just as meticulously cared for as the rest of the place. We went on to find a little breakfast room off the kitchen, and that's where we finally stopped.

"Do you know where the liquor cabinet is?" asked Hadley.

"As a matter of fact I do," I said.

"Do you think Constance would mind if we had a drink?"

"Constance always says the only rule in her house is that there are no rules. What's your pleasure?"

"You decide," she said. "I'll have whatever you're having."

I headed out through the kitchen, where the clock's second hand sounded like a gun being cocked again and again. There was enough ticking in my head already, so I took the clock off the wall, popped out the battery, and was left with silence as bad as the noise.

I found a bottle of Cristal in the half refrigerator under the bar in Constance's den. I grabbed two slim champagne glasses and returned to the breakfast room.

"Your favorite," I said and popped the cork.

"That's what Margo told me," Hadley said. "And I did like it but…" I'd seen the look on her face a couple of times before. If she were a man, I'd call it a thousand-mile stare.

"…but it's so expensive," she went on, "I would never buy it—unless it's some special occasion…"

"Good," I said, filling our glasses, feeling like her memory was on the verge of catching up to the present. "You remember that you're careful with money."

"I'm not so virtuous," she said.

We'd knocked off almost the whole bottle when Hadley asked if she could see the rest of the apartment. She'd already seen all of the first floor. I knew that on the second floor, aside from the little room where Constance wrote letters, there was nothing but her bedroom and the guest rooms.

The staircase circled upstairs, where Constance's bedroom lay on the other side of an art deco glass door. A pair of lovers had been etched lightly into the pale-blue opaque glass.

Hadley decided that Constance wouldn't mind if she looked inside.

"What a beautiful room," she said when she opened the door. "I was expecting something else."

The large bedroom was stark, white, and spare with what I learned on my original tour were white-on-white paintings by Agnes Martin, who had been Constance's friend years earlier.

I opened the windows, turned, and saw Hadley walking over to Constance's bed. She sat down, and after a few beats she looked at me and her violet eyes were clear as fresh water.

"Come sit with me," she said.

Familiar music from somewhere nearby floated in through the open window.

"Not here," I said and took her hand.

In a guest room down the hall I finally touched the dancer's smooth body, felt her soft skin, her practiced hands…

But it was Julia in my arms. This one last time with Julia.

Hadley was upstairs in the shower and I was sitting in the den with a glass of Jameson, neat, when the house phone rang. And rang. There was one upstairs, so Hadley must have heard it too.

Getting up out of the chair gave me a conscious sense of defying gravity. Or the chair was a magnet and I was steel shavings.

"Yes," I said, picking up the receiver in the front hall.

"Mr. Sutro is on his way up," said the doorman.

It struck me that Hadley's hair would be wet in the middle of the afternoon at a stranger's apartment and what would Sutro think and what would Hadley do.

It was not my problem anymore. Hadley knew what she was doing, and I didn't give a fuck about what Sutro thought.

Since the elevator was powered by molasses, there was time to run up to the second floor. I knocked on the guest room door once before I opened it and saw the open bathroom door across the room.

"Hadley, he's here—so please make it fast," I said. "I don't feel like entertaining him."

She didn't say anything, and I didn't wait for a reply because Constance's doorbell started to chime.

Nile Sutro was a satisfying two inches shorter than me. He had thin lips, which, according to Rue, denote everything from bad manners to mass murder.

His pale-blond hair was artistically long, and his eyes were hidden behind the sunglasses he probably wore day and night.

He had a white linen shirt on, tight black jeans, no socks. His alligator shoes looked like Sloane's velvet bedroom slippers without the crest, and he was wearing a long, featherweight gray scarf. Draped casually. As casual as a man's scarf can be at the end of August.

He didn't offer to shake hands, and I was tempted to ask if that was policy. Being careful about his hands. Maybe they were insured. Like Jennifer Lopez's ass used to be.

I walked him into the den.

"You're Nick Sayler," he said, and I nodded. "I don't know how we can thank you for everything you've done."

"Just take care of her," I said.

"Don't worry," he said evenly, picking up on my tone. "May I have your office address so I can pay the bill?"

"There's no bill," I said.

"I can't accept so much generosity," he said.

"Well you can't pay a bill if you don't get a bill."

"Why no charge?" he asked.

"Call it karmic kickback."

"This is a beautiful place," he said, looking around. "Is it yours?"

How long had it taken for him to show what a fuck he was?

"No," I said, "it belongs to a friend."

"Oh right—I forgot," he said. "You live on a boat—in New Jersey."

Yeah, I thought. I drop anchor in downtown Hoboken.

"Exactly," I said.

"What can you tell me about the attack?" he asked.

"I don't know anything more than Detective Fallon knows," I said.

"Of course," said Sutro. "But you took her out of the hospital. You saw her first—do you know why she had your card?"

"I really don't," I said.

"I can't believe this has been going on for days," said Sutro. "Are you sure she doesn't remember anything?"

"I think she'll be the judge of that," I said. "So far it doesn't seem like it and—"

"What's she doing?" Sutro interrupted, checking the time on his cell phone. "She's always late." He forced a smile onto his face. "Sorry," he went on. "What were you saying?"

"Nothing," I said. "Do you want me to go up and get her?"

"Yes, thanks," he said, and I was glad he didn't argue.

67

"Hadley," I said when I reached the open guest room door, "come on—he's waiting. You have to come down...or he'll probably want to come up."

Nothing.

"Hadley," I said again.

The room was empty, and when I walked over and saw the bathroom was empty too, my heart picked up speed.

She'd taken off. I almost laughed. Maybe she remembered what an asshole Sutro was.

On the barge, she'd been in the cupboard. In Connecticut she'd been having a smoke with Margo Holderness. There were a lot of nooks and crannies and closets in Constance's big, quiet apartment.

The building superintendent must have been instructed to disable the alarms for our visit. So there'd be no loud alert when a door or window was opened.

And without an armed alarm system, the arrangement of unlocked front and back hall fire doors in some of these classic old buildings made for less than ideal security. Even worse in Constance's case, since she was in the penthouse, where additional fire doors led to the terrace and gave access to the roof.

If Hadley suddenly wanted out, there were a lot of choices—but no reasons. There were also choices if somebody wanted in.

My blood could've run out of my body and I wouldn't have noticed because I felt like it was already gone. I was cold. My scalp tingled.

All right. Think where she is. Both other times before, she'd been somewhere safe. And she'd gone on her own. It would have been stupid to climb out of any guest room or bathroom window. Stupid and dangerous. Nevertheless, I would check each room on the floor before considering anything else. It was procedure. It was the thing to do.

First I went to Constance's room and opened the deco door.

"Nick," she said, stepping away from the window with its view over Central Park.

"I thought I lost you," I said.

"No, you've got that wrong," she said. "I lost you."

I never claimed to be a decent guy or a disciplined guy. I'm an addict. I can always recognize a drug. And that would be Hadley. The glassine envelope. The paradise key.

"Are you ready?" I asked coldly, and she fixed her eyes on me. That day they were lilac colored. A beat passed. And then another. Until I looked away.

"Ten minutes," she said.

She walked ahead, and as I closed Constance's bedroom door behind us, I glimpsed the two motionless lovers permanently fixed in glass.

Thankfully, Sutro, like every other insufferable asshole, went off into the living room to make calls on his cell phone and I wasn't forced to talk to him.

True to her word, Hadley was ready in ten minutes. From the door of the den I watched the prima ballerina coming down the stairs. Even dressed in her old blue jeans and a white T-shirt, she seemed, unearthly. Surreal. Bright eyes looking straight ahead. Pale skin. The bruise subsiding. The cuts healing.

Her long hair was twisted and piled on her head, fastened with invisible pins. If it was still wet you couldn't tell by looking.

Before she reached the last step, Sutro ran up and threw his arms around her.

"Darling," he said. "I'm sorry I wasn't there for you. I'm sorry about everything."

Hadley put her arms around him.

I couldn't leave the penthouse first, so I turned away from the tableau and went into the den. I heard her say, "I'm all right…Nile. Don't worry. Everything is fine."

I poured a drink, and as I was downing the Jameson I heard Hadley.

"Nick," she said. "We're going."

I knew she wouldn't be making any long good-byes, and I was grateful.

"OK Hadley," I said, put my empty glass down, and joined them in the hall. "I'll walk you to the elevator."

"Thanks," said Sutro, and to Hadley, "Do you have a bag?"

"I don't have anything," she said.

After I rang for the elevator, Hadley said, "Tom and Linda said they'd be in touch with me every day."

"And they will," I said. "And you can call them anytime you want." I didn't need to add that she could also call me.

"Tom and Linda?" said Sutro.

"NYPD detectives," I said. "Tom Fallon, the guy who met you at JFK, and Linda Goode, his partner."

"Oh yes," said Sutro. "You never think they have first names."

Although I don't hit people anymore, I'd have made an exception and punched Sutro square in his smug face if the old man in the elevator hadn't arrived just then.

Sutro stood back so Hadley could enter first, but she stopped and turned to me and extended her hand. As I took her hand we looked each other directly in the eye.

"Thank you, Nick," she said.

People who are very close can send powerful silent messages. Her violet eyes said we have a secret. My eyes said the same.

"Good luck," I said.

"And good luck to you as well," said Sutro. "Let's go."

They got in the elevator, the old elevator operator tipped his hat, and the door closed.

I probably would have stood there for twenty minutes if my cell phone hadn't started barking.

"How're you doing?" Fallon asked in a tone that made me think he was calling from one of the airport bars. Not a good sign.

"What can I tell you?" I said. "She's gone."

"Where'd she go?"

"I don't know where she went," I said testily. "Sutro picked her up and they left."

"Nick," said Fallon, his voice suddenly flat and icy, "that wasn't Sutro."

Constance's walls were spinning.

"What the fuck are you talking about?" I said.

"Sutro's plane was delayed," said Fallon. "It's not gonna touch down for another hour."

6 8

I crammed my cell phone in my pocket as I raced through the fire door in Constance's foyer. The front elevator was so slow, it was possible they hadn't gotten all the way down yet, so I hit the stairs running, taking three at a time.

There was a landing on each floor where one flight stopped before angling into the one below it. I swung around each landing and kept going, fourteen, eleven, nine, five, four, and finally the ground floor service area, which was separated from the lobby by a locked door, reinforced by a steel panel.

I pounded the door, kicked it, called for the doorman. Had my hand on the Beretta, knowing it was useless against the steel.

"Open the door," I yelled. "It's Nick Sayler from Mrs. Cohen's apartment. Come on, open the door. Goddammit, now! Right now!"

I didn't see the building's super and the big guy at his side until they were on me.

"Sir, please come with us," said the super, who was a short man with a sad comb-over. As he put a hand on my arm, I pulled away and the big guy took a tentative step forward. It was clear by his uniform and tool belt that he was a handyman, not a guard.

"Don't do it," I said. And to the super, "I'm Constance Cohen's guest."

"I don't want to bring the authorities to this building," said the super, "so I need to see some identification."

Instead he saw the Beretta. "Get that door open," I said.

Before they moved, there were two sharp clicks as the doorman finally unlocked the heavy door.

I turned into the lobby and slammed the door shut again, closing the super and his sidekick out. They immediately began pounding, and I got in front of the doorman.

"Don't open it," I said, knowing in an instant one of them would find the key to unlock the door. "Just trust me."

"Mr. Sayler," he said, "what happened?"

"Long story," I said. "The lady I went up with—where did she go?"

"Miss Fielding," he said. "Yes, she and Mr. Sutro left, about two minutes ago."

"Only two minutes—"

"Yes," said the doorman, following me when I ran out onto the sidewalk, "just after they got out of the elevator, she said she'd forgotten something upstairs. Said she'd be quick. Mr. Sutro asked her not to go back up because his driver was double-parked and he didn't want to get a ticket and he'd get her another one of whatever she forgot. Finally she went with him. You just missed them."

"Did you see the car?" I asked.

The pounding on the lobby door had stopped, meaning the super and handyman or decided to use another exit.

"Yes," said the doorman. "And it wasn't double-parked—"

"Tell me what it looked like," I said. There's no time.

"Black BMW sedan—"

"Plates?"

"No sir," said the doorman.

"I promise you won't get in trouble," I said. "Call the Thirteenth Precinct—say it's urgent. Ask for Detective Goode. Tell her what happened. She'll understand."

The Madison Avenue Fair had just ended, and all the traffic on Fifth Avenue was moving slowly—but I knew better than to start running. It could pick up at any time and leave me far behind. I needed a car.

"I'm sorry Mr. Sayler," the doorman said, coming toward me, "after Miss Fielding went out to the car, Mr. Sutro said you were drunk and smoking cigarettes and he was afraid you'd set Mrs. Cohen's apartment on fire. It was my duty to tell the super—"

"Forget it," I said.

I heard a siren and figured the super had called the cops. But I couldn't depend on them not to haul me in. And even if Fallon sent for backup, there wouldn't be enough to close off streets and box in the BMW.

Exactly when traffic began to move faster, the Widow Luck decided to give me a break and the shiny black limo that pulled up was it.

A big, stoner-looking kid jumped out, and, as he helped an elegant old lady to the sidewalk, I yanked open the driver's door and dragged the uniformed chauffeur out of his seat. I got him onto the street, but when I tried to get in the car, the kid tackled me. At least he wasn't a pussy, and if I'd had time to think, I would've been sorry I had to punch him so hard in the gut. I had lost a minute; I'd taken my eyes off the traffic.

I slid into the limo, hit the gas, and, lurching away from the curb, sideswiped an SUV before I pulled the door shut and heard the locks snap into place.

Then I sideswiped a cab to cross into the bus lane because my only hope of getting through the traffic was there.

I turned the driver's wheel with white knuckles, and my concentration was so intense, I was staggered when I heard a familiar voice, saw a familiar face in the rearview mirror.

"Jesus fucking Christ!" I said. "Meriwether."

"I decided to back you up anyway," said Meriwether. "I was in the hall outside the kitchen. I took the fire stairs down to the service entrance and broke through the fence to Fifth—I got in the limo when you were dumping the driver and the kid. What happened?"

I told him, and in the mirror I caught a glimpse of his impassive face turning hard. As hard as I'd ever seen it. And anyone who was strong enough to break through a ten-foot-tall chain-link fence made of galvanized iron was strong enough to break a man's neck. Easily. He wouldn't do it though, or kill him with a knife. I wouldn't kill anybody either.

We wanted to be sure the men who took the dancer lived. Just barely. Just enough to go to jail and rot there.

69

The Widow Luck tossed me another biscuit that day because the bus lane was empty, allowing us to fly past all the traffic until Meriwether said, "I see the car."

One-way going south, Fifth Avenue is wide enough to accommodate three lanes, so what the bus lane had given us in speed was diminished by the lane of traffic between us and the BMW.

As soon as they got a chance, the two 44s would turn off Fifth by going east toward Madison Avenue or west into Central Park. If they wanted to get out of the city, the fastest way would be heading through the Midtown Tunnel or over the Queensboro Bridge. Or they might ditch the car.

They couldn't make a run for it with Hadley in tow unless she was unconscious. Or dead. There was no way to keep the thought out of my head.

Even if they got out of Manhattan they couldn't go upstate or to Connecticut or Long Island or to one of the airports in the BMW. You didn't need to be as smart as they were to know the cops were closing in.

Up in the blank blue sky, I first heard and then saw a chopper. I couldn't read its call letters, but it had to be NYPD. It was against federal law for civilians to fly so low.

Fallon told me once that the earliest NYPD aircraft carried three seats: the pilot's seat, the copilot's seat, and the angel's seat. That seat was always empty, ready for the angel the crew hoped would ride with them on every flight.

Currently, the police department maintains a fleet of about half a dozen helicopters. None of them carries an angel seat, nor do fancy limos like the one I was driving.

And even though there were only nine angels in the entire Bible and Apocrypha, Sister Mary A used to tell me one of them would always be around to protect me when I needed him.

I learned early to save a lot of time by not arguing with her about crap like that, but in the stolen limo trying to keep up with two killers who had gotten the better of me at every turn, I was ready to accept good luck under any name it went by, including Gabriel, Michael, or Raphael.

Of course Satan had once been an angel too.

My phone barked, and I handed it over to Meriwether.

Fallon was on his way back from JFK, and as soon as he learned our location he clicked off so he could contact the chopper and direct the squad cars that were already swarming through Midtown.

Cutting across Fifth trying to get closer to the BMW, I forced the limo in front of three cars, took a hit on the passenger side, and heard the squeal of metal against metal as I sideswiped a little MINI Cooper and sent it swiveling into the Mercedes behind it.

The 44s shot left at Fifty-Seventh Street almost into an old couple dressed like tourists, right down to the man's white belt and white shoes, and a pack of teenagers who were looking everywhere but where they were going.

Crossing Lexington, the 44s hit a bike messenger hard enough to hurtle him into the plate glass window of a shoe store.

Hadley was no match for two men under any conditions, and these two were fueled by craziness.

She must have had second thoughts or a premonition or maybe something he said or did scared her enough to try and go back up to Constance's penthouse—where she knew she hadn't left anything.

By the time the BMW fishtailed onto Second Avenue going south, the chopper hovered above it and three squad cars, lights flashing and sirens wailing, were closing in from three sides.

When my cell barked again, Meriwether switched to speakerphone.

"I'm almost to the tollbooths," rasped Fallon, meaning the ones on the Queens side of the Midtown Tunnel, which is divided in half. Two lanes in each direction with a wall in between.

"They've just reached the tunnel," I said.

"Yeah," Fallon went on. "We can't get in front of them, but we got cars coming from the other side and the chopper's flying over. I don't want you in this, Nick. You hear me, Meriwether? Do *not* follow them through the tunnel."

"Yeah, I hear you," I said as I drove the limo into the tunnel, crashing past one of the additional squad cars sent to block the entrance.

The Manhattan entrance to the tunnel, behind us, was now closed, so it was the BMW, the limo, and three squad cars, heading toward the exit.

The Midtown Tunnel is just over a mile long, and I reckoned the cops could easily send in a SWAT team on foot from the Queens side.

"Nick," said Meriwether, "something's wrong."

"I know," I said. "They're too smart for this. Nobody had eyes on them for the first couple of minutes after they left the building."

"They were stuck in traffic," said Meriwether.

"Doesn't matter," I said. "I don't think she's in the car."

"There's no third accomplice," said Meriwether.

"I agree," I said. "I think one of them took her out of the car and the other one's driving now. He's been driving the whole time."

"Suicide by police," said Meriwether. "It's been done before."

"Many times," I said. "Or he'll give himself up—figuring to make a deal—him for her."

"Where would the other one take her?" asked Meriwether.

"I don't know," I said with the same sense of helplessness I felt ten years earlier. Maybe worse because I knew I was letting it happen.

"You did everything you could," said Meriwether.

"Bullshit," I said. "I've killed her."

The BMW suddenly slowed to a crawl as we saw daylight.

"I'm on the other side of the tollbooths," said Fallon, back again on speaker. "Goode's here with a hostage negotiator."

"I don't think Hadley's in the car," I said.

We were emerging from the semidark tunnel into the bright sunlight. For once the mayor meant what he said about the full force of his office. He and the police commissioner wanted that *Number One without a Bullet* designation back.

There was an army of police between the tunnel and the tollbooths. SWAT teams in heavy gear. Helmets, body armor, and a complement of weapons from semiautomatic to fully automatic. I saw Emergency Service Unit trucks and an armored Lenco BearCat rescue truck. A second chopper was flying low.

A dozen SWAT team guys started circling the BMW, and three other members of the team, who'd been heading toward us, stopped.

"I see you," said Fallon. "I told them to leave you alone."

"We're going to run out of time," I said, "if the other one has her."

"Give me the odds," Fallon said. "Gut odds."

I was looking at the controlled chaos between the exit from the tunnel and on both sides of the tollbooths.

"Fifty-fifty," I said. I didn't know.

"Then we can't take a chance," said Fallon. "We have to treat it like she's in the car."

"But if she's not in the car," I said, "we can't spare the time—I want to know where she is."

"Nick—"

I couldn't hear the next thing Fallon said because I was out of the limo, running toward the BMW. With Meriwether behind me. I wheeled around.

"No," I said to Meriwether. "I'm asking you. If I get hit, you've got to find her."

Meriwether stopped and stepped back toward the limo. I slowed to a walk, amazed that nobody tackled me. I didn't know what Fallon was telling them or what authority he could summon up over a SWAT team.

It didn't matter. They were leaving me alone as I got closer to the BMW with its blacked-out windows shimmering in the blinding bright sun. Three figures in plainclothes came out in front of the tollbooths through a crowd of uniforms. Goode, Fallon, and another man, very slight, shorter than Goode, who must have been the hostage negotiator.

70

I stopped about six feet from the car and put my hands up. What did I have that I could trade for information? Nothing but lies.

Where was Sloane to accuse me of attempting suicide by psychopath? He'd be wrong. I was digging deep for tricks since once I had been very good, and lying, I'd recently found, like a foreign language not spoken for years, could come back in a crisis. I would think of something. Or the guy would kill me.

I felt deadly calm. *Ashes to ashes.* But maybe not. I heard Julia's voice. *Dust to dust.* But maybe not. *To some people love is given, to others only heaven.* One of her poets said that. Maybe it was true.

"Sayler," Goode yelled, "get back. Right now. Get back."

I took three steps forward, and the driver's side window lowered a few inches.

"Don't move," said a man's voice. "Let's see your gun."

Fallon raised his hand, which was a signal for his people to hold. The cops stood immobile, waiting.

I took the Beretta from the small of my back, dropped it on the ground. Kicked it away.

"Now the other one," the voice said. What did that voice sound like?

I took the other Beretta out of my pocket, dropped it, and kicked it.

"Let's see your ankles," he said.

I showed that there were no guns.

"All I want to know is where she is," I said. "They'll go easier on you if you tell us where she is."

"Dead or alive?" asked the cocksucker.

"Just where she is," I said.

"I'm trying to remember where we put her," he said. In a Southern accent.

I turned to look at Meriwether, who was on his haunches, still as a cat.

"How long will it take you to remember?" I asked very calmly, entering the fugue state I use to deal with pain.

"I'll tell you when I'm ready," he said. When *Ah'm* ready.

I waited immobile, like the battalion of men who made a large semicircle behind me across from the same large semicircle behind the car.

"She's right here," the voice said and put two gun barrels through the space at the top of the window. *Rahght heah.* A moment later, he pulled the guns back and raised the window.

"Let her say something," I yelled at the closed window. I moved closer to the car. And the man with Goode and Fallon approached from in front of the tollbooths, walking at a casual pace that definitely belied his job.

"All right," he said to me quietly. "Get out of here. Move."

"I'm not going anywhere," I told him softly. "He said she was in the car, but there's no proof."

"Get the fuck out," whispered the slight man in the short-sleeved shirt, and then he continued loudly, "I'm Bill Drabek, I want to work out a plan with you."

There is a classic psychopathology of someone like Emil Kane who killed redheads because his redheaded mother tortured him by forcing him into simultaneous feelings of extreme pleasure and extreme guilt.

Here there was no empirical evidence to rely on. Not for me anyway. There was only projection. Only guessing. And not informed guessing.

I bent down, picked up my guns, and moved toward the BMW.

"Sayler," hissed Drabek the negotiator, "you're going to get everyone fucking killed."

"Get out of my way," I said.

I hadn't realized how bad I felt. How ready I was to do penance. How long I'd been waiting. Nothing could stop me, and the guy in the car wasn't prepared for someone as crazy as he was. There was no playbook.

None of the snipers would take me down. If the 44 in the car got me, they would get him. But then no one would know where the other one took the dancer.

I was three paces from the car when the driver's door flew open and the man who had been Nile Sutro at Constance's apartment jumped out, holding a gun in each hand.

Two seconds later the driver's side back door opened and an almost identical-looking man got out, pulling Hadley Fielding by her long hair. Her hands and feet were tied, and she couldn't do anything to avoid scraping along the black tarmac, where he dragged her next to the first man. And dropped her. Her cheek and bare arms were bleeding. He kept a gun to her head.

She really was going to die. They set out to kill her, and now why wouldn't they? There was no way out for her. The best snipers in the world couldn't protect her. There was only me. Like any other human, I was hardwired for survival. All the other times. Not now.

Each blond-haired man knelt on one knee on either side of the girl. The motion was simultaneous and graceful, and I wondered if they too were dancers.

"We're going to kill her," the driver drawled. "There are two of us, as you can see. You can't get both of us before we put a bullet in her head."

Fallon and Goode were inching toward the car from the other side.

"Can we talk about this?" said Drabek, the hostage negotiator.

"You can talk till kingdom come," said the driver. His Southern accent became more pronounced each time he spoke.

"Why?" I asked, ignoring looks from the hostage negotiator.

"She ruined our lives," the other man said. "Destroyed our lives."

Exactly what Lolek the nanny had said—and was totally off the mark.

"How did she destroy your lives?" I asked.

"Well," he said conversationally and gave Hadley a hard elbow in the ribs, "it's a kind of long story. A pretty long, dreary story. And we don't want to go there because we're having too much fun here and we deserve it after everything."

"Everything," I said, not a question.

"You want to know," he said. "Don't you? You want to hear all the sticky details."

"Listen pal," I said conversationally, slowly, almost pleasantly, "I don't give a fat fuck what you did or why you did it. You know how this negotiation ends. It's not a negotiation. It's bullshit. You're going to kill her, you're going to kill me, and those guys"—I looked at the snipers—"are going to kill you. Looks like that's what you want. But nobody gives a rat's ass about your story. In half an hour you'll both be wrapped up in plastic and they'll haul your asses over to the morgue. They'll find out who you are, and that's nobody."

If I could ever look back on this I would laugh. Because what I said actually got to the first one, the Sutro impersonator. After they had us all almost believing they were supermen, this one falls for a comic-book ploy.

"We're going to tell you anyway," he said. And I looked up at the sky in theatrical boredom, so when I dropped my head I could glance at Hadley. Whose eye I caught just before the second guy gave her hair a vicious yank.

"And you're going to fucking listen," the phony Sutro said. I had definitely gotten to him. But to what end?

"We didn't give a fuck about the two other little cunts," he said. I shrugged my shoulders. Why not go for broke?

"As far as I can see, you two are the only little cunts around here."

"Shut up," he screeched. "Shut your piehole and listen." *Pah-hole.* "We had a plan to throw you ass wipes off the track. That's why we killed the nigra and the spickchickaboo. Every six months another dancer. Somebody was killing dancers. But nobody would think it was us."

"I got news for you, my friend." I was pushing it. "Nobody knows who you are, and in a couple of minutes it won't matter."

"Well ah guess you're right," he said, suddenly calming down, calling my bluff. "It sure ain't gonna matter to you. You're the pricksucker who decided to be a hero. We don't like imitators. We're the heroes. And we're all going down together. You, me, my brother, and this bitch."

As he spoke I saw Fallon and Goode inching toward the BMW from the other side.

71

The Sutro imposter smashed his elbow into Hadley again, his brother followed suit, and I turned my head, half expecting Meriwether to break away from the cops. The brothers must have taken their eyes off her for an instant to see what I was looking at. And one instant was all she needed to execute a move like a diver would make in midair. With her bound arms and legs perfectly aligned, she arched up off the ground, twisting her body into the kneeling driver, who lost his balance. She rolled under the car, and I went for the other guy. I took him down with the one killer punch I never knew I had.

In a split second the driver recovered and put a bullet in my bad leg before he swung toward the car's hood and continued firing at Fallon and Goode.

Then he was on the ground. The sound of so much simultaneous gunfire was deafening, but it was quick. The two blond-haired killers were dead with maybe two dozen officers around them as I rolled under the car to Hadley and carefully rolled her out the other side toward more waiting cops.

"Nick," she cried, "thank God, thank God." And as the police came at her she screamed at them, "Don't touch me. Don't put a hand on me."

With a penknife I cut the zip cuffs away from her wrists and ankles. She threw her arms around me, and we rose up from the ground, until I lost my balance. Protocol went to hell as Meriwether came from nowhere to pick her up and carry her away from the BMW and from the Emergency Service people. Two minutes hadn't passed since the first gunshot.

I turned to look for Fallon and Goode, and what I saw straight ahead froze me.

Linda Goode hadn't been wearing a vest. This one time, the only time. She'd been shot in the chest. Her white shirt was soaked in bright-red blood, her skin was pallid, and her breathing was shallow.

Fallon was next to her on the ground, cradling her head, smoothing her hair, and touching her cheek.

"Linda," he said. "You can't leave me. Do you hear? Linda… Nick, for fuck's sake, what can we do?"

The medics were approaching, and Fallon snarled at them as they put her on a stretcher.

"Be careful, for fuck's sake," he said and bent close to Goode again. "You're a brave girl Linda. Don't give in. Listen to me goddammit. I'll take care of you. I promise. You can't fucking die."

But it was too late to get through to her. He lightly kissed her lips. The one thing she wanted. I saw them carry her away. So still. Limp. And lifeless.

Fallon followed them. I couldn't watch.

Over by our stolen limo, I saw Meriwether holding Hadley as he had when he scooped her off the ground. As I tried to walk toward them, I felt wet blood on my leg and in my shoe.

The sun was setting over the city, and heaven would have to wait for another day. My cell phone was ringing. *"J'ai Passé Devant Ta Porte."*

72

Explanations, even those dealing with psychopaths, become logical in context. Without a context they are like cards in search of a deck.

I'd run through some of the answers before the questions were fully formed. The victim in Staten Island and the victim in the Bronx were murdered as distractions for the police.

The men would get the satisfaction of torturing and killing Hadley. But by creating an imaginary serial killer, it wouldn't look like Hadley was the specific target.

A vicious hoax like this was one of my first thoughts when Goode mentioned how odd it was that there was no sexual element in the attacks. Since the killers were dedicated to their crimes, they obviously realized that no sexual element could ruin their story, and that is why I got the call with the heavy breathing.

The two killers were not in any state or federal systems because they had never been arrested before. Neither one, not once.

I didn't know their names, at the time, but they had been on my list of implausible twosomes. Hadley's two brothers, Margo's two brothers, Victorine's two brothers.

Temple and Parrish Campbell were Victorine Campbell's brothers. The runners who gave up the shot they thought they had at the Olympics. The younger sister gave up her own dream of becoming a ballerina and OD'd on heroin. All for Victorine. There was so much anger. But with Victorine gone, they needed to find someone else to blame.

Years went by, and their anger became distorted. Everything became Hadley's fault. She took Victorine's place in the ballet; she took Victorine's lover. She took everything, and they were left with nothing.

Why they couldn't change their lives and why they thought punishing Hadley for Victorine's death would do it for them doesn't make any sense, but carving and killing people doesn't either.

They followed Hadley's and Nile's lives on Internet gossip sites, and the way they got Nile's flight number was simply by Temple posing on the phone as a *Vanity Fair* writer.

The only insight into what drove Temple and Parrish Campbell obviously came secondhand from people who knew them. And from diaries in which Parrish claimed he could fly and had fucked Nijinsky—a famous dancer who died before he was born.

Hadley went back to Nile. I went to Justin Greenburg's memorial service at Temple Beth El in West Hartford, Connecticut, and the tower Po Digger and I thought we saw on the BMW's license plate turned out to be the Biloxi Lighthouse. I never found out why Mildred was more familiar with Billy Holderness's schedule than his wife was, but I did learn that my ballerina friend Allegra Trent was calling so urgently because she thought I could hook her up with a coke dealer.

As for the number 44: it was on the list Meriwether originally compiled. Like Psalm 44 or Jeremiah 44, Ezekiel 44 came from the Bible. To me, the Bible had been the least promising place to find an answer. I thought I had seen that movie before. Obviously I forgot one of Sister Mary A's staples, which goes: There are only seven stories under the sun.

It was accepted pretty conclusively that a page, torn from the Bible, found folded in Parrish Campbell's pocket was a big piece in the puzzle.

Maybe there was a shred of humanity left in the Campbells' deadly folie à deux. At some point they, or at least Parrish, knew killing was a sin. An unforgivable, profane sin.

By the time they were ready to commit the first murder, they saw themselves as heroes. Why not see themselves as priests too if they could find some holy vindication? They settled on a passage that wouldn't hold up to close interpretation.

What the fuck. Why should anything make sense? They were crazy.

Ezekiel 44

A priest must not defile himself by going near a dead person; however, if the dead person was his father or mother, son or daughter, brother or unmarried sister, then he may defile himself.

ONE YEAR LATER

Some prices are just too high, no matter how much you may want the prize. The one thing you can't trade for your heart's desire is your heart.
— *L. M. Bujold*
Memory

On a hot evening toward the end of the following August, I was on the deck of the barge reading *The Art of War*.

Meriwether was out there too, getting ready to grill the monkfish we were having for dinner, and Sloane was still in the South of France with Constance Cohen.

When Larry started to bark, I looked up the hill to where a FedEx truck had just pulled in. The FedEx guy was always in a sour mood when he came to the *Dumb Luck*, since he had no choice but to find his way down the embankment and across the beach with whatever envelope or package he was delivering. He always complained about the sand or mud or wind or something.

I decided to make his day by meeting him halfway, so Larry and I walked around the deck to the other side of the barge and down the ramp to the beach.

It turned out the crotchety man had been replaced—at least that day—by a young girl with thick auburn braids. She practically skipped down the incline.

"Wow," she said. "This is awesome. Look at the river, it's so smooth."

"Yeah, I like it," I said.

"Are you"—she looked at the package she was carrying—"Nick Sayler?"

I nodded, and she handed over the package.

"Could you sign please?" she asked, giving me her clipboard with a receipt on it. Then she pointed to the barge. "You live there? What is that thing?"

"It's a barge," I said. "It's called the *Dumb Luck*."

"I love it," she said and took back her clipboard, then turned and started toward the incline. "Have a great day."

"You too," I mumbled, looking at the package with a London return address I didn't recognize.

Larry had been carrying a rubber ball and kept dropping it at my feet as I walked, then picking it up and trying again. Finally I heaved it far enough away so he could get a run, and I went up the ramp and headed back around to my chair on the deck.

When I got there I saw Rue, who'd just come out of the shower with her hair wrapped up in a white towel, looking particularly beautiful, backlit by the setting sun. She had poured a glass of wine for me and brought it over.

"What's that?" she asked, pointing to the package.

"Don't know," I said.

"Then wait a minute," she said. "Maybe Meriwether should look at it first."

Rue was not generally nervous, but I could tell she was remembering the time just after we met when somebody sent a letter bomb—which never detonated because Meriwether was inspecting everything that came into the barge.

"Those days are long gone Rue."

"Sorry," she said. "Sometimes it just comes back to me."

"Well you can rest easy now," I said.

"Three minutes," said Meriwether, turning the fish on the grill.

"I'll get the salad," Rue said and kissed my cheek. "Be right back, *cher.*"

I opened the package and found another one inside. Gift wrapped, with a note. Slanted handwriting on pale-blue paper.

Dear Nick,

Please forgive me for not being in touch till now.

Nile and I couldn't make it work. I moved to London, where I have some good friends, and I'm giving a few classes at the Royal Ballet.

I get headaches sometimes and my memory still plays tricks, but I feel pretty well in general and I remembered something I want to tell you.

When Margo called to give me her new phone number, I was in Central Park, up at the Conservatory Garden, my favorite place. I had a pen but no paper. It was that very still, hot August day, before the storm.

A breeze came out of nowhere and blew a white business card toward me. I remember thinking, that's lucky. I didn't read the name, just wrote Margo's number on the back and put it in my pocket.

You saved me last summer and I got better, but if I were to forget everything again, I would never forget you. You are in my heart.

Hadley

I pulled the wrapping paper away from a small silver box engraved with the initials *N.S.*

There was only one thing in it. A battered, dirty business card. Sayler Security.

"Hey, what's for dinner?"

It was Fallon's unmistakable rasp.

He had two dates that night. A blonde girl like all the blonde girls before and all the blonde girls to come. And his partner, who turned out to be tougher than the bullet that hit her in the chest, Homicide Detective Linda Goode.

ACKNOWLEDGMENTS

I would like to thank William Clarke, Andy Bartlett, Michael Daly, Michael Featherston, Jerome Gary, Victoria Grifffith, Charlotte Hercher, Kay Kendall, Suzanne Maas, Samira and Jeff Sine, Andrew Slaby, and the Stonington Historical Society.

Nick, Thomas, and Terry McDonell.

Richard Price.

Irma Rivera-Duffy, without whose generosity this book couldn't have been written.

And most grateful thanks to the brilliant, ineffable Ed Victor.

Agus buíochas le A.W. ar shon gach rud. Suaimhneas sioraí a chara dhílis.

JM
Amagansett, NY
March, 2013